WHISPERS OF PASSION

"The water is much more effective if you remove your clothes," she said, not recognizing her voice in its huskiness.

"For what? Ridding the body of fleas? Or giving my woman more access to it?" Ashton teased, unfastening the buttons of his breeches with his free hand and lowering his breeches down away from him. The fire was raging within him as his fingers traveled hotly down her body, caressing and arousing.

He then jerked her next to him. Their bodies strained together hungrily. "I love you, Sasha," he whispered. He ran his tongue slowly over the perfect contours of her face. "Tell me that you love me." He framed her face between his hands and gazed down at her with passion-filled eyes as she inched away from him. "Tell me, Sasha. Tell me."

"CASSIE EDWARDS IS A SHINING TALENT!"
—Romantic Times

TOUCH THE WILD WIND

CASSIE EDWARDS

LEISURE BOOKS   NEW YORK CITY

To Jane Thornton, a specially dedicated editor and friend.

And to Glenna (Highland) Brown, with many special memories of long ago—Lytle Park and pool; the telephone company; double dates and dances at Stable's (now Tomaso's); the Fifinellas; and a longtime friendship!

And to Donna Ingersoll and her family—Tim, Stephanie, and Tim II, with much love.

A LEISURE BOOK ®

February 1991

Published by

Dorchester Publishing Co., Inc.
276 Fifth Avenue
New York, NY 10001

Printed in the United States of America.

POEM

If I had never known your face at all,
Had only heard you speak, beyond thick screen
Of leaves, in an old garden, when the sheen
Of morning dwelt on dial and ivied wall,
I think your voice had been enough to call
Yourself before me, in living vision seen,
So pregnant with your Essence had it been,
So charged with you, in each soft rise and fall,
At least I know, that when upon the night
With chanted word your voice lets loose your soul,
I am pierced, I am pierced and cloven, with Delight
That hath all Pain within it, and the whole
World's tears, all ecstasy of inward sight
And the blind cry of all the seas that roll.

—WILLIAM WATSON

Chapter One

"Come, mates, and suck it up!" a voice yelled from outside York's Pub. "Come one, come all, and get your taste of champagne! Melbourne's finest!"

Barefoot, Sasha Seymour hurried to the pub window. She groaned as she stared outside at a shabbily dressed, thick-whiskered gold prospector just in from the fields, pouring one bottle of champagne after another into a horse trough. Though it had been five years since the first major sighting of gold in Australia, Melbourne was still a round-the-clock orgy conducted by the diggers, their mates, and their red-faced doxies drinking the gold away.

From morning till night, miners lurched in and out of the luxury shops, jamming huge, tawdry rings on their girls' fingers, lighting their pipes with notes, and pouring gold dust from their matchboxes

7

or tobacco tins into the cupped hands of hackney drivers. Perhaps a man with a celebrating spirit today had bought out a hotel's entire stock of champagne, ready to share it with all and sundry.

His pet dingo pup following at his heels and heavy revolvers holstered at his hips, Ashton York sauntered to Sasha's side to gaze intently through the window at the spectacle at the horse trough. "I smell trouble in the air," he said, his spine stiffening when he recognized two of the men joining in on the fun. Not only were they Ashton's friends, but they had also recently been employed by him to help establish his and Sasha's sheep station. They were supposed to be tending to business now— business that was paid for from Ashton's meager daily earnings as the proprietor of a pub.

Recognizing Crispin Tilford and Rufus Ackley, and realizing what they were up to, Sasha placed a hand to her throat. "Oh, Ashton," she gasped. "Surely Crispin and Rufus have more sense than to get mixed up with those ruffians."

She turned and gazed up at Ashton, no less intrigued by him now than the first time she had seen him. He was thirty and dangerously single, with violet eyes that melted Sasha's insides every time she looked into them. His golden-red hair was pulled back and tied at the nape of his neck. He was a lithe six feet, a golden beard hiding the true mysteries of his face behind it. His broad, muscled shoulders filled out his shirt of soft kangaroo hide, and his long, lean legs were sheathed in snug-fitting dark breeches.

To Sasha, Ashton York was the epitome of man,

and she found herself constantly fighting her feelings for him.

Loud laughter and jeers caused her to look away from Ashton and out the window again. Her eyes widened as Rufus playfully knocked Crispin into the champagne in the horse trough, only to be dragged in after him.

"Doggone them," Ashton grumbled. He looked at Sasha, then down at his nervous pet dingo. "Sasha, hold onto Lightning. If the pup gets mixed up with that mess out there, she's liable to get shot for being a dingo, no matter that she is tamed and mine. I didn't go through hell taming the pup these past two months just to get her blown away by some drunken fool."

Sasha nodded eagerly and grabbed the dog up into her arms. She cuddled the pup close, recalling the day that Ashton had brought the dear thing to the pub after having found her running loose and half-starved on the outskirts of Melbourne. Sasha's heart had gone out to the pup with the short soft fur, bushy tail, and erect, pointed ears. Its color varied between yellowish and reddish brown, with white underparts, feet, and tail tip, and a marking on its head that set it apart from all the other dogs in town—a patch of white in the shape of a star.

Ashton had no trouble convincing Sasha that wild dingoes, although bold and suspicious, could be tamed, and those raised from puppies could become affectionate pets. She loved the pup at first sight! She laughed to herself when she recalled the day the pup was named. It was during a fierce electrical storm. The lightning was snapping and popping everywhere from the sky, thunder shaking the earth like dynamite exploding. Excited by this, the pup leapt and leapt into the air, trying to bite the lightning.

Thus she had been christened with the name.

Ashton pushed the swinging doors open and stepped outside. He elbowed his way through the throng of drunken men, most of whom were dressed in sweat-stained tartan jackets and woolen shirts. Reaching into the horse trough, he dragged Crispin out by the shirt collar, glaring at Rufus with angry eyes.

"Fun's over, mates," he grumbled. "It'll take a month of Sundays to get this stink off you two."

With everyone guffawing and pointing at him, Crispin jerked clumsily away from Ashton. His ringlets of wet, dark hair were clinging to his brow, making him look much less than his age of twenty-seven. A mischievous look bounced across a face covered with a coarse, dark stubble of beard. He licked one finger and then another. "Who cares about the smell," he chuckled. "It tastes mighty good."

"I hope it'll satisfy your appetite for champagne and all sorts of spirits for some time to come, mates," Ashton said, helping thin and lanky Rufus from the trough. He took a step back when Rufus began to shake the champagne from his body, much the way a dog did after a bath. "Once we're in the outback, working from sunup to sunset, there'll be no drinking except for strong tea and creek water."

"So, Ashton? Sasha's agreed to go with us?" Crispin asked, forking his fingers through his tangled, sticky hair. "She's finally put that aristocrat from her mind?"

"Not quite," Ashton said, glaring from Rufus to Crispin. "And from the looks of things, perhaps it's best. If I can't depend on you to keep out of mischief, how can she be expected to put her trust in you?"

"Ashton, for gawd sake," Crispin fussed. "Have I ever let you down?"

"Excluding this foolishness today, not yet."

"And I won't."

"I don't think it's me that needs convincing, mate."

"Then I'll go and sweet-talk Sasha into believing in me."

Ashton took Crispin by the elbow and, with Rufus following close behind them, walked away from the merriment at the horse trough. He leaned close to his friends and spoke more softly, casting occasional glances across his shoulder, not wanting to be heard by troublemakers. There were plenty of them in this crazed city of wild prospectors.

"I'll worry about Sasha's feelings," Ashton said. "And I'll forget today's incident—that is, if you've come to tell me that everything's been taken care of, as instructed."

"Everything," Crispin said, his hollow-cheeked face serious now. "All 'cept for the time and date. When will you know, Ashton? Sasha can't expect you to wait on her decision forever."

"Sasha's given me her pub earnings for the venture," Ashton said, looking through the pub window. "I'm not about to let her change her mind."

Through the purplish haze of cigar smoke he could see Sasha at the bar, gazing raptly at a picture above it. It portrayed a ship at sea, tossed by stormy waters. He knew her thoughts without asking. She was thinking of that damned aristocrat, Woodrow Rutherford!

Damn it, Ashton thought. He wished that he could purge Sasha's mind of that man. Ashton wanted her all to himself! He gazed admiringly at her lovely breasts curved above the low, rounded neckline of her homespun dress, which also displayed a tiny waist and gently rounded hips. She was blessed with dark eyes and long, flowing raven-black hair; her smile was charming.

She was the sort who melted a man's insides, clear into the core of his being!

His jaw set, Ashton glared at Crispin. "No, by damn, no matter what, I won't let her change her mind."

"Not even if the fancy aristocrat shows up to claim 'er?" Rufus asked, his adam's apple bobbing in his scrawny, long neck.

"Damn it, mate, he's been gone three years now," Ashton said in an agitated rumble. "It's plain to see he's not coming back. But it's something that Sasha hasn't accepted yet." He swallowed hard. "Perhaps she never will."

"Who could abandon anyone as sweet and pretty as Sasha?" Rufus asked, looking at Sasha through the window, never failing to appreciate her vivacious curves and lovely face.

"Aye, how could any man turn his back on Sasha?" Ashton said, following Rufus's gaze. Then he laughed lightly. "She's so damn pretty it hurts.

But sweet?" He rubbed his bearded chin. "I've learned not to give her cause to grow impatient or angry. That angelic face and mood of hers can change quickly from sweet to a strange blaze of fury when she's crossed. She's restless and indefatigably curious."

"She'd liven up any man's life," Crispin said, envy thick in his voice. He laughed awkwardly. "But it's hands off for me, mate. I understand that she's spoken for."

"That she is, and by damn, by me, not the aristocrat," Ashton said, his violet eyes gleaming over his thick bush of neatly trimmed beard. "But I won't rest easy until I get her out of Melbourne. Tonight isn't soon enough as far as I'm concerned."

"Maybe you'd best have a go with another lady," Rufus said, wringing the remainder of the champagne from his shoulder-length hair. "Someone who's willin' to share more than a business partnership with you, if you know what I mean."

"Aw, Ashton, don't pay this drongo no mind," Crispin encouraged. "She'll be right, it'll work out."

Ashton patted Crispin on the shoulder. "Thanks for the vote of confidence, mate," he said. "Sasha's the only one for me and I'd best go and protect my investment." He nodded toward a steep flight of stairs at the side of the building. "Go on upstairs to my room and get cleaned up. I'll talk to you later when you're smelling better. Right now you're no better than two street-rowdy rascals."

Chuckling, Rufus and Crispin ambled off and climbed the rickety stairs. Ashton turned and stared at the men who had their heads dipped low into the horse trough, gulping down the champagne. Ignoring them, he walked back inside the pub, his eyes never leaving Sasha. Though barefoot and dressed poorly, she seemed misplaced in this miasma of blue and black smoke. She was a slim, black-haired beauty with a face like a quiet meadow, and she was graceful in all her movements, as though brought up in a house of aristocrats.

In truth, she had learned her most genteel, refined ways from another man—the man she was pining for even now, as she continued staring pensively up at the painting over the bar. Exhausted from the never-ending excitement of the pub, Lightning snoozed peacefully at Sasha's feet.

Ashton's pub was one of the boozier and bawdier in Melbourne, so he did not have time to concentrate on Sasha's woes. Sam, his assistant, was being run ragged by diggers from the goldfields with their gaudy women hanging on their arms in colored silks and enormous earrings like those the gypsies wore.

Making his way through the congestion, Ashton went behind the bar and began slopping out ales, "old toms," whiskey, and a popular, explosive mixture called "Thunder and Lightning." But the common solace was gin. This white grain spirit, flavored with crushed juniper berries, cost next to nothing. They said a man could get drunk for a penny—dead drunk for twopence.

As more miners flung their nuggets on the bar and ordered their drinks, Ashton balanced a row of tumblers on his arm from his fingertips to his elbow, filled them all at the same time with ale from a row of cocks, and flung them out to the customers without spilling even one bubble.

A slight clapping of hands drew Ashton's gaze to Sasha. "Bravo!" she said, her hair swirling around her shoulders as she stepped up to the bar where Ashton was now arcing liquor from tumbler to tumbler. "Ashton, you've missed your calling. You should join the circus. My word, your performance would surely make a circus juggler blush in shame."

"Anything to keep my lady entertained," Ashton said, continuing to perform his feats with the alcohol, cheers and applause proving that his efforts were appreciated by more than just Sasha. He glanced at the painting. "Sweet darlin', I dedicate my performance to you today. It seems that you need something to get your mind off Woodrow Rutherford. You can't give up on him, can you?"

Blood rushed to Sasha's cheeks. "Ashton, he promised that he'd be back," she said, her lower lip curving into a sensual pout. "He must have met with some tragedy. Perhaps . . . perhaps the ship on which he was traveling to England was wrecked in a storm at sea. I . . . would never know, would I?"

She toyed with the tiny cameo ring on her left hand, recalling the moment Woodrow gave it to her. It was a promise ring, of sorts.

"I can't believe he's dead," she added pensively. "A man as kind as he should live forever."

"Sasha, I think it's best if you concentrate on our partnership, not on the aristocrat and what may have happened to him," Ashton said, jealousy scalding his insides. He paused from his bartending to lean across the counter, only a whisper away from

15

her lustrous lips. "That's reality, sweet darlin'—
what we are planning to share."

"It's purely a business agreement," Sasha said,
lifting her chin stubbornly. "Nothing else, Ashton.
Remember that." Whenever Ashton looked at her
with his brooding, violet eyes and got so close that
she could smell his pleasant, manly scent, she
became unnerved about the agreement they had
made with each other. His nearness always made
her heart frolic within her chest, and there were
dangers in that. She had promised Woodrow that
she would remain faithful to him, and upon his
return from England would marry him. She had
been wrongly labeled his paramour in London.

In Australia, she would be his *wife*—legitimate
and respectable in every way!

"I know what we agreed to," Ashton grumbled.
"But it'd be much simpler if we'd make it a perma-
nent arrangement as man and wife."

"As long as there's hope that Woodrow is alive, I
feel unclean even speaking of marriage to another
man," Sasha said, fingering the ring nervously
again. "He was so good and kind to me. I owe him
my life."

Ashton groaned. "Sasha, it's been three long years
since he left," he said, leaning closer to her. "I can't
wait three more years for your decision about when
you'll go with me. No matter how you choose to
live, be it married or single, I need to know soon.
We've arrangements to make."

"Do you think we have enough money saved up
yet, Ashton, to purchase all of the supplies?" Sasha
asked, staring down at her bare feet. She had not
spent one coin of her earnings on even a pair of

shoes. Those that Woodrow had purchased for her were too fancy to wear while laboring in Ashton's pub. She wanted to split the cost with Ashton as evenly as possible so that she would feel like a true partner.

In her heart she had given up hope that Woodrow would return. She was torn as to how to feel about that. Sad that harm may have come to him? Or bitter because he may have chosen to abandon her?

Either way, she was near to admitting that her future lay with Ashton York—but not as his wife. Only as a legitimate business partner. She had given her heart to one man. Did she dare to love another? Trust was weakening within her for any man.

She would guard her investment, that was for sure!

"We're pretty damn close to having everything we need to head for the outback in search of prime land for a sheep station," Ashton said. "But you must remember—few ways of life demand more financial prudence than stockfarming."

He nodded toward the crowd that was swelling in his pub. "There's lots of gold in those pockets tonight, sweet darlin'," he drawled. "Let's work it all out of them. Who knows? Maybe we can leave for the outback tomorrow. Being a squatter has its compensations. We'll awaken every morning breathing the free, open air—not the stench of ale!"

And, he thought, he would have Sasha away from the temptation of always being on the lookout for the aristocrat. Once in the outback on their sheep station, Ashton would make sure she never had cause to think about Woodrow Rutherford again!

Also, Ashton could perhaps put another man from his mind. Superintendent Silas Howland. While in Melbourne, Ashton was forced to keep an eye out for him day and night even though he wore a beard to help hide his identity. If Superintendent Howland's wounds ever healed, it was for certain that he would strive to seek vengeance on the man who had half crippled him—Ashton York!

The dingo pup following her, Sasha gave Ashton a half smile and began making her way around the room, taking orders and filling them. She had become adept at avoiding the raucous, foul-talking miners who tried to sneak in strokes and pinches. She was no less skilled tonight even though her mind was elsewhere, on another time—four years ago, when she was fifteen, in London . . . .

Sasha's father had been a metalfounder who died paralyzed with lead poisoning. Her mother had preceded her father in death by three years in childbirth, the stillborn infant joining his mother in the grave.

As the only surviving child, with no close cousins or uncles to care for her, Sasha had been forced to fend for herself on the streets of London, begging for even the tiniest morsel to keep herself alive. Bedraggled, barefoot, and half-starved, she wandered to an affluent section of the city and curled up on the steps of a grand mansion, only to be awakened by the sound of coins dropping close to her feet. When she discovered two of the brightest gold coins she had ever seen, and then a man wearing elegant patent-leather boots standing beside them, she looked slowly up into dark and questioning eyes.

Her gaze swept quickly over the man. From his elegant attire and the diamonds sparkling on the fingers of both his hands, she realized that he must live in this mansion on whose steps she had taken refuge for the night. She bolted to her feet to run away, but the man grabbed her by the wrist and stopped her. After she explained her sad circumstances to him, he took her inside his home.

This man, Woodrow Rutherford, was a scion of a rich and highly respected English family, a bachelor in his late thirties. Intrigued by Sasha, and pitying her state of affairs, he made her his ward, proposing to instruct her in all the skills and arts necessary to become a refined and proper lady. . . .

Sasha stooped to pet Lightning, her troubled thoughts brought quickly back to the present when she heard the clinking of coins landing at her bare feet. She stared unblinkingly down at the two shiny gold coins, her heart lurching when she saw just beside them a pair of elegant patent-leather boots that were surely worn by a man of distinction. Could it be? Had Woodrow returned and was he teasing her with a repeat performance of their first meeting?

Sasha slowly lifted her eyes, a part of her truly dreading Woodrow's return, for she had never loved him the way a woman should when she gave her promise of marriage. Now, at this moment of truth, she knew that she loved Ashton York with all of her heart! Not only did she love Ashton, but he had taken her under his wing and employed her as a tavern maid in his pub. They were even planning an exciting adventure together! She had saved all of the money she had earned, and she and

Ashton were going to own and run a sheep station together!

Now if Woodrow had returned, what should she do?

She had promised to marry him.

Her gaze stopped on the man's face and she gasped when she found dark, questioning eyes peering down at her. . . .

Chapter Two

Lightning's growling at Sasha's side drew Ashton quickly from behind the bar. He rushed to Lightning and grabbed her collar, stopping her just as she was ready to make a lunge for the man who had obviously startled Sasha.

Ashton grew cold inside when he was able to see the man's full facial features. His free hand went to his beard and stroked it nervously, wondering if the beard was enough disguise, for this man had known Ashton when he had not worn one.

"Is this man bothering you?" Ashton asked, knowing there was no way to disguise his voice. That alone could give him away. Was it possible that after two years of pretending to be somebody else, he was going to be discovered? The name Lawrence Proffitt was dead to him now, and once he had chosen his new name—Ashton York—he had decided never to fall back on the old identity again. There were too many dangers in that.

"No," Sasha murmured, rising slowly to her full height. "I—I took him for someone else. How foolish I feel!"

She could not believe that she had let herself think that the man being generous with the gold coins could be Woodrow. If it had been he, he would have swept her away from the pub without playing games with coins! He would have been appalled to find her there, barefoot and tending to drunken, rowdy prospectors—no matter that he was the reason for her situation.

Ashton slipped a possessive arm around Sasha's waist and drew her close to him. He glared at the man who still smugly stood his ground, his thick lips curved into a sly grin. "Mate, I would suggest you be on your way," he said flatly, challenging the man he knew as Stanford Sidwell. Ashton had never been certain if that was Stanford's true name. A confidence man and ex-convict, Stanford could fool anyone—surely even his own mother.

Ashton's gaze swept over Stanford and saw that his leisurely pastime of thinking about how to get money—scheming, planning, plotting, organizing, and dreaming of it—seemed to be working for him since his recent departure from prison. His dark hair oiled and scented, his midnight-black eyes confident, he played the role of a man of dignity well. Today he was dressed resplendently in a crisp white ruffled shirt, a silk embroidered, white Marseilles waistcoat, and dark, snug-fitting breeches. A diamond stickpin sparkled from the folds of his white silk cravat and an expensive cigar was stuffed into his breast pocket.

Ashton's eyes locked on the lone pistol tucked under Stanford's belt, then caught a glimpse of a sheathed knife at his waist beneath his coat. His insides tightened, recalling the feel of that cold steel against his flesh, and then the warm trickle of blood. . . .

He slowly met Stanford's gaze again, knowing not to trust the pompous swindler, no matter how respectable he looked.

While Sasha watched the quiet communication and the sense of challenge between Ashton and the stranger, she momentarily forgot the gold coins at her feet. Her eyes wide in disbelief, she watched the man now take a ten-dollar note from his rear pocket and strike a match, holding the flame to the note.

Lightning began to growl again, straining at the leash as Ashton held tightly to it. "I think my pup is a good judge of character," Ashton said, his teeth clenched, ignoring the game that Stanford was playing. "And if you don't want me to sic her on you, I suggest you take your notes to burn elsewhere." He glanced down at the coins at Sasha's feet. He scooted them toward Stanford with the toe of his boot. "And take your coins with you. Sasha doesn't take handouts. She earns her pay."

His eyes gleaming, still smiling roguishly, Stanford dropped the flaming note to the floor, grinding it out with the heel of his fine patent-leather boot. "The coins are hers," he said, winking down at her. "Seems her pay isn't enough for her to own a pair of shoes."

Feeling left out of this fray which had started because of her, and wanting to defend her character to this man who seemed not to be a stranger at all to Ashton, Sasha jerked away from Ashton's possessive hold. Kneeling, she scooped the coins up into her hands, then straightened her back proudly and took it upon herself to drop the coins in the stranger's waistcoat pocket.

"Sir, I am barefoot by choice," she snapped. "Please take your coins and take leave of this pub. It seems you took a wrong turn when you entered. The hotels where whores would find your generosity and flamboyance amusing are just up the street."

Not swayed by either Ashton's or Sasha's rebuff, Stanford slipped his cigar from his pocket and lit it. He took a long drag from it, then gave Sasha a slow smile. "I find you much more fascinating than any whore I could pay to lift her skirts for the night," he said smoothly. "My dear, there are so many stories that I would like to amuse you with if you would so desire to listen."

Ashton circled his free hand into a tight fist at his side, tempted to let Lightning loose on this vain, damned persistent man. "Sasha doesn't need to hear any of your tall tales," he said, his jaw tight. It was taking all the willpower he could muster up not to slam a fist into Stanford's smug face. It was obvious what the con man was trying to do. He was going to get on Sasha's good side, eventually to get her to reveal secrets about Ashton York—secrets that Sasha did not even know and Ashton had hoped never to have to tell her!

"Sasha," Stanford said, delicately flicking the ash from his cigar. "What a lovely name. But of course it would be. A beautiful woman deserves a beautiful name."

Ashton sucked in a trembling, angry breath of air. He took a step forward, Lightning jerking at the leash and snarling close to Stanford's feet.

But Stanford was not to be dissuaded by the threats of a dingo pup—or an Ashton York. He stood his ground, oblivious of anything or anyone but Sasha.

Sasha was astounded by the man's persistence and knew that all she had to do to stop it was to turn and walk away. But there was something about the man and the strained behavior between him and Ashton that made her stay. Her lips parted when the man began to spin a tale that soon caught her in its spell.

"My dear Sasha, have you ever heard the tale of the seaside dairies where mermaids come up to be milked every morning?" Stanford said smoothly, his eyes twinkling.

"My word, no I haven't," Sasha said, always susceptible to fantastic fables. "Mermaids? Are there truly mermaids? Can they actually be milked?"

Ashton was at the limit of his patience. He grabbed Sasha's elbow and jerked her away from Stanford, walking her and Lightning toward the bar. "For God's sake, Sasha, don't you know when someone is pulling your leg?" he said angrily. "How can you be so naive as to believe anything that son of a bitch says?"

"He sounded so sincere," Sasha said, looking over her shoulder as the man continued to watch her with his sly grin. "And the story—the beginning of the story—was so beautiful. I could just envision a beautiful mermaid. . . ."

"If you believed that, then you'd believe the man if he told you you could buy a Sydney Harbor ferry boat for that same ten-dollar note he burned to impress you," Ashton fussed, securing Lightning's leash to the leg of a stool and taking Sasha over to the far side of the room to talk with her in private.

"Ashton, you seem to know so much about the man," Sasha said, searching his eyes for answers.

"Everyone knows a confidence man when they see one," Ashton said, then forked an eyebrow. "Except you, it seems."

"Ashton, I sensed more in your meeting than the recognition of a confidence man," Sasha ventured, knowing by Ashton's reaction that she had guessed correctly. Her questioning caused Ashton to tense up and look guardedly over at the man who had strolled casually to the bar, ordering drinks for everyone. "Who is he, Ashton? You have met before, haven't you?"

"Aye, I know of him," Ashton grumbled, his eyes squinting angrily as he watched Stanford. "His reputation precedes him, you might say." He nodded toward Stanford. "Look at him. See how free and easy he spends his money?"

"Yes," Sasha said, nodding. "It seems that he is quite an affluent man. Yet how can he remain wealthy if he so easily squanders his money? Why Ashton, I have never seen such a spendthrift as he!"

Ashton laughed throatily as he leaned his back against the wall. "It's all a part of the con game, sweet darlin'," he said, folding his arms across his chest. "The greasy swindler. Just watch him. He'll dangle his money before the prospectors' eyes and tell them how they can make big money fast."

"How?" Sasha asked, unable to keep from being intrigued by the stranger with the smooth, flamboyant manner. But she knew to be wary of him. Any man who sported such wealth was not to be trusted. She had trusted Woodrow Rutherford.

Ashton gave Sasha a quiet, disbelieving stare, wishing that she wasn't so innocent and sweet. Now that Stanford had shown up, the man would stop at nothing to learn all of Ashton's movements since they had had their last fiery entanglement. Sasha was going to be suckered into liking the man—into trusting him! And there wasn't one damn thing Ashton could do about it, short of killing the son-of-a-bitch confidence man. Stanford Sidwell had been a thorn in Ashton's side in the past and was surely planning to sink deeper and deeper into his flesh now, until he got what he wanted.

Information.

Information that could make the confidence man richer than anyone ever dreamed possible!

"Sasha, haven't you heard anything I've said about that man?" Ashton groaned. "He'd sell his own mother if he could make a profit on the transaction." He glowered as he watched Stanford in action. "Just look at him. I can just hear his spiel. He's probably selling one of those prospectors the sundial in the city garden, or offering to sell him a gold brick in a brown paper wrapper for a ten dollar note. You can bet he's got a dozen tricks up his sleeves tonight."

"I can see why you didn't want him in your pub,"

Sasha said, casting Ashton a look of sympathy. "You asked him to leave and he didn't. Are you going to have him thrown out?"

Not wanting to stir up any more trouble with Stanford tonight, and realizing the risks he would be taking, Ashton saw no choice but to ignore the man. "Naw, I don't think so," he said, leaning away from the wall. He started back toward the bar. "I'll just close the place down for a while. That way I'll get no arguments from anyone in particular."

Sasha scampered after him, the skirt of her dress whirling around her legs. "Ashton, if you close down the pub, we'll lose out on too many wages," she argued. She grabbed him by the arm, stopping him. She looked up into his eyes. "Ashton, it's not just because he's a confidence man that you don't like him. What else? You've never let any man intimidate you. You've never hesitated for a moment to throw a troublemaker out of your pub. Now you're going out of your way to keep from doing it." She paused, her heart pounding. "Why, Ashton? What aren't you telling me?"

Ashton glowered down at her, his pulse racing, aware that he had let his guard down too much tonight. As astute as Sasha was, she had picked up on too much that he had kept hidden from her.

His future—their future—might be in jeopardy because of it.

It was best to ignore her implorings and hope that she would soon forget her questions—and Stanford Sidwell too.

Yet, would Stanford let her forget him?

Not likely!

Setting his lips tightly, Ashton moved away from

Sasha and began informing everyone that the pub was going to be closed for a while. The drinkers and their clinging women began to leave, but not without first fussing about it. To Ashton's chagrin, Stanford was the last at the bar. He was slowly sipping on a drink, looking over the rim of the mug at Ashton.

"Damn it, I said clear out," Ashton said, resting his palms against the top of the counter. He leaned into Stanford's face, now almost certain that he had been recognized. He waited to see exactly what the con man had on his mind.

Stanford lowered the mug from his mouth and wiped his lips with the back of his hand, then shoved the mug toward Ashton. "Have an ale, mate?" he taunted. He placed two shillings on the counter. "Or do you prefer whiskey?"

"If I wanted a drink, I sure as hell wouldn't share it with you," Ashton said in a low hiss. "I'm not one of your suckers, Sidwell. Now move on."

"So you've heard of me, eh?" Stanford said slyly. "You know what my game is, eh?"

"Who doesn't?" Ashton challenged.

"Now, mate, can you blame me for being good at my trade?" Stanford boasted, his eyes gleaming. "After all, if somebody loses some money here and there, well, it's no worse losing it to me than losing it to somebody else."

Ashton's jaw tightened. "Take a look around you, mate," he grumbled. "Do you see anyone left for you to fleece?" He placed a hand on one of his revolvers. "Most certainly not me." His eyes became dark squints. "And for damn certain not Sasha."

"I hear tell you are the owner of this pub and that

29

your name is Ashton York," Stanford said, ignoring the threat of Ashton's revolver. He smiled sardonically as Sasha moved to Ashton's side.

"That's true," Ashton said. "You want to make something of it?" The next thing he expected was for the ex-convict to breathe the name Lawrence Proffitt across his thick lips. If so, Ashton's world would be turned upside down again, just as it was the last time he got mixed up with this damn con artist.

"Naw," Stanford said, slipping a hand inside his front breeches pocket for a coin. He flipped it on the counter, and leaned toward Ashton. "But it's strange as hell how that name Ashton York just doesn't seem to match the color of your eyes."

Stanford mocked a salute as he rose from the bar stool. "Good day to the both of you," he said, laughing boisterously as he walked toward the swinging doors.

Lightning yelped and howled until the confidence man stepped outside, out of sight. Ashton turned slowly and met Sasha's questioning stare, then looked quickly away. He was waiting for her to bombard him with questions and searching for a way to avoid them.

His gaze stopped at the painting over the bar. Remembering her earlier concentration on the portrait, and knowing why, he found an escape from her questions—for a while, at least.

"Sasha, earlier you were fretting over Woodrow and I scolded you for it," he said, going to close and lock the front door. He went back to her and took her hands. "For so long you've been wanting to talk about it and I haven't let you. We have a respite from the drinkers for a while. Why not spend it just sitting and talking? Then perhaps you'll feel better about things."

The confidence man's words about Ashton's eyes and name not matching had sent more waves of questions through Sasha's mind. She wanted to rush Ashton with the questions, yet she knew when he was purposely avoiding being open with her. And this time he must be more desperate than usual if he was willing to hear her discuss her life with Woodrow. She knew the jealousy this caused him!

She felt no less jealous herself now, knowing that Ashton had had a past, perhaps a questionable one, that he had not shared with her. Did the past include not only the confidence man, but also a woman?

Perhaps many?

Guilt washed through her for feeling that she had any claim at all on Ashton York. She was still spoken for. And until she knew that she wasn't, she had no right to feel jealousy over Ashton—or the sensual feelings that he aroused within her sometimes.

Oh, but love him she must! Never had she felt these emotions with Woodrow! She had experienced only a great sense of gratitude and peace while with the rich aristocrat who had chosen her over all the other women in his world. She had to remember! Above all else, even though he may have betrayed her, she had to remember that she owed him so much!

"Come," Ashton encouraged her. He stopped to release Lightning's leash, setting her free to roam as she pleased around the room. Then he guided Sasha by the hand to a table and chairs. He eased her down onto a chair, then sat down opposite her. "Talk. Talk it all out. Then perhaps you will even feel like setting a date for leaving for the outback."

"Are you sure you want to hear me talk about Woodrow again?" Sasha murmured, blinking her thick eyelashes at Ashton. "At the beginning, when we first became acquainted, you listened intensely. But since then, you . . . you do not. I understand, Ashton, if you would rather I didn't worry aloud again about my awkward situation with Woodrow."

Ashton reached for her hand and patted it. "I understand that it makes you feel better to talk out your worries," Ashton said, now circling his fingers around her hand, relishing the touch of her flesh against his. He had yet to kiss her, and his mouth hungered for her lips more than he would have thought possible.

Even now, every fiber of his being cried out to hold her and tell her that no matter how many promises she had made to that rich aristocrat, it was Ashton York she loved! He could see it in her every look! He could feel it when they stood close, as though her soul was merging into his!

He knew she loved him. And in time, she would admit it and allow him to return that love in every way known to man!

"Go ahead, Sasha," Ashton further encouraged her. "Talk it out. I'm here to listen."

"I explained to you about being orphaned and that Woodrow took me in to be his ward," Sasha said, watching Ashton closely to see whether or not she should truly go on. He seemed to be controlling his mood better than the last time she

32

had attempted to talk to him about her past, so she continued.

"Woodrow kept his word," she said, patting Lightning as the pup came and lapped at her bare feet. "Because of his kindness I learned how to read and write, how to dance, and to be skilled with the loveliest of needlework." She stopped and lowered her eyes, blushing, then looked at Ashton again. "But instead of people calling me Woodrow's ward, I was called his paramour by many." She circled her fingers around Ashton's clasped hand. "But Ashton, I never ever slept with Woodrow. He wanted more than for me to be his mistress. He had grown fond enough of me to want me to be his wife."

Ashton's eyes darkened moodily. He glanced away from Sasha, glad that Lightning had jumped onto his lap, to divert attention away from the true feelings that were jarring his insides. "Go on," he said thickly, running his free hand through the pup's soft fur. "Get it all out, Sasha. Perhaps you won't have the need to tell it again."

"If you wish," Sasha murmured. "Ashton, no matter how cultivated and refined I became, in the class-conscious opinion of the British aristocracy I could never be accepted as Woodrow's wife. He was a man with a background and breeding. I . . . I was the daughter of a mere metalfounder."

Wanting her to get through with the story, Ashton interrupted her. "So the aristocrat was forced to bring you to Australia, where he would be free to marry and love you," he said, his voice solemn.

"Yes," Sasha said, nodding. "But before the vows were exchanged, he was summoned back to England. His father had died. He was to return to inherit the family estates and become Sir Woodrow Rutherford, baronet."

Ashton interrupted again. "He promised to return for you," he said. "Soon to be a titled man, he would have all the privileges that he had not had before."

"Yes, and he was kind enough to leave me enough money to last the eighteen months that we had planned to be separated," Sasha said, interrupting Ashton. She held out her ring finger, the cameo small and white beneath the dull lamplight of the room. "He gave me this cameo ring the day he left. It was to seal his promise to me."

"And you couldn't part with the ring when your luck ran out," Ashton grumbled.

"You came to my rescue just in time," Sasha said, laughing softly. "I would've hocked the ring the very next day. But you offered me a job. Then you became my—very best friend in the world. I shall always remember that, Ashton. Always."

Her description of their relationship as only 'best friends' rankled Ashton. He wanted much more than that!

But he had been patient with her feelings up to now. Surely he could be patient a while longer. Come hell or high water, they would soon be out of this damn pub, living a much different sort of life out on a sheep station. *Their* sheep station. . . .

Sasha took her hand from Ashton's and rose from the chair. She went to peer from the window, feeling suddenly alone and empty. "Oh, Ashton, I feel so torn," she said, her voice breaking. "Should I be bitter because Woodrow has not returned as promised? Has he deserted me for money and title? Or has something happened to him?"

Warm arms encircling her waist made Sasha's knees grow weak and her insides become strangely quivery. Never had he done this before. And now she understood why she had not wanted him to. The feelings that his arms were stirring within her were frighteningly wonderful! Frighteningly wrong—for she was promised to another man!

When Ashton turned her slowly around, locking her within his powerful arms, she looked up into his heart-melting violet eyes. She could not find it within herself to struggle to get away from him. She was becoming quickly lost to an ecstasy that she had never known before.

Oh, how deliciously sweet it was!

Nor did she attempt to move away from him when she saw his lips lowering toward hers. She needed him.

Oh, how she needed him!

He was like a balm to her wounded pride—pride that had been slowly ebbing away as the days and weeks passed without Woodward proving that he had not made a fool of her.

Ashton moved his hands to Sasha's long and flowing hair. Weaving his fingers through the silken tresses, he drew her mouth closer. . . .

And then they kissed. Sasha had never experienced anything as glorious as Ashton's kiss. It sent spirals of rapture through her, from her head to her toes. She twined her arms around his neck and clung to him, very aware of his body molding into hers, and of the strength of him at the juncture of his thighs. Slowly he pressed himself against her, erasing everything from her mind but the rapture that his body was conveying to her.

Everything seemed to be whirling inside Ashton. Filled with such heated passion, he could hardly bear not to lower her to the floor to fulfill the manly needs that she had aroused within him from that very first moment he had seen her. It would not take much to carry him over the brink into total ecstasy. . . .

Frisky and ready to play, Lightning wormed her way between Ashton and Sasha. Looking up at them, from one to the other, she began whining. When that got no response, she let out a mind-grabbing howl.

Sasha and Ashton were jerked apart by the howling. Sasha looked up at Ashton, her face flushed with sensual excitement. His heart pounding, Ashton touched her face reverently, then laughed when Lightning began jumping up at him for serious attention.

"Seems Lightning is jealous," Ashton said, grabbing the pup up in his arms. "Is there anything to be jealous of, Sasha? The kiss said that there is."

Tormented by her true feelings, yet angry at herself for having allowed Ashton to discover them, Sasha turned to walk away from him.

With the pup in his arms, Ashton followed her. "Deny it all you want, Sasha, but I won't believe that you don't have feelings for me," he argued. "And, damn it, I can't go on this way. Either you come to your senses and stop fretting over Woodrow, or by damn I'm going to forget our arrangement. It's bad enough loving you like hell and not being able to do anything about it, let alone have you continue to refuse to give me an answer about when we can sell this pub and buy up some grazing land far from this crazed city of Melbourne.''

Sasha swung around and faced him. "But Ashton, if you care so much for me, won't it be awkward working with me as partners at the sheep station?'' she asked, her voice weak and troubled.

"Damn it, Sasha, don't you know that's exactly why I decided to join in this adventure with you?'' Ashton grumbled. "If I couldn't have you for a wife, at least I could have you for a partner!''

Sasha's eyes widened and she swallowed hard. "Oh, but, Ashton, will that be enough for you?'' she murmured.

"Will it for you?'' he questioned, his voice deep and strained.

Sasha ignored his question, knowing that she could not give him an honest answer about anything, personal or business. She now knew that every moment with Ashton out on the sheep station would be a struggle—a struggle to keep her wits as far as he was concerned. Now that she had tasted his kiss, she would always hunger for it again—and again!

"You asked for an answer,'' she said softly. "Give me one more month, Ashton. Please? Then I promise, if I've heard nothing from Woodrow, I will leave Melbourne with you.''

Ashton's heart skipped a beat, finding it hard to believe that she was finally making an actual commitment! "Fine,'' he said a bit awkwardly. He set Lightning to the floor. "That would be fine.''

Sasha went to a cracked mirror on the wall. She lifted her black hair and studied it. "Ashton, I've been thinking about cutting my hair before we start out for the outback," she said, then thrilled all over when he came to her and tenderly kissed the nape of her neck. She closed her eyes. "Oh, Ashton, please don't do that. Please?"

Ashton stepped away from her. He grabbed a pair of scissors from the back of the bar and forced them into her hand. "Go ahead and cut your hair," he said angrily. "What does it matter if you look like a man or woman, anyhow?"

He stormed away. Lightning went to Sasha and looked up at her with trusting eyes, looking as though they were smiling. Sasha placed the scissors on the bar, shuddering at the thought of ever actually having to cut her long hair, then knelt to her knees and hugged Lightning.

"I continue to hurt Ashton, Lightning," she whispered. "Will it ever be any different? Will I ever truly feel free enough to allow him to love me?"

She watched Ashton as he began moving glasses from the tables, slamming them on the bar. When he looked her way, his expression and mood quickly softened. Their eyes locked and there was no denying what was being said between them, no matter that Sasha would not allow it to be said aloud.

Chapter Three

ONE MONTH LATER

Standing at a mirror in her drab room across the corridor from Ashton's above York's Pub, Sasha gazed at her reflection. She giggled as she ran her hands down the loose-fitting red woolen shirt, and then the trousers that hung loosely from her body and were secured at the waist with a length of rope. Would Ashton even recognize her once she plopped the wide-brimmed kangaroo-hide hat on her head? Down to the shining new boots on her feet she looked like a man—the best way for a lone woman to travel with a group of men into the out-back.

She eyed the scissors that lay on a table beside her bed, then looked back at her reflection in the mirror and ran her fingers through her lustrously long hair. Without it she would feel naked.

Yet, wouldn't it be a bother on the journey? To

keep it hidden beneath her hat, she would be fighting it constantly.

And in his anger hadn't Ashton told her to go ahead and cut it?

She should, just to spite him!

While looking in the mirror, she caught sight of her naked ring finger. She held it out before her, missing the cameo ring, but not what it had stood for. She was more bitter than sad now that Woodrow had not returned for her. Surely he had abandoned her. Even if it had been at the advice of his attorneys, he had abandoned her no less! She was worth less to him than being a baronet. Had his title been threatened because of his association with her, he surely would have chosen it over her!

"No matter why he has not returned for me, I shall never wholly trust a man again," she whispered harshly. "Even Ashton. He would surely abandon me also if there were monetary rewards in doing so!"

"Did I hear someone speak my name?"

Ashton's voice behind her drew Sasha around to face him. She had not heard him enter the room. How much had he overheard while she was fussing to herself?

Her face colored, but she soon discovered that it was not what she had been doing or saying that had caught Ashton's attention. She could tell by the way his eyes were raking over her that her attire had completely caught him off guard. She had talked of dressing as a man for the journey. But never had he thought that she had been serious.

"Damn," Ashton said, ambling toward her, his

eyes still taking her in as though they were drinking her. "Where on earth did you get those clothes? Is that truly you?" A slow smile lifted his lips. "Do I call you Patrick? Or Aaron?"

"Do I truly look that horrid?" Sasha gasped, wounded by his reaction. "I kind of . . . like the way I look." She turned and faced the mirror, then spun around, giggling. "I think I like the name Spike better. Would you like to call me Spike, Ashton? Does that fit my appearance well enough?"

"Spike?" Ashton said, laughing softly. "I don't know. Perhaps we'd better ask Lightning." He whistled, and Lightning bounded into the room from the corridor. The pup seemed to stop in mid-air when she saw Sasha, then emitted a low snarl, her teeth baring. The pup sidled up next to Ashton's leg, her tail tucked between her leg.

"My word," Sasha said, placing a hand to her throat. "She doesn't seem to recognize me at all."

Ashton nodded toward the huge hat lying on the bed. "Once you get that damn thing on, nobody'll know you," he said, his eyes dancing.

"Good!" Sasha said, grabbing the hat. She plopped it on her head and leaned down into Lightning's face. "Boo!" she teased.

Both Sasha and Ashton flew into a fit of laughter when Lightning cowered, dropping to the floor to cover her eyes with her paws, a trick that Ashton had taught the pup.

"Well, that's that," Sasha said, removing the hat as her laughter faded. "I've chosen right. Now I can travel with the rest of the men as though I'm one of them. Though those who travel with us will know who I am, I most certainly will fool any other men who may pass by us on our way in search of land for our sheep station."

Ashton took the hat from Sasha and tossed it on the bed. He lifted her hand up to his eyes and gazed at her empty ring finger. "Just as I thought," he said. "You hocked your ring to buy this outfit." His eyes implored her. "You didn't tell me you were going to do that. We could've come up with some spare money, somehow, to buy the clothes."

Sasha kicked out a leg. "And boots," she said proudly. "Aren't they grand, Ashton?"

"Sasha, the ring," Ashton persisted. "You cherished it. I am amazed that you parted with it. Are you sure you truly don't mind having done so?"

A strange sort of pain circled Sasha's heart as she recalled the exact moment the ring had been given to her. A promise ring—a promise ring given to her by a liar!

"I had no further use for it," she said, swinging away from Ashton. She picked up the scissors and stood before the mirror again. "Now do I? Or don't I?"

"Do you or don't you what?" Ashton said, aghast at what she was considering doing, pretending that he didn't know.

"Just a few snips, Ashton, and I wouldn't have to be bothered with my long hair any longer," Sasha teased, giving him a sidewise glance. She knew that he adored her hair. She had seen him admiring it often enough. The one time he had woven his fingers through it had been done with such reverence! "Wouldn't it be simpler, Ashton, just to cut my hair and throw it away?"

Teasingly she pulled out a long length of hair and placed the scissors to it. She was startled speechless at Ashton's quick, violent reaction.

In a blink of an eye he grabbed the scissors from her hand and took them to the door, pitching them out into the corridor. Then he turned to face her, his doubled fists on his hips. "Now are you ready to go, or not?"

For a moment Sasha was speechless. In so many ways, Ashton proved his devotion to her. Surely he could be trusted. Surely she could entrust her love to him! Yet, there would always be the nagging doubt that had been instilled in her by Woodrow Rutherford!

Her gaze traveled over Ashton. Every inch of him stirred her with a keen passion! His deerhide breeches and shirt clung to him the way a glove fits a hand, revealing his muscled shoulders and chest and his lean, magnificent torso. His wide-brimmed hat hid his golden-red hair and shadowed his violet eyes and whiskered face. As usual, as though they had been born with him, Ashton's revolvers were holstered at his hips.

"I'll be just a minute," Sasha murmured, drawing herself from her reverie. Turning toward the mirror again, she busied her fingers by plaiting her thick hair into two braids, coiling them on top of her head, and pinning them there. Suddenly Ashton's reflection was in the mirror behind her, and she sucked in a nervous breath when he gently placed her hat on her head over the coil of hair.

"It's gonna take a lot of getting used to," Ashton said, frowning down at her. "I may up and burn those clothes if I ever catch them off you."

"You wouldn't!" Sasha gasped.

"Sweet darlin', it's a crime to hide such a body beneath such garb as you're wearing today," Ashton said, reaching to touch her face.

Sasha tensed and stepped away from him, and his hand dropped awkwardly to his side. She could see the passion in his eyes. She had heard the need in his voice.

Oh, but Lord, it matched her own!

But since their one wild embrace, she had avoided letting it happen again.

Slipping away from him, Sasha took one last look around the drab room, but not because she was going to miss it. The bed was leaning precariously sideways, the mattress flat and hard. There was only one chair, a table on which sat a washbasin and a pitcher of water. The window was bare of curtains.

A dark shade hung at the window, tattered and torn; wallpaper was peeling from the walls, plaster crumbling from beneath it. A trunk sat empty at the foot of the bed, the silken and satin clothes that had once filled it sold long ago. She had placed her few cotton frocks, which were more appropriate for the life that she was heading for, in her valise.

"Sasha, are you ready to go?" Ashton asked, breaking through her thoughts. "Are you ready to seek our fortune in the thriving wool trade?"

She turned to him and smiled wanly. "I am if you are," she murmured. "I don't think I'm going to miss this place one bit." She moved to him and peered up at him. "Ashton, are you sure we're doing the right thing? At least, running the pub, you knew from one day to the next where the next meal was coming from. There are so many unknowns ahead of us."

Ashton placed his hands gently to her shoulders. "It's a mite late to begin doubting our decision, isn't it?" he said, his eyes devouring her lovely face. "Sam has already bought our pub. Looks like we have no choice but to leave Melbourne in search of our dreams."

Sasha's lips fluttered into a smile. "Our dreams," she said softly. "I like the sound of that."

"Then let's go and mount our horses, sweet darlin', and be on our way," he said, touching the brim of her hat delicately. "We've a ways to go before finding that dream."

He reached down and lifted his pup into his arms, then eyed Sasha questioningly. "You can ride a horse, can't you?" he asked, forking an eyebrow.

"I guess you're just going to have to wait and find out, aren't you?" Sasha said, grabbing up her packed valise. She walked briskly toward the door. "But I bet you're going to find out that I can out-ride you any day."

She was transported back in time, to the days when she had looked forward to afternoons after school with her best friend Priscilla. Priscilla had shared her gifts from her over-generous father with Sasha—including her horses. On their proud steeds, they had ridden many an afternoon, touching the wild winds, oh, so often! She had felt as if she belonged in that world, at least for a while. . . .

She stopped in mid-step and looked at Ashton, her eyes wide with a sudden new thought. This was now. There was plenty to worry about now and tomorrow, without wasting thought on yesteryears!

"Ashton, how on earth did you find enough men to ride with us, to join us on our sheep station?" she marveled. "So many single men are still looking for their fortunes in gold. Lordy, I daresay the wages we'll be able to pay them may not be enough to clothe them adequately, much less have any left over for a man's sort of entertainment."

"Most of the men who have signed up with us are those who have been rich for one day, poor the next," Ashton said, weaving an arm around Sasha's waist, ushering her from the room. "They saw the follies in that sort of life and are ready to enjoy the pleasures of the life of the outback."

He gave her an uneasy look, one that he hoped she would not recognize. In truth, most of the men joining him and Sasha on this adventure were reformed convicts and bushrangers—friends of Ashton's past. He fervently hoped they were reformed in all ways, including their behavior toward ladies.

"You said that Crispin and Rufus have gone ahead," Sasha said, walking beside Ashton down the steep flight of stairs outside the building, to the wooden sidewalk. "Why would they? How will we ever find them if they aren't aware of where we are going to claim our squatter's rights? Where are the sheep? Have they been purchased?"

"We've a meeting place planned," Ashton said, setting Lightning to the ground, then whistling to her as the pup started to dash across the thoroughfare in front of a horseman. "That's all that I can say about it. I guess you're just going to have to trust that I know what I'm doing."

Lightning came and wagged her tail as she looked up at Ashton. Ashton reached to pat her, then stiffened and rose to his full height again when he saw Stanford Sidwell dismount across the street. For a moment their eyes met and held. Then Stanford strode away, puffing on a cigar.

Sasha placed her hands on her hips. She glared up at Ashton. "Ashton York, you should not be keeping any secrets from me about our sheep station," she reminded him. "Do you forget so soon that I am your partner? I should be apprised of everything you have planned and do. Is that understood?"

"Aye, understood," Ashton said, his eyes twinkling. "Now, Spike, have you finished scolding me? Can we get on our way?"

He glanced across the street, searching for Stanford and sighing with relief when he was nowhere to be seen. It was apparent, Ashton thought, that he was not getting out of town any too soon. If he didn't have enough to worry about now that Stanford had discovered his whereabouts, it would be his luck if Superintendent Silas Howland also suddenly appeared from his past to wreak havoc in his life again—just as Ashton was beginning to hope that he was not only going to have the life he wanted, but also the woman of his heart.

"Ashton, forevermore dispense with that horrid nickname," Sasha said, sighing. As she stepped out onto the dirt street, she dodged horse droppings and broken bottles. "Heaven knows what I am going to be forced to endure on this venture. I most certainly do not need that name to contend with as well."

Ashton took her by an elbow and guided her

toward a saddled horse. "I think you'll not find it hard to get used to this lovely creature, will you?" he asked, stopping to pat the sleek white horse, its mane about him like a cloud. "He was once a brumby, one of Australia's wild mustangs. But now he's tamed and I bought him just for you." He turned to Sasha. "I hope you two become the greatest of friends."

Sasha's breath was taken away by the horse with its wide, rigid nostrils and flaming eyes. She reached a hand to its nose and let it nuzzle her palm. "We already are friends, aren't we, Cloud?" she murmured. "Do you like that name? I think it's as pretty as you are."

Ashton shoved a rifle into the saddleboot on Sasha's horse. "Time's awastin', Spike," he teased, flashing a wide grin at Sasha. "I'd advise you to mount your horse without assistance or you might get labeled a sissy if you ask for help."

"Spike?" Sasha said, giving Ashton an annoyed stare. "Truly, Ashton, I abhore that name!"

Ashton shrugged. "You're the one who chose it," he taunted. "Not I."

"Perhaps I did," Sasha pouted. "But I'm asking you please not to call me that again."

Ashton laughed throatily. "All right," he said. "Whatever my lady wants, she gets."

"Good," Sasha said, giving Ashton a victorious look. She placed her foot in the stirrup and swung herself into the saddle, watching Ashton mount a red roan beside her, a horse that he had said was fast and easy riding—afraid of nothing.

Then she looked down at Lightning. Never had she seen the pup filled with such friskiness. She seemed to sense the adventure, also, and was eager to be a part of it. Perhaps the pup realized that she was going to be traveling to a place where she might one day mingle with those of her own kind. Would both Sasha's and Lightning's destinies be found in the mysteries of the outback?

Goosebumps rose along Sasha's flesh at the thought, already knowing deep down inside her that Ashton York, alone, was her destiny!

Turning sideways in her saddle, Sasha looked over the group of horsemen that Ashton had hired to be a part of this adventure. They were waiting with a dray and two bullocks and several pack horses heavy with supplies.

A keen thrill soared through Sasha to realize that she was truly going to be a part of a much different sort of life than she had ever known. With Woodrow, she would have lived in luxury, being waited on hand and foot by maids and servants. With Ashton, she was not sure what the future held, except for the ultimate excitement of adventure.

And passion—if she allowed it to happen!

As she flicked her horse's reins and began riding down the street with a proud and lifted chin, she wondered again briefly if Woodrow was alive—and hating him if he was!

A smirk on his thick lips, Stanford watched the procession led by Ashton and Sasha leave town. He dumped his cigar from his fingers and ground it out in the dirt with the heel of his boot. "Now who does she think she's foolin'?" he whispered to himself, having gotten all the information he needed about Sasha and Ashton's plans from the new owner of York's Pub. "No one can hide such female attributes in a man's breeches and shirt. At least not from me."

He glanced toward the far end of the road and mocked a half salute at the men waiting for him, then smiled smugly at the packhorses, dray and bullocks that he had made sure were stocked well enough for the journey into the outback. He planned to be Ashton's shadow, at least until Ashton became careless and revealed where he had stashed the chest of coins and jewels that Stanford had overheard him talking about to his sidekick, Crispin Tilford, when he had visited Ashton in prison.

Not wanting to let Ashton and Sasha get too far ahead of him, wanting them to be so close he could smell them in the breeze, Stanford straightened his ascot, cleared his throat, and made his way through the section of Melbourne that had been nicknamed Canvas Town. He had been there countless times and it made his skin crawl no less now than before. It was a place of squalor. The immigrants who were too listless to dig or dolly for gold, or too poor to pay their coach fares to the diggings a hundred miles north of Melbourne, lived crowded together in rough timber huts, mud and wattle humpies, bark lean-to's, and tents. The people who infested these makeshift shelters were rough, tough men in woolen shirts, women in Wellington boots, and squabbling children, mixed generally with pigs, goats, dogs, geese, and hens.

Picking his way through broken bottles, rusty tins, gin jars, and the wreckage of brandy cases, Stanford ignored the lean, hungry-eyed children who came to grab at him. He kicked dogs aside and spat at beggars as they rattled their empty tins at him.

He looked from side to side, glad that he had risen above living like this long ago. He was from this sort of environment in London. It was hardly any different here. In a grubby little hut in Canvas Town, a person could buy a half pint of dirty coffee for a couple of cents, along with, as a chalked notice said, "Plenty Bread."

Other huts advertised "Beds to Let." For as little as ten cents a night one could hire a canvas stretcher out in the open, with the assured prospect of sleeping within a couple of feet of a drunk, a lunatic, a garroter, or a hard-working harlot.

A part-time barber, with a crudely painted red-and-white pole jutting out like a crazy bowsprit from the lintel of his mud-and-wattle hut, undertook to set razors, draw teeth, and let blood. He guaranteed that in his absence his wife would look after any hapless customers.

A little farther along was a timber shanty leaning perilously to one side and swarming with blowflies. A proud placard promised, "Take in joints for baking."

Another placard advertised an eating house— "Hot Soups and Stews Always On Hand!"

And then Stanford's heart raced faster when he gazed upon a grass hut set back from the other establishments. He had frequented this dwelling since his first day in Melbourne, and now he could not think of leaving without the woman he had grown to depend on for his carnal needs. Though a lowly prostitute who lifted her skirts to any man who paid her the price, the thrill of being with her made him forget about the others she took to her bed. He had come to take her away, if not willingly, then by force. The outback was a lonely place without a woman. For a while at least, Bianca Whitelaw would have to do.

He stepped inside the dark hovel, where a lone candle flickered low on a table. A blanket hung between the front and back rooms, and he knew that when it was drawn closed, Bianca was not to be disturbed—that she was busy with a client.

Frowning, nervous perspiration beading his brow, Stanford glared at the drawn blanket. There was no denying what was transpiring behind it. The grunts and groans and the squeaking of the bed played with Stanford's vivid imagination, and he could hardly bear the thought of Bianca's legs wrapped around another man's waist, meeting his eager thrusts with her own.

Gifted with a body that could make a man's heart stop, Bianca knew the ways to make a man lose his senses. Apparently she was practicing her skills eagerly today. The recipient of her charms was now howling like a wolf.

Bianca was screaming, a part of her ritual in the bed.

Unable to take any more, Stanford jerked the blanket aside and stormed into the back room. Blinded with jealous fury, he yanked the man away from Bianca and tossed him so that he thudded hard against the wall.

"Get out, damn you," Stanford shouted at the

man, his eyes wild. He scooped up the man's clothes and threw them at him, laughing throatily when the man stumbled from the room, panting.

Bianca scooted back on the bed, fear turning her insides cold. She reached for a blanket to cover herself, but Stanford was too quick. He grabbed the blanket and threw it across the room, then circled his fingers around Bianca's wrists and pulled her up before him.

"Whore," he hissed, his gaze absorbing her nudity, hungering for her now, even though she had just copulated with that dirty-haired runt. A half-breed —her mother an Aborigine, her father a white man whose identity was unknown to her—she was exotically beautiful. Her brown hair was so long it reached the floor, her skin was dark and velvety, and her eyes were green. Her body was well-rounded—much more than most Aborigines Stanford had ever seen—and it gave him plenty to fill his hands with.

"Do you always have to enjoy it so much with the other men?" he asked, his voice tormented. "Do you?"

"Bianca pretends," she murmured, swallowing hard. Then she told a lie, fearing that if she didn't, he might cut her throat with the knife he kept hidden beneath the tail of his coat. "It is only for money that I—I do like I enjoy it. Stanford, it is only you who make me feel alive inside."

"Liar!" Stanford shouted. He drew a hand back and slapped her across her face, regretting it the instant he had done it, for blood began to run in a tiny stream from her nose.

"Please don't hurt me," Bianca begged, tears pooling in her eyes as she wiped the blood from her face with the back of a hand. "You know I do what I do so that I can exist. Mama lives a nomadic life with our people. I do not know who my Papa is so I cannot ask him to help me. It is only myself that I must depend on to put food in my mouth and clothes on my back!"

"That's going to change," Stanford said, picking up her meager cotton dress and thrusting it into her arms. "Get dressed. You're going with me."

Bianca's breath was stolen in her throat, fear spiraling through her. "You take me away?" she said, her voice lilting. "Where to?"

"Anything is better than this hellhole," Stanford grumbled, grabbing more of her clothes and thrusting them into a valise he found under the bed.

"I'm not sure if I want to go," Bianca said, clutching her clothes to her chest as she cowered away from Stanford.

Then she felt something grab her at her heart when another thought came to her. She was pregnant. If she did not cooperate with him he might beat her and make her lose her child. At this moment, her child was the only thing that gave her a reason to live! Giving a child life would be the first time she had ever done anything decent in her own life.

Stanford's face reddened as anger flared within him. "Let me give you cause to want to go with me," he said. He cupped her face between his hands and lowered his mouth to her lips. "I'll give you all the lovin' you need without having to be pestered by all of the faceless gents you bed up with each day and night."

He kissed her long and hard, his arms encircling her waist. He drew her close, feeling her magnificent breasts crushing against him. It was hard not to take her sexually at this very moment. But he would have her every day and night from now on.

Until he tired of her.

"My little half-breed," Stanford whispered against her lips. "I'm taking you with me to the outback. We are going to live on a sheep station. You will be there for me at my beck and call."

He leaned her away from him, looking into her green eyes. "But you are never to talk about me to anyone," he warned. "Do you understand? No one."

Bianca nodded anxiously, unsure of what he truly expected of her. Whatever it was, she knew that she had no choice but to go with him. If she refused, who could say what he would do to force her to? But was she delaying the inevitable? How would he treat her when she began to show with child? Fleshy by nature, she was six months along already and was not showing. She had no idea how long she could fool him, or what to expect when he did finally find out.

"I understand that I speak to no one about you," she said, hurrying into her dress.

"If anyone other than those who will live at my sheep station should ask, you belong to a sheepherder under my employ," Stanford further warned. "It is imperative, Bianca, that you do as I ask."

Bianca nodded again. Believing that she truly understood, Stanford picked up her valise, locked an arm around her waist, and escorted her from her dreary hut. He had everything planned out so carefully, surely nothing would go awry.

He smiled slyly, hardly able to wait until the day came that Ashton York—no, in truth, Lawrence Proffitt—would discover that he had a close neighbor, and who it was. . . .

Chapter Four

THE OUTBACK

Twilight had drained out of the western sky, which slowly changed from light orange to deep red, and finally to gray. The trees were filled with the thumping, scrabbling, and chittering of nocturnal creatures. Sugar-gliders with wide, furry airfoils slung between their fore and hind feet parachuted from tree to tree in wobbly swoops. Camouflaged against the fleshy, gray burl of a eucalyptus tree, a koala sprawled sedately, slumbering trustingly in one of the forks of the tree.

A campfire beside a serene river close to these trees cast its fluttering light on Sasha as she was sullenly eating from a tin plate of sinewy kangaroo stew and bread. The excitement of the journey had waned with each mile she had traveled along rough track cut by hand through the gum-tree

forests. She ached unmercifully all over, so much
that it had been hard for her to slip from the saddle
to put her feet on solid ground.

But she was glad to be able to discard the
sweat-stained hat for the evening so that her hair
could breathe again as it hung loose and free
around her shoulders and down her back.

"Hey, Spike," Ashton said, drawing Sasha's head
quickly up. "Want a refill on the stew or tea?"

Sasha gazed angrily at him as he stood over a
smoking stewpot, busily ladling himself a refill of
the kangaroo stew into his tin plate. "I asked you
not to call me that," she snapped, startled at her
snippiness. Normally she did not become annoyed
at anyone so quickly—especially Ashton.

But she had been on a horse all day fighting off
fatigue and all sorts of insects stinging her face and
neck, and now all she had for tending to her private
needs was her bush bathroom.

What respectable woman wouldn't be irritated
and short tempered?

She was definitely in no mood to be teased.

She glanced from side to side, hearing the snickering of the men who were lounging around the fire,
either eating or smoking. She especially did not
want those complete strangers to get in on the
taunting! It was bad enough that because of them
she did not feel free to take the bath she needed so
badly.

She then gazed angrily up at Ashton again, who
was now pouring himself a tin cup of tea from a
billy.

"As I said before, I don't find that nickname

amusing at all," she added. "If you call me that again, I—I—"

Ashton settled down on the ground beside Sasha. He dove into the stew, scooping large spoonfuls into his mouth. "You'll what?" he teased, chewing hungrily. "The name seems to be growing on you, sweet darlin'. Those breeches and shirt just tend to make a man forget you're a lady."

A slow boil heating up her insides, Sasha gave Ashton a fiery stare. "That is my intention, you dimwit," she hissed. She set her dish down on the ground and rose quickly to her feet. She placed her hands on her hips and gave Ashton another angry stare. "And as far as nicknames go, you can stop calling me sweet darlin'." She exhaled a nervous breath. "That has annoyed me for months, Ashton! For months!"

Ashton's lips curved into a slow smile, and he laughed throatily as Sasha turned and fled into the shadows of night. Then he frowned as he set his own dish and tin cup aside, not wanting her to wander too far alone where all sorts of dangers could be lurking.

He began following her through the tangled undergrowth, but kept his distance. He did not want her to know that he was guarding her this closely. She seemed annoyed enough at him of late.

Especially since they had shared that sizzling embrace and kiss!

Time. Time was now on his side. There was no reason why Sasha could not totally forget the aristocrat and concentrate her full attentions on the man who truly loved her.

"And that man is me," Ashton whispered to himself, walking amid the stuttering whirr of cicadas, their throbbing croak seeming to be coming from all around him.

The world brimming with moonlight, every tree splashed with silver, he was able to keep his eyes on Sasha, but he stopped and stepped quickly behind a tree when she turned and looked over her shoulder in his direction.

Then, as she moved onward, he followed her. He stepped behind a tree again when she stopped beside the river, wattle trees bowing under the weight of their golden blooms, bending above the river like lovers.

Peering around the tree, Ashton watched as Sasha fell to her knees and scooped water from the river, splashing her face with it, then wove her fingers through her lustrous hair. Ashton's heart went wild as she turned her face up to the moonlight and its glow illuminated her exquisite loveliness. It was a picture that he could not expect to see more than once in a lifetime—the most beautiful woman in the world sitting amidst the tangles of exotic willows and tea trees shimmering like thousands of moonbeams in the pale night air.

A scampering behind him drew Ashton quickly around. When Lightning bounded into view, his eyes widened. He glanced at Sasha, then at the pup. Knowing the dog's friskiness, there was no way that Sasha could help but discover that he was near.

The dingo's playful yelps silenced all the activity in the trees. Ashton swept his pup up into his arms and stepped out into view as Sasha rose quickly to her feet and turned to discover him there.

"I see you've come to continue annoying me," Sasha said, her spine stiffening. She flung her hair back from her shoulders. "I guess the only reprieve I can have from you is to just go on to bed in my tent." She spun on a heel to face him. "If you please, do allow me that privacy, Ashton."

His jaw tight, his eyes filled with rage, Ashton set his pup to the ground and flung a hand frustratingly in the air. "Damn it, Sasha, go and have all the privacy you want," he said, his voice a near shout.

Stung by Ashton's rage, Sasha gazed at him for a moment, her lips parted, then she turned and rushed back to the campsite. Without hesitation she crawled into her tent and became as comfortable as possible in her bedroll.

She lay and watched the shadows of the men outside and listened to their jokes and laughter. Her eyes narrowed and she felt the heat of a blush rising to her cheeks when she recognized Ashton's voice, his jokes no less raunchy or shocking than the other men's.

Flopping over on her stomach, covering her ears with her hands, she tried not to hear this side of Ashton that she had never known before. She had somehow set him aside from all other men, as though putting him on a pedestal, because he had been so kind and gentle to her.

But now she was seeing that a part of him was just like any other man. Did that mean that he was like other men in other respects?

Would he be like Woodrow?

Would he tire of her and eventually abandon her?

A soft whimpering noise and a nudging at the bedroll at her feet drew Sasha's attention, and she mellowed when she looked down at Lightning, who was trying to get comfortable beside her. "Come here, sweet puppy," Sasha whispered, beckoning with a hand. "Just because I'm sore at Ashton doesn't mean that I am at you."

Lightning's tail began to wag. The pup scooted on her stomach up to Sasha's hand and curled up next to her as she began to stroke her soft fur. "Thank you for coming to make me feel better," Sasha whispered. "I'm glad you are finally used to seeing me in clothes other than a dress." She sighed. "Now I think I can go to sleep. But only if you will stay with me."

The horses grazed peacefully among the snow gums, and the voices around the campfire faded as the men went to their tents. Sasha watched a tall shadow moving around outside her tent—Ashton. Her pulse began to beat faster. He was going to be sleeping in the tent next to hers—so close, yet so far.

A part of her wanted to stick her head from her tent and apologize for being so cross with him tonight, yet another part of her warned her to be as distant with him as was civil, for she needed to prove her independence. They were partners. She had to prove her worth. To do so she must not allow herself to behave like a schoolgirl with a crush.

Sasha drew Lightning closer. "I do have a crush on him, Lightning," she whispered. "But you'll keep my secret, won't you?"

Everyone but Sasha seemed to be asleep. Hugging Lightning to her, she stared at the sides of the tent. The flickering shadows from the outdoor campfire were writing weird lines on the thin canvas; the trees outside gave off queer noises as the breeze stirred through them.

And then fear quickened her heartbeat. She raised up on an elbow, leaning her ear toward the side of the tent. She listened intently, having heard what sounded like men's voices breaking through the silence of the night. She had thought that everyone else was asleep.

Wanting to investigate, Sasha slipped from her bedroll and crawled around the sleeping dingo pup to the opening at the front of the tent. Her heart thudding, her mouth dry from fear, she stuck her head out and peered slowly from side to side. She looked toward the forest, where the shadows made a blue and purple jungle, seeing nothing. She looked heavenward. Clouds were thickening around the moon, giving an eerie radiance to the night.

Then she looked cautiously around her again, no longer hearing anything that resembled voices. Had she been imagining things? Did the outback cause the mind to play tricks?

Or had it been the touch of the wild wind whispering through the trees?

Determined to find out, she crawled on her hands and knees from her tent across the crushed and tangled brush that led to Ashton's. When she reached his tent, she slowly lifted the flap and crawled inside. She was jolted with alarm when he bolted suddenly to a sitting position, then gave a startled gasp when he discovered Sasha in the shadows, staring at him.

"What the—?" he said, squinting his eyes as he gazed up at her. "Why are you here? Is something wrong?"

Embarrassed to be there, now wishing that she had thought twice before entering his tent, Sasha could scarcely move, much less speak. It was as though she were a child being caught stealing from a cookie jar!

"I heard noises," she finally said. "I—I became afraid."

Ashton shoved his bedroll aside and crawled to Sasha. "What sort of noises?" he asked, grabbing a revolver. He moved past her, outside. He rose to his full height, his gaze moving slowly around the ring of tents. "I see nothing threatening out here."

Sasha left the tent and stood beside him, feeling foolish for having let night noises frighten her. If she was going to learn to exist in the outback, she realized that she would have more than noises to get used to!

Ashton turned his gaze back to Sasha. "Well?" he said, forking an eyebrow. "Are you going to tell me? What did you hear that brought you to my tent?"

Sasha lowered her eyes. "It was nothing," she murmured, fidgeting with the tail of her shirt. "I was just being foolish."

She looked slowly up at him. "It's my first night away from the city," she explained. "I guess I am just a bit nervous."

"I can understand that," he said, taking her by the elbow and leading her back to her tent. He helped her inside, smiling when he saw Lightning sleeping soundly beside Sasha's bedroll. "I guessed it was you I had lost my pup to tonight."

"I suppose Lightning was too tired from the long journey today to come on to your tent after snuggling down with me," Sasha murmured, slipping back inside her bedroll. She forced a yawn and stretched her arms over her head. "Just like me. I've never been so sleepy."

Ashton placed a hand to her cheek, his insides melting at the silken feel of her flesh. "I'm glad you're no longer sore at me and that you came to me tonight when you were afraid," he said thickly. "Remember, Sasha, I am always here for you."

Sasha swallowed hard, her head spinning from the rapture pressing in on her heart. She nodded her head, afraid to speak lest she reveal her feelings to him.

"Sasha," Ashton said thickly. "Do you truly hate for me to call you sweet darlin' all that much?"

A blush rose from Sasha's neck to her cheeks. She blinked up at Ashton. "Not really," she murmured. "I don't know why I said that. I—I think that nickname is sweet. Honestly, I do."

A slow smile touched Ashton's lips. "Good," he said, running his fingers through her hair. Then he drew his hand away from her when Sasha turned to her side and closed her eyes, apparently so tired that she was already drifting into a sound sleep.

Sasha cuddled into her bedroll, pretending to be asleep. In truth, her heart was pounding too hard for her ever to go to sleep tonight. She could still feel Ashton there, his eyes on her.

Only when he left did she exhale a nervous breath. Oh, how he did affect her! Perhaps she had made a mistake by coming with him. She was afraid that her heart was going to win over her common sense—and her fear of men!

Ashton walked back to his tent and crawled inside, but his desire for Sasha would not allow him to go to sleep again all that easily. The fact that she was only a heartbeat away in the next tent was enough to stir fires within him that only being with her could extinguish.

But he must proceed slowly to win her. That damned aristocrat had spoiled her trust where men were concerned. If he ever got his hands on the son of a bitch . . . !

Tired of wrestling with his thoughts, Ashton eyed the razor and strop that he had removed from his saddlebag earlier in the evening. The time had come for him to resume his normal identity. Away from the city and watchful eyes, he was free to remove the itchy beard. With every traveler's mind on his own passion for land or gold, the identity of one Ashton York would not be any concern.

But what of Sasha? Without the beard, would she be more or less attracted to him? Would she be repelled by the long slash of scar that would be revealed with a clean-shaven face?

"I've learned to live with many risks," he whispered to himself, grabbing the razor and strop. "I guess one more won't hurt me."

He left his tent and stopped to stare at Sasha's tent for a long moment. Then he went to the river and splashed his face with water. He ran his fingers one last time through his beard.

Adding two more shadows to the moonlit night, Stanford Sidwell rode his bay mare with one of his hired gunmen through the gum tree forest. The campfire up just ahead was like a beacon in the night, leading them to Ashton. Stanford's own camp had been set up across the river, far enough back so that none of Ashton's men would realize they were being followed. Stanford had waited two more long years in prison after Lawrence Proffitt was released on good behavior—waiting to find him, not to let him get out of his sight again. There was a fortune at stake here—a fortune that would never be the ex-convict's, no matter what name Lawrence was answering to these days.

"I'm going to get the best of him, that's for sure," Stanford said to his companion. "But first I'm going to pay some attention to his little lady! Once we reach the sheep station, my true fun will begin."

Seeing someone standing beside the river, Stanford and his companion reined in their horses and quickly dismounted. Tethering their mounts to a tree, they moved stealthily through the darkness, then stopped and hid behind a tree.

His eyes dancing, Stanford watched Ashton pulling the razor through his thick stubble of beard. Soon he would see if the knife wound he had inflicted on Lawrence Proffitt's face in prison had healed grotesquely enough.

Chapter Five

The sound of thunder and howling winds drew Sasha quickly awake early the next morning. She searched the tent for the dingo pup, but the approaching storm had apparently already drawn Lightning's attention. She was yelping just outside the tent, excited by the snapping and the crackling of the lightning.

Shifting her mussed braids back atop her head, Sasha flinched when an even brighter flash of lightning lit up the interior of her tent, the boom of thunder reverberating in the air soon after.

"It's going to be a terrible storm," Sasha whispered, crawling to the flap of the tent and lifting it. As she stuck her head outside, the wind almost knocked her down. The tent was leaning against the incessantly moaning wind, straining at the stakes pounded into the ground to hold it in place. She winced when great zigzags of lightning flared across the purple sky.

Just as Sasha caught a glimpse of Ashton scurrying around, helping to gather up the cooking and camping paraphanalia, a great gust of wind ripped the tent from around her. Her lips parted with surprise, she watched the tent and her hat flip and flop across the ground, then land in the river and float away in the current.

Scrambling to her feet, Sasha ran to Ashton, whose back was still to her as he gathered supplies up into his arms. "Ashton, I'm frightened," she said breathlessly, watching other tents being stripped from their stakes. She then glanced up at the sky and flinched when lightning flared over and over again. "I don't think I've ever seen such winds—or lightning."

"Well, sweet darlin', you'd best hold onto your hat because you haven't seen anything yet," Ashton said, still not looking her way.

"Ashton, my hat blew away with the tent," Sasha said, her eyes wide. "It ended up in the river."

Ashton chuckled low and stopped his desperate rescue of whatever could be protected from the vicious wind and the rain that threatened to fall at any moment. He turned to Sasha, glad to hand over what he was holding when one of his men came and emptied his arms. "Well at least you didn't blow away with the tent," he teased.

Then his heart skipped a beat, realizing that Sasha was staring at his clean-shaven face, and at the scar that he had kept hidden beneath his beard. He searched her eyes, trying to read her feelings about the discovery. All he could see was astonishment, which he was thankful for. He had expected her to perhaps be repelled by the imperfection of his face—an imperfection inflicted by a man Ashton despised!

Sasha's stomach did a strange sort of churning when she saw the white scar that shaving had uncovered on Ashton's lower right cheek. Yet it was not so much the scar that caused her reaction. It was something else that his having shaved had uncovered—Ashton was the most handsome man she had ever seen! She had fallen in love with a man who not only had heart-melting violet eyes, but also a kind and intelligent face with lean lines and smooth features, a straight nose and a square jaw.

Then her attention was drawn back to the scar when a flash of lightning lit it up as though it were a part of the lightning itself. "Ashton, how did you get the—?" she blurted, but was interrupted by a great clap of thunder that was followed by a sudden torrential downpour.

Ashton sighed with relief, realizing that he had just been saved from her questions, at least for the moment. He swept an arm around Sasha's waist and ushered her quickly away. "Get beneath the dray," he shouted above the howling winds. "It's strong. The winds won't be able to budge it."

Already soaked clean through to the bone, Sasha did not argue the point. She crawled beneath the dray and hugged her wet arms, shivering, as she peered from beneath it to see Ashton run to the horses to make sure they were secured.

Then she screamed and almost fainted when lightning cracked somewhere close by and a tree snapped in two as though it were only a twig and began falling where Ashton was standing.

Sasha scurried from beneath the dray and stumbled and slid in the mud as she tried to reach Ashton to warn him. "Ashton!" she screamed, her feet suddenly slipping from beneath her. She landed with a loud splat in the mud.

"The tree!" she screamed. "Ashton!"

The tree landed several yards from Ashton, but although he survived the tree, a horse did not. Sasha felt a sickness spiraling through her as she watched the horse writhe on its side, smashed by the fallen tree.

Ashton's horse neighed and whinnied, jerking at the reins, its dark eyes wild. Ashton held the animal firmly around its neck, talking soothingly into its ear, all the while looking at the horse that was filled with misery.

"Well? Don't just everyone stand around gawking! Shoot the horse!" Ashton shouted to his men. "Put the animal out of its misery!"

Sasha turned her eyes away and winced as a shot rang out. She looked slowly Ashton's way again, then at the slain horse, knowing that it could have been Ashton if the tree had fallen a few feet more to the side than it had.

Pushing herself up from the mud, almost blinded now by the driving rain, Sasha fought against the wind and finally managed to get to Ashton. She helped him hold his horse steady on the opposite side from where Ashton stood bracing himself in the wind and rain.

"Oh, Ashton!" Sasha cried. "That could have been you!"

"Never in a hundred years!" Ashton tried to

reassure her. "I'm around for a while longer, sweet darlin', so you'd just better get used to me."

"And you think I'm not?" Sasha shouted back.

"I certainly hope so," Ashton said, laughing into the wind.

Sasha's gaze went to the white scar. She wanted to question him about it, but knew this was not the right time. The wild wind and rain seemed bent on destroying as much of the camp as it could, as though purposely trying to make everyone return to the life that they had left behind in Melbourne.

But Sasha hoped that it would take more than winds and rains to send Ashton back to being a pubkeep, she his tavern maid. Their journey had just begun into the unknown and she wanted nothing to stand in the way—not even unanswered questions about the man she now knew she loved.

Suddenly the squall subsided as quickly as it had begun, but not before it had turned the whole encampment into a rain-lashed bog.

"The storm is over so quickly?" Sasha exclaimed, moving away from Ashton's horse. She looked incredulously around her. The sun was standing high above the treetops. The drenched ground was steaming.

"Not any too soon," Ashton grumbled, giving his horse one last pat before turning to assess the damage done to the camp. His eyes narrowed when he heard the rush of water through the trees and he discovered that the river was in flood—a river that must be crossed to continue their journey.

Sasha heard Ashton whisper several obscenities beneath his breath and followed his gaze to see why he was angry. She gasped when she saw the raging waters of the river rushing over the bank, swirling and muddy, and grabbing up anything that might be in its way to suck it beneath the water and carry it away.

"Ashton, we're stranded," Sasha said, watching the men as they began gathering beside the river, studying the situation. "At least until the river subsides. It would be too risky to cross it as it is now."

"That would mean missing a full day of travel," Ashton said, looking over at Sasha. They knew the risks, and they had known to expect some perils while traveling through land rarely touched by man. "But Sasha, we've waited too long to have our sheep station to let mother nature get in our way."

Sasha swallowed hard as she continued watching the raging, swirling waters. "What are you saying, Ashton?" she murmured, wringing out the tail of her shirt. "Though perhaps I don't want to hear."

"We're crossing the river today," Ashton said, brushing several damp strands of golden-red hair back from his brow. "As soon as we gather up the blown-away tents and camping paraphernalia, by damn, we're going to cross the river."

He raised his voice, drawing the attention of his men. "Did you all hear what I said?" he shouted. "We're going to cross the river. Today!"

Sasha began unbraiding her tangled hair. She looked guardedly at the men whose expressions showed that they did not agree with Ashton's decision to tackle a river that seemed to be lashing out at the world with its furious swirlings and thrashings, taking everything within reach into its dark and muddy bowels. The thought of crossing that torrent caused a crawling sensation at the back of her neck, quickening her heartbeat with fear.

But before she could voice her opinion, the men rushed all around, picking up equipment and tents, quickly loading them in the dray. The two bullocks were attached to the dray and the driver climbed aboard, eyeing the river nervously as he slapped a whip across the young bulls' backs.

"Climb aboard the dray," Ashton said, taking Sasha's arm and guiding her to it. "You'll be safer there."

"But what about my horse?" Sasha queried, looking over at Cloud, who was pawing nervously at the soaked ground.

"I'll see that Cloud gets over okay," Ashton said, taking Sasha by the waist and lifting her up to the seat. "Michael here will take care of you, won't you, Michael?"

The young driver looked at Ashton with a nervous smile. "I can't guarantee anything, Ashton," he said. "I can't even get the damn animals to budge. They sense the dangers of the river. I doubt if I'll ever get them across."

Flipping her long, unbraided hair back from her shoulders, Sasha stared at the river. "Ashton, they would probably drown if you force them to cross," she said, knowing for sure that she did not wish to enter the crazed water. She looked slowly over at Ashton, her thick lashes fluttering anxiously. "Ashton, perhaps it would be best if we camped here another night and crossed the river tomorrow."

"I have made my mind up and that is the way it shall be," Ashton said, his jaw tight. He grabbed the whip from Michael and sent several lashes across the bulls' backs, then held the whip motionlessly in the air, surprised that the animals not only balked, but refused to move one inch ahead.

"Now what do we do?" Michael asked, idly scratching his brow.

"We'll lighten the load and then try again," Ashton said, throwing supplies from the dray. He looked over his shoulder at the men who were gaping disbelievingly at him. He grabbed a large tub and set it down beside him. "You don't get paid to watch. Get busy and start filling the tub with the supplies. I'll be damned if I'm going to let two young bulls get the best of me."

Sasha climbed from the dray. She looked down at Ashton, then at the tub, and then at the water. She was getting a bad feeling about what Ashton might have planned. As bullheaded as he was, it would be just like him!

Falling to her knees, Sasha grabbed Ashton by the arm. "Ashton, what are you planning to do?" she demanded. "Or need I ask?"

"I think you may have it figured out," Ashton said, smiling when he saw that the tub was filled. He rose to his feet, then bent over and grabbed the tub by its handles and began toting it toward the river.

Sasha stared blankly at him, but when he got to the river and placed the tub in the water, panic seized her. With Lightning yelping at her heels she ran to the river—but she was too late. Ashton had already dived headfirst into the water. Sasha's eyes searched frantically for Ashton. When he bobbed to the surface and swam for the tub, soon overtaking it, she breathed more easily. But not for long. She could see the muscle that it was taking for Ashton to keep afloat, the waters seemingly eager to swallow him and the tub whole.

Sasha turned to eye the men who stood alongside the river watching Ashton. She doubled her fists at her sides and glared at them. "Are you going to just stand there and let him drown?" she cried. "Isn't there a brave one among you? Does Ashton have to do it all?"

There was no response and she truly understood why. Ashton had taken on this chore by himself. No one could do anything to help him at the moment. But then, to her surprise and satisfaction, both finally reached the other side of the river unharmed.

Ashton dragged the tub to shore. He hung his head for a moment and took several deep breaths, his lungs aching from the battle with the water.

Then he turned and looked across the river. "Now you see how it's done!" he shouted. "I suggest you follow my lead. There was more than one tub in the dray. Fill them full. Bring them across!"

After making sure the tub was far enough from the bank so that the water could not reach it, Ashton dove into the river and fought the current as he swam back across. Dripping wet, he climbed on land and stared at the bullocks. Sasha came to him and placed a hand to his cheek.

"Please don't do that again," she begged softly. "I died a thousand deaths watching you in that water."

"There's much to get across," Ashton said, wiping a hand across his brow and shaking water from it. "Just stand aside, sweet darlin'. I'll come for you later."

"Ashton . . ." Sasha argued, then drew in a quivering breath when he ignored her and instead began working with the bullocks. With Lightning barking at the bullocks and Ashton giving them slaps on their rumps, the animals finally decided to cooperate.

"Want us to remove the flour before tryin' to take the bulls across?" Michael asked, eyeing the tarpaulins that were wrapped around the bundles of flour.

Ashton jumped up on the seat and began flicking the whips against the bullocks' backs. "No, don't bother," he shouted. "Now that we have the bulls cooperating, we'd best get them on into the water."

Sasha held her breath as Ashton led the bulls into the river. They bellowed and fussed but braved the water well enough and were soon at the other side.

But another obstacle stood in the way. The animals became bogged in the mud on the far bank. Sasha could hear Ashton's curses fill the air. She stiffened and watched him work with the young bulls, scarcely noticing that all the horses and the rest of the equipment had also made it to the opposite shore.

All except her and Lightning.

Not wanting to cause Ashton any more trouble by reminding him that she had been left behind, she eyed the water speculatively. Everyone else had gotten across without a mishap. Surely she could also. She was a skilled swimmer. And the current seemed to have subsided somewhat.

"It truly isn't that far across," she whispered, yet she could not deny the chills that were encompassing her at the thought of diving into the river. She glanced down at Lightning and back at the river. "She's too little to swim across."

Bending to kneel, Sasha hugged Lightning to her. "I'll send one of the men back for you as soon as I reach the other side," she promised. She patted Lightning and kissed her on the tip of the nose.

Sasha rose to her full height and looked commandingly down at the pup. "Stay, Lightning," she said firmly. "Do you hear? Stay!"

Lightning looked trustingly up at her, wagging her tail. Sasha turned and swallowed hard as she edged toward the water.

Then, fiercely fearing her decision to do this, she dove in, headfirst.

The moment she hit the water and was sucked deep into what seemed a dark, never-ending void, she knew that she had made a mistake.

Chapter Six

*Sasha had misjudged the current. Its force was suck-*ing her down, farther and farther into the dark water. Her lungs ached and burned as she fought to rise back to the surface. She was beginning to feel lightheaded—even saw remnants of her past flash before her mind's eye.

But suddenly she popped back to the surface. Thrashing her arms in the water, almost crazed from the need for air, she inhaled deeply, the air going down her throat like an elixir to her aching lungs.

Her eyes wild, she looked toward the bank on which Ashton was still struggling with the bullocks. She realized that he had no idea that she was in trouble. And if she didn't get help soon, she would be washed away like the debris that was floating past her.

Fighting against the rush of the current, unable to swim in it, Sasha treaded water and began waving an arm. "Ashton!" she screamed. "Oh, God, Ashton, please see me! I'm here in the water!"

Ashton's spine stiffened when he recognized Sasha's voice. Extricating himself from the mire at his feet he turned around and stared disbelievingly. What he saw made his heart turn to stone.

Sasha was in trouble in the river!

Then his gaze swept past her, upriver just a few yards. Racing toward her was a tangled pile of twisted limbs. In a matter of moments she would become a part of the mass, more than likely ripped to shreds by it.

Without further thought, Ashton dove into the river and began swimming desperately toward Sasha, his heart pounding out his fear that he might not reach her in time. If she died, it would be his fault. And he would want to die alongside her. Without her, his existence was worthless!

Sasha was weakening. But she had seen Ashton dive into the water. She could see him taking long and masterful strokes as he swam toward her.

Then her gaze was drawn elsewhere. She swallowed a great gulp of water when she saw the pile of twisted debris headed toward her. A paralyzing fear seized her, for she did not believe that Ashton could get to her before—

Suddenly Ashton's arm swept around Sasha's waist. In concentrating on the approach of the debris she had not seen him come up behind her. She splashed her arms wildly in the water as she tried to anchor herself against him. When she finally managed to wrap her arms around his neck,

he began swimming away with her just as the
twisted limbs and debris floated past with a loud
sucking noise.

Tears streamed from Sasha's eyes as she clung to
Ashton, his one arm so powerfully wrapped around
her, the other taking long strokes in the water.
"Ashton, oh, Ashton, thank God you saw me," she
sobbed weakly. "Had you not, I—"

"Don't think about it," Ashton said, glad to be
able to place his feet on the bottom of the river at
last. He lifted Sasha into his powerful arms and
fought the mud at his feet to carry her to dry land.
"But what I would like to know is why you were in
the river in the first place?"

Her hair in massive tangles around her shoulders,
loose strands hanging in her eyes, Sasha sighed with
the weariness of her fight with the river. "I thought
the river had become calmer," she said. "I was the
only one left on the opposite shore. I wanted to
prove that I could fend for myself as well as any of
you men."

"And you almost got yourself killed while doing
it," Ashton grumbled.

He held her tightly to him, looking down into her
tearful eyes and at her flushed cheeks. "I came close
to losing you," he said thickly. "Promise never to do
anything as foolish as that again."

"At the time I did not see it as foolish," Sasha
defended herself. "The next time I may not either."

"I was afraid that's what you would say," he
said, frowning down at her. "What am I to do with
you?"

"Right now I would like nothing more than to stay
snuggled in your arms," Sasha said, closing her eyes

as she placed her cheek against his chest, his muscles prominent through his wet and clinging shirt.

Loud shouts and the bellowing of the two young bulls drew Ashton's eyes elsewhere. "Oh, no," he groaned, quickly placing Sasha on her feet. "I thought the bullocks were going to pull the dray free of the mud without this sort of mishap." He shook his head. "All of the flour supply is gone. What else can happen today? What?"

Sasha combed her fingers through her unbraided hair and watched along with Ashton as the flour that had spilled from the dray began floating past like snow in the water, followed by the tarpaulins that had been wrapped around it to protect it.

Ashton swung away from her and went to the young bulls. He angrily grabbed one by the head and began yanking. "Get out of that mud, damn you!" he shouted. To his surprise the animals began moving forward. He lost his balance and fell close to their hooves, then rolled free as it ambled on past.

Lying in the mud, taking in a shaky, annoyed breath, Ashton waited until the bullocks and the dray had gone on past him, then he pushed himself up from the ground, mud covering him from head to toe.

Sasha came to him and her eyes twinkled as she fought against laughing at Ashton's appearance.

"Don't say a word," he said, wiping his hands down the front of his breeches, mud oozing between his fingers. "Not a word, Sasha."

"Now do you think I'd laugh at the man who just

84

saved my life?" she teased, realizing that she did not truly look much better than he. Her soaked shirt and breeches were soiled with all sorts of river muck and mire. "Now that wouldn't be showing my gratitude in a very nice way, would it?"

"I can think of a way that I would like to be shown your gratitude, but I don't think you would want to hear it," Ashton said, giving her a knowing look.

Sasha's face was consumed with a blush, knowing what he most surely had to mean as his eyes raked over her. She was very aware of how her wet clothes clung to her like a second skin, and of how the nipples of her breasts were clearly defined beneath the shirt. If any travelers would happen along now, there would be no way to disguise herself as a man. At this moment, she would not even want to pretend. The way Ashton was looking at her was enough to make her very aware that she was a total woman. His violet eyes were causing her insides to become aflame with passion, yet she knew that this was not the time, or the place, to let him realize how much he disturbed her.

If ever. The bitterness that Woodrow had caused within her was still festering like an open wound. She had trusted him. She had been wrong.

Loud yelps drew Sasha and Ashton's thoughts elsewhere. Together they turned and gaped disbelievingly at Lightning as the dingo pup floated past on a barrel in the middle of the river.

"Lightning," Sasha said in a low gasp, covering her mouth with her hand. "I forgot about Lightning!"

Ashton bolted into the water. Sasha watched him

swimming toward the barrel, a cold sweat of fear covering her as she so vividly recalled the suction of the current and the dangerous threat of the debris that could suddenly come from out of nowhere.

When Ashton reached the barrel and grabbed Lightning into his arms, Sasha drew an audible breath of relief. She waited anxiously and went to her knees to pull the soaked pup into her arms as Ashton came to shore and set Lightning to the ground.

"Lightning," Sasha murmured, stroking the pup's wet fur. She brought the pup's nose up so that their eyes met. "I'm sorry, Lightning. I'll never forget about you again."

Sasha's gaze moved upward. She smiled at Ashton. "Twice in one day you are a hero," she said, her voice trembling. "Thank you, Ashton. Thank you for both me and Lightning."

Ashton ran the back of his arm across his wet brow. "If I had listened to you in the first place, none of this would've happened," he said hoarsely. His eyes sought hers in a quiet apology. "You were right when you tried to encourage me to wait another day, or at least until the river was at a more decent depth."

He cleared his throat nervously and placed his fists on his hips, looking around at the disarray of his men and the equipment. Everything that was of any worth was either gone or soaked. Because of his haste to put more distance between himself and Melbourne and the likes of Stanford Sidwell and Superintendent Silas Howland, he had made too hasty a decision today.

And it had almost proven fatal.

Sasha patted Lightning one last time, then went and stood beside Ashton, her eyes assessing the damage around her. "Ashton, what are you going to do now?" she asked, smoothing a wet lock of hair back from her eyes.

"It seems we've no choice but to stay here for a while," he said, angrily kicking a rock into the river. "We've got to spread out and dry all of the bedding and clothes." Disgruntled, he looked at the bullocks and dray. "Some of our men will have to return to Melbourne for fresh supplies to cover what was lost in the storm."

"How long will our journey be delayed?" she asked, knowing how anxious he had been not to be delayed at all.

"Only today," Ashton said bluntly. "We'll move on early tomorrow morning. That should give the bedrolls and clothes the full day to get dry and us a full night to get rested up after today's ordeal. The men should not take more than a full day and night to get to Melbourne and back." He kneaded his chin contemplatively. "As I see it, we won't have lost all that much time after all."

Sasha swung away from him. "I'll start collecting the bedrolls and spread them out on the sand beneath the sun," she said, Lightning at her heels. "Surely they will be dry by evening."

She was glad that the rest of the men were busy doing their own chores, for she could feel her shirt getting tighter and tighter as it dried, leaving nothing to the imagination.

* * *

The sky was darkening and the noise of the cicadas was almost deafening as Stanford Sidwell sat by a campfire pitching his pocket knife over and over again into the ground. A smile played on his lips. From a distance, he had watched Ashton York's perilous adventures at the river. He had hoped that Ashton would lose everything, forcing him to uncover the hiding place of the chest filled with coins and jewels. That would have been the only way for him to survive had he lost everything in the river!

Somehow, some day, Stanford or mother nature would force Ashton's hand.

"You find something funny?" Bianca asked, seeing the evil glint in Stanford's dark eyes. She pulled her knees up to her chest and wrapped her arms around them, hoping that Stanford would be too occupied again tonight to approach her sexually. She had grown to detest his hands, his lips, his manhood. . . .

Stanford folded his knife and slipped it into its sheath. With a firm grip, he wrapped his fingers around Bianca's wrist and drew her onto his lap. His tongue sought her lips and teasingly tasted them, as his free hand roamed beneath her low-cut, white drawstring blouse. He circled his hand around one of her breasts, and the soft feel of her flesh started a fire within his loins.

"What am I finding funny?" he said, brushing a kiss across her lips, his gaze taking in the loveliness of her dark face. "Do you really care?"

"Bianca is always ready to laugh if given cause to," she said, hoping to avoid what was beginning. Although they were not alone, he was touching her breasts and kissing her, not caring that he might be stirring the other men to lusty needs. "Tell me something funny, Stanford. Make me laugh."

She sucked in a wild breath of air when he lay her down on the ground and held her there forcibly with one hand while his other hand sought her moistness beneath her skirt. "Please," she whispered harshly, her face flooding with color. "Do not humiliate me in such a way. Please?"

"A whore is begging not to be humiliated?" Stanford said huskily, spreading himself over her. He kissed her wetly along the dark planes of her face, down the gentle slope of her neck, and then the upper lobes of her breasts. "Let's show the men just how a whore makes her money, Bianca. Loosen up. Kiss me. Touch me."

"You were going to tell me something funny," Bianca pleaded. "This is not funny, Stanford. Please stop!"

Having had his fun with her for the moment, Stanford jerked away from her and left her lying there panting with fright. He laughed to himself when he detected a deep hatred in her eyes. She did not know it, but that made him even more excited and willing to wait for the right moment to have her.

"Get up," he ordered flatly. "I'm in no mood for you right now. I've got a lot of thinking to do."

Meekly straightening her blouse and skirt, Bianca scooted to a sitting position. Tears shone in the corners of her eyes. One day she would find a way to make Stanford pay for treating her so unkindly. She would have been better off staying in Melbourne! Yet she knew that he would have never allowed it.

He would have forced her to leave by gunpoint.

Perhaps she should have forced his hand and let him shoot her. Surely she would be better off dead.

She lay a hand on her abdomen. But what of the child? Could there ever be a future for her unborn child? She would search for a way. Until the day she died, she would strive for a happy future for her child!

Stanford sat down beside the fire again and lit a cigar. As the smoke spiraled up into his eyes he became lost in thoughts of another time, another place. He had tried many sorts of entertaining careers in his lifetime, most of which had had a part in landing him in prison. But he had paid his dues and had walked away from the prison a smarter man. It had not taken him long to dig up enough nuggets in the goldfields to buy fancy clothes, a horse, weapons, and enough men to ride with him for the meager wages that it had taken to supply them with enough ale to last them for a month of Sundays in the outback. They made him look legitimate. They didn't know that their usefulness would run out once he was led by Ashton to a chest that far exceeded any amount of gold that could be found in a year's diggings!

A smug smile curled Stanford's lips. "But first things first," he whispered to himself. "I learned the art of patience well while in prison. And so shall I practice it a while longer."

He leaned back and rested on an elbow, giving Bianca a sly wink. "My dear Bianca, if only you knew what had truly brought me to the outback," he said, taking on a faraway look. "If you only knew."

She gave him a dark frown, not caring about anything now except to find a way to have the sort of freedom that he would never allow—short of killing him.

Chapter Seven

The moon was lighting the land with its silver sheen.
The sound of men snoring resonantly disturbed the
tranquility of a slow-burning campfire. Her eyelids
heavy with the need for sleep, Sasha gazed as
though drugged into the fire, then looked over at the
tent in which Ashton was sleeping soundly. Since
her tent had blown away in the storm, he had tried
to persuade her to use his. But she had stubbornly
refused and now lay outside beside the campfire,
Lightning snuggled close to her, asleep.

"I think I'm the only one awake," she whispered to herself. She listened to the rumbling of the
snores reverberating through the air from tent to
tent. "Oh, if I could only go to sleep like everyone
else!"

Her bedroll was stiff and itchy with sand, and
Sasha moaned as she tried to get more comfortable.

But nothing seemed to help, for it was not just the bedroll that had become an annoyance to her—it was the tightness of her clothes. The rain and the river water had caused the material of her breeches and shirt to shrink.

"Do I detect in the way you are tossing in your bedroll that you are having problems going to sleep?" Ashton suddenly said from behind her.

Sasha jumped with alarm. She had thought that she was totally alone in her misery. She sprang to a sitting position, her blankets falling down away from her. Lightning awakened with a low, snappish growl, then wagged her tail when she saw Ashton.

"Lord, Ashton, you scared both me and Lightning to death," Sasha scolded, patting the dingo pup. "I thought you were sound asleep. Everyone else is."

"No," he said, bending to a knee beside her. "I was faking it. I thought I'd give you enough time to realize that you chose unwisely when you said no to my offer of my tent tonight. Seems I was right in my calculations."

Sasha lifted her chin stubbornly, yet melted inside as she looked into Ashton's violet eyes. The reflection of the fire in them was turning them a strange sort of mellow purple-gold that threatened to tear down all of her defenses against him. It was as though he were looking clean into her soul, burning a path of desire to her heart.

"It is not where I am sleeping that is the bother," she said, hating herself when her voice broke with the sensual emotions that were awash within her. "It is you, Ashton. Now go on back to your tent. I am fine. Just a bit restless—but fine."

She twisted and turned her shoulders, trying to get more comfortable in her tight, shrunken shirt. But in doing so she only drew the shirt more tightly against her breasts—so much that a button popped loose and flipped awkwardly through the air, hitting Ashton in the face.

Sasha covered a gasp behind her hand. "I'm— I'm sorry, Ashton," she said, her eyes wide. "I had no idea the button was loose." She had to stifle a giggle behind her hand, for it was amusing to see Ashton's expression when the button hit him.

Ashton chuckled low as his gaze moved to the gap in her shirt where the strain had snapped the button off. The fire's glow revealed quite a magnificent cleavage, her rounded breasts all but exposed to his feasting eyes. "I don't think a loose button was the problem," he said thickly. "It seems they were battling something quite out of their control."

"Oh, yes," Sasha said, sighing. "My shirt. It shrank today. Also my breeches." When Ashton continued to stare openly at her, she followed his gaze, stopping where her shirt gaped open, and realized why he had not been able to peel his eyes away from the sight.

A blush rose hot to her cheeks as she tried in vain to pull the shirt closed, then finally drew a blanket up around her shoulders and glared at Ashton.

"Sweet darlin', so you see what I meant," Ashton said, touching her cheek gently. "The next time you purchase a shirt make sure it is adequate in size to cover your beautiful breasts."

"I told you that the shirt shrank," she said heatedly. She slapped his hand from her face. "And also my breeches." She paled. "Oh, Lord, what if I pop the buttons on my breeches also? I don't have another pair, nor do I have another shirt. I could only afford this one outfit!"

"I think I can offer assistance if you would allow it," Ashton said, his eyes twinkling.

"No, thank you," Sasha said, avoiding his eyes as he implored her with them. "I will manage. Somehow."

Ashton shrugged as he moved to his feet. He stretched his arms over his head. "Whatever you say," he said, yawning. "Goodnight, Sasha."

Sasha watched him saunter off to his tent, the play of muscles on his legs and shoulders making her heart race. When he bent to crawl inside his tent, she looked quickly away, embarrassed. She placed a hand over her heart, wishing that it would quit pounding. It was too much proof of just how much she loved Ashton York—and that she mustn't!

Sighing heavily and feeling the need to walk off her frustrations, Sasha slipped out of her bedroll. As she stood she winced and groaned, for what she had feared came to pass. One step from the bedroll and a button popped from her breeches.

And then another!

She looked incredulously down at her awkward situation, her stomach all but exposed where the breeches gaped open in front, her breasts all but hanging out where the shirt strained against them. The breeches were now up past her ankles, and so tight that every step was an effort.

"What am I to do?" she whispered, raking her fingers nervously through her unbraided hair.

Firm hands on her waist made Sasha's knees weaken, for she did not have to look to see who it was. Ashton. He was not one to give up so easily. And this time, she had no choice but to welcome any assistance that he might offer.

In truth, she was now totally at Ashton's mercy!

She slowly turned and faced him. Her lashes blinked nervously up at him as she smiled. "You were right," she hated to confess. "I do need a change of clothes. Do you truly have something that I can wear? I would still rather not travel in a dress."

Ashton smiled down at her. "I think we can manage something for you," he said, chuckling. "You may look a mite comical, but you can pretend you are a circus clown traveling with this outfit solely for our entertainment."

He paused for a moment, his eyes gleaming with amusement. "But, sweet darlin', you may have to let us call you Spike again," he teased. "That name would fit a circus entertainer well enough, don't you think?"

Not finding any of what he was saying amusing, Sasha jerked away from Ashton. "On second thought," she said dryly. "A dress will do me just fine." She turned to storm away from him, but he stepped in front of her.

"All right," he said, frowning down at her. "I won't tease you anymore tonight. Come on. Come to my tent. We'll go through my clothes and find something that'll do."

Sasha searched his eyes, then acquiesced. She walked with him to his tent, then became tense and wary when she felt the intimacy of his quarters as they crawled in together. The fire's glow was weaving dancing designs on the outside of the tent that were reflected on the inside. The night was so quiet—the moon so bright and romantic!

And Ashton was looking at her with his wondrous violet eyes, his hand reaching to her face, tracing the outline of her lips.

"Sasha, damn it, you're so beautiful," he said huskily. "Do you know how long I have wanted you? How badly?"

Sasha's heart skipped a beat as alarm set in. She was battling wild, rapturous feelings that were dangerous under the circumstances. He was too close. She could almost feel his heartbeat, as though the sides of the tent were breathing in and out with it. She could smell the manly scent of him.

And the way his finger was tracing her lips—oh, how it was causing her to become weak all over, as though she just might collapse at any moment and be consumed by him!

"Please don't," she finally managed to say. She shoved his hand away from her face, but sucked in a quavering breath when this same hand suddenly reached inside her shirt and cupped a breast. Never had she felt anything so deliriously wonderful!

"I did not bring you here to seduce you," Ashton whispered, his loins on fire with need of her. His hand enveloped her breast, the softness against his flesh like nothing he had ever before felt. His head was spinning with passion—a passion that had plagued him for too long.

"The clothes," he quickly added. "I must get you . . . the clothes."

When Ashton pinched the nipple of her breast between his thumb and forefinger, Sasha closed her eyes with ecstasy. "Yes," she managed to whisper. "The . . . clothes. You must . . ."

His mouth seized her lips, silencing her words and any protests that may have been lying beneath the surface of her consciousness. She drifted toward him and became a part of him as he embraced her. She twined her arms around his neck as he lay her down on his spread-out blankets. She kissed him with abandon, her breath quickening with yearning as once again his hand sought and found her breast and began kneading it.

Without much thought as to what she was doing, Sasha unlocked her arms around his neck and tore at the front of her blouse until her breasts were fully freed. When his lips left her mouth and brushed against her throat, and then went lower and sucked a nipple between his teeth, Sasha moaned, pleasure spreading into a delicious tingling heat throughout her.

"Sasha," Ashton whispered reverently against her flesh. "My sweet Sasha. I have waited so long for this."

Sasha wove her fingers through his hair, breathless with anticipation as his hands worked at disrobing her. There was no fight left in her. Her heart had won the battle. And all that was left was the promise of paradise that he had to offer.

Her clothes and boots tossed aside, Ashton leaned over Sasha. He took her hand and guided it to the buttons of his shirt. "Undress me," he whispered huskily.

Embarrassed at the thought, yet eager to see his unclothed body, Sasha complied with his wishes. Slowly, almost meditatingly, she unbuttoned his shirt. When she drew it aside to slip it down from his shoulders, she inhaled a nervous breath. Nestled within a thick crop of golden-red hair were two dark, tight nipples.

Remembering how wonderful it had felt when he had sucked one of her nipples between his teeth, she wrapped her arms around him and drew him down over her. As though practiced, she flicked a tongue across one of his nipples, then nipped it with her teeth, drawing a sensual groan from deep within Ashton.

Smiling seductively up at him, strangely not bashful in her nudity with a man for the first time, she smoothed his shirt on away from him, then ran her fingers down the flat plane of his stomach until she reached the buttons of his breeches.

Her heart thundered inside her, echoing in her ears like massive drumbeats, as she unfastened one button, then another—and another.

Her pulse raced as she slipped her hand beneath the waistband of the breeches and began urging them over his slim, tight hips.

The campfire's glow lit up the tent enough to reveal Ashton's manly strength as it jutted out from a thick crop of reddish hair at the juncture of his thighs. Sasha was almost spellbound by the sight. His manhood was distended and tight, and when she accidentally brushed her hand against it as she attempted to finish disrobing him, it jumped as though it had life in itself.

Ashton stiffened, the mere touch of her driving him wild. Unable to bear much more of this waiting, he finished undressing himself, then leaned fully over her and took her mouth by storm. One kiss blended into another as he parted her thighs with a knee. He moaned throatily when his hardness touched the core of her womanhood.

But knowing that this was the first time for her, he momentarily moved his hardness over her love bud, evoking a sigh of pleasure from between her lips.

"I need you," he whispered, his tongue brushing her lips lightly. He held her wrists above her head and looked down at her with haunted eyes. "Sasha, I love you. I've loved you for so long. Tell me that you love me. Tell me."

For the first time since this had begun between the two of them tonight, Sasha was catapulted back to the real world. She looked frantically up at him, scarcely believing she had let this go so far. A moment of madness had claimed her! A moment when nothing mattered but the wonderful feelings that Ashton aroused within her!

But she had been wrong. She had forgotten that she should not let her guard down with him. Though loving him with all her heart, she could not bear to give herself to him, then lose him in the end.

One man had tricked her. She couldn't let another do the same!

Shoving at his chest, Sasha tried to squirm from beneath him. But the more she moved, the more she was put in contact with his powerful body and his intriguing manhood, which her hands brushed against more than she intended. It was this part of his anatomy that seemed to make her heart swallow her whole whenever she caught glimpses of it or felt it against her flesh. A part of her hungered to discover the true mysteries of it, yet a part of her knew that she should not.

"Sasha, damn it," Ashton said, pinioning her to the ground. "Just stop and think of what you're doing, will you? You know that you love me. A woman does not kiss a man like you do unless she loves him. And feel your heartbeat. I know it isn't beating this wildly because of fear of me. It is because you want me, Sasha. As badly as I want you."

Sasha began to thrash her head from side to side. "No," she cried. "I don't." She tried to get her wrists free. "Let me go, Ashton. Surely you don't plan to take me against my will. You don't plan to—to rape me."

The thought, the accusation, made Ashton grow pale. He lurched back away from Sasha, eyeing her almost venomously. He grabbed his breeches and hurried into them, then reached for his satchel of clothes. Angrily, he began flinging shirts and breeches from it.

"Take what you want and get out of here," he growled. After the satchel was empty, he turned and glared at Sasha. "Better yet, I'm the one who is leaving." He doubled a fist at his side. "And don't follow me, Sasha. The tent is yours for the night and every night as far as I'm concerned."

Sasha cowered away from him as he grabbed his shirt, boots, and gunbelt. She flinched as he gave her another angry stare and bolted from the tent, leaving her there in an awkward silence, her body still warmed from his caresses, her mouth still swollen from his kisses.

"What have I done?" she whispered to herself, tears pooling in her eyes. "Oh, Ashton, what have I done? I do love you. I do."

Never had she felt so alone.

Chapter Eight

Rocking gently back and forth with her horse's stride,
Sasha traveled in silence a few yards back from
Ashton. She refused to look his way. They had not
spoken at breakfast, nor did she expect they would
speak when they stopped and made camp for the
evening. In one of Ashton's wide-brimmed hats and
in his borrowed clothes that were twice her size, she
felt no less comical than she had expected. Though
she had rolled up the sleeves of her shirt and the
legs of her breeches, and a rope secured the
breeches at her waist, they were still so large and
bulky they almost swallowed her whole.

She knew that she was a sight, but Ashton had not
laughed and teased her about it today. He was
ignoring her as much as she was ignoring him.
Their brief sensual moments together had placed a
barrier between them—perhaps so high a barri-

er that neither could, or would, ever try to scale it.

It was a high summer's day in January when the trees kept their leaves but shed their bark. In them, squat brown birds roared with laughter. The dragon of the outback, a carrion-eating lizard known as a goanna, rushed up a tree at Sasha's right side and clung there staring at her as she passed by, its throat puffed out in soundless alarm. Other animals crept, slid, and waddled through the dry brush ahead. A silvery-coated eastern gray kangaroo bounded away, emitting a faint, querulous sort of bleat.

A persistent itching drew Sasha's fingers to her neck. She scratched and scratched, then found herself itching in other unspeakable places that she could not touch in the presence of the men who rode on each side of her. Nervous perspiration beaded up on her brow as the itching worsened. She scratched everywhere that she could reach, then noticed that everyone else seemed to be spending a lot of time scratching, also.

She looked at Ashton, whose back was to her. Smiling devilishly, she watched his hands flutter along his neck, his arms, and his legs as he also scratched himself incessantly.

Arching an eyebrow, Sasha looked at the other men again. Not one of them were without eager fingers clawing at their skin and clothes.

Suddenly Ashton stopped his horse and turned to face everyone. "So what do you think is causing this damnable itch?" he shouted. "Ever since I woke up, it seems like something is crawling all over me. And I see it is the same for you. Do any of you have any idea of what we may have been exposed to?" He rolled up a shirt sleeve and examined his arm. "I see no rash. But I do—" He gasped.

Sasha moved her horse toward Ashton's. "Ashton, what is it?" she asked, having seen that he had discovered something on his arm. "What did you find?"

"Fleas," Ashton said in disgust. Then he shouted as he looked incredulously up at Sasha. "Damn fleas! I'm infested with fleas!"

Sasha drew her reins taut and stopped her horse. "Fleas?" she said, a shudder of distaste rushing through her.

She looked quickly down at her arm as she rolled her sleeve up, then gasped anew, for even though they were no larger than the head of a pin, she could make out the little black pests jumping along her flesh.

"Lord," she whispered, paling. When she thought of all the places on her that were itching, she felt an urge to retch.

Fleas!

"I've heard about bush fleas," Ashton said, dismounting. He secured his horse's reins on a tree limb, then began unloading his belongings from the horse. "Seems we have quite a battle on our hands."

Sasha dismounted. "Ashton, I'm willing to do anything to get rid of these dratted things," she said, screwing her face up in a frown. "Tell me! I'll do it!"

"First we've got to figure out where the fleas came from," Ashton said, spreading his bedding out on the ground. He knelt on a knee and examined it. His jaw tightened as he glanced up at Sasha. "These blankets are full of them." He nodded toward her neatly bundled pack on the back of her horse. "Get yours. Check them." He nodded toward the men who were off their horses, itching frantically. "Check your blankets. See if they are infested!"

Low grumblings and cursings filled the air as blankets were spread out on the ground. Sasha knelt to the ground and examined hers, then looked slowly up at Ashton and smiled awkwardly. "I've never seen so many obnoxious tiny creatures in my life," she said.

She rubbed her ankles, wishing for enough privacy to scratch at the juncture of her thighs. "The blankets do seem to be the source of the trouble," she said, as all the men confirmed that their blankets were as infested as hers and Ashton's. "Why, Ashton? Where did the pests come from?"

Ashton rose to his full height. He frowned thoughtfully, then his eyes brightened. "Those are sand fleas," he said. "Don't you remember? You spread everything out to dry on the sand. That sand must have been filled with fleas. Those little blood-suckers probably leaped on our blankets the minute you laid them down."

"Blood-suckers?" Sasha said, shuddering.

"That's why we're itching so bad," Ashton said, shrugging.

"How utterly horrible," Sasha said, gagging.

"We'd best get busy ridding ourselves of the creatures while the sun is still high in the sky," Ashton said, pushing his broad-brimmed hat back from his brow to study the position of the sun.

"What can we do?" Sasha asked, endlessly scratching. She had easily forgotten that she and Ashton had had differences which had led to silence between them. They were partners again, trying to solve a problem on their trek to their new land.

"First we've got to kill us several opossums and skin them," Ashton said, yanking a revolver from its holster. He waved his firearm in the air. "Opossums are a'plenty in the outback. Every man for himself. We need a lot of skins if we're to get rid of those damn fleas." He lowered his gun and looked at Sasha. "It's up to you to search and find us several ant hills. While we're preparing the 'possums, you find the ant hills and then start carrying everyone's blankets to them."

"Whatever on earth for?" Sasha asked, giving him a quizzical stare.

"Just do your part, Sasha," Ashton said gruffly. "You wanted to be my partner? Now's the time to prove it."

Stung by his attitude, Sasha placed her hands on her hips. "As if I haven't proven time and time again that I am capable of being here with you and—and those men," she spat.

She ignored Ashton's amused grin and began walking through the tangled brush, her eyes peeled for the ant hills. As she walked, the ground became mantled in a crackling skin of dry gum leaves and grasses. The fallen strips of eucalyptus bark were like a stretched drum, a delicate resonator that informed every animal of Sasha's approach.

She moved stealthily onward. A wombat, a marsupial resembling a squat, blunt-skulled bear, peeked from a hole, then dove headfirst into it when Sasha came closer.

Then she spied the ant hills. They were like large sand castles beneath the hot, broiling sun, sculpted beautifully by the never-tiring ants.

"First fleas and now ants," she fussed to herself, turning to return for the blankets. As she made her way back, several gunshots broke through the silence. She flinched when some of the men returned with a couple of dead opossums dangling from their hands. She turned her eyes away and did not watch as they began skinning them. She gathered up the blankets in her arms and smiled wanly at Ashton as he appeared with an opposum skin, having skinned it where he had shot it.

"I found several ant hills," Sasha said, walking on past Ashton. "I hope they will do, for I refuse to look for more. I cannot see why I must bother. As far as I'm concerned, ants are as bad as fleas."

"Sweet darlin', ants eat fleas," Ashton said, taking the blankets from her arms and slinging them over his shoulder. "And so we shall give them a feast they will never forget."

"I still don't see how," Sasha said, feverishly itching her stomach. "I think the fleas are on me to stay!"

"Well, I must admit that we can't use the same technique to rid ourselves of the fleas as we use on the blankets," Ashton said, chuckling. Over his shoulder he nodded to the men who were following, also carrying their opossum skins. "But first things first."

When they reached the ant hills, she watched in silent awe as Ashton went through the procedure which he vowed would take care of the flea problem on the blankets. First he and his men spread the blankets out on the ant hills. After that, they put the opossum skins over the blankets, fleshy side up.

"The fleas will go for the opossum skin, but the

sun gets too hot for them," Ashton explained as he continued to arrange the blankets and skins. "It drives the fleas from the skin back to the blankets. The ants will be waiting to snatch them up. Then all we will have to do is shake the rest of the ants out of the blankets."

Sasha was surprised to see that this was exactly what happened. The ants appeared and acted frenzied while grabbing up the fleas. She took a quick step back when all of the blankets were snatched up and shaken, then hesitated when Ashton offered her one.

"It's safe to hold them now," he said, scratching his left thigh.

"All right, you got rid of the fleas in the blankets," Sasha said, draping a blanket over her arm. "How are we to get them off of us?"

"It seems that we all must take a swim in the river, clothes and all," Ashton said, chuckling as he saw a look of doubt in Sasha's eyes. "Now don't fret, Sasha. My clothes won't shrink on you. They've been washed countless times before."

"I had not even thought to worry about that," Sasha said, lifting her chin stubbornly. "It's that I—I don't relish the thought of bathing with all of you men. Not even to rid myself of these dreaded fleas."

Ashton shrugged. "I'm not going to force you," he said, then his eyes locked with Sasha's. "I shall never force you to do anything that you don't want to do. Anything," he said, and she knew what he meant.

Sasha blushed. She turned away, but the shine of the river beckoned at her through the trees. She had no choice but to take a swim. She could not bear to live with the itch of the fleas another minute!

But she would choose an isolated spot so that she could bathe in private.

She watched in which direction the men were going, then moved quickly in the opposite direction along the riverbank. After only a short distance she began to feel that she was perhaps a little too alone, and stopped. In case some animal decided to taste her for its supper, she did not want to go beyond screaming range of the men.

Yet she thought she had found a private enough cove away from the searching eyes of the men and felt it was safe enough for her to remove her clothes so that she could give her body a good dousing in the water. Even so, she feared that she might be scratching for the next year because of the bites already inflicted on her flesh!

First she slipped her boots off, then her shirt and breeches. The boots were laid aside. She carried her clothes into the water with her, steadying herself on the rocky bottom. Moving out into the current, she stopped when she was waist-deep in the river and began furiously scrubbing her clothes together in the water.

As she labored to rid the clothes of their infestation, she looked guardedly around her, then relaxed when she realized that she was still very much alone. It was a place of total serenity. The current of the river was slow; the warm, brown water seemed to stand still as it murmured and meandered through intermittent deep pools and gravel-filled shallows. It seemed a secret place. There in the deep shade, enclosed in the dense, overhanging growth of the banks, her eyes became fixed on the wings of a dragonfly, and then the flitting motion of a water strider.

A frog leaped from the far bank and broke the image apart, and also Sasha's moment of reverie. She shook her head, as though to clear her thoughts, suddenly aware that it was not smart to stay away from the others very long. There were too many dangers in being alone, naked—and a woman.

After pitching her washed shirt and breeches ashore, she took a deep breath and dove beneath the surface of the water. She swam fully immersed, her skin already feeling soothed of its tormented itchings. Enjoying these moments of weightlessness and itch-free skin, she broke to the surface to get a gulp of air, then dove back deep into the water again.

She glided through the water, her arms stroking smoothly, her legs kicking. And just as her lungs told her that they needed another reprieve and she was ready to rush back to the surface for a breath of air, her heartbeat seemed to lodge in her throat when a hand suddenly grabbed her around one of her ankles and held her in place beneath the water.

Desperately afraid, Sasha twisted herself around so that she could see who had joined her, but the water was too dark to make out anything except for that hand still locked around her ankle.

And then the hand was gone and she was trying to reach the surface for that badly needed breath of air, but she was caught off guard a second time. Before she reached the surface, a hand was on her breast, caressing it.

Wild with rage and fright, she slapped the hand

away. Breathing hard, she finally bobbed to the surface.

Gasping for breath, her breasts heaving, Sasha stood on the rocky bottom and looked frantically around her, waiting for her assailant to show himself.

She knew that it could be anyone. . . .

Chapter Nine

Bubbles surfacing close to Sasha made her aware that someone was still there beneath the water. She wanted to run, and she eyed the shore anxiously, but her knees were too weak from fear to move.

She gasped and looked quickly around when Ashton burst through the surface, breathing harshly. "You!" she said, folding her arms over her breasts in an attempt to cover them. "All along it was you!"

He inhaled a deep breath of air and forked his fingers through his hair to draw it back from his face. His kangaroo-hide shirt clinging to his shoulders and chest. "What can I say?" he said. "This was all done in innocence, Sasha. I didn't mean to frighten you."

Sasha's eyes were aflame with rage, and her nostrils flared angrily as she glared up at Ashton.

"How else would you expect a person to react when someone grabs their ankles beneath the water?" she said in a rush. "And, Ashton, how—how dare you take such liberties with me beneath the water. You—you touched my breasts!"

"I don't guess you would believe me if I said that none of this was planned, would you?" he asked. His heart pounded erratically as his eyes took in the sweet innocence of her face. Surely she was only pretending to be angry.

Ashton had been sidetracked more than once by the force of nature on this journey to his sheep station, but his need of Sasha was the most painful of all these experiences. He had dared to take that first kiss from her that day in Melbourne, and it had triggered in him a fire that would never be extinguished. He would never stop hungering for Sasha. Never.

"Are you saying that you did not know that I was bathing here?" she snapped. She tried not to be unnerved by the way he continued to look at her, with strange lights moving in the depths of his eyes. It was not so much that he was seeing more of her body than was decent. It was that he was there, so close, only a mere wondrous kiss away!

"You are the one who told everyone to wash in the river," she added quickly, lest he read her thoughts and know that he had won a victory over her that she did not want to give in to again.

A slow smile tugged at the corners of Ashton's lips as he looked slowly over her again. "But I believe my instructions were to keep your clothes on," he said, his eyes glittering dangerously.

"Am I to believe that you did not follow me and

even watch me undress before I entered the river?"

Ashton's jaw tightened. He took a step closer to Sasha, flinching when she took a step back. "I swear to you that I was not aware of which part of the river you were swimming in," he said. "Nor was I aware that you were swimming nude."

Forgetting her need to cover her breasts, Sasha placed her hands on her hips. "And, kind sir, are you going to tell me that you did not know it was my ankle that you were holding, nor—nor my breast that you were touching?" she hissed. "How could you not know it was me? No other woman is traveling with us."

"The water is not clear enough to see an inch ahead of you and you know it," Ashton said, tiring of this bantering. "I was swimming beneath the water minding my own business when my hands just happened upon you swimming ahead of me."

He flung a hand in the air. "And, damn it, at that moment I did know who it was," he said in a near shout. "No man I know has such delicately tapered ankles."

His eyes lowered and he cleared his throat. "Now I must admit that when I touched your breast, that was done deliberately," he said softly.

He looked slowly up at her. "How could I not?" he said, his voice drawn. "Sasha, damn it, I need you. I love you."

A dull ache knotted within Sasha's chest. Something compelled her not to pull away when his hands were suddenly on her throat, framing her face. Her pulse raced and her knees weakened with rapture when he bent and pressed a warm, tender kiss to her parted lips. Just as quickly, all of her reserves, all of her denials, melted away. She curled her arms around his neck and kissed him with longing too long denied, sighing from the pleasurable sensations that were claiming her.

Sasha moaned and became pliant in Ashton's arms as one of his hands moved down to curve over her breast, then lower where she ached so strangely between the thighs. When he began stroking her, her entire body seemed to be throbbing with an unbearable sweetness.

She needed to touch him all over. She drew her lips from his and looked up at him with drugged passion as she began smoothing his shirt up over his chest.

"The water is much more effective if you remove your clothes," she said, not recognizing her voice in its huskiness.

"For what? Ridding the body of fleas? Or giving my woman more access to it?" Ashton teased, unfastening the buttons of his breeches with his free hand and lowering his breeches down away from him. He lifted them from the water and tossed them ashore along with his shirt that Sasha had already thrown there. The fire was raging within him as his fingers traveled hotly down her body, caressing and arousing.

He then jerked her next to him. Their bodies strained together hungrily. "I love you, Sasha," he whispered. He ran his tongue slowly over the perfect contours of her face. "Tell me that you love me." He framed her face between his hands and gazed down at her with passion-filled eyes as she inched away from him. "Tell me, Sasha. Tell me."

Sasha stared at him questioningly for a moment,

torn over what she should do. Then, with a sob of fury, she flung herself back into his arms and clung to him. "Oh, Ashton, I don't want to love you," she cried. "I don't! I don't!"

"I think I can understand why," he whispered, caressing the soft and creamy flesh of her back. "And don't say it until you can feel comfortable with it. Seeing it in your eyes and hearing it in your voice is enough for me now. In time, Sasha, you will be free of your fears and doubts. Then you will show me fiercely the depths of your love for me."

"I feel so wicked, Ashton," Sasha whispered, her breath taken away when she felt his manhood probing between her thighs. If she did not stop him now, it would be too late. She could not control the beating of her heart nor the desperate needs that were encompassing her. To have him inside her was surely the ultimate of ultimates! To stop him, all she had to say was no!

But every fiber of her being was screaming yes!— yes!—yes!

"Nothing that we ever share can be called wicked," Ashton whispered against her cheek as his fingers cupped her buttocks, drawing her closer to his throbbing hardness. He forced her hips in at his, then stifled her cry of sensual shock with a kiss as he plunged inside her. Their naked bodies fused, sucking at each other in the water, flesh against flesh, Ashton's passion rising, his whole body seeming to be fluid with fire.

Only half aware of making whimpering sounds, Sasha hid her blush of pleasure against the broad column of Ashton's throat. Sinking into a chasm of desire from which she felt she might never rise again, her hands clung to his sinewed shoulders. She closed her eyes and let him guide her legs around his waist. In this position she was even more aware of how he filled her. And as he surged into her, she met each of his strokes with abandon, each fresh stab within her awakening her to exquisite agony.

Ashton found her breasts and stroked them, causing Sasha to gasp with pleasure. She was now delirious with sensation, feeling the last vestiges of her rational mind floating away. And when he kissed her again, his mouth sucking her tongue through her parted lips, a surge of tingling heat flooded from her breasts to her toes.

Then her whole universe seemed to start spinning around as she went over the edge into total ecstasy, the spinning sensation and surges of warmth flooding through her body.

When Ashton plunged harder and harder into her, breathing his groans of pleasure against her neck, she knew that he had also found the same paradise as she and she did not want to feel ashamed of what she had just done.

It had seemed so right, so very, very wonderful— this total sharing with the man she loved!

Sasha clung to Ashton, breathing hard. When he looked down at her, his eyes filled with a tender loving, she smiled weakly up at him, then turned her eyes away. Although it had seemed right to love him in such a way, because she felt so deeply about him, she was now beginning to feel as she had before. She could never fully trust a man again. Not even a man who had just taken her to heaven and back! And she was angry at herself for having let down her guard! Now he would expect her always to give in to his needs, no matter that her own matched his.

Slipping from his embrace, Sasha suddenly felt shy beneath his searching eyes. He had touched her all over and surely had her every curve and dip memorized, but now, after having shared the ultimate of embraces with him, she felt awkward.

"Sasha, what's the matter?" Ashton asked, reaching gently to touch her cheek. When she moved away from him and left the water, almost frantically scrambling into her wet clothes, his heart sank. He knew that the battle with her, to win her, was not yet over. Perhaps he was worse off than before now that he had made love to her. Perhaps his timing had been all wrong!

Circling his hands into tight fists, as if that way he could hold in the sadness that washed through him, he left the water and pulled on his clothes, feeling the silence between them like a heavy weight pressing in on him.

Then, unable to bear this, he took Sasha by a wrist and turned her to face him. "Is this the way it's going to be now?" he asked, frowning down at her. "Because we made love, you are going to treat me like the plague? I guess I should be used to it by now, but damn it, Sasha, I'm not. Why can't you come to your senses and admit that you love me? Why, Sasha?"

Her face flooding with color, her body still throbbing from the passion they had shared, Sasha found it hard not to lunge into his arms and beg him to hold her and never let her go.

But she had too much to sort out inside her mind,

even deep within her soul, to make any more foolish blunders today.

"I would rather not talk about it, Ashton," she said, her voice quavering. "Please honor my wishes."

Ashton looked incredulously down at her. "You would rather not talk about it?" he said, his voice rising in volume as his anger flared. "You ask that I honor your wishes?" He grabbed her by the shoulders and yanked her to him so that their bodies were crushed together. He looked down into her eyes. "Sweet darlin', I may have just misinterpreted our little affair in the water a moment ago. I had thought that it meant something to you."

He released her so abruptly that she stumbled back away from him, almost falling. Shocked, she covered her mouth with her hands. She had never seen Ashton so quickly angered before.

"Well, little lady, I'm not misinterpreting your behavior now," he said heatedly. "I'm sorry to have been a disappointment to you!"

Stunned as though she had been slapped, Sasha released a sob of remorse against the palm of her hand. Although she wanted to run after him and beg his forgiveness, she watched unmoving as Ashton stormed away through the brush. Memories of the wondrous time with him in the water only moments before swept through her, knowing that it was only the first of so many more exchanged passions if she would just say the words to Ashton that would prove to him that what he had just said was so wrong. He had not disappointed her. He was a masterful lover. He had awakened her to so many wonderful feelings!

But the memory of her betrayal by one man kept her from going after Ashton and accepting fate as it was handed to her.

She sat down on the ground and yanked on her boots, then dispiritedly moved through the tangled brush back to the camp. At least that dratted itching had stopped. Looking guardedly around her, she was almost afraid to see if any of the men would look knowingly up at her, knowing, somehow, that she had just lost her virginity.

But to her relief, all of the men were hard at work rolling up blankets and securing their bedrolls on their horses. Some were already in their saddles, ready to ride onward.

Hoping to make it up to Ashton, knowing that was best since their futures were linked by agreements and commitments, Sasha walked meekly over to him as he tied his bedroll behind his saddle. "Did you give Lightning a bath?" she asked softly, seeing the pup licking her wet fur.

"What does it look like?" Ashton said. His expression was sad and brooding, and there was a searing hurt in his eyes as he glanced at her. "She's wet isn't she? I would think means she's had a bath." He walked past Sasha and bent to grab up another bedroll. He came back to her and thrust it forcefully into her arms. "Here's your bedroll." He turned his back to her to bend and pet Lightning. "And, no, I didn't bathe her. She had enough sense to jump into the river herself."

"Oh, I see," Sasha said, taking her bedroll and securing it at the back of her horse. She grabbed her hat from the ground and plopped it on her head, then went back to Ashton. "When are we going to be seeing Rufus and Crispin? I still don't understand why they didn't travel with us."

She eyed his scar. The water had made it turn a sort of purplish white, which intensified her interest in it. It made him look so much a man of mystery. Would he ever tell her how he had become scarred? Who had inflicted the scar? Did she even want to know? Perhaps she would not be able to accept his past!

"We've just a few days of travel ahead of us and then you'll know the answers to all your questions," Ashton said bluntly. He swung himself up into his saddle. "It's time to leave. I presume you've not changed your mind about traveling with me."

Sasha paled and her lips parted with surprise. "Why, no, Ashton, I haven't changed my mind," she murmured.

He nodded toward her horse. "Then if you don't want to be left behind, I suggest you get on your horse," he said flatly.

Shaken by his coldness, Sasha stared at him a moment longer, then, without looking at Ashton again, swung herself into the saddle. When she heard Lightning barking excitedly, she knew that Ashton had taken the pup up onto his lap.

Her chin held high, Sasha flicked her reins against Cloud's snow-white mane and rode away. As she rode past Ashton she could feel the heat of his eyes on her, as though branding her.

Two approaching horsemen made Stanford Sidwell draw rein and wait for their arrival. He chewed on a half-smoked cigar and squinted his eyes beneath the brilliant rays of the sun.

"Stanford, can't we stop for the day?" Bianca asked, drooping in the saddle on a horse next to Stanford's. She placed a hand to her abdomen, the unborn child so still within her. "I need some rest. Please, Stanford, let's not go any farther."

Stanford took the cigar from between his lips and tossed it to the ground. He scrutinized Bianca carefully as he leaned closer to her. "You are a bit drawn," he said, forking an eyebrow. "I guess travel on a horse is too hard for a woman who used to spend all her time spreading her legs on a bed." He chuckled and shrugged. "You'll get used to it, Bianca. You'll get used to it."

The two horsemen drew rein next to Stanford. "So? What'd you two find out?" he asked, turning away from Bianca.

"Sir, we found it," one of the men said, sucking on his yellow, jagged teeth as he laughed. "It's two-days ride north."

"Don't test my patience," Stanford growled. "Tell me all about it. What exactly did you find?"

"We found Ashton York's sheep run," the other man said, his dark eyes gleaming. "There's a house already built, fences set up, and at least four hundred sheep on property staked off by his men."

"So he did this all in secret, eh?" Stanford said, kneading his chin contemplatively. "I thought he would. That's why I sent you ahead."

"We did everything you asked," the yellow-toothed man said. "We marked off acreage across the river from Ashton York's."

"Were you seen doing it?" Stanford asked guardedly.

"No, and there ain't no way of telling we were

125

there except for the markers, and we made sure they were too tiny for anyone to find except us when the time is right," the dark-eyed man said, laughing throatily.

"Then all we have to do is wait until Ashton arrives at his sheep station. Then we can settle down at ours all legal-like the next day, as though it is all by accident that we are there," Stanford said, pulling a fresh cigar from his pocket. He thrust it between his teeth and lit it, puffing confidently.

"Do you want the men who are already at the sheep station to meet with an accident?" the yellow-toothed man asked, spittle rolling from the corner of his mouth. Greed for killing made his eyes darken.

"Naw," Stanford said, squaring his shoulders. "There's plenty of time for that later."

"Whatever you say."

The men rode away and joined the others.

Bianca looked at Stanford with fear, now realizing that he was more evil and calculating than she had ever guessed.

Chapter Ten

The evening sky was streaked with long, uncertain bands of red. Sasha was weary in the saddle, but relieved that they had finally reached the plain beyond the gum tree forest. She gazed around her, wondering about this land that was dust-colored but liberally sprinkled with the gray-green of water-conserving mulga and mallee shrubs. Ashton had taught her that sheep grazing in mallee scrub, patches of which extended for miles, could get lost because the tough bushes of *eucalyptus dumosa* were too high for a man to see across, even from horseback. Sasha shuddered when she heard dingoes howling in the middle distance, recalling also that Ashton had told her that the mallee was known as *dingo shrub* because it sheltered the wild dogs that shepherds had learned to fear most.

She eyed Lightning. The pup's ears were perked

up and her eyes were alert. Sasha had to wonder if Lightning might one day decide to return to the wild and become a hunter of sheep.

Riding onward, her backside sore from being in the saddle so long, Sasha sighed. Then her eyes widened in disbelief when she found herself riding beside a six-foot-high fence which ambled into the distance. At least four hundred beautiful Merino sheep grazed peacefully within its safe confines.

She had heard about the outback's millions of rolling acres that were covered in box, a shrub whose thirsty roots pulled every drop of surface moisture out of the soil and prevented the grass from growing. The solution for the graziers was ringbarking. This killed the box without using up extra labor felling it and grubbing out the tree stumps. Grass then sprouted in abundance on these spectral landscapes of gesticulating, claw-white dead box branches, the sort that Sasha could see now and then across the pasture land that was spread out before her.

She nudged her horse with her knees and rode up next to Ashton. "Ashton, we are most certainly not the first to arrive here," she said, tipping her wide-brimmed hat back from her brow with a finger. "Will we settle close by? Will these squatters be our neighbors?"

Ashton looked at her with a strange sort of gleam in his eyes. "Yes to both of your questions," he said, resting a hand on his saddle horn. "What do you say we go and give these folks a hello right now? Let's see just what sort of neighbors we are going to have to deal with."

An anxiousness stirred within Sasha to think that

she just might have a woman neighbor with whom to exchange female talk from time to time. She had expected never to see another woman out here in the outback. She had heard the outback referred to as almost exclusively a man's world, lonely and robbing robust men of home, wife, and children. It was said that the outback was no place for women and children, for there was no medical service, schools, or community activities of any kind.

But knowing this had not stopped Sasha. She had longed for the adventure, the challenge.

"Yes, let's do go and meet those who are soon to be our neighbors," she murmured, then glanced down at her attire and frowned. "Oh, but look at me. Not only am I dressed in men's breeches and shirt, but they are also so dusty and dirty from the long journey."

She jerked her hat from her head and thrust it inside her saddlebag, then quickly stroked her slim fingers through her hair.

Ashton chuckled. "Sweet darlin', don't fret so over your appearance," he said. "I doubt if it makes much difference at all to these people how you look. Out here at the end of nowhere everyone tends to look the same anyway."

Sasha gave him an annoyed look, hoping that he was not sincere in suggesting that she looked no better to him than the men of his acquaintance. She flicked her reins and rode on ahead of him.

Lightning following dutifully behind him, Ashton sank his heels into the flanks of his horse and caught up with Sasha. "I hope that soon we can declare peace between us," he said. "There's more to do out here in the outback than to argue. We're partners,

Sasha. We've lots of planning ahead of us."

"I am sure that we do have," she snapped. She cast him an angry look. "It seems that Rufus and Crispin have deserted us. Some friends they turned out to be, Ashton."

Lightning suddenly seemed to go crazed. Yelping, the pup ran ahead of Sasha and Ashton toward the gate that led through the fence and crawled beneath it. Then Sasha and Ashton saw the cause. A sheep dog, a kelpie, bounded into view from the throng of sheep and was racing toward Lightning.

"Damn it," Ashton said, swinging himself from his saddle. He ran to the gate and opened it. But before he could reach Lightning to stop her confrontation with the kelpie, the two dogs had met nose to nose and were quickly getting acquainted without a fight.

Sasha dismounted and ran to Ashton and stood by his side, breathless. "I don't think they are going to fight, do you?" she whispered. "Perhaps they can become friends."

"It seems that the only fight here is between you and me," Ashton said beneath his breath.

Sasha looked up at him. "Did you say something?" she asked, forking an eyebrow.

Ashton laughed nervously. "Not really," he said, his gaze drawn to an approaching horseman, recognizing him. It was Crispin. He knew that Rufus would be tending to the sheep.

His heart swelled with pride that his two friends had done him proud—the fence, the sheep, the loyal kelpie. He only hoped that the house was presentable enough to put his future bride in.

Sasha saw the approaching horseman. She

squinted her eyes into the shadowy dusk, at first unable to tell who it was. Then her mouth fell open in astonishment. She knew the man! He was not a stranger at all—it was Crispin.

But what was he doing at this sheep station?

Crispin wheeled his horse to a halt next to Ashton and dismounted. Ashton went to him and shook his hand, then hugged him readily. "Damn good job, Crispin," he said proudly. "I knew I could depend on you."

Sasha looked from one to the other, stunned. And then she stepped forward, her hands on her hips. "Is there anyone among you who might let me in on what is going on here?" she snapped. She then narrowed her eyes at Ashton. "Ashton? Do you have anything to say?"

Ashton's eyes wavered. He looked at Crispin, hoping that he might intervene and save him. But he was silent—suddenly turned coward before a demanding lady.

"Well, it's like this," Ashton finally said, taking Sasha by an elbow and guiding her away from his friend so that any tongue-lashing he might get from Sasha would be in privacy. "I made an advance trip and secretly marked out this run."

"When did you?" Sasha gasped.

"Before you and I met," Ashton said, imploring her with his violet eyes. "I bought the pub to earn enough money to eventually stock my land with sheep. I guess I should've told you."

"Yes, I would say so," Sasha fumed. "All along I have been told that I would be traveling with you to find appropriate land for our sheep station. *Our* sheep station, Ashton. Yours and mine! And you already had the land." She swallowed hard. "Just what other secrets have you held from me, Ashton?" She eyed the scar with flashing eyes. "What terrible secret even lies beneath that scar on your face?"

Ashton's hand went to his scar and traced its outline. Stung by her words, he stared at her for a moment longer, then swung himself into his saddle.

"I want to see everything," he shouted at Crispin. "Take me to Rufus. I'd like to see just how he's taken to sheepherding." He gave Sasha a brooding look, then rode on past her.

Lightning came to Sasha and offered her a paw. Choked with confusion, Sasha bent to one knee and took the pup into her arms. "I've done it again, Lightning," she whispered. "Why can't I control my temper?" She swallowed back a rising lump in her throat. "But why can't Ashton be totally truthful with me? I do fear so much what he has not yet told me!"

She waited until the long line of men, packhorses, and dray and bullocks moved past her through the gate, then went to her horse and drew herself up into the saddle and rode in a lope along the land.

At first her ride was a dispirited one, but the farther she rode across land that she knew was part hers, and saw exactly what some of her hard-earned money had purchased, pride began to swell within her. It was even possible to forget why she had been angry at Ashton. Even though he had lied to her about many things, she knew that everything he had done was for her benefit—to make things easier on her once they arrived at their new home in the outback.

The house came suddenly into view. It was set off

from the pasture land, a long building with a bank of yellow flowers growing in front and the stockmen's quarters farther back from it. Her heart raced when she saw a garden filled with vegetables and farm animals grazing within a fence close beside a barn, and even more cattle grazing midst the sheep in the distance.

Ashton had thought of everything!

And she had been wrong about Crispin and Rufus. No one could be more loyal than they! They had labored hard to get the sheep station ready.

Ashton was lost to her sight, having gone with Crispin to survey the property and to meet with Rufus. Sasha rode up to the house and dismounted. Not taking her eyes off the small, hipped-roof dwelling with two windows like eyes on either side of the doorway, she looped her reins around a post. Ashton had forewarned her somewhat about the sort of house that she would be living in. He had said that the only good building timber came from the cabbage-tree palms, which were straight and easy to work with. The wall slats were cut from mimosa saplings—the "golden tree" of the Australian summer. The roof was reed thatch, gathered from the tidal marshes.

Her stomach quivering strangely with excitement, she moved up the front steps onto a porch, then on inside the house shadowed with dusk. There was just enough light left for her to find a candle and matches. Lighting the candle, she held the candleholder up and began moving it slowly around so that she could take in everything about the house. Although it was small and crude, she could not help but be proud of it, because it was hers!

"And Ashton's," she whispered to herself, her gaze settling on the one bed in the room against the far wall. A blush rose to her cheeks. There was only one bed—only one room! Where on earth would she find any privacy?

Momentarily catapulted back to those intimate moments with Ashton, Sasha looked quickly away from the bed and looked over the rest of the room, assessing all that Crispin and Rufus had done to prepare the house for occupancy. A fireplace had been built opposite the door, and an iron cooking pot hung over the grate. The walls were of unpainted planking, the mortar, she learned later, a mixture of sheep hair and mud; the floor was made of wide wooden planks.

All the furniture was handmade. The table was a split slab on four legs set in auger holes, the three-legged stools at the table made in the same way. Rough cupboards stood in one corner of the room, and pegs had been driven around the wall to hold clothes and on both sides of the fireplace to hold cooking utensils. Wooden shelves held food-stuffs and other utensils—whittled wooden knives, forks, plates, cups, butter paddles, buckets and dippers. A broom of fine birch splints tied together with a strip of hide rested against the wall.

Two armchairs sat before the fireplace, flanked by small tables with fresh, unburned candles in brass candleholders on the top of each.

"It's not much, but it's the best we can do for now," Ashton said from suddenly behind Sasha.

Startled, Sasha turned quickly to face him. "I didn't hear you come in," she murmured, glad that he no longer seemed to be angry at her for what she had said about his scar—and everything else.

"I saw the candlelight," Ashton said, hanging his hat on a peg on the wall. "It seemed inviting." He went to the fireplace and bent to a knee before it. Wood lay on the grate, ready to be lit. Striking a match, he touched it to the bits of kindling. "Somehow this all seems natural, Sasha. I guess it's because we dreamed of it for so long." He waved a hand over the flames that were taking hold.

"It's a lovely house, Ashton," Sasha said, nervously fidgeting with the tail of her shirt as she glanced toward the bed. "But, Ashton, I had expected at least two rooms and—two beds."

Ashton rose to his full height and went to the bed and pressed down on the tick of kangaroo skin filled with dry cornhusks and leaves, testing it. "Seems comfortable enough," he said, avoiding Sasha's set stare. "And big enough to hold two without being too crowded."

Sasha gasped. "Ashton, it is not my intention to sleep with anyone," she said, squaring her shoulders. Her voice waned in strength as she added, "Not even you."

Ashton turned to her, removing his gunbelt and hanging it on a peg on the wall close beside the bed. "Well, then, it looks as though one of us will be sleeping on the floor," he said. "I'm sorry I can't accommodate all of your wishes, sweet darlin'. But this is a new venture and I thought it best to curtail expenses wherever and whenever possible." He nodded toward the bed. "Even when it came to sleeping arrangements."

"You know very well that you did this only to be sure that I would sleep with you," Sasha said, her eyes flashing. "I would have settled for fewer sheep in exchange for a bed and a room of my own!"

Ashton glared at her, then stomped outside to stand on the porch. Sasha bit her lower lip in frustration. She didn't want to start their first evening at their sheep station with a quarrel. This should be a time for celebration! Ashton had even managed to bring a bottle of champagne with him for the occasion. He had guarded the champagne with his life through their daily battles with the forest and rivers. Not to open it and share it seemed a crime and she seemed to be at fault here. She should be grateful instead of being a whining shrew!

She went outside and stood beside Ashton on the porch. The sky was now filled with moonlight and flecked with stars. As far as the eye could see, the moon's glow revealed grazing sheep. The air was filled with the music of the bleating flock and the bassoon-like sound of the distant kangaroo.

A shiver raced up and down Sasha's spine when she heard the howling of dingoes in the far distance. She looked down at Lightning, who seemed still not disturbed by her own breed. The pup was curled up and peacefully asleep at Ashton's feet.

"We're finally here," she murmured. "Ashton, I am so glad." She looked up at him. "And, Ashton, I apologize for being so ungrateful. Will you forgive me?"

She warmed clear through when his answer was to place his arm around her waist, drawing her next to him. That was enough, for she knew that this gesture for him was not a small one.

"We've our own piece of heaven on earth,"

Ashton said, smiling down at her. "Your being with me makes my contentment complete."

"Oh, Ashton," Sasha said, leaning more into his embrace. "I am so content, also. I am at this moment more at total peace with myself than ever before in my life. We have so much to be happy for, don't we?"

"Everything," Ashton said huskily. "Everything."

"I'd like to call our sheep station The Homestead," he said, smiling down at Sasha. "Do you approve of the name?"

"The Homestead," Sasha said, as though testing the name on her lips. She smiled up at Ashton. "Why, yes, Ashton, I think that's a lovely name."

"Good," he said, nodding. "Then The Homestead it will be. It means more if you give your place a name."

"The sheep are beautiful," Sasha said, looking out at the flock beneath the moonlight. "Did you see Rufus? Does he enjoy his sheepherding duties?"

"Rufus seems made for the job," Ashton said, laughing softly. "He's always been a dreamer and being isolated with a flock of sheep day in and out gives a man plenty of time for dreaming."

"He stays with the sheep even at night?" Sasha asked, looking up at Ashton.

"Aye, he does," Ashton said. "It's not safe to leave the sheep untended for even an hour." The hair at the nape of his neck seemed to bristle at the sound of the dingoes' haunting refrain in the distance.

"In a good season, the life of the flocks can be idyllic, saved by man from the dangers that can beset them, such as the dingo and the blow fly," he continued in a monotone. "And also fire."

"Fire?" Sasha gasped, fear spiraling through her at the mere thought of a fire.

"The Aborigines run around through the outback half starved all of the time," he grumbled. "They are known to fire a province for a single meal."

"What do you mean?" Sasha asked, her eyes wide.

"The Aborigines do not hesitate to burn off a few square miles of territory just to catch a dozen or so goannas and marsupial rats at the cost of destroying all slow-moving animals and trees of the forest within that area," he explained. "The one advantage to these fires is that they promote new grass in the open country."

He glanced down at his trusting dingo pup sleeping at his feet, then looked back into the moonlit distance. "The worst enemy of the sheep is Australia's native dog, the dingo. Once one gets into a flock, it might kill thirty or forty sheep before the shepherd can come to their rescue."

Sasha looked down at Lightning, everything within her loving the pup. "Lightning is a dingo," she said, her voice drawn. "Do you think she will ever become an enemy of our sheep?"

Ashton looked down at the pup. "I don't think we have anything to fear from Lightning," he said. "Though a dingo, she wasn't reared and taught to kill sheep. She doesn't need the flesh of the sheep or any other wild thing to survive." He laughed. "I think that she sometimes forgets that she's a dog."

"Today she remembered," Sasha said, smiling at the memory of Lightning meeting the kelpie nose to nose. "She and the kelpie seemed to become instant friends."

"That's good," Ashton said, turning to look at the sheep again.

"Perhaps the kelpie will teach Lightning how to become a sheep dog," Sasha said, flicking her hair back from her shoulders.

"Crispin chose wisely when he chose that dog," Ashton said, leaning his weight on the porch rail with his hands. "The kelpie is a hard-working dog that can handle our Merino sheep. They are a tricky and delicate breed, but these that we have at our sheep station are healthy and should bring top dollar for their wool in England's textile market."

Crispin appeared from around the corner of the house, grunting as he labored at carrying a large copper tub to the foot of the steps. He set it down and smiled up at Sasha. "This is my welcoming surprise for you, Sasha," he said, wiping beads of perspiration from his brow. "I've already ordered some of the men to go to the river to bring up several buckets of water."

"Why, how sweet of you," Sasha said, placing her hands to her throat. "My word, how I do need a bath!" Then she looked shyly at Ashton. "But how can I take a bath? There is no privacy in our house."

Ashton went down the steps and grabbed the tub. He carried it past Sasha. "Sweet Darlin', whenever you need privacy, you can have it," he said, taking the tub in the house and setting it before the fire as Sasha came to stand beside him. "The whole outdoors is my second home, don't you know?"

Crispin leaned his head inside. "And there's a large pot of kangaroo stew cookin' for supper in the bunkhouse," he said. "So there'll be no cookin' for you tonight, Sasha."

Sasha could not believe Crispin's thoughtfulness. She went to him and slung her arms around his neck and gave him a big hug. "Thank you so much," she murmured. When she stepped away from him, she giggled, for she had made Crispin blush.

The men started carrying buckets of water into the house. Sasha stood back and watched them. Though the water would be cold, it would be welcome. And she could not wait to get into a dress.

Chapter Eleven

A fire was burning low and cozy in the fire-
place. Sasha was sitting on the floor beside Ashton
enjoying the first night in their new home. They
were drinking champagne from tin cups. The bub-
bly, effervescent drink seemed to be out of place in
the rustic cabin, yet it was still fitting as a symbol
that they had met their dreams head-on and now
looked to a future of even more adventures and
challenges.

Attired in a yellow cotton dress, smelling fresh
and clean from the river water, her stomach comfortably full, Sasha smiled to herself when she
remembered how proud Crispin had been when he
had ladled out a large dish of his kangaroo stew for
her. Not wanting to hurt his feelings about the
supper he had prepared for her and Ashton, Sasha
had forced herself to eat the stew, though everything

in her had been repelled by the thought of more of the tough and sinewy kangaroo meat. On the journey from Melbourne kangaroo stew had been their main meal, and she had hoped never to have to eat it again.

"Was it worth it?" Ashton suddenly blurted out.

His sudden break into the silence took Sasha off guard. She looked with a start at him. "Was what worth it?" she asked, her eyes wide.

Ashton set his empty tin cup aside and moved closer to Sasha. "Were the waiting and the grueling days of travel worth it?" he asked, reaching to smooth her dark hair back from her shoulders so that it tumbled long and free down her back. "You aren't too disappointed?"

"Disappointed?" Sasha said, looking quickly away from him when she realized that the way he was looking at her was making her heart pound almost out of control. And he smelled so wonderful after his bath, fresh shave and change of clothes! "No. Not at all, Ashton."

"It is only the beginning, you know," Ashton said, reaching to take her hand, which she quickly took away from him. He frowned at her and his heart felt the sting of her rejection. "One day, Sasha, I promise you that you shall have a much nicer house, and we will bring plenty of bright, overstuffed furniture from Melbourne for your comfort."

He cleared his throat nervously. "You will have a room of your own, if at that time you still prefer it," he said. "It will be decorated in fine white lace, for that is how I see you, Sasha. A pretty thing who should always wear beautiful white lace."

Sasha swallowed hard, scarcely able to stop herself from being pulled into feelings that she wanted to deny. "That's lovely, Ashton," she murmured, her pulse racing as he again tried to claim her hand. This time she allowed it.

She looked slowly his way. Their eyes met and held, then she grabbed her hand away again and rose quickly to her feet. "I am suddenly so tired," she said, her voice drawn, not wanting to let her emotions run free again with him. Faking a yawn, she purposely stretched her arms over her head. "Truly, I must retire for the night, Ashton, or be a fright tomorrow when I want to be alert for my first full day on our sheep station."

Frustrated by her continued evasions, Ashton rose to his feet and grabbed some blankets from the bed. "I'll go and sleep outside," he said. "Get a good night's sleep, Sasha."

He began to walk away, but Sasha was suddenly there, blankets thick in her arms. "Ashton, no," she said in a rush. "There is no need for you to go outside. I shall sleep on the floor. You can have the bed." She began spreading her blankets. "Tomorrow night we shall exchange places."

Ashton frowned at her and swept up her blankets and tossed them on the bed. He took her gently by the wrist and led her to the bed. "Sasha, will you quit being so stubborn?" he said, giving her a gentle shove toward the bed. "You sleep on the bed and I'll sleep on the floor."

Tired of bantering with him, and at least winning one victory—he wouldn't sleep outside on the cold ground—Sasha smiled wanly up at him. "If you insist," she murmured, yet wishing that she felt free enough to remove her dress so that she could get more comfortable in a nightgown. Perhaps in time she would become more used to this awkward situation and be able to wear what she pleased at night.

She plumped up her pillow and pulled blankets over her, bashfully watching as Ashton stretched out on the floor before the fire. She did not think much about it when he sat up and removed his boots, but she gasped and felt a blush rising to her cheeks when he yanked his shirt up over his head, revealing his bare, magnificently muscled chest.

Her breathing quickened when she watched his hands go to the waist of his breeches. Knowing what might be bared to her next, she turned over on her stomach and buried her face in her pillow.

Her heart racing, she listened for him to become quiet. And when he did, she was able to relax somewhat herself. Fighting the tumultuous feelings within her, she finally drifted off, but her sleep was no less restless than when she was awake. She began to dream—dreams of being in Ashton's arms. He was kissing her, his hands eagerly disrobing her. She felt a soft, melting energy warm her insides when he began to stroke her breasts. But when he moved over her and entered her with a passion that drew her lips apart in a gasp, she awakened with a start, her heart beating so wildly she felt as though she might faint.

"It was only a dream," she whispered to herself, leaning up on an elbow.

When she looked across the room and saw Ashton, she caught her breath. She had momentarily forgotten that he was sleeping in the same room.

And what a mind-shattering reminder! He was nude, a blanket draped over him not covering the part of him that in Sasha's dreams only a moment ago had catapulted her to overwhelming heights of ecstasy.

Her pulse raced as she stared at him a moment longer, then she tore herself from her reverie and realized what she must do. She could not sleep in the same room with him—not with him so close and so tempting. If she were ever to get over these feelings for him so that she could become a partner in the true sense of the word she must learn to separate her heart from her mind!

Moving from the bed, she began to creep across the room. She breathed shallowly, her eyes wide as she inched past Ashton and Lightning curled up at his side. The door was close, and she hurried her pace—but a scream froze in her throat when she felt a hand on one of her ankles.

"Where do you think you're going?" Ashton growled, keeping a firm hold on her.

She refused to look his way, knowing the dangers. "Outside," she said, her voice tremoring. "Ashton, I—just couldn't sleep. Perhaps if I got a breath of fresh air—"

"And it takes an armload of blankets to get a breath of air?" Ashton said, letting go of her ankle. He wrapped a blanket around his waist and rose from the floor. He went to Sasha and placed a hand on her shoulder, urging her around to face him. "You're going outside to sleep, aren't you? Why, Sasha? What about this cabin disturbs you so much that you can't bear to sleep in it?"

Sasha breathed a sigh of relief when she realized

that he had been polite enough to cover the lower part of his anatomy. Perhaps now she could keep her sanity while talking to him.

"Ashton, you know that the sleeping arrangement is the problem," she said softly. She nodded at him. "You—you could have at least kept your clothes on." She felt the heat of a blush rise to her cheeks again. "Why, it is shameful the way you have chosen to sleep. Especially in the same room as I."

Ashton laughed awkwardly, looking down at himself, then slowly up at her. "It never occurred to me to sleep any other way," he said good-naturedly. "Sweet darlin', we're here at our sheep station to stay. Don't you think you're going to have to find a way to overlook a few things—like sleeping arrangements and what one chooses to sleep in?"

Sasha thrust her chin up stubbornly. "You can argue the point all you want," she said. "But never shall I be comfortable with these arrangements."

"Should I hang blankets across the room?" Ashton said, his anger beginning to rise. "Shall I divide the room so that one half is yours and the other is mine?"

Sasha's eyes widened innocently. "Why, that is a wonderful idea, Ashton," Sasha said. Then her lips curved into a pout. "But there is still only one bed."

"Isn't that so!" Ashton said sarcastically, stepping away from her. He went to the bed and scooted it angrily across the room so that it was hugging the far wall. He turned and glared at Sasha. "Now does that solve the problem? That side of the cabin can be yours. I don't need a damn bed." He frowned down at her. "Or are blankets still required to give you the privacy you desire?"

Feeling frustration and even a trace of shame for causing Ashton such a fretful time on his first night at the sheep station, Sasha sighed and shook her head dispiritedly. "None of this is right," she said, letting her blankets tumble from her arms. She sat down before the fire, cupping her chin in her hands as she leaned her elbows into her legs. "I'm ruining it for us, Ashton. Absolutely ruining it."

Taken aback by Sasha's sudden change of heart, Ashton stared at her for a moment, then went and sat down beside her. "I think we both are a bit to blame, sweet darlin'," he murmured. "I'm sure it's because we are feeling the strain of the trip."

She smiled wanly. "And perhaps because we are uneasy about the future?" she murmured. "Though I am eager for the challenge, so much depends on us, Ashton, to make sure that our dream does not fall into disaster."

"Do not fret so, Sasha," Ashton said, leaning to place another log on the fire. "As you have discovered, everything has been well planned out. The only thing that we need fear now is mother nature and wild dingoes." He leaned closer to her, daring to slip an arm around her waist. "Now I can't do much about mother nature, but as for the dingoes, we'll do all we can to keep them at bay. The kelpie is well trained."

"But the kelpie is only one dog," Sasha murmured. "From the sound of the howling in the distance, I would say there are many dingoes."

"Remember the fence, sweet darlin'," Ashton said. He drew her closer and tipped her chin up with a forefinger. "And remember that worrying can make you old too soon." He lowered a kiss to

147

the tip of her nose. "Let me do the worrying, Sasha. I'd better be plagued by worry wrinkles than you." His hand cupped her chin, and her eyelashes fluttered nervously as she met his steady gaze. "I don't want anything ever to mar that lovely face of yours. Damn, Sasha, do you know how breathtakingly beautiful you are?"

Sasha smiled softly up at him. "I may not be all that beautiful," she whispered. "But, Ashton, I do feel it deep inside my soul whenever you look at me like that." Her heart seemed to be melting when he flicked his tongue across her lips teasingly. She inhaled a nervous breath of air and closed her eyes. "Please, Ashton, don't" she softly begged, realizing where this was going to lead if she did not nip it in the bud now. She could feel her reserves weakening.

"Why, Sasha?" Ashton whispered huskily, his lips now at the hollow of her throat. "Why must you always fight the passion? Just relax. Let your feelings take hold. Let me . . . love you."

"I did not follow you to the outback for . . . this," she protested, trembling when Ashton cupped a hand around one of her breasts, the heat of his flesh penetrating the thin cotton material of her dress.

"I did not bring you to the outback with the intention of rendering you helpless to my commands, either," Ashton whispered. "I had hoped that you would quit fighting your emotions and would come to me willingly—would want me as badly as I want you." He began easing her to the floor. "And you do, Sasha, but are too stubborn to admit it."

Ashton held her within his arms only inches from the floor, his fingers at the buttons at the back of her dress, deftly unbuttoning it. Sasha knew that this was the moment to set herself free. But his lips trailing heated kisses along the column of her neck made her no longer care that she had only moments ago protested his nearness. Now she hungered for it more than ever she had hungered for anything in her life. She knew that any protests she might utter now would betray her, for she wanted nothing more than to make love with Ashton at this moment. She was awash with so many pleasurable feelings—how could she deny herself any of them?

Giddy with rapture, Sasha let Ashton disrobe her, his lips never ceasing to madden her with longing. She trembled with ecstasy when he moved over her and pressed his body against hers, the feel of his muscled strength stealing her breath away.

And then he entered her gently and began his slow thrusts. She locked her legs around his waist and, as though they had done this many times before, she began to move her body with his. His hands set her afire as they moved tantalizingly over her flesh.

She had known the magic of his lovemaking only once and had thought nothing could ever compare with it. But this time, with him sculpting himself to her moist body, pressing endlessly into her and thrusting his tongue into her mouth, flicking it in and out, she was lost in an incredible sweetness quite new to her. Her whole body quivered with the ecstasy.

"It could always be this way, Sasha," Ashton whispered against her lips. "If you would just allow it."

His words momentarily interrupted the flow of

wondrous feelings, but Sasha would not allow them to take away from this moment of sweet togetherness. "Please don't talk," she whispered. "Just love me, Ashton. Just . . . love . . . me."

"Oh, how much I do love you," Ashton whispered. "Never could a man love you as much as I."

He nestled her close and loved her in a long and leisurely fashion, wanting to savor every moment with her, for he knew her well and expected her to regret having let down her guard with him in this way once he released her from his arms. He could only hope that each time they made love, it would bring her closer to accepting a future of loving from him. He would banish everything in his life but her if that was what it took to have her totally.

"Oh, Ashton!" Sasha cried, gripping his shoulders when a great surge of ecstasy suddenly swam through her. "Oh, Ashton, this is so—so wonderful!"

Her body shook and quaked against his. Perspiration beaded up on Ashton's brow as he thrust himself more determinedly into her, the pleasure rising, then exploding as he reached the same summit of passion as she.

They clung for a moment. Then Sasha's eyes flickered open, and it was as though a bolt of lightning struck her when she realized exactly where her needs had led her again. She could not believe that she had no more control of herself than this! She had participated in the lovemaking as wantonly as a whore—had perhaps enjoyed it even more!

She groped for a blanket and drew it around herself, then scrambled to her feet and turned her back to Ashton, her breathing shallow.

Ashton looked up at her, disappointed yet again. Even though he had expected her to behave like this again, it did not make it any easier for him to accept. It made him feel less than a man not to be able to draw her into a comfortable relationship with him, to get her to treat him as though he was worthy of the loving she had just given him!

"You took advantage of me," Sasha suddenly blurted out, turning to look down at him with accusing eyes. "You knew just how to make me forget my true purpose for being here. You are very skilled, Ashton York, in making a woman forget everything except—except for pleasures of the flesh."

A heated anger raged through Ashton. He rose quickly to his feet, not taking the time to care that he was still nude in front of a lady who seemed to care less about that part of his anatomy than most women he had known.

"I try to understand you," he said, his fists clenched at his sides. "But by God, Sasha, I am beginning to doubt that I ever shall. If Woodrow Rutherford is the cause for your erratic behavior, I damn the day you met him!"

He flung an angry hand in the air. "I should've left you wandering on the streets of Melbourne longing for the damn aristocrat," he shouted. "At least my life wouldn't be guided by the misfortune the man wreaked on your life!"

Sasha gasped and covered her mouth with a hand. Tears pooled in her eyes as she watched Ashton angrily grab his clothes and blankets, then leave the house in a fury. She sobbed when Lightning followed him dutifully from the house, leaving her all alone—and desperately empty!

She flung herself on the bed, sobs wracking her body. She did not like hurting Ashton, yet it seemed that she was becoming quite skilled at it. If she persisted, she might lose him totally. But she was afraid to let him have control of her feelings and body. He was a man—and so far, she had found them all untrustworthy! Although she felt she had almost succeeded at making him believe that she did not care for him enough to make a total commitment to him, she had to find a way to prove it, once and for all—to prove that she was here for business purposes alone!

At least until she was convinced beyond a shadow of a doubt that he could be trusted!

Ah, but then, how wonderful things could be! He did know how to send her into a world of wonder!

A shiver coursed through her. "I am taking a chance of never sharing such wondrous feelings again with him," she whispered to herself. "But it is a gamble I must take . . ."

Stanford Sidwell stood bathed in moonlight across the river from Ashton and Sasha's sheep station. A smug smile lifted his lips. A cigar hung loosely from one corner of his mouth. "This'll do just fine," he said, surveying his staked-off property. "Just fine."

Bianca walked beside him as he grabbed his camping paraphernalia from the back of his horse, then Bianca's. He turned and faced his men who stood silently by, awaiting orders. "Some of you get busy building my house first thing in the morning," he commanded. "The others go back into Melbourne and pick me out some prime sheep and cattle. To fool Ashton York, I've got to make this look legitimate."

Never questioning Stanford's reasons for hating Ashton, only concerned over the pay they were receiving for obeying Stanford's orders, the men nodded and separated. Some rode away on horses; some took bedrolls and settled down close to the river.

Stanford turned to Bianca and his eyes glistened as he smiled at her. "We're home," he said, moving to stand over her so that their breaths mingled. "And I guess you know what I'm expectin' from you tonight, don't you? A homecoming present from my pretty half-breed."

Ripples of fear crept along Bianca's flesh. She knew the art of Stanford's lovemaking, and it was in no way gentle. Though she had shared a bed with many a man in her lifetime, never had any enjoyed inflicting pain while making love the way Stanford Sidwell did. And she feared not for herself alone now. She had her unborn child's welfare to consider!

Curled up with Lightning close to the house, Ashton was suddenly awakened by a sharp, piercing scream in the distance. He grabbed one of his revolvers and bolted to his feet, peering into the darkness, waiting to hear the scream again. Soon he began to think that he had not heard it at all, for never had he heard a night as quiet and peaceful as this one was now. Even the dingoes had ceased their howling.

Yawning, Ashton settled back down into his blankets and scooted Lightning into his arms again. "Damn Sasha," he whispered to his pup. "She's causing me to hear things in my sleep. Damn her."

He closed his eyes but could not go to sleep again. Something troubled him about the scream. It had been too real to be imagined. Perhaps it was an animal being slain by another.

"Aye," he whispered to himself. "That must have been where the scream came from. An animal taking advantage of another of its own kind."

Chapter Twelve

Sasha swirled a thickly bristled brush gingerly around in the soap suds spread across the wide planks of the flooring, fearful of getting splinters in her knees through the thin cotton material of her dress. Her hair pulled back from her face and tied with a bow, sweat pearling on her brow, she ignored Ashton as he came into the cabin.

But when he began to cross the freshly-scrubbed floor, she dropped the brush angrily into the bucket of water and rose to face him with her hands on her hips.

"Ashton York, all day long you have been getting in my way," she said, her eyes flashing. "If I am outdoors airing the bedding, you are there falling over it. If I am in the garden, you are there scaring the living daylights out of me when your shadow suddenly falls over the vegetables. Must I go on? You know how bothersome this entire day has been." She nodded toward her wet floor. "And now you dirty up the floor faster than I can clean it. Ashton, don't you have better things to do?"

Still disgruntled over the previous night, when Sasha had again stung his heart, Ashton walked on across the wet floor. He grabbed a tin cup from a peg on the wall, bent to one knee before the fireplace, and took the coffeepot from the hot coals of the fire. Ignoring Sasha's angry breathing behind him, he poured himself a cup of coffee.

Replacing the coffeepot in the hot coals, he rose to his full height and started to walk past Sasha to leave, but suddenly his feet slipped on the slick floor and as coffee splattered everywhere, he fell with a splat on his rear. As he landed, one of his hands hit the bucket of water, knocking it over. Sudsy, dirty water began spilling in dark streamers across the already cleansed floor, drawing an appalled gasp from Sasha.

"How can you be so clumsy?" she stormed, reaching quickly to try to right the bucket. But her eyes widened when she felt her feet slipping beneath her. Before she could steady herself she found herself falling awkwardly on Ashton, landing face to face with him.

"You were saying?" Ashton said, a slow smile quivering on his lips. He was inclined to help her up, but then thought better of it, enjoying her embarrassment. He could not deny, either, how much he relished the feel of her breasts crushing into his chest. For a moment he was catapulted back to the previous night when she had shared so much with him so willingly.

Feeling ridiculously awkward, Sasha glared at
Ashton. Then her nose began to twitch when a smell
so vile she could hardly stand it began stinging her
nostrils.

"Whatever am I smelling, Ashton?" she said,
screwing her face up into a frown as she leaned
away from him. "Why, you smell like a pig!"

She rose from him, holding her nose as she stared
incredulously down at him.

He got up from the floor and deliberately stepped
closer to her so that she could get a better whiff of
him. "Why, sweet darlin', I thought you would like
my new cologne," he teased, a smile tugging at his
lips. "It's the only sort a man can find here in the
outback."

Sasha took an unsteady step back from him, still
holding her nose. "Stay away from me," she said.
"You didn't come in here to get a cup of coffee. You
came in here to torment me with that—that horrid
stench. It would serve you right if I never got the
smell out of our cabin."

"It doesn't matter to me how this place smells or
looks," Ashton grumbled. "You aren't going to let
me spend enough time in it to care. If you recall, I
spent the night outside beneath the stars."

"Only because you chose to," Sasha said, lifting
her chin defensively.

"Only because you gave me no other choice,"
Ashton said, taking another step toward her.

The stench wafted more strongly toward Sasha.
She choked on a cough as she placed her back to
Ashton. Then she cringed when she felt his arms
snaking around her waist, drawing her backside
against the front of him. "Oh, no," she groaned.

"Why did you have to do that, Ashton? Now I shall smell as bad as you do!" She tried to jerk away from him but he held her firmly in place.

"Best you get used to my new fragrance," Ashton said gruffly. "Little darlin', mixing with the sheep and caring for them like I have to is a very dirty job."

His lips crinkled into a tormenting smile. "But I reckon I can count on you to keep my clothes clean for me."

"I wouldn't count on that if I were you," Sasha said. "I am not your maid, you know."

"No, you aren't my maid," Ashton grumbled. "But there are certain things a woman does better than a man."

"Washing clothes is one of them, I presume," Sasha said haughtily. "Perhaps I could prove you wrong. Why don't we exchange our duties for just one day and see who does what best?"

Ashton smiled smugly down at her. "I would be willing to give it a try," he said, chuckling. "That is, if you prefer to be the one who smells, not the one who is doing the smelling."

Sasha's reserve weakened beneath his steady gaze. She swallowed hard, then gulped when with that swallow came the sting of the awful odor of his clothes. She jerked herself free and scrambled to the door to suck in several breaths of fresh air.

"So?" Ashton teased her as he came to stand beside her. "Do you want to change places today? I think I could mop the floor adequately enough. Do you think you can rope a few stray cattle?"

"You ought to have to mop the floor while I watch, laughing," Sasha said, sweeping a loose strand of hair back from her eyes as she glanced up at Ashton. "You are the one who spoiled what I had already done."

"And you would deny a hard-working man a cup of coffee?" Ashton said, himself brushing back the strand of hair that persisted in dangling across her brow.

"There is a time and place for everything," Sasha argued, slapping his hand aside. "Won't you please, the next time you saunter into our cabin for anything, look and see if the floor is wet or dry? It might save both of us a lot of extra work."

Ashton shrugged. "I guess I see no harm in that."

Sasha's eyes traveled over him, seeing the thin layer of dust on his clothes and again pinching her nose closed. "I doubt if ever those clothes will smell decent again."

"Or me?" he said, leaning down into her face, smiling.

"I doubt that even the river water and a dozen bars of soap will make you pleasant-smelling again," Sasha said, then giggled. "As I recall, you spoke favorably of leaving the stench of ale in the pub to come to these great outdoors to work in the clean, fresh air. You glorified too much the way it would truly be, didn't you?"

Ashton raked his fingers through his hair as he laughed softly. "Perhaps," he said. "Perhaps."

Then his eyes were drawn away from Sasha, to the window and an approaching horseman. He placed a hand on one of his holstered revolvers, stiffening when he suddenly recognized the rider. "How in the hell can it be him?" he said, more to himself, than to Sasha. "Stanford Sidwell . . ."

Sasha tried to make out who the lone horseman

was, as Crispin quickly caught up with him on his proud mare. "Who is it, Ashton?" she said, shadowing her eyes with a hand as she stepped out onto the porch beside him.

She sucked in a wild gulp of air when she recognized the man that Crispin had stopped before he reached the house. "Why, Ashton, that is the con man who caused you trouble at your pub," she exclaimed, but Ashton did not hear her. He had left the porch and was walking in wide strides toward the con artist. It seemed that Ashton had some past relationship with this man—and that his past had followed him to the outback.

Sasha circled her hands around the rail of the porch and watched as Ashton stepped up beside the man, who had not dismounted and whose fancy clothes seemed misplaced in the outback.

She could not hear what was being said between them, but she could tell by the looks on their faces that it was not a congenial conversation by any means!

"Ashton, should I send the son of a bitch on his way by gunpoint?" Crispin asked, his hand resting threateningly on his holstered revolver.

"Let's hear what he has to say first," Ashton said, meeting Stanford's steady stare with his own. "Sidwell, what're you doing out here? How'd you know where to find me?"

Stanford reached for a cigar in his front pocket and thrust it between his lips. With this same hand he took a match from his pocket and scraped a very carefully manicured thumbnail across the head of the match, igniting it. As though there was meaning in it, he slowly lit his cigar and blew the smoke into the wind, then flicked the match away as he leaned his face down closer to Ashton's.

"You knew back at your pub that the beard did not work, and that your eyes were all that were needed to give you away," he gloated. "But don't fret. My being here has nothing to do with you. I've come to call on Sasha—to court her. She's some find, wouldn't you say?"

A slow burning was beginning in Ashton. His jaw tightened, and his hand clasped hard onto the handle of his revolver. "Now let's get this straight," he said between clenched teeth. "You've come all the way out here—just happened to find our sheep station without any trouble—to court Sasha?" He laughed throatily. "Now do you think I'm stupid enough to believe that? I guess you forget that I know all about your con games. You should know better than to try one on me."

"You are not the only one to squat on land in the outback," Stanford said, flicking ashes from his cigar close to Ashton. He motioned with his head toward the river. "I've got my own spread across the river. There are no sheep yet, but my men should be arriving soon with around a hundred head." He smiled wickedly down at Ashton, his white teeth flashing in the sun. "Seems you've got competition for more than a woman, Lawrence. Or I guess I'd better call you Ashton, or your pretty lady might get wind of your past name and deeds."

Ashton doubled a fist. "I don't know what your game is," he said. "But whatever you've got up your sleeve, it's best not to include Sasha. She's mine and

I won't allow her to get near the likes of you."

"Does she wear your wedding band?" Stanford taunted, his eyes gleaming.

Ashton glared at Stanford icily. "Whether or not she wears my wedding band, you stay away from her," he said. "If you don't heed my warning, I'll—"

Stanford reached a hand beneath his coat and rested it on his sheathed knife. "I wouldn't make threats," he said, glowering at Ashton. "I wouldn't want to reshape your face again with my knife."

Ashton's hand went automatically to his scar, recalling the instant it was inflicted. It had been easy enough for the con artist to sneak a knife into the cell they had shared.

"Ashton? Is everything all right?" Sasha said suddenly behind him.

Paling, Ashton swung around to face her, wondering if she had heard Stanford's remarks about his face. Relief flooded him when he could tell that she hadn't. There was only a look of absolute puzzlement as she gazed up at Stanford. She had wondered about him in the pub. Now her questions would be redoubled!

"I have everything under control," he said, frowning down at her. "Sasha, go on back to the house."

She gave him a stubborn look and stood her ground. Smoothing her hands down the front of her dress, she took a bold step toward Stanford's horse. "Sir, it is quite a surprise to find you in these parts," she said. "How is it that you are here? Or do your con games take you to all corners of the outback as well as the city of Melbourne?"

Stanford chuckled beneath his breath. He took a long, lazy drag from his cigar, then took it from his mouth again. "I see Ashton has told you a little about my past activities," he said, his dark eyes gleaming down into hers.

"Yes, a little," Sasha said, squaring her shoulders.

"That is unfortunate," Stanford said, giving Ashton a slow, smug smile. "I would much rather speak for myself."

"You have not said why you are at our sheep station," Sasha persisted, ignoring Ashton's hand that had deftly circled her wrist, trying to pull her back to his side.

Stanford's eyebrows rose. "You speak as though you and Ashton jointly own the sheep station," he said, looking from Sasha to Ashton. Then he focused his eyes purposely on the ring finger of her left hand. "How can that be? You are not married. I see no wedding band."

"One does not have to be married to be in joint partnership," Sasha told him. She gave Ashton a half glance, then looked up at Stanford again. "And, no, sir, we are not man and wife. Only business partners."

"Then that means that you are free to let a man come to call?" Stanford asked, smiling down at Sasha.

Sasha's mouth fell open. She would never have expected such a question from a man of such a questionable background and personality. "Why, sir, I—" Sasha began, but Ashton quickly interceded.

"Get the hell off our property," Ashton warned darkly. "Sasha wants nothing to do with the likes of you."

"Oh?" Stanford said, arching a dark eyebrow. "Do

you always speak for her? Isn't she free to make her own decisions? Do you own her after all?"

Those words burned into Sasha's consciousness. She had wanted to devise a plan to prove to Ashton that their having made love meant nothing—and that he did not lay claim on her because of it! This man, this stranger, was the perfect answer. The fact, even, that he and Ashton were bitter enemies made everything just perfect for the scheme that had just this moment hatched inside her brain! If she accepted this man's invitation to let him come calling, it would prove to Ashton once and for all that she did not want an intimate relationship with him.

Stanford slipped from his saddle and went to Sasha. He took her hand and lifted it to his lips, gallantly kissing it. He then gazed determinedly into her eyes. "Stanford Sidwell at your service, ma'am. It would be my pleasure if you would accept an invitation to go on a buggy ride with me tomorrow," he said smoothly. "I have just settled on land across the river from you. Since we are both new to these parts, we could become acquainted with the terrain at the same time."

Ashton's face was red with anger. His violet eyes were dark, his jaw tight. "Stanford, I'm warning you—" he hissed between clenched teeth.

"Ashton!" Sasha said, giving him a scolding glance. "You are being impolite to my caller. I would think that you would treat him with the respect that befits a man whom I have chosen to become better acquainted with."

Ashton's breath was taken away, as though someone had slammed a doubled fist into his chest. He looked disbelievingly at Sasha, not understanding her motive behind this sudden decision to be with a man that he so openly detested!

"Then you are saying that you will accept my invitation?" Stanford asked, surprised himself, that she would agree. He had hoped to use her as a ploy to get what he wanted from Ashton, but he had never guessed that it would be this simple.

He looked at Ashton, seeing the rage and confusion in his eyes, then smiled triumphantly down at Sasha, once again lifting her hand to his lips, kissing it. "Until tomorrow, beautiful lady," he murmured. "I shall arrive promptly after breakfast, if that time fits your schedule."

"That would be delightful," Sasha said in a purr, smiling devilishly at Ashton. She slipped her hand from Stanford's, placing it behind her so that he could not capture it again to cover it with his cold, wet lips. He disgusted her. She even feared him, yet knew that he was the only way to make Ashton think that she did not care for him in the way he wished— even though all the while she loved him so much that she could hardly bear it!

"Until tomorrow," Stanford said, swinging away from Sasha and quickly mounting. He gave her and Ashton a mock salute, then wheeled his horse around and rode away.

Crispin dismounted and went to study Sasha with troubled eyes. "Did I hear right?" he said. "You agreed to go on an outing with that—that man?"

"I see no crime in it," Sasha said, then turned on a heel and walked briskly back to the house. Her heart was pounding, feeling Ashton's eyes on her. She now knew that her performance may have been too grand—too convincing.

Chapter Thirteen

Carrying a clean change of clothes, a towel, and a fragrant piece of soap, Sasha moved toward the river. Ashton's stench had most certainly rubbed off on her, and she did not believe a mere bath in her tub could make her smell decently clean again. She would take a swim, and then a bath, in the river. That would give her not only the opportunity to get clean, but the time to think about her decision to go on an outing with the confidence man whom Ashton so obviously detested. Would he, in the end, despise her as much? Deep within her, that was not at all what she wanted. Oh, Lord, she wanted him! Him!

Bending low beneath a eucalyptus branch, Sasha was separating some tall weeds with her hands when her footsteps faltered and she was surprised to discover that someone else was bathing in the river.

"A woman?" she whispered, staring down at the dark-skinned figure. Only her face was exposed above the water, her magnificently long hair drifting in the water behind her. When the woman looked up at her, her dark eyes revealed the shock of seeing Sasha suddenly there, and Sasha immediately recognized her. And it was obvious that the woman had recognized her as well.

"Bianca?" Sasha said, walking on to the riverbank.

"Sasha?" Bianca said, staring disbelievingly up at her. "I know you from York's Pub. Why are you here?"

Sasha blushed, not wanting to reveal to Bianca how she knew her—the prostitute everyone had talked about in Melbourne, the half-breed prostitute who knew well the art of pleasing a man!

"I have recently moved to the outback," Sasha said. She motioned with a hand toward the sheep station. "I live just through those trees." She paused, absently dropping her hand to her side. "And you, Bianca? What are you doing in these parts?"

Bianca smoothed her hands through her hair, drawing it back from her face. She looked nervously up at Sasha, recalling Stanford's threat and instructions. "I, too, live close by," she said, her voice drawn. She motioned with a hand toward the other side of the river. "Through those trees. I come with my husband to a sheep station. He is the sheepherder."

Sasha's lips parted with surprise for more than

one reason. It seemed as incredible that Bianca would be married as that she was living on a sheep station so close to—

Then a thought came to her. The only other sheep station she knew of was Stanford Sidwell's. Bianca must be living there.

Yet, still—with a husband?

No. It did not ring true. Bianca's reputation was surely too questionable for any man ever to marry her.

But at this moment it did not matter at all to Sasha why Bianca was there—or whom she was with. She was another woman in this outback of men! Bianca would be someone to share woman-talk with. Even if Bianca's conversations up to now mainly centered on men and how to please them, Bianca was a woman, and might become a friend! It was not Sasha's place to condemn this beautiful, dark-skinned lady for her past deeds!

"I have come to bathe in the river," Sasha explained, showing Bianca her towel and soap. "Would you mind if I share the water with you?"

Bianca laughed softly, her eyes alight with a strange sort of relief. "Do come in," she said, pulling up a strap of her undergarment that had slipped from her shoulder. "It is very warm and inviting."

"Thank you," Sasha said, curling up her nose at the vile stench of her dress as she drew it over her head. "If you only knew how badly I need one. Ashton was mean to rub his filthy clothes against mine."

"Ashton?" Bianca said, her eyebrow forking. "You speak of Ashton York? You have come to the outback with him? He is your husband?"

Sasha's eyes wavered and she felt another blush troubling her cheeks. "Yes, I have come to the outback with Ashton," she murmured, slipping off one shoe, and then the other. "But we are not married. Ours is a—a business relationship only. That is all."

Bianca studied Sasha closely, not believing that any woman could live with Ashton York as no more than a business partner. Sasha was trying to hide her true feelings just as Bianca was forced to hide hers! Oh, but she wanted to open up and tell Sasha exactly why she was in the outback, that she had accompanied Stanford with the hope of bettering herself. In truth, it was becoming a living hell with the man who had no true feelings for her, but wanted only her body.

Now barefoot and wearing only her cotton shift edged with eyelet lace, Sasha dunked her dress in the river, then spread it out on a rock and scrubbed it with her bar of soap to get the stench out. She then rinsed it thoroughly, hung it on a branch, and slipped into the water herself, the soap clutched in her hand. She immediately relaxed and enjoyed the soothing caress of the water as she waded in, to stand at shoulder level in it.

"You say that you live at a nearby sheep station," she said, gliding the soap up and down an arm. She looked guardedly at Bianca, who was also running a bar of soap up and down an arm. "Is that Stanford Sidwell's sheep station that you are speaking of?" She winced when Bianca's eyes reflected a true fear in their depths at the question, and she had to wonder again why Bianca was there.

"It is Stanford Sidwell's sheep station where I live," Bianca said, her voice shallow. "You know of him?"

"Not very well," Sasha said, shrugging. She continued to watch Bianca. "How long have you known him? How long has your husband been in his employ?"

Bianca looked away from Sasha, feeling trapped. She started walking toward the riverbank, her hair trailing behind her in the water. "Not long," she said, giving Sasha a quick glance over her shoulder. "But long enough to know that I do not like the man!"

"Oh?" Sasha said, watching Bianca leave the water to dry herself off with a towel. Her gaze settled on Bianca's stomach, and an uneasy feeling breezed through her. This woman who was known for prostitution was pregnant! Was that why the sheepherder had married her? To give the child a name? But how would he have known it was his?

"Bianca should not have said that," she murmured, lifting her heavy hair and moving a towel over it. "Please never say that I said that about Stanford. He would not like it."

A keen wonder filled Sasha, seeing the genuine fear that even speaking Stanford Sidwell's name caused Bianca. Sasha was beginning to have second thoughts about going on an outing with such a man. Well, she would simply not allow him to travel all that far from The Homestead. But she must go with him to prove a point to Ashton!

Not wanting to chance losing this newly found friendship, Sasha followed Bianca to the riverbank, wondering why her clothes were on this side of the river, instead of on the side where she made residence. She must have found a way across other than swimming.

"Don't worry, Bianca," Sasha said, searching for a sunny spot among the trees to stand in, to ward off the chill that was quickly encompassing her drenched body. "I won't tell a soul what you said." She turned and faced Bianca, her mood somber. "And always feel free to confide in me. It is wonderful to have a woman nearby. I had thought I was the only woman for miles around."

Unashamedly, Bianca removed her wet shift and dropped it to the ground. As she dried her stomach, she looked down at it meditatively, then looked slowly over at Sasha. "I fear so for my unborn child," she confessed, then bit her lower lip in frustration when she realized what she had said.

Bianca grabbed a dry shift from the ground and quickly slipped into it. "Please forget that I said that," she said, her eyes anxious. "It is only because I am far from the city that I fear for my unborn child. You understand, don't you?"

"I believe I do," Sasha said softly, not finding Bianca's reasons for such a fear to be justified. Why had she come to the outback at all? Even married, she could have begged her husband to allow her to stay behind. Her pregnancy would have been reason enough.

"My body has only just begun to show that I am with child. I have told no one about my pregnancy," Bianca revealed. She looked quickly up at Sasha, paling. "But of course I have told my husband." She swallowed hard, pulling a dress over her head. "But it is good to have a woman to share this special time with." She reached behind her and began buttoning her dress. "We will meet like this often? It would mean so much to me."

"I would find that delightful," Sasha said, silently admiring Bianca's hair, which touched the ground. "I shall look forward to it, Bianca."

Bianca came suddenly to her and hugged her fiercely. "Thank you," Bianca whispered, then fled, leaving a strange sort of awkward silence behind her.

Sasha had the urge to follow, to see where she had crossed the river. But the wet shift clinging to her body was reminder enough of what she must do. She walked back into the river and finished bathing, then hurried into her now dry clothes.

Puzzling still over Bianca's presence in the outback, and her pregnancy, Sasha hurried toward The Homestead. Suddenly she stopped, struck dumb over what she found being built under Ashton's supervision. Even though they had a wide stretch of fence that separated their land from the wilds, where dingoes awaited the chance to feed on sheep, another huge fence was being erected closer to the house. And it was not just any fence—it looked like the sort that was used around forts!

Shaking herself out of her surprised state, Sasha hurried to Ashton's side. She looked incredulously around her again at the huge stockade fence more than half built around the perimeter of the house.

"Ashton, what is going on here?" Sasha finally demanded. "I came out here to the middle of nowhere to live on a sheep station—not inside a fortress! Why are you having this dreadful fence built so close to the house?"

"Sweet darlin', this fence is for protection," Ashton drawled. He frowned down at her. "There is more to fear out here than wild dingoes."

"You never spoke of erecting such a fence until—until Stanford Sidwell showed up here," she accused him. She placed a hand on her hip and exhaled a shaky, breath. "It is because of my decision to go on an outing with him, isn't it? You don't want me to go, so you are trying to frighten me into not going."

"I think you have it all figured out," Ashton said icily.

"Well, I am going to show you just how much that fence will stop my activities," she raged. "I will go wherever and with whomever I please, no matter how large a fence you erect, Ashton York!"

The skirt of her dress fluttering wildly around her ankles, Sasha marched off defiantly. Yet she could not shake the fear of Stanford Sidwell that was building within her. Ashton was not the sort to despise a man unless he had cause to. What was there between those two men? Would she ever find out?

She smiled slyly as a thought came to her. Perhaps she could worm some answers out of Stanford. . . .

Shadows were thickening and lengthening. In the distant growths of karri and jarrah, unseen birds repeated their wild lyrics, the chirps, trills, and twitters the sweetest Bianca had ever heard. She tried to concentrate on this, to ignore Stanford, who was placing a log on the fire in the fireplace. She had prayed that it would take his men longer to build the house, but with many muscles behind the labor, it had taken only one day. Now they had complete privacy, and the four walls of the make-shift shack separated her from those who might hear her screams for mercy should Stanford choose to torment her again tonight. She could not hope that someone would pity her and rescue her from the man whose heart was made of stone.

Stanford rose to his full height. He turned and smiled wickedly at Bianca, his hands at the buttons of his shirt. "My pretty half-breed, are you ready for a night of lovin'?" he said, snickering.

"There is no bed," Bianca said, trying to find any excuse to delay what was coming, yet knowing this was a lame one, if ever there was one. "Let us wait until one is brought to us. It will make lovemaking better, Stanford."

"Now, Bianca, you have to know that the men won't be arriving with the furniture for another couple of days," he argued. "It's more important to get the sheep and cattle moved on our sheep station. Furniture is only a minor detail."

His shirt off, he placed his thumbs at the waist of his breeches and began slipping them down his narrow hips. "But half-breed, if you object to not having a bed, perhaps we could delay making love to another night. You could entertain me in a different sort of way tonight." Nude, he went and stood over her where she sat before the fire on a blanket. "Take off your clothes, Bianca," he said thickly, reaching for one of her wrists and yanking her to her feet.

"But you just said that we could make love another time," Bianca said, her voice quivering. "Why must I undress?"

"Because you are going to perform that spider

belly dance for me that you do so well," Stanford said, placing a hand at the bodice of her dress and yanking at it. The sound of cloth ripping mingled with Bianca's low gasp. "I want to see you go through your gyrations," he chuckled. "I might even toss a few gold nuggets at your feet to show my appreciation."

She grew limply cold with fear inside, knowing that if she was forced to dance before him in such a way, there would be no way of her keeping the pregnancy from him any longer. And once he knew, what then?

"There," Stanford said matter-of-factly. He stepped back away from her, his fists on his hips. "I got you started. Now finish undressing."

Pale, her heart pounding, Bianca knew that she had no choice but to comply with his wishes. Slowly she began disrobing, her fingers trembling. When she was nude, his eyes locked on her abdomen and she knew that there would be no dancing tonight. His eyes had already discovered the secret.

"What the hell?" Stanford said, stammering. He went to Bianca and ran his hands over the swell of her stomach, then looked darkly into her eyes. "You didn't tell me that you were with child! Why didn't you?"

Bianca began inching away from him. "I don't know," she whispered, her heartbeats almost swallowing her whole. "I now know that I should have. Please, Stanford, don't hurt me or the child. I—I already love my baby! It is all that I have ever had that I could call my own!"

"Whose child is it?" Stanford shouted, inching toward her, his hands circled into fists at his sides.

"I . . . don't know," Bianca softly cried.

"Of course you wouldn't," Stanford hissed. Then he smiled slowly, his eyes gleaming. "Well, half-breed whore, I'm going to teach you not to lie to me. I don't want no bastard child running around my sheep station!"

Bianca's back was to the wall now. She placed her hands to her cheeks, her eyes wild. "What are you going to do?" she asked desperately.

"Teach you obedience," Stanford said, reaching to yank his belt from his breeches.

Bianca tried to run away from him, but she wasn't quick enough. The first blow from the belt landed right across her abdomen.

Chapter Fourteen

The night had been long. Eating breakfast with Ashton had been uncomfortably strained and quiet. When he left the house without uttering that first word to her, Sasha felt as though he had thrown cold water on her. No rejection by anyone could have been as bone-cutting as Ashton's since she had accepted Stanford Sidwell's invitation.

Was this only the beginning?

Would Ashton now treat her forever as though she did not exist?

Or was this a ploy to make her fret herself into the grave over her decision to go with Stanford?

Determinedly, Sasha tied on a frilly bonnet and slipped a shawl around her shoulders. Though uneasy, she was not going to let Ashton's cool behavior stop what she had already started.

Anyhow, wasn't this her objective? To prove to him that she did not care for him in the way that she had so carelessly led him to believe?

Until she could learn to trust again, this was the only way it could be.

Perhaps she could at least pull some answers out of Stanford about his relationship with Ashton. She might learn at least about Ashton's past. Until she had seen the scar on his face, until he had behaved so strangely around Stanford Sidwell, she had not even wondered about his past. Now she wanted to learn everything about him—enough to prove to her whether or not he could be trusted!

She wanted so badly to cast aside all her doubts and give herself to him wholly—to be his wife, to shed all doubts and wonder, would make her the happiest woman in the world.

A sound outside in the distance, like rolling thunder, drew Sasha's eyes to the open door. Her heartbeat quickened when she realized this was the sound of many horses and they were approaching The Homestead.

"Stanford?" she whispered to herself, placing a hand to her mouth. It was time for him to arrive, but why would he not be arriving alone? Surely he would come for her in a buggy.

Gathering the hem of her skirt up into her arms, her shawl draped loosely around her shoulders, Sasha hurried onto the porch. There she saw that the fortress fence that was only half finished did not stop at least twenty horsemen from riding on through the opened gate, stopping only a few yards from the house.

Sasha's breath was taken away when she looked up into the steel-gray eyes of a man who was surely some kind of criminal. He wore a filthy, roughly-sewn garment and moccasins of kangaroo hide. His dark hair was long and tangled, his beard was thick, and a pistol was stuck in his rope belt. He was close enough for Sasha to realize that he smelled like a polecat.

"Where's the man of the house?" the man asked, his yellow, jagged teeth showing beneath his thick mustache.

The sight of the man and his filthy, leering companions made Sasha quickly forget about her planned outing with Stanford. Looking slowly around the men, her skin crawled with fear, wondering where Ashton was—or at least Crispin. Or Rufus. Or anyone!

"What do you want here?" Sasha managed to ask, gulping hard.

"I don't waste my time talkin' business with women," the man growled. "Now I don't have all day. Where's your mister?"

"I think you're speaking of me?" Ashton said, stepping suddenly from behind the house and moving into the shadows beside Sasha. He snaked an arm protectively around her waist.

"Well, now, ain't this a surprise?" the man said, laughing throatily. "If it ain't Lawrence Proffitt. It's a small world, ain't it?"

Sasha looked quickly up at Ashton. "Lawrence . . .?" she murmured.

"Seems this man has made a mistake," Ashton said, avoiding Sasha's questioning stare. "But I don't make mistakes all that easily. I've heard of you and your kangarooers. The name is Ajax, isn't it?"

Ajax shrugged and smiled crookedly down at Ashton. "I don't know what your game is," he said. "If you ain't called by Proffitt these days, how should the likes of me address you?"

"The name doesn't matter," Ashton said, his voice drawn. Lightning bounded suddenly to his side and growled as she looked up at Ajax. "What matters, Ajax, is that you and your convict kangaroo hunters get off my land. Your smell might frighten my dingo pup."

Ajax leaned his weight against the saddle horn and smiled wickedly down at Lightning. "Your pet, huh?" he said. "Afraid it might get frightened, huh?" His gaze moved slowly to Ashton. "I'd think hard on what might happen to that pup if you don't cooperate with me."

"I've heard that you're good at making threats," Ashton said, taking a step closer to Ajax's horse. "Well, Ajax, you're threatening the wrong person this time." Ashton placed a hand on one of his holstered revolvers. "Now get out of here. Don't come back."

"Ashton, be careful," Sasha whispered, stepping quickly to his side. "He looks so mean."

Ajax had heard her. "Ashton, is it?" he said, chuckling. His smile faded. "Aye, most say I do look mean." He focused his eyes on Sasha. "And most know that I am." He looked slowly back at Ashton again. "You know that I'd kill a man as soon as a kangaroo." He laughed again, his eyes gleaming. "Why, only yesterday I strung up a corpse of a man by the heels on a gum tree as if I was hangin' a boomer for skinning."

A shudder coursed through Sasha, and she edged closer to Ashton, glad to be standing in his shadow.

"If you don't get the hell out of here, Ajax, you and every one of your men will be the ones hanging from the heels in gum trees," Crispin said, stepping suddenly into view with twelve armed men, Crispin's revolver cocked and aimed at Ajax's chest.

Ashton flipped his revolver from its holster and smiled smugly up at Ajax. "I'm tempted to give the order to shoot every last one of you now, on the spot," he threatened. "That'd keep you from going to the next innocent grazier, forcing him to cooperate with you, forcing him to buy the skin and meats of the kangaroo directly from you and your stinking men. But since I'm not the law, I'm forced to let you ride away."

Lightning picked up on Ashton's anger. She began leaping at Ajax's horse, causing the horse to whinny and paw at the ground nervously.

"You'd best get that damn dog away from my horse or I'll see to it that no matter what you do to me, the dog'll go first," Ajax warned, his eyes dark with hate.

"You're not happy picking on the poor graziers and families on the sheep stations, now you pick on a defenseless pup?" Ashton said contemptuously.

Sasha bent and reached for Lightning and held her protectively in her arms.

"We'll leave," Ajax snarled, meeting Ashton's stare with one matching in venom. "But stay out of my way, Proffitt. Don't cause me no trouble, do you hear? I've got a good business goin' out here. I just never planned on comin' face to face with you."

Sasha gaped openly at Ashton. She could tell that his acquaintance with this filthy kangarooer was of long standing. As with Stanford Sidwell, they seemed to have a history of knowing one another—and not on friendly terms.

Each day it seemed that she was discovering more and more mysteries about the man she loved.

Ajax wheeled his horse around and rode away, his men following him. Ashton flipped his revolver back in its holster and ran to his horse. "Come on, Crispin!" he shouted, swinging himself into his saddle. "Let's make sure they don't circle around and come back!"

Numbly, Sasha watched Ashton and Crispin ride away, then watched the rest of the men return to their duties. "Lightning, I doubt if I'll ever get bored out here in the outback," she said, smoothing her hand along the pup's soft fur. "Every day there seems to be someone different appearing out of nowhere."

The sound of a horse and buggy approaching made Sasha grow cold inside, knowing without looking who it was. Stanford Sidwell. Setting Lightning to the ground, she turned and awaited his arrival. Her pulse raced, knowing that this was the time to change her mind. With Ashton not there to witness her leaving with Stanford, how would he even know whether or not she had? Wouldn't it be easy to say that she had? It would be only a small lie.

The horse and buggy wheeled to a halt beside Sasha. She smiled weakly up at Stanford, yet she could not help but admire the fancy way he was dressed. Today he even wore white kid gloves.

But the clothes did not always reveal the true personality of the man. She would never forget how immaculately Woodrow had always been dressed, and she had learned that he was not at all the gentleman that he had appeared to be. He had proven himself to be not at all trustworthy!

"Good-day, Sasha," Stanford said, stepping down from the buggy. He lifted her hand to his lips and kissed it. "I am glad you chose to go on this outing with me. It will be delightful to have a lovely lady such as yourself sitting by my side while I take in some of the wonders of this outback."

His lips were cold and wet on her hand, and Sasha wished that she had worn gloves to protect herself from his kisses. She drew her hand away and held it behind her. "I can be gone for only a little while," she murmured, now having fully committed herself to this project that she dreaded with every fiber of her being. "I shouldn't even be going with you today. I have many chores to do." She winced when he took her by the elbow and helped her into the buggy.

"If it were up to me, you would never soil your lovely hands with menial chores," Stanford said, climbing aboard the buggy beside her. He lifted the reins and slapped them against the horse's back, urging it around, then into a gentle lope as it passed through the high fortress gate. Stanford eyed the fence with a lifted brow, then smiled in amusement, as if he understood why Ashton had constructed it.

"It is of my own choosing that I live on the sheep

station and perform the duties that are required of me," Sasha said, hanging onto her bonnet as the wind whipped at the bow tied beneath her chin.

Sending his horse on past the outer boundaries of the fence that outlined the land that Sasha could say was partially hers, Stanford cast her a glittering look. "then you do not miss the city?" he asked smoothly. "You do not miss working barefoot in that smelly pub?"

Sasha cast him a quick, angry look. "As I said, I am here of my own choosing," she said abruptly. "If I had wanted to remain in the city, I would have."

A strained silence fell between them. Sasha squirmed uneasily on the seat, trying now to focus on everything but this man at her side, who knew well how to grate against her nerves. Stanford turned the buggy toward the river, where blackberry vines crowded out tree ferns and lignum bushes and rushes choked large areas, much to the satisfaction of the ibises that gathered there to nest. Two plumed egrets, the plumes on their backs and chests rising like lacy veils, stood at their nest, touching each other tenderly. Chest to chest, beaks together, they momentarily entwined their necks.

"Do you see those birds? It's not often you see humans display such affection toward one another," Stanford said, his jaw tight. He looked Sasha's way again, studying her. "How is it with you and Ashton? Do you plan on marrying him?"

His sudden question about Ashton made Sasha tense up. She cleared her throat nervously. She had intended to ask the questions—not be questioned herself. "Sir, my personal life is none of your concern," she murmured, tilting her chin stubbornly. Then she slowly looked his way. "But I would like to know how it is that you know Ashton. Why are there such bitter feelings between you?"

Stanford chuckled. He reined his horse to a halt beneath the shade of a leafy coolibah tree. "I'd suggest you ask Ashton about our past relationship," he said. "But I doubt if he will answer you, nor do I intend to."

Flustered, Sasha exhaled nervously. When Stanford stepped from the buggy and came to her side to offer her a hand, she momentarily refused to budge. But when he persisted, she saw no other choice but to acquiesce. Perhaps she could get on with this and leave much sooner if she cooperated with his wishes—to a point!

Stepping from the buggy, her shawl loose around her shoulders, Sasha refused to let her eyes meet Stanford's admiring stare. When she had her footing on the ground, she moved on to the river, then stiffened when she heard him behind her.

"Lovely lady, turn around and see what I have to offer you," Stanford said insinuatingly.

Almost afraid to, not sure what he had on his mind now that he had gotten her away from her sheep station, Sasha turned slowly around. Her lips parted when she saw a bottle of wine in one hand and a small wicker basket containing long-stemmed glasses in the other.

"Just a bit of sweet nourishment, and then I shall return you to your sheep station," Stanford said.

"The Homestead," Sasha corrected. "We call our sheep station The Homestead."

Stanford shrugged and set the basket on the ground. He stooped to one knee and took the glasses from the basket. He poured wine in one of them and offered it to Sasha.

"Thank you," she said coolly. She settled down on the ground beside the river and began sipping the wine as he poured himself a glass and sat down beside her.

"Are you sorry you came?" Stanford asked, finding himself being caught up in feelings he had not wanted to allow himself. He had wanted only the opportunity that knowing Sasha might eventually afford him.

"I truly shouldn't have," Sasha said, guilt tugging at her heart when she thought of Ashton and how much he had been against her going with Stanford. "I doubt if I shall again. I did not come to the outback to become lazy and frivolous. I came here to share a partnership with Ashton." She got a faraway look in her eyes. "It could be such a wonderful relationship, if . . ."

Stanford's eyebrows forked when Sasha's words trailed off to nothing. "If what?" he prodded.

Sasha shook her head, as though clearing her thoughts. "Nothing," she said, laughing awkwardly. "I was thinking out loud. That's all."

"If ever you need a friend, I am close by," Stanford said, his softness surprising Sasha.

She gaped openly at him, wondering if she had been wrong about him. And when he spied a wild mustang grazing not too far from them and began speaking so gently about it, Sasha's wonder of him grew even more.

"Do you see that horse yonder?" Stanford said, placing his empty glass in the wicker basket. "One never sees a horse so well as when he is grazing close by, intent upon the grass, oblivious of man.

"Look how he moves his ears, how he blows through his soft nostrils, how his casual movements are made," he continued. "He moves from clump to clump, making his selection by standards of his own, never still, yet entirely free of the restlessness of a stalled horse."

He looked at Sasha. She met his gaze and did not even notice when he took the wineglass from her hand, for his beautiful words about the horse had momentarily mesmerized her.

"Gentle animals make peace," Stanford said, setting the glass into the basket beside his. He took both of Sasha's hands and drew her close. "Listen to the soft noises of the horse—its hooves in the grass, its teeth crunching the grass."

Before she could stop him, Stanford had Sasha in a tight embrace, his lips pressing hard into hers. The kiss brought her back to reality and the sort of man she was with. One of his hands was now wildly caressing one of her breasts through her dress.

"Sasha . . ." he whispered as he drew his lips away. "Let me make love to you. I need you. God, how I—"

Sasha was near to gagging from his wet kiss and his groping hands. She shoved hard against his chest, knocking him off balance as he fell away from her.

"Take me home at once," she said, scrambling to her feet. Breathing hard, she glared down at him. "I did not come here to be manhandled. Take me home now, Stanford. Do you hear?"

A cold chill coursed through her when he looked up at her with hate-filled eyes, his cheeks red with a mounting rage. "Gladly," he muttered. He rose to his feet, grabbing the small basket and the bottle of wine. "I'll take you back but I won't give up this easily, Sasha. If you must know, I followed you to the outback. And, by damn, I'm not planning to share you with Ashton York."

"You made a wrong decision when you chose to follow me," Sasha said, hurrying to the buggy and onto the seat. She glared at him as he settled down beside her. "And I am not a mindless ninny. I will never believe that you moved to the outback just because of me. It has something to do with Ashton, and I plan to find out what it is."

He chuckled. "I don't think you'd want to know these answers you are seeking," he said. "You just might get disillusioned about this man you call your partner."

Sasha's eyes wavered.

A basket handle looped over her left arm, Bianca moved along the river, the image of Stanford and Sasha riding in the buggy together locked in her mind. Hate filled her at the thought, but not jealousy. She could hardly bear to think that Sasha would be at the mercy of such a madman as Stanford Sidwell.

"I want to warn her, but I can't," Bianca whispered to herself. "Stanford might kill me if he found out!"

She moved to her knees, smiling as she spied

what she had come searching for nestled in some rocks near the river. What she planned for Stanford would at least give her a reprieve for one night. As soon as he drank the coffee she prepared for him for supper, he would be too ill to touch her.

With trembling fingers, Bianca picked up a drab green object—hard shelled, but cracked, the size of a small ball. It was the seed of the *idiospermum*, nicknamed idiot fruit, for it was a hallucinogen, and poisonous.

"Tonight I shall sleep peacefully," she whispered to herself, placing several of the seeds into her basket. She smiled. "Stanford will enter the pits of hell, begging to be dead!"

The fire in the fireplace was burned down to dying, glowing embers. Sasha lay on the bed, covers drawn to her chin as she listened to Ashton's even breathing. She scooted to the edge of the bed and gazed pensively down at him, Lightning curled up in his arms on the floor close to the fireplace. She was haunted by Stanford's words about Ashton. She was haunted by the kangarooers calling him by the name Lawrence Proffitt. She had hoped that they would ease into a gentle conversation about it at the supper table, but Ashton had taken his plate of food and had eaten outside. His cold behavior toward her was unchanged.

Flopping over on her stomach, Sasha tried to will herself to sleep, knowing that she should be feeling victorious. She had gone with Stanford Sidwell to prove a point to Ashton and it seemed that she had succeeded.

* * *

Stanford walked through the flock of sheep that his men had just brought from Melbourne—sheep that most would shoot on first sight. These particular sheep had been purchased cheap for his special treat for Ashton.

"These'll do just fine," he said, smiling devilishly from man to man. "Take them. Mingle them in with our neighbors' sheep." He laughed throatily. One way or another he was going to break Lawrence Proffitt's will, forcing him to go to the hidden chest of riches.

Bianca cowered as he walked into the cabin. He grabbed her by the wrist and jerked her to him. "How's my little half-breed?" he said huskily, looking past the bruises that he had inflicted on her face the previous night. "Are you tamed enough? Can I expect cooperation from you tonight?"

Bianca looked up at him, shaking her head wildly. "Yes, yes!" she sobbed. She eyed the coffee pot, now fearing that he wasn't going to drink it before taking her.

Suddenly he released her and went to stand before the fire. "Pour me a cup of coffee, Bianca," he ordered. "It's been a long day."

Bianca's heart raced, but she couldn't appear too anxious to give him the coffee. He must be given no reason to suspect that she was to blame for the seizures caused by the seed of the idiot fruit!

Trying to control the trembling of her hand, Bianca poured a cup of coffee and handed it to Stanford. She watched him guardedly as he began sipping it, his mind seeming to be on something else as he stared into the flames of the fire. When his body began twitching strangely, she smiled to herself. When he stumbled to the bed and fell upon it, sweat pouring down his face, his eyes wild, Bianca knew that the idiot fruit was working.

Soon. Soon . . .

Chapter Fifteen

The ripe pumpkins had been plucked from the garden and put on the roof of the cabin to be mellowed by frost. Disconsolately, Sasha was now gathering eggs in the chicken house, placing them carefully in a small basket. Ashton had left early for the pasture, ignoring her as though she meant nothing at all to him any longer. Day by day her loneliness was compounded, and she was beginning to regret how she had chosen to treat Ashton. She could hardly bear to think of another full day and night ahead of her without his speaking to her, without his taking her into his arms and holding her.

Oh, but dare she cast her doubts aside and take from Ashton whatever love he wanted to share with her and only pray and hope that in the end he wouldn't be another Woodrow Rutherford?

The chickens clucking at her fingertips, Sasha took comfort in the warmth of the eggs against the palm of her hand as she lifted each one from its nest. Then she left the chicken house, her basket bulging with eggs, and began searching around the yard for Lightning. She was beginning to get worried. The pup usually escorted her to the chicken house, but this morning she had been nowhere in sight.

Sasha's shoulders sagged as she walked on toward the cabin. "She probably decided to abandon me also," she whispered to herself. "How can I bear this loneliness?"

Inside the cabin, Sasha placed the basket of eggs on the kitchen table and was preparing to make a custard when the sound of heavy iron wagon wheels pounding like a giant hammer along the land in the distance reached her. She could hear the shouts of the driver to the animals pulling the vehicle.

"Now what?" Sasha said, sighing. Grabbing the rifle she now kept loaded and standing beside the door for quick use, she ran outside, the skirt of her cotton dress whipping around her legs as she ran toward the gate of the massive fence. She looked around her for signs of any hired help that may have heard the approaching wagon, but saw no one. Had everyone left? Was she more alone today than she had even imagined?

Upset at Ashton for this carelessness, and recalling the threats of the kangarooer the day before, Sasha poised herself with the rifle. Then, reeling from side to side like a cork tossing in a storm-swept sea, the wagon came into sight around a bend and began bearing down upon the sheep station in a swirl of dust and noise.

From this distance, Sasha could see that the wagon was being pulled by two snorting, sweating horses whipped on by the driver. She could hear the slap of the leather and the creaking of the timber and bolts that held the whole thing together.

"Why, it's Jacob, the Syrian hawker," Sasha gasped, lowering her rifle to her side. Her eyes danced as the wagon continued on its way toward her.

Sasha had seen the peddlar often on the streets of Melbourne and knew that he was liked by everyone, especially those in the outback who could not get into town often enough to shop for their needs. In his wagon he carried the usual stock of clothing, scents, soaps, red flannelette to ward off pneumonia, and much, much more!

The hawker drew rein next to Sasha. "Good-day, miss," he said, tipping his sweat-stained hat to her. "Can I interest you in something fine today for yourself, or your husband?"

"Good morning, sir," Sasha said, her heart pounding. The day which only moments ago had been flat as a pastry board was now exciting. "I would love to see your wares. But I am not sure I can afford anything that you show me."

The hawker was dark, with blue tattoo marks on his hands; his eyes were deep and dark in the bones of his face. He climbed down from his seat and ambled, stiff-legged, to the back of his wagon. "Most say they can't afford much, yet they end up buyin' one or two of my items," he said, uncovering his shiny white teeth in a smile.

Sasha's breath was taken away when the hawker lifted the old tarpaulin covering and began bringing out openwork stockings, ribbons, and shawls for her close scrutiny.

"Now those are items most ladies are interested in," the hawker said smoothly. When Sasha only looked and didn't offer to buy any of the finery, the hawker placed them back in the wagon.

He pointed to a mouth organ, but reached for a pen knife, its handle made of pearl. He handed it toward Sasha. "Most men entertain thoughts of owning one of these handy gadgets," he said.

Sasha was taken quickly with an idea. If she could purchase this lovely pen knife for Ashton, perhaps he would accept it as a peace offering!

"Take it," the Syrian urged. "Run your hands over the smoothness of the pearl handle. It'll seduce you into buyin' it for your mister, it will."

Her pulse racing, Sasha took the knife and did as the hawker suggested. As she ran her fingers over the pearl handle, another thought seized her. The scar on Ashton's face! It had surely been inflicted by a knife of some sort. What if it had been a pen knife? Surely he would detest such a gift!

Quickly she handed the knife back to the hawker. "No," she said, "I don't think that will do."

The hawker frowned at her with his dark eyes, then turned and placed the pen knife with the other items.

Sasha's attention was drawn away from the man and his wares by the sound of an approaching horse and buggy. Her heart grew cold when she recognized Stanford Sidwell as the driver. He had said that he would not give up on her—and he had meant it!

The hawker turned his eyes to Stanford as the horse and buggy wheeled to a stop close to Sasha. "And good-day to you, mate," he said, ambling to Stanford to offer a handshake. "You have come to see what I have to sell today? That is good. I fear this young lady has no means with which to purchase anything from me."

The hawker's dark eyes gleamed as Stanford stepped from the wagon and accepted his handshake. A diamond stickpin glittered in the folds of his ascot—and in the eyes of the hawker.

"You are a man of means, I see," the hawker continued. He cast Sasha a look over his shoulder, then turned from Stanford and went back to his wagon. He chose the finest of linen handkerchiefs with the finest of lace gracing its edges and held it out to Stanford. "This would be a perfect gift for such a lady as this, wouldn't you say?"

Sasha was feeling trapped, almost desperate. She clutched the rifle hard, not liking being at the mercy of Stanford Sidwell, whose smug smile was making a sick feeling sweep through her. Oh, how could she have gotten herself involved with such a man? Would she ever be able to shake herself free of him? Was he going to cling like a leech? How could she rid herself of him short of threatening him with the barrel of a rifle?

Stanford took the handkerchief and eyed it admiringly. "Yes, I think I will take this handkerchief— and let me take a look at your hair ribbons," he said, walking to the wagon and sorting through the colorful ribbons with his eyes. His gaze settled on a scarlet ribbon. He smiled and picked it up. "Perfect," he pronounced, fishing in his breeches pocket for several coins.

The hawker mentally counted the coins as Stanford placed them in the palm of his hand. He paled, for this man had paid him twice what the items were worth.

"Now, fellow, be on your way," Stanford said, taking the hawker by an elbow and leading him back to his wagon.

The hawker climbed aboard, tipped his hat, and rode away, singing into the wind.

Sasha stood square-shouldered and tight-jawed as Stanford smiled down at her. "Sasha, I hope to make a peace offering with these gifts," he said, holding them out toward her. "It seems we got off on the wrong footing yesterday. I have come to apologize. Will you accept the apology?"

"I do not wish any gifts from you, nor apologies," Sasha said icily, her hand tightening on the rifle. "Please leave." She looked more closely at him, seeing a strange sort of tiredness in his eyes and in the way his jowls sagged. Had he gotten drunk the previous evening because of her? He most certainly looked as if he had had a hard night!

A quick anger flared within Stanford. "I am trying to be nice to you," he said, his teeth clenched. "Or is that the wrong approach?" He thrust the handkerchief and ribbon into his waistcoat pocket. "Do you like a man to be rough? If so, I'm just the man you're lookin' for. I'd be happy to do you the honor."

Before Sasha could even think to raise the rifle to defend herself, Stanford had grabbed it from her hand and had tossed it aside. She was too suddenly in his tight arms—too suddenly assaulted by his wet, cold lips—to even get a grip on her senses!

When he began shoving her to the ground, a fierce panic seized her, and all that she could think of was Ashton!

Where was Ashton?

Or would Ashton even care that she was being attacked by this vile man?

Would he laugh at her and tell her that she had asked for it—that she deserved whatever happened to her?

A clicking noise from somewhere close by made the hair at Stanford's neck rise and his gropings stop. He knew the sound well. Someone had just cocked a gun. He stiffened when he saw a tall shadow suddenly fall over him and Sasha. He flinched when the hard steel of a shotgun's barrel was thrust between his shoulder blades.

"I think that's enough, unless you want a hole blasted into your back large enough for me to run my fist through," Ashton warned, his voice filled with a cold threat. "Get up, Sidwell. Get away from Sasha. And if you value your life at all, you'll start running until you're off my land."

Sasha's breathing was shallow. She peered up at Ashton, weak with relief. Then she looked up into the leering face of Stanford and screamed when he suddenly flipped over and grabbed the shotgun from Ashton, causing Ashton to fall awkwardly to the ground.

"Ashton!" Sasha cried, grabbing for Stanford when he lunged for Ashton and had him quickly pinned to the ground.

"You son of a bitch," Stanford growled, quickly slipping his knife from its sheath at his waist. "You continue to pay no heed to my warnings. Are you wantin' another scar on that ugly face of yours? I'll oblige, if you are."

Sasha crept to her feet, trembling. She sucked in a wild breath of air when Stanford lowered his knife to Ashton's throat. "No!" she whispered harshly. She looked quickly at the shotgun. She grabbed it up before Stanford noticed and soon had the barrel thrust against the back of his neck.

"Get off Ashton or I'll blow your head clear off your body," Sasha warned, her voice quivering. Her stance wavered when Stanford didn't budge. "Do it, Stanford, or I'll shoot you."

"You don't have the nerve," Stanford chuckled. He began easing the knife back towards his sheath. "But to save testin' you, I'll do as you say." He gave her a slow look. "I'm puttin' the knife away. Now you lower that damn shotgun."

"Not on your life," Sasha said, steadying the shotgun as she fought the continued trembling of her fingers.

"How in the hell can I move with a shotgun poked against my head?" Stanford argued, not taking a chance on trying to move. He never trusted a woman's skills with a firearm. Especially a woman with the spirit of a wildcat!

"As I move the shotgun slowly away, you move with me," Sasha said, inching around so that she was standing more at Stanford's side than his back. She felt Ashton's eyes on her, making her feel suddenly awkward and shy. Never had he seen this side of her—nor had she, in fact!

"All right, all right," Stanford grumbled. He followed her movements, and as soon as he was free from the threat of the shotgun he fled to his horse and buggy and was soon gone in a fury of uprooted grass beneath the horse's hooves.

Heaving a sigh of relief, Ashton rolled over and stretched out on the ground. He looked up at Sasha, his lips tugging into a smile. "Well, now," he said. "Aren't you full of surprises?"

"I'm not the only one," Sasha said, dropping the shotgun to the ground. She sat down beside Ashton, still weak from the ordeal. "Where did you come from? I thought you were way out in the pasture."

"I was, but when I saw the Syrian hawker riding across the land with his wagon of foolishness, I thought I'd better come to the rescue of our bankroll," Ashton teased. "I know the ribbons and fancy things Jacob sells to the women of the outback. I thought you'd be tempted to buy something pretty for yourself."

Sasha combed her hands through her hair, taking it back from her face and shoulders. "Would you believe I found something for you instead?" she murmured, eluding his steady stare, now knowing exactly what she must do. She would no longer deny her love for Ashton! That had made her too miserable!

And hadn't she just proven to herself that she would always protect him with her life?

She would, indeed, make the ultimate sacrifice for him.

She would allow herself to trust him!

Ashton leaned up on an elbow. "Oh?" he said, eyes wide. "You bought something for me? What?"

Sasha lowered her eyelashes. "I didn't say I bought anything," she said, slowly looking up at him again. "I just said that I found something."

"Oh, you didn't buy it because you worried about how much it cost?" Ashton said, scooting over to sit beside Sasha. He snaked an arm around her waist, glad that she did not draw away from him.

She looked innocently up at him, her gaze settling on the scar. "No, that was not the reason I chose not to buy it," she murmured. "It was something I had second thoughts about. I thought that perhaps it might not be something you'd want."

"And that was?" he persisted.

"A pen knife," she blurted out, looking quickly away from him again. "I—I thought that perhaps you might detest all forms of knives. Surely that is how you were scarred—by someone's knife."

Ashton's hand went automatically to his scar. He always forgot about it until there was someone to remind him. Sasha's reminder was like a splash of cold water on his face. He knew that she must be filled with many questions but was glad that she, thus far, had refrained from pouncing on him with them.

"A pen knife would have been a nice gift," he said, trying to smooth over the awkwardness of the moment. "Thank you for thinking of me."

"You would have wanted it?" Sasha asked, her

heart thundering wildly as Ashton placed a forefinger to her chin to direct her eyes at him.

"It would not have been the gift so much that I wanted," Ashton said softly. "But the person who gave it to me." He lowered his mouth to her lips. "Sasha, moments ago you gave me a gift and I thank you for it."

"What . . . sort . . . of gift?" Sasha murmured, his breath hot on her lips. She ached for his arms! For his kiss! To be wholly with him!

"The gift of yourself," he whispered, suddenly on his feet and sweeping her up into his arms. "When you defended me, you proved that you loved me. All of these recent petty arguments were forced, weren't they? Tell me that you meant nothing by them—that you went with Stanford Sidwell only to make me jealous!"

Jealousy had not been her true intention, yet it did seem like a way out without having to go into the full truth of how she would not let herself trust him. Yes, this was an easier out. And by the way he was looking at her and holding her as he walked toward the cabin, she knew that she was being allowed a fresh beginning with him.

"Yes, it was all to make you jealous," she murmured. She looked playfully up at him. "Did it work?"

"What do you think?" Ashton growled, taking her on into the cabin. He placed her on the bed and smiled down at her as he hurriedly removed his shirt.

"Why, Ashton, this is only mid-morning," Sasha teased, her fingers eagerly unbuttoning her dress.

"What will the hired hands think?"

"To hell with the hired hands," Ashton said, leaping onto the bed, nude. His lips bore down onto Sasha's.

Her whole world once again melted away into something blissfully sweet.

Chapter Sixteen

ONE WEEK LATER

The early morning light was just beginning to stream through the cabin window. Sipping coffee, Sasha sat cuddled close beside Ashton on the floor before a cozy fire. "Ashton, except for my worries about Lightning since she has been missing, this past week has been the happiest of my life," she murmured, still warmed clear through with rapture from their lovemaking of only moments ago.

"It could have been that way every morning since I met you had you just allowed it," Ashton said, setting his tin cup on the floor. He took Sasha's cup and set it aside, then lifted her chin with a forefinger, brushing a kiss across her lips. "But, darling, you were too stubborn."

Not wanting to break the spell of happiness, Sasha wove her fingers through his hair and drew his lips fully into hers to silence him. She kissed him with passion, sucking in a wild breath of ecstasy when he eased her down to the floor and crept a hand up the skirt of her dress, caressing that part of her that became inflamed so easily with need of him.

Her hands moved down the wide breadth of his chest and to his buttocks, reveling in the feel of the tightness of his muscles through the kangaroo-hide fabric of his breeches. Brazenly, her hands wandered on around and touched the bulge in front, and she realized by its size that he was awakened, again, with need of her.

Sasha slipped her lips from his, looking seductively up into his violet eyes. "Oh, Ashton, aren't we shameful to want to do this again so soon?" she teased.

"However you describe—" he began, but his words were cut short by the sound of voices shouting outside the cabin.

"What the—?" Ashton sprang away from Sasha, to his feet. He grabbed his gunbelt and fastened it around his waist.

Sasha scrambled to her feet, smoothing her hands down the skirt of her dress to straighten it. "That's Crispin and Rufus," she said, eyeing the door speculatively. She could hear the desperation and fear in their voices. What came to mind sent her heart into a tailspin.

"Oh, Ashton, what if they've found Lightning?" she cried, grasping hard onto Ashton's arm. "They probably found her—dead!"

Ashton gripped Sasha by the shoulders and eased

her away from him. "I won't believe that Lightning is dead," he said, his voice drawn. "She'll come home again, Sasha. You'll see."

"But then what is wrong with Crispin and Rufus?" Sasha said, rushing alongside Ashton to the door, then outside to the porch. She held her breath as she looked down at the two faces etched with concern. She gazed quickly around, then exhaled a nervous breath of relief when she didn't see Lightning's body anywhere.

"What's this all about?" Ashton said, hurrying from the porch. "What's happened?"

Rufus stepped forward, his head hung. "It ain't my fault, Ashton," he said, twisting a sweat-stained hat round and round between his long, lean fingers. "I did my job." He looked quickly up at Ashton, painful regret in the depths of his eyes. "But damn it, Ashton, somehow it happened."

Frustrated and growing impatient, Ashton ran his fingers through his hair. "Rufus, damn it all to hell tell me," he shouted. "What happened? Is it Lightning? Did you find her? Is she dead?"

"No, we didn't find Lightning," Crispin said, edging Rufus aside. "It's the sheep, Ashton. It's the damn sheep."

Ashton paled slightly. "What about the sheep?" he asked, looking from Rufus to Crispin. "Has something happened to them?"

"You might say that," Crispin said, his eyes wavering as he met Ashton's steady, questioning gaze.

"Well?" Ashton demanded. "What about them?" He looked past the two men at the flock of sheep grazing peacefully in the distance. He did not think there were enough missing to stir up this commotion and concern.

Still wringing his hat, Rufus edged Crispin aside. He knew that a single act of neglect or inattention on the shepherd's part might in a moment blast the prospects of his employer. He had been attentive to the sheep—more so than a mere stranger working in the capacity of a sheepherder would. Yet—the proof was there that somehow the sheep had been neglected.

"Ashton, Lord knows I'd never neglect my duties as sheepherder," Rufus said, his voice quavering. "But, by God, somehow some of our sheep have become infested with scab."

For Ashton and all graziers, the word scab was synonomous with doom. It was the terror of the sheep stations. Scab was a highly infectious disease that ruined the wool, inhibited breeding, and had no known cure.

"How many?" Ashton asked, trying to keep calm. He could not figure out how his sheep could have become infected. Rufus and Crispin had chosen their flock with great care.

"I'd say a dozen or so," Crispin said, turning to look at the grazing sheep. "We've already separated them from the rest."

"How could this have happened?" Ashton asked.

"The neighboring sheep station has a flock of sheep grazing across the river from us," Rufus said, looking in the direction of the river. "Perhaps they brought scab to the area with them." He scratched his brow idly. "But the river separates our two patches of land. There ain't no way those sheep could have mingled with ours."

A coldness surged through Ashton. "Are you saying that Stanford Sidwell now has sheep at his station?" he asked guardedly. "Has anyone seen them? Are they of prime stock?"

"I ain't seen them," Rufus said, shrugging. "I ain't had no reason to want to."

"I haven't seen them either," Crispin said, his eyes narrowing as he began to understand Ashton's suspicions. "You don't think he might have . . ."

". . . moved some infected sheep in with ours in the middle of the night while we all were sleeping?" Ashton interrupted, completing Crispin's words.

Sasha gasped lightly. "Do you think he would do something as mean as that?" she asked, guilt washing through her for having given Stanford a good excuse for coming onto their property at all.

Ashton laughed. "Stanford Sidwell do something mean?" he said sarcastically. "Naw."

"That man's got the morals of a snake," Crispin interjected.

"There is no way to prove Stanford did this," Ashton said bitterly, his brow knit into a deep frown. "But if I ever discover that he's been up to his usual dirty tricks, it will be his last trick!"

"What are you going to do about the sheep?" Sasha asked softly.

"We'll kill and bury those that are infected the worst, and the others will be treated," Ashton said. He took her hands. "I suggest you don't watch the procedure. It might be unpleasant for you."

"Perhaps so," Sasha said. She lifted her chin

stubbornly. "But as I see it, it is my responsibility to be taught every procedure used on this sheep station, be it pleasant or ugly."

Taking the hem of her skirt up into her arms, she walked determinedly toward the sheep. "Are you coming?" she said over her shoulder. "Time's a wastin'."

Ashton shook his head, but could not help smiling at Sasha's courage and fortitude. More than any woman he had ever known, Sasha had the strength of mind that enabled her to meet danger or bear the pain of adversity with courage. She was a woman of grit, backbone, pluck!

"All right, if you insist," Ashton said, following Sasha. He motioned for Crispin and Rufus. "Take us to the sick sheep. Let's hope we don't have to kill many of them."

"There ain't no question about ten of them," Crispin said, falling into step beside Ashton. "No amount of treatment will help them."

"I still smell something foul here," Ashton grumbled. "And the stench comes to me from Stanford Sidwell. That bastard. Why couldn't he have rotted in prison?"

Sasha's eyes widened. "Prison?" she said quickly. "How would you know about his being in prison?"

"Sweet darlin', it's not a guarded secret," Ashton said, giving Sasha a harried look.

"Oh, I see," Sasha said faintly, her gaze settling on Ashton's scar. If anyone kept secrets about himself, it was most certainly Ashton York. Why didn't he just tell her that he had gotten the wound as a child? It would be so simple to say something as innocent as that to put her mind at ease.

But no, he avoided any comments at all about the scar—and his past which did not include her. Just how much of it had included Stanford Sidwell? It was too obvious that these two men hated each other with a vengeance!

"Over here," Rufus said, guiding everyone to a small, fenced-off area in which stood the infected sheep. "Take a look. The wool is ruined. I'd say kill them all or take a chance on it spreading. From all I've heard about the scab, it is practically incurable."

Sasha's heart went out to the pitiful-looking, timid sheep that looked up at her with their dark, trusting eyes. She could hardly bear to think that they would have to be slain, yet she understood why it was necessary. Through their fleece she could see thick, crusty scabs on their bodies, some worse than the others. Their fleece was matted and ugly, and sparse where the scabs were the most prominent.

"How terrible," Sasha said, sighing.

"Well, I've seen enough," Ashton said, after a close examination. He began shoving the sheep in separate directions. "This one must go," he said. "We'll do what we can about this one."

When Ashton had made his final decisions, five of the sheep had been given the death sentence.

"Do you want me to do it?" Crispin asked, jerking a revolver from his gunbelt.

Ashton glanced over at Sasha. "I told you it wouldn't be pretty," he said. "Do you still want to stay?"

Sasha swallowed hard, then turned without saying anything and fled back to the house. She covered her ears with her hands when the shots rang out.

Then she grabbed a basket and left the house to busy herself with a much more pleasant chore. She would try to place her worries over Lightning's disappearance and the plight of the sheep from her mind by going to the river to gather wild spinach and the licorice-flavored creeper called sweet tea.

Also, she hoped to see Bianca. She had not seen her again since their first meeting, and it gave Sasha a fretful feeling to think of Bianca living at Stanford's sheep station. Even though she was married to another man, surely she was at Stanford Sidwell's mercy by just living there!

Sweat dampened Ashton's brow as he shouted out orders to his men. The slain sheep were buried. The other animals were immersed in a large tub of disinfectant and then laid, one by one, on a sheet of bark and scraped down with an iron hoop.

"That's about all we can do," Ashton said to Crispin, wiping his hands clean on his breeches. "Only time will tell if any more of the sheep are infected." He looked at Rufus. "Just make sure these are kept separate from the others and keep an eye out for any more that might show signs of scab."

"Sure thing," Rufus said. He shuffled his feet nervously. "I'm sorry as hell about this, Ashton. I'd give a year's pay to have kept it from happening."

Ashton swung an arm around Crispin's shoulder. "You know I'm not blaming you for any of this," he said, looking toward the river—farther still, at land now occupied by Stanford Sidwell. "If I ever do find out who is responsible, he'll pay and pay good."

"Want us to go snoopin' around Stanford's place

to get a look at his sheep?" Crispin said, resting a hand on the handle of his holstered pistol.

"No, there's no use in doing that, mate," Ashton said. "We won't be able to trace the blame to him. He'd not leave any diseased sheep at his station. He's smarter than that."

"It must have been done real quiet-like," Rufus mumbled, remembering with pride his nights beneath the stars among the sheep. "I never heard nothin'."

"That bastard can move around in the dark like a spook and no one is ever the wiser," Ashton said, recalling the night that Stanford had suddenly been straddling him in the jail cell, the blade of his knife cold on his cheek until the blood began to run warm across his flesh. . . .

"He'll slip up if he tries anything else around here," Crispin growled. "I'll be on the lookout for him and his men. I won't stop to ask questions, neither. I'll be shootin' to kill."

"I think that bastard has nine lives," Ashton said, wiping sweat from his brow with the back of his hand. "I don't know how many times he's escaped the clutches of the law and the bounty hunters in these parts. Now he looks like he's livin' legal-like. But never a breath escapes from that man's mouth when he isn't involved in one rotten scheme or another."

"Perhaps this time it ain't so much what he's involved in," Crispin said, keeping his voice low so that it would not carry in the wind to the men working around him. "Maybe he's snoopin' around here, purposely causin' trouble, to get in on the

215

whereabouts of that chest you hid. Think so, Ashton?"

Ashton frowned from Crispin to Rufus. "I damn well know so," he said flatly. "But you're here to help me keep it a secret, aren't you, mates?"

"Aye," Crispin said.

Rufus's eyes became anxious. "When are you goin' to show us where you hid it, Ashton?" he asked. "When are you goin' to dig it up?"

"It's not in my plans ever to touch that damnable chest," Ashton grumbled. "It's best kept away from those who might squander it."

"If Silas Howland ever gets well enough to travel again and hears where you are, he'll come and force you to tell," Crispin said solemnly.

"I doubt that," Ashton said. "He would be a condemned man for sure, if he ever got possession of the chest that I stole from his premises. That would be all the proof I needed to point an accusing finger at him."

"Maybe he wouldn't care," Rufus interjected. "Since you wounded him, he ain't fit for much, anyhow. I'd think he'd take a chance of trying to get the chest back, at least to enjoy for his final days on this earth."

Ashton laughed. "Rufus, I may have wounded Superintendent Howland, but I'm sure he's far from being on his death bed," he said. "I would say that being accused and condemned of cheating the people of Melbourne out of thousands of dollars would assure his demise quicker than anything."

Rufus shrugged. "Aay, I'm sure you're right," he mumbled.

Ashton didn't want to admit to his friend that he always carried the dread of coming face to face with Silas Howland again. The man who once boasted of being a pillar of the community surely hated Ashton much more than Stanford Sidwell ever could. Ashton had robbed the superintendent of a comfortable future. He had only robbed Stanford Sidwell of two years of his life.

Ashton glanced up at the sky. The sun was lowering behind the eucalyptus trees in the distance. The birds were fluttering overhead, returning to their nightly nesting spots. "You'd best get these sheep seen to for the night and return to your post in the pasture, Rufus," he said, sighing heavily. "It's been a long day—and not one of the best."

Ashton spied Sasha as she stepped outside to stand on the porch. The wind lifted her hair from her shoulders, fluttering it long and free down her back. The skirt of her dress occasionally lifted above her knees with the breeze, revealing her tiny ankles and shapely legs. Seeing her, knowing that she was waiting for him, made him move in haste from his friends.

"Good day, mates," he said, waving at them. "I'm going to see what my lady has done all day to keep herself occupied."

He hurried to the porch and swept his arms around Sasha and leaned his lips close to hers. "Are you all right?" he asked, seeing that she looked pensively withdrawn.

"Yes, I'm fine," Sasha whispered, lowering her eyes. She could not tell Ashton that she had been worrying about not seeing Bianca again. Earlier, while taking her stroll down by the river, she had heard something like a scream echo across the river from Stanford Sidwell's sheep station. The scream had been brief, but most definitely a woman's. The only other woman in this part of the scrub was Bianca. If Sasha confided in Ashton about the scream, he would watch her like a hawk, and she would not be able to go to Stanford's sheep station to investigate tomorrow. And she wanted to do this alone. If Bianca was in some sort of trouble, it would look less conspicuous if a woman friend came to call without being escorted by a man holstered heavily with revolvers.

"Then give me a smile," Ashton said, slipping a finger beneath her chin and lifting it so that their eyes met.

Sasha forced a smile.

"Now that's more like it," Ashton said, then playfully swept her up into his arms and carried her inside the cabin. "What's for supper, sweet darlin'?"

"Fried chicken and spinach," Sasha said, clinging around his neck, adoring him.

Ashton groaned. "Spinach?" he said, visibly shuddering. "When I left Melbourne, I thought I'd never have to eat another leaf of spinach. Where on earth did you find it out here?"

"I have my ways," Sasha said, giggling.

"Spinach?" Ashton repeated, screwing up his face with distaste again. Then he smiled down at Sasha before placing her to her feet. "But, sweet darlin', what's for dessert? Or need I ask?"

Sasha twined her arms more tightly around his neck and drew his lips to her mouth. "Let me give you a small sampling now, my love," she whispered.

She kissed him sweetly.

Chapter Seventeen

As Sasha stepped out onto the porch with a dish of food for Lightning, hoping that the dingo pup might choose this day to return home, she flinched and glanced quickly up when lightning flared across the purple sky. The wind was still. The morning was oppressive with a sultry, muggy weight to it.

"That's sweet of you to place fresh food on the porch every day for Lightning," Ashton said, reining his horse to a stop close to the porch. He leaned his full weight against his saddle horn, smiling down at Sasha. "And you're right to. She will come home."

Sasha stooped and placed the dish on the porch, then straightened back up, touched with a deep sadness over the loss of the special animal. "I can't help but think that someone is responsible for her being gone," she murmured, reaching to smooth her hair back from her brow. "You know how Stanford and that—that kangarooer person named Ajax immediately disliked Lightning. What if one of them abducted and killed her?"

"It's a thought, but I don't want to labor over it," Ashton said, his jaw tight. "It's best to think positive, Sasha, than to envision Lightning at the hands of either of those sons of bitches."

His gaze raked over her. She wore a fancier dress than seemed necessary for doing chores at the sheep station. The fully gathered yellow dress displayed eyelet trimming on her sleeves and at her lowswept bodice. Her hair was lustrous from a fresh brushing and spilled over her shoulders and tumbled down her graceful back. And there was something about her eyes today. They were luminous, yet vague, as though she were hiding something from him.

"You said earlier this morning that you had a lot to keep you busy today, Sasha," Ashton asked. "What might that include?"

Sasha grew tense, not wanting him to know that she was going to go and check on Bianca. When she had put on her best dress for her visit with Bianca, she thought that Ashton had left for the pastures and would not return until later in the day.

"Why do you ask?" she asked, defying him with a set stare.

Again Ashton raked his eyes over her, then challenged her with a stare of his own. "If I didn't know better, I'd think you were dressed up for a gentleman caller," he said. "Sweet darlin', you look damn pretty this morning—all fresh and dolled up like something out of a picture book."

"Thank you," Sasha said, her lashes casting shadows on her cheeks as she cast her eyes downward. She then looked up at him again.

"You didn't say why you are dressed so pretty, Sasha," Ashton persisted, his eyes too dark and knowing.

"Ashton, I assure you that my reason for putting on a pretty dress today is perfectly innocent," Sasha murmured, feeling trapped. She was afraid that if she didn't tell him the truth, he might surmise that she planned to go driving again with Stanford Sidwell. She did not want to ever make Ashton jealous again over such a terrible man. Yet if she told him that she was concerned over a woman who lived on Stanford's sheep station, he would not allow her to go there. She had not even thought to mention Bianca to him!

"Then do you mind telling me why you are acting so damned uneasy because of my questions about the way you look today?" Ashton persisted, scowling down at her. His jaw tightened and his eyes narrowed. "Don't tell me that you've accepted an invitation to go on another buggy ride with Stanford Sidwell. I thought you and I had come to an understanding, Sasha. I thought you were perfectly happy with me."

The truth out, the hurt there in Ashton's eyes and in his voice, Sasha felt no other recourse than to confess the full truth to him. She left the porch and went to the horse's side, reaching for Ashton's hand. "My darling, never would I wish for another man's company now that I have made peace within my heart over my feelings for you," she said softly.

Ashton slipped from the saddle and swept her into his arms, cuddling her close. He placed his nose into the wondrous scent of her hair. "You don't know what hearing you say that means to me," he said. "For so long you fought your feelings because of that damned aristocrat Woodrow Rutherford. I would hate to think that a man like Stanford Sidwell could ever stand in the way of our happiness."

Sasha stiffened somewhat within his arms. She looked woefully up at him. "Darling, what I had planned today did, in a small measure, include Stanford," she said, gazing up at him.

Ashton's eyes became charged with dark emotion. "But I thought you just said . . ." he began, but was stopped when Sasha placed a finger to his lips, silencing his words.

"Darling, let me finish," she encouraged softly. "Let me try and explain."

Ashton took her hand from his mouth and circled it with his tight fingers as he urged it back to her side. "I'm not sure if I want to hear," he growled. Lightning zigzagged across the purple sky. Thunder boomed in the distance.

"I should have told you about her before now," Sasha said, slipping from his embrace and leaning against the hitching rail.

"Her?" Ashton asked. He stepped around her so that they were eye to eye again. "Who are you talking about?"

Sasha looked innocently up at him. "Bianca," she said, not surprised at his reaction when his lips opened with surprise. He knew who Bianca was. Everyone knew Bianca. She did not even require a last name!

"What about Bianca?" he asked.

"She's living at Stanford's sheep station with her

husband, a sheepherder," Sasha said in a rush of words. "I discovered her at the river a few days ago when I went there for a swim and bath."

Ashton forked his fingers through his hair. "Well, I'll be damned," he said. "Bianca? Married? And living at Stanford's sheep station? Nothing could surprise me more. She's got the most notorious reputation of all the women in Melbourne."

Sasha felt a blush rush to her cheeks. "I know," she murmured. "But that is in the past, Ashton. She is married and pregnant." She looked in the direction of the river. "And I'm worried about her."

"I think she's capable of taking care of herself," Ashton said, laughing. "She did for years, you know."

"Perhaps so," Sasha said, sighing heavily. "But Ashton, although she was a prostitute, I saw many redeeming qualities in her the day we became acquainted. I liked her. Immediately."

She screwed her face up into a frown. "And I can't help but be worried about her," she continued. "I haven't seen her since that one day. What if she is in trouble?"

She swallowed hard. "Ashton, I heard a woman screaming the other day. It had to be Bianca. She and I are the only women in these parts."

She paused, measuring her next words very carefully, knowing what Ashton's response would be. "And I plan to go over to Stanford's sheep station today and check on her welfare," she finally blurted out.

When Ashton's eyes flashed angrily, she quickly added, "No matter what you say, I am going," she said, tilting her chin stubbornly. She swallowed hard again, daring him with unwavering eyes. "I am, Ashton. I am."

"The hell you are," Ashton said. He took her by the wrist and led her up the steps, across the porch, and into the house. "Now this is where you belong. Not poking around over at Stanford Sidwell's. Mind your own affairs, Sasha. It's healthier that way."

A slow boil rose within Sasha. She jerked herself free from Ashton and placed her hands on her hips. "How dare you," she hissed, unable to control her temper. "Although I have confessed to loving you and have been happier these past few days than ever before in my life, I cannot let you rule my life, Ashton York. I must feel free to come and go as I please. I would hope that was a part of our bargain, Ashton—that I be treated like someone with brains and common sense. I am not a mindless ninny, Ashton York. And I don't want to feel as though I am always having to prove it to you. Do you understand?"

Ashton was taken aback by her defensive attitude, yet he should not have been surprised. This was a part of why he had always been attracted to her— her perseverance, her stubbornness! And she was always so damn pretty when she was mad!

But no matter what she said, he could not allow her to get mixed up further in Stanford Sidwell's affairs. And knowing Stanford and his lust for loose women, Bianca was not at his sheep station only because she was married to one of his men. Stanford was surely lifting her skirts and taking his share of enjoyment from her.

Then his insides tightened as he recalled also having heard what sounded like a woman's scream one night not long ago. Had that been Bianca? Or had it been an animal in the outback?

He hoped for the latter.

But right now he was concerned only for Sasha's welfare.

"Sasha, I think it's time for you to understand something," Ashton said, taking her hands from her hips and holding them. "I want you to listen and listen good. When I am through you will see why I don't want you to get anywhere near Stanford Sidwell again—or anyone associated with him."

Sasha tried to free her hands but Ashton's were locked around them too tightly. "Ashton, I . . ." she began to protest, but was interrupted too quickly by him.

"Sasha, before Stanford earned the reputation of being a confidence man he was a bushranger, pickpocket, and card sharp," Ashton explained. "For those offenses he got a couple of light prison terms in Melbourne." He hesitated briefly, then continued. "You see, I became acquainted with Stanford when we shared a prison cell."

Struck numb by the discovery that Ashton had been in prison, Sasha grew pale. "Ashton, you?" she gasped. "No, Ashton. No."

Ashton held more tightly to her hands, afraid that if he released her, she would flee and perhaps never return. The shock was in her eyes, in her voice! Now he wished that he had been truthful with her sooner. They had just made their peace, and how wonderful it had become! To lose her now would be like losing his own soul!

"Don't condemn me too soon, Sasha," he said, searching her eyes as he spoke. "Listen carefully to what I have to say. When I was a small lad, my father abandoned me and my mother. Soon after my mother died, I came to Australia with my Uncle Jason. He was killed a few years later by a lone gunman over a gambling debt. I stayed in Australia. I saw the corrupt ways of some of the so-called lawmen and decided to fight for the people's rights," he said.

He stopped and cleared his throat nervously before continuing. "You see, I became a leader of a gang a few years ago, fighting the corrupt English rule in Australia led by Superintendent Silas Howland. My gang was wrongly labeled bushrangers."

He did not want to tell her about the hidden chest filled with a fortune, preferring to leave that in his past along with everything else that had almost ruined his life. "For my supposed crimes I was imprisoned, Sasha," he continued. "But not for long. I was lucky not to be assigned to a chain gang thanks to the skills I learned in school in England studying to become a government clerk. I paid my dues and was released on good behavior with the few dollars I had saved up during my convict sentence. Those few dollars I invested in my pub."

Having listened raptly to Ashton, Sasha was momentarily stunned by his confession. Then she flung herself into his arms and hugged him. "Oh, Ashton, why didn't you tell me sooner?" she cried. "You should have known that I would understand. And oh, but I do! I do!"

Ashton held her away from him and looked down at her, his eyes filled with emotion. "Sasha, that isn't all I wanted to tell you," he said. "Stanford Sidwell's prison term was lengthened by two years for having attacked me with a knife in prison, slashing my face. That man hates me with a passion because of this and is out to ruin me.''

"The scar," Sasha said, smoothing a hand over the long welt on his cheek, relieved to know that there was nothing in Ashton's past that was all that dark and sinister. "So that is why it is there. Because—because of Stanford.'' She tilted her head and gazed up at Ashton. "But, why, Ashton, did he do this to you? It is such a terrible thing.''

"Sasha, there was no true cause," Ashton lied. "Sometimes hate comes naturally to such a man as Stanford who is so filled with such hate himself. It is obvious that he hates me no less now than then.''

"Yes, I have noticed," Sasha murmured.

Ashton framed her face between his hands. "This is why, sweet darlin', he followed me here," he said. "To finish what had started between us while we were imprisoned together. This is why you must be careful and stay away from him at all costs.''

Ashton looked at her guardedly, hoping that he had told her enough to satisfy her curiosity and to give her cause to do as he asked of her. He did not want to be forced to tell the true reason that Stanford had followed him to the outback—the fortune! The damned fortune!

"But you allowed me to go with him on an outing," Sasha said, so relieved to finally know about his past—about the scar. He had been imprisoned wrongly! Stanford had attacked him wrongly!

Ashton chuckled low. "Allowed?" he said. "Sweet darlin', if I recall correctly, a team of horses couldn't have kept you from going with him that day.'' He frowned down at her. "Don't you know I wasn't ever that far from you? I wouldn't have ever let that man harm you."

Sasha blushed. "Do you mean you saw him try to—?"

"Aye, I saw."

"And you did not intercede?"

Ashton chuckled again. "You seemed to be doing quite well on your own," he said, his eyes dancing.

"As I could even today," Sasha said stubbornly. She pleaded up at him with her eyes. "Ashton, I have heard your warnings and understand exactly how careful I must be, and I shall be when I go and check on Bianca today. I shall be all right. I shall."

Ashton inhaled a shaky, irritated breath. He clasped hard onto her shoulders. "Haven't you heard anything I've said?" he demanded. "Sasha, this is not the time to be so stubborn. This time I find it less than amusing."

"But, Ashton, I wouldn't be gone long," Sasha pleaded. "I shall be traveling just across the river. Once I see that Bianca is all right then I shall return home."

The cabin lit up with a vivid sheen of light as lightning flashed incessantly outside. The floor shook beneath Sasha's feet, and her fear of the approaching storm was stronger than her fear of Stanford Sidwell. She would take her rifle. She would shoot him if he even threatened to come near her this time.

Crispin appeared suddenly at the door, his eyes wild. "Ashton, come quick!" he said breathlessly. "It's going to take all of us to keep the sheep and cattle from scattering. That damn lightning is spookin' them something fierce! They might even tear the fence down!"

Ashton shook his head, feeling torn by two different sorts of duties. One to his woman—and one to his sheep station! But he had no choice except to depend on Sasha's common sense. "All right, Crispin," he said, drawing Sasha closer to peer determinedly down at her. "I'll be there in a minute."

Crispin gave Ashton a mock salute and turned and ran back to his horse, mounting it in one leap. Ashton still gazed down at Sasha. "Now I can't tie you to the bedpost to make sure you stay here," he said. "So I've got to depend on you to think this through and do what you have to realize is logical. Do you want to take a chance of throwing all of this away because of Bianca? Would she do the same for you?"

More lurid flashes of lightning and the sound of men shouting in the distance tore Ashton away from Sasha. He gave her another long look, then rushed from the cabin.

Sasha wrung her hands as she went to the door and watched Ashton ride away. She continued to watch him until he was far into the distance, riding through the sea of sheep to join his men.

Then Sasha turned her eyes away, going over everything that Ashton had said to her. She now understood about his scar, and so much more, and she loved him no less for the truths he had spoken to her today.

But now, knowing so much more about Stanford Sidwell than before, Sasha could not help but be worried about Bianca more than ever. Bianca was living on a sheep station owned by a crazed, evil man! Surely she must be in danger! And though

Bianca was disliked by many because she had been a prostitute for most of her adult life, Sasha could not let that dissuade her from caring for her.

And she could not forget that Bianca was with child! The unborn child's welfare was at stake, also.

"I must go!" she whispered to herself. She marched across the cabin and grabbed her rifle.

Chapter Eighteen

As lightning flared overhead in continuous flashes, Sasha urged her horse into a canter up a slope where yellow grass waved. She drew Cloud to a halt atop one of the low ridges that, in this country, was as close as one got to a hill. From this vantage point she searched the river for a crossing point, knowing that Stanford had to have found a way since he had arrived at the sheep station more than once with his horse and buggy—and Bianca had also found a way across, somewhere.

Smiling, Sasha spied a ford where the river consisted of caked clay to the other side and a thick row of acacias lined its southeast bank. "That ought to do it," she whispered to herself. Clucking to her horse, she gave the reins a slap.

Blowing out a snort, Cloud galloped toward the river. There, Sasha's spine stiffened, hoping that she was not miscalculating the firmness of the clay beneath her horse's feet as she began inching Cloud across it. On each side of her, the river gleamed like a large hand mirror, lightning reflecting off it in deep purple flashes.

The wind moaned around her, and the air was muggy with the approaching rain. Sasha was glad to finally reach the other side, but she could not shake off the paralyzing dread that had seized her at the thought of bringing herself face to face with Stanford Sidwell again. Now that she knew of his criminal activities, she could not help but feel dispirited and uneasy.

Touching the rifle thrust into her gunboot, Sasha took from its nearness the courage that had driven her this far to check on Bianca's welfare. "I pray that I am worrying for naught," she whispered to herself.

A hare burst from a clump of grass ten yards away and raced for heavy cover, causing Sasha's heart to palpitate wildly.

Then, feeling foolish for letting herself be frightened so easily, she rode onward, then drew her horse into a gentle lope as she spied Stanford's cabin across a straight stretch of open field up just ahead.

With a sense of uneasiness hovering over her, she continued toward it, her gaze moving slowly around her. She did not see very many sheep grazing close to the cabin. Nor did she see a sheepherder tending the meager flock. And as she drew closer to the cabin, she discovered that it was cruder than her own, apparently just thrown together, as though it was meant only to be temporary.

It was hard to envision Stanford in such a setting. He was always well-dressed and dignified appearing —most likely a deliberate attempt to mislead those who did not know the full truth about him.

Inhaling a deep, nervous breath, Sasha traveled onward.

Taking an armload of dishes from the kitchen table to the washpan that stood on a wobbly stand across from the fireplace, Bianca cowered as Stanford made a move toward her. The previous night had been one of pain and humiliation—and worry about her unborn child. Now that Stanford knew she was pregnant, his fondness for inflicting pain on her while forcing himself upon her sexually had worsened. He was obviously trying to make her go into early labor so that she would lose her child.

The sound of a horse approaching outside was Bianca's reprieve this morning. It was the hour that most of Stanford's hired hands were still in the bunkhouse sleeping off their drunken stupors of the night before. The fact that Stanford called this place cut out of the outback a sheep station was a joke, to say the least. The men he had brought with him were for the most part retired bushrangers or lazy, shiftless tramps taken from the streets of Melbourne for low wages, if any at all. A bottle of whiskey seemed to be enough for them in the way of pay.

"Who the hell is that?" Stanford grumbled, fastening his sheathed knife at his waist. He went to the window and drew aside its sheepskin covering, taken aback when he discovered Sasha reining in her horse in front of the cabin.

"Well, I'll be damned," he said, smiling smugly. "Sasha has decided that she likes my company after all. What a willful woman! She's come searching me out."

"Sasha?" Bianca said softly, paling.

Stanford squared his shoulders as he turned to face Bianca. "Yes, Sasha," he said. "It seems that I won't have to depend solely on your bedroom activity to amuse me. Sasha will be my plaything for a while." He went and talked down into Bianca's face. "And she ain't no whore. She's a woman with class."

Bianca was cold with fear and this time it was not for herself and her unborn child. She was afraid for Sasha. Stanford had a heart of stone, and Sasha was too sweet and gentle to be a recipient of the sort of cruelties that he enjoyed inflicting on women.

Yet Bianca still could not speak up in Sasha's defense. As far as Stanford knew, Bianca and Sasha had never met.

Then a fearful thought suddenly came to Bianca. What if Sasha had come to see her—not Stanford! Then he would know that they had met and had talked. Would he believe Bianca when she told him that she had lied to Sasha about who her husband was, just as Stanford had ordered her to do? Or would he accuse her of lying to him?

Either way, she expected another beating as soon as Sasha left.

Stanford ignored the marked fear in Bianca's eyes, having grown used to it since they arrived in the outback, and sauntered from the cabin.

Sitting stiffly in the saddle, Sasha met Stanford's stare courageously as he moved toward her. She could tell by the smirk on his face that he thought she had come to see him. A shiver coursed through her when he stepped up to the horse and reached for her hand.

"Let me assist you from your mount," Stanford said, flinching when Sasha jerked her hand away from him. His smile wavered. "All right, stay on the damned horse." He placed his fists on his hips and glared up at her. "Why are you here?"

"I want to make it perfectly clear right now that I am not here to see you," Sasha said icily. She peered around her for any signs of Bianca, narrowing in on the makeshift bunkhouse that sat far back from the cabin. She hated to think that Bianca was having to share the bunkhouse with more than her husband. Surely her reputation had preceded her and she would be fair game for any man who had the notion to bed her. Sometimes even a husband could not protect his wife if a man's lusts were heightened.

"Then why have you come?" Stanford asked in a throaty growl. "Did Ashton send you with a message? I thought he got his piece said well enough to me the last time I saw him."

"Ashton does not even know that I am here," Sasha said, then regretted having been so truthful when Stanford's lips smoothed into another slow, smug smile.

"Oh, he doesn't, does he?" Stanford said, a hand moving to his sheathed knife, his fingers circling its handle. "Do you think that's smart, Sasha? Ain't you scared to death of the likes of me?"

Sasha shifted nervously in her saddle. Her fingers tightened on the horse's reins. "I do not frighten all that easily," she said, jumping with alarm when a great bolt of lightning streaked the heavens white above her.

"You ain't afraid, huh?" Stanford said, laughing. "Then why'd a mere streak of lightning almost scare the pants off you?" His laughter faded and his eyes narrowed. "Sasha, you're choosin' the wrong things to be afraid of. Now take me for example . . ."

Tired of bantering with him and wanting to get to her reason for coming, Sasha interrupted, "I have come to see Bianca," she said. "I'm worried about her."

Rage suddenly lit Stanford's eyes. He doubled a fist to his side. "How do you know about Bianca being here?" he growled.

"Is it supposed to be some sort of deep, dark secret?" Sasha taunted bravely.

"How did you know she was here?" Stanford demanded again, glancing at the cabin, then back at Sasha.

"If you insist, Bianca and I met one day while bathing in the river," Sasha said, awash again with a feeling of uneasiness. "But I saw her only that one day. Is she ill?"

"No, she ain't ill," Stanford said, frustration setting in. How was he to know what Bianca had said to Sasha? He was beginning to realize that it had been a mistake to bring her to the outback with him. She could cause his plans to get his hands on the chest of riches to go awry.

"Then perhaps you don't mind if Bianca and I talk for a while," Sasha said, boldly swinging herself out of the saddle. She looked again at the bunkhouse as men began to amble from the dwelling.

Sasha looked up at Stanford. She set her jaw and squared her shoulders stubbornly. "I presume that you would have no reason not to let me go to the bunkhouse and see her," she said. "It is rather nice to have a woman in thcse parts to have conversation with."

Stanford laughed at that. "You call her a woman?" he said. "I call her a whore." He thrust his hands uneasily inside his front breeches pockets. "Why would a woman of your breeding want anything to do with the likes of Bianca, anyhow?"

"I do not set myself above anyone," Sasha said, anger flaring in her eyes. "Now if you will excuse me I shall show myself to the bunkhouse and see Bianca. I see no need to await your permission."

Stanford swung around in front of Sasha, blocking her way and stopping her as she boldly moved toward the bunkhouse. "She ain't in the bunkhouse," hc said.

Surprised, Sasha stared up at him. "Then . . . whcre is she?" she murmured. "She told me that she was married to one of your sheepherders. I see no other cabins, so that must mean that she shares the bunkhouse with not only her husband, but—but also the rest of your hired hands."

The sky was darkening overhead. Thunderheads were billowing along the horizon in deep grays against the velvety black heavens. Lightning forked incessantly across the sky, and the ground shook threateningly beneath Sasha's feet, unnerving her even more. She feared her return journey across the river. If the rain wetted the jut of clay that she had used to ford the river, she might not be able to make it back across safely. She did not want to be forced to swim across. If the water deepened due to the storm, the rapids could become fierce. She had almost lost her life once already due to crazed waters in the outback!

Stanford quickly thought up a lie that could seem convincing enough. "She ain't there right now," he said quickly. "Early every mornin' she comes to my cabin and prepares my breakfast and cleans things up for me." He chuckled beneath his breath. "You might call her my maid."

"Oh?" Sasha said, forking an eyebrow. "Then would you please tell her that I am here? I don't have long. The storm is getting closer. I fear it is going to be a bad one."

"We can't have you gettin' more scared by the storm, can we?" Stanford taunted. He spun around and walked toward his cabin. "I'll get Bianca, but don't keep her long. I've better things for her to do than to waste time in idle chit-chat with you."

Sasha frowned. Something deep within her made her believe that Bianca was not in Stanford's cabin in the capacity of a maid at all. He was too possessive of her.

And was the child his instead of a sheepherder's?

Was Bianca even married to a sheepherder?

Sasha could not sort out the truth among what seemed to be too many deceptions.

Stanford stormed into the cabin. He grabbed Bianca by the hair and yanked her face close to his as he leaned down into it. "You bitch," he hissed. "You didn't tell me that you were at the river with

Sasha. What'd you tell her? She surely ain't come here today just from the goodness of her heart. She's usin' you to spy on me. What'd you tell her?" He yanked her hair harder, causing Bianca to stifle a cry of pain behind her hand.

"I told her nothing, Stanford," Bianca sobbed. "Except what you told me to. I told her I was married to your sheepherder. That's all."

"And you saw her only once?" he demanded, his breath hot on her face.

"I purposely did not return to the river so I could avoid seeing her," Bianca said, tears streaming from her eyes. "I knew the danger of opening up too much to her. And she is so nice! I did not want to endanger her by becoming too friendly with her. I am innocent of any wrongdoing, Stanford. Innocent!"

Stanford ran his fingers over the contusions on Bianca's face and neck. "I'll let you go and talk with her, but as for your bruises, should she ask, tell her you fell off a horse," he said, snickering. He released her hair and gave her a shove toward the door. "Now get out there and satisfy her curiosity. Then get rid of her."

"I will," Bianca said, giving him occasional glances over her shoulder as she inched her way toward the door. "I will."

She fled outside, for the moment free of Stanford's abuses. If only she could confide in Sasha! If only she could plead for her help! But both she and Sasha would be in danger, and it was not fair to include Sasha in her own sad, perilous affairs.

She forced a smile as she walked in a slow gait

toward Sasha. Her fingers went to her neck in an attempt to hide the worst bruises. But she could tell by Sasha's astonished look that she had seen the bruises—all of them.

And she knew that Sasha was too astute to believe that they had been caused by a fall from a horse.

Chapter Nineteen

The sight of at least a dozen horsemen leaving Stanford's sheep station was momentarily distracting, causing Sasha to look toward them as they rode in the direction of the river.

Then her thoughts were brought back to Bianca. Sasha's first impulse was to embrace her, but she held herself at bay when she saw how uneasy Bianca was, not making any effort herself to offer such a welcome.

Sasha was badly shaken when she discovered the contusions on Bianca's lovely, dark face. It was obvious that she had been beaten.

But by whom? Surely by Stanford! He was the sort who could be guilty of such a crime—had he not left Ashton scarred for life?

Sasha's gaze went past Bianca and her insides grew cold when she saw Stanford standing in the door of the cabin leering at them both. At this distance he would be able to hear anything that was said and because of this Sasha would have to guard her every word. Perhaps by coming today, she had already placed Bianca in jeopardy. Sasha felt utterly helpless.

"You shouldn't have come," Bianca whispered, her back to Stanford so that she had some semblance of freedom to speak.

"You haven't been at the river," Sasha said. "I was concerned."

"I have been too ill," Bianca said, her voice breaking. She placed a hand on her abdomen. "My baby. I feared for my baby after a fall from . . . from a horse."

Sasha paled. She wanted to reach out for Bianca to comfort her, yet again she refrained from doing so. Stanford staring at her was like having the eyes of the devil on her. "You fell from a horse?" she gasped. She searched Bianca's face and neck again, studying the contusions. Could that be how she had truly become bruised?

Sasha's jaw tightened. She very much doubted if Bianca was being truthful. Surely she had been coerced into lying. "I see," she murmured. "I am so sorry." She gazed down at Bianca's swollen abdomen. "Did the fall harm the child?" She wanted to ask if her beatings had harmed the child!

But she had to hope that she was coming to all the wrong conclusions and that Bianca had indeed fallen from a horse. It would be simpler.

But one usually fell from a horse only once. Beatings from a man could be repeated numerous times!

Bianca rested her hands on her abdomen. "I am a lucky woman," she said, smiling weakly at Sasha. "My child is still moving within my womb."

"More rest would be good for your health," Sasha said, looking uneasily past Bianca at Stanford. She then looked into Bianca's green eyes. She leaned into her face, blocking Stanford's view of her lips. "Meet me again soon at the river. I shall be looking for you."

"I don't know," Bianca whispered back.

"Are you afraid of someone?" Sasha dared to ask, then jumped with alarm when Stanford was suddenly there, standing threateningly at Bianca's side.

"There's been enough talk between you two," he said, glaring down at Sasha. "If you want to beat the storm, you'd best leave now."

"Yes, I'd best go," Sasha murmured, knowing that he did not want her to leave because of his concern over her welfare. He wanted to get rid of her for his own selfish, evil reasons.

She glanced up at the sky as another flash of lightning streaked across the heavens, then looked back at Bianca. "I hope all will be well with you," she said, wanting to say so much more, yet forced not to. She prayed she would get a chance later.

Bianca said nothing. With her heart aching to go with Sasha, to be freed of this madman at her side, she watched Sasha mount her horse and ride away.

Then she winced with pain as Stanford grabbed her wrist and twisted it behind her, forcing her toward the cabin.

"You should've told me about meeting Sasha at the river," he growled. "Bianca, you should've told me. Now you're going to pay for your negligence.

I'm going to give you a beating you'll never forget."

Bianca knew better than to beg for mercy. That always made Stanford inflict more pain than when she took her punishment in silence.

But with every beating and tongue lashing, her hate for him swelled. In time, she would reach her limits, and she hoped she would have the courage to make him pay then.

The first drop of rain hit Sasha's face just as her horse gained a solid footing after successfully crossing the river again without a mishap. Badly wanting to reach home before the worst of the storm hit, she gave the reins a slap. One lightning bolt after another flashed overhead in lurid zigzags, and then it was as though the heavens had been ripped open by the lightning when the rain began to fall in a torrent.

Soaked to the bone, Sasha pressed her heels into the flanks of her horse, leaning low over its wild and flying mane. The wind was blowing and howling around her, threatening to topple her from the saddle. Bits and pieces of debris sailed past her, some hitting her face in stinging bites.

"At last!" she cried, seeing through the haze of rain the fence that outlined her sheep station. She slapped her reins again, sending her horse into a harder gallop. She locked her knees to the horse, trying not to slip from the wet saddle.

Finally within the safe confines of the fence, she rode onward, not unaware of the commotion around her. Through the sheets of rain she could see many horsemen trying to keep the frightened sheep and cattle from scattering. A sick feeling grabbed her at the pit of her stomach when she saw several dead sheep trampled by those that were running crazed in all directions.

Then she spied Ashton among the men. Wiping the streamers of rain from her face, she wheeled her horse around and rode toward him. When she reached him, he gave her a frenzied look.

"What the hell are you doing out here in this damnable storm?" he shouted, reining in beside her.

She gave him a silent stare, knowing it was best not to tell him the truth, yet hating to have to lie. He had told her not to go to Stanford's sheep station.

Yet how could she not tell him? Bianca was obviously in some sort of trouble. She needed help!

She started to tell him the truth, but was stopped when Crispin came riding suddenly up to Ashton, his face a mask of despair.

Ashton turned to Crispin, searching his friend's eyes and seeing too much there that made his insides knot up. Crispin had gone to check on Rufus. By the look on Crispin's face he had not brought back a favorable report.

"Well?" Ashton shouted through the howling wind and pouring rain. "How's he doing, Crispin? Did some of the men stay behind to give him a helping hand? Damn it! I should've gone there myself at the first signs of this storm. Out there all alone in such weather, Rufus is defenseless."

Crispin lowered his eyes, then looked slowly back up at Ashton. "I'm sorry, Ashton," he said, his voice haunted. He emitted a loud sob, then choked back another one. "Ashton, when I got there the sheep were gone and—and Rufus's neck was broken!"

Ashton teetered in his saddle. He stared disbelievingly at Crispin. "His . . . neck . . . broken?" he gasped. He looked away from Crispin, his pulse racing. In his mind's eye he was seeing Rufus laughing and joking—the gentlest man Ashton had ever known.

And now, killed by a flock of sheep?

What in life was fair?

"Someone killed him, Ashton," Crispin offered bitterly. "He was murdered, Ashton. Murdered!" He swallowed hard. "And those sheep he was in charge of are not among those that are scattering. Those sheep that Rufus was watching are gone! Stolen!"

Sasha inched her horse closer to Ashton's. She reached for his hand and clasped it comfortingly. "Ashton, this is so terrible," she murmured, tears swelling in her eyes. She blinked raindrops from her lashes. "Who could . . . ?"

She suddenly recalled seeing several horsemen leaving Stanford's sheep station, headed in the direction of the river. Could they . . . ?

Now she knew that she had no choice but to tell why she was out in the rain and where she had been. She had to tell Ashton about the horsemen! Perhaps they were responsible for Rufus's murder and the theft of the sheep!

"Ashton, I think I may know who is responsible for everything," she blurted out.

Ashton looked over at her with squinted eyes. "How could you know anything about this?" he asked, wiping rain from his face with the back of his sleeve.

"Ashton, I was over at Stanford's sheep station talking with Bianca and—and I saw several men ride away in the direction of the river," she said, glad that the rain and howling winds had slowed down somewhat.

Ashton's jaw tightened. "You went there after I told you not to?" he said, anger flaring in his eyes.

"You knew that I would," was all that Sasha could think to say.

"You're impossible, Sasha," Ashton grumbled. "I warned you of the dangers!"

"But, Ashton, if I hadn't been there, I wouldn't have seen Stanford's hired hands leaving his sheep station in the direction of ours," Sasha defended herself. "Why would they be riding toward our land if not to cause some sort of trouble?" She swallowed a lump in her throat at the mention of Rufus— sweet, gentle Rufus. "Could Stanford hate you so much that he would order that Rufus be killed?"

"Stanford Sidwell is capable of anything, especially vile acts against another human being," Ashton said, shaking his head. He looked in the distance where the rain had now stopped. "But I also have other enemies. Ajax. And . . ."

He did not voice his worries about Silas Howland possibly being behind Rufus's death. There had been no signs that Silas knew of his whereabouts. At least, not yet. . . .

He spun his horse around and began riding away. "Come with me, Crispin!" he shouted. "We'll go and see what Stanford has to say about this." He gave Sasha a harried look. "You stay home and out of trouble, Sasha. Damn it, you'd best listen to me this time!"

Sasha nodded. Dispirited, deeply saddened over Rufus's death, worried over Bianca's welfare, and missing the dingo pup so much that it cut into her bruised heart even more, she rode on toward the cabin. Suddenly she heard a terrible bawling. She wheeled her horse to a stop and looked around her, trying to find the source of the sound. Her insides froze when she discovered a cow that had gotten its head snagged between the rails of the fence that circled the barn, its horns keeping the animal from being able to jerk itself free.

"Oh, no," Sasha moaned, looking around her for anyone who could free the cow. Everyone was out in the pasture worrying about the sheep. She was the only one to offer this pitiful creature assistance.

But how? Its horns were totally locked between the slats of the fence!

Weary, her shoulders sagging, Sasha dismounted. She guided Cloud into the barn and secured her in a stall, then went back outside and studied the cow's dilemma again. Continuously bawling, the cow looked up at her with its big, woeful eyes.

"Settle down," Sasha murmured, petting the cow on its rump. "I'll get you free. Somehow."

She bent low over the animal and studied the horns, then gave the cow a despairing look. "I see no other choice but to remove your horns," she whispered, sighing heavily.

She shuddered at the thought.

But she had chosen to come out to the wilds of the outback and live on a sheep station, in partnership with Ashton, which meant that she had the responsibility of seeing to the animals under her care.

Desperately, she looked around her again, hoping

to find someone else to do the honor of sawing off this poor cow's horns.

But no one was in sight. They all had their own duties to attend to today.

Her thoughts went to Ashton, wondering if he would find out anything at Stanford's sheep station. She doubted it. Stanford had ways of covering up all of his dirty deeds. Even Bianca had surely been coerced by Stanford to lie to Sasha about her bruises.

Sasha hurried into the barn and searched for a hand saw. When she found one hanging on a peg on the wall, she took it down with trembling fingers. Clutching its handle, she went back outside to the cow. She felt a sick feeling at the pit of her stomach. When she began sawing on one of the horns, the cow not only bawled now, but emitted loud screams that made shivers race up and down Sasha's spine.

The cow kicked and jerked, and its eyes were wild, but finally one of its horns dropped to the ground.

Sasha tried to reassure the cow. "Perhaps I won't have to saw the other one off," she said, placing the saw on the ground. She tried to force the cow's head back through the fence, but it would not budge.

"I'm sorry," Sasha whispered, now sawing on the other horn. "But you will soon be free. That's all that matters."

Finally the other horn dropped to the ground. The cow lurched and bucked, and when it discovered that it was free, it backed up and ran in a crazed circle until it got its bearings, then wandered peacefully into the barn. Sasha followed it and replaced the saw on its peg.

Her wet hair stringing down her back, she went to the cabin. Shivering and chilled clear through to the bone, she stood at the fireplace and held her hands over the flames. Again she was filled with worry for Ashton. Just how far would Stanford go with this hate he had for Ashton? Just how much would Ashton stand for before retaliating in kind?

"Oh, Ashton, please keep safe," she whispered to herself, choking back a sob of fear.

Chapter Twenty

The river had risen. Holding his rifle up in the air away from the suction of the current, Ashton moved waist-high through the water on his horse. When he finally reached the bank, he nudged his horse's sides with his knees, urging it up the slippery, muddy bank to level, drier ground.

Crispin following his lead, Ashton snapped his reins and urged his horse into a gallop through tall, waving grasses, his hand still clutching his rifle. Suddenly several horsemen appeared ahead, riding at neck-breaking speed toward Ashton and Crispin, Stanford Sidwell at the lead.

"Looks as though we're goin' to meet trouble head on," Crispin shouted at Ashton. "What say we take a stand, Ashton, and show them we can't be intimidated by them?"

"Sounds fine to me," Ashton said, wheeling his horse to a shuddering halt beside Crispin. They both held their rifles steady, aiming into the center of the oncoming horsemen.

As Stanford came close enough to Ashton and Crispin to almost smell their horses' breaths, he raised a fist into the air, giving the signal for his men to stop.

He then inched his horse slowly forward, smiling crookedly from Ashton to Crispin. "Seems you two are a mite lost, wouldn't you say?" he said. "I lay claim to this parcel of land now. It don't need the likes of you two contaminating it."

He peered intently at the aimed rifles. "And I don't think it's wise to keep pointin' those firearms at my men," he warned. "It might cause one of them to get trigger-happy."

"I welcome anyone who might want to try drawing his firearm against me," Ashton said. His finger was planted solidly on the trigger of his rifle. "It'd be my pleasure to teach him a few tricks of my own when it comes to firearms."

Stanford shifted in his saddle as Ashton slowly moved the barrel of his rifle so that it was now directed squarely at him. He gave his men a look across his shoulder. "Don't do nothin' foolish," he said, his voice drawn. "We can handle this thing peacefully. Don't do nothin' till I tell you to. Do you hear?"

Ashton's violet eyes danced as he smiled smugly at Stanford. "Now that's more like it," he said, still not lowering his rifle. "I like a man who cooperates."

"Aim that rifle somewhere else," Stanford grumbled, sweat pearling his brow. "One slip of the finger and—"

"And you'd be history?" Ashton said, chuckling. "I don't think anyone would miss you."

"Get on with why you saw fit to come on my land," Stanford said, wiping the nervous perspiration from his brow with the back of a hand.

"Are you going to try to pretend that you don't know?" Crispin exclaimed, astonished. In his mind's eye he could still see Rufus lying lifeless, his neck broken, his eyes staring blankly upwards. "Are you going to deny that one of your men came on our property and killed Rufus and stole some of our sheep? Sidwell, if I had my druthers I wouldn't have come by day to see you. I'd have sneaked up on you in the middle of the night and broke your neck just like you ordered Rufus's to be broken!"

Stanford was not touched or swayed by Crispin's threats. "So one of your men died during the storm, eh?" he said, leaning his weight on his saddle horn. "Why, I'm sure sorry to hear it." He looked over his shoulder at his men again. "Is there anyone among you who wants to come forward and admit to the dastardly crime?"

Low rumblings of laughter wafted through the air. Ashton's insides tightened as fury mounted within him. "You son of a bitch," he growled. "Your smugness proves your guilt. You'll pay for this. You'll pay."

Stanford inched his horse a fraction closer to Ashton's. "All kidding aside," he said threateningly, "you aren't the only one who has a murder to report today. One of my men was murdered also. And several of my sheep were stolen."

Ashton was taken aback by what Stanford said, then he squinted his eyes at him. "Do you expect me to believe that?" he questioned.

Stanford waved a hand toward one of his men. "Go and bring the body so that we can prove that what I say is the truth!" he shouted. "And make it snappy. We've got two men here who need convincin'."

One of Stanford's men swung around and rode away toward his sheep station. Stanford's lips curled into a slow smile, having expected Ashton's arrival and prepared himself for it. Stanford knew that he would need a body to prove his point and he had not batted an eye when he had ordered one of his most devoted followers to break the neck of the most lazy and useless of his hired hands while he was sleeping off a drunken stupor.

As for Ashton's stolen sheep—to hide the evidence, Stanford had ordered his men to kill and bury them.

The waiting was filled with a strained silence, and then Ashton sat taller in his saddle to watch as Stanford's hired hand reappeared in the distance, leading a horse on which a body lay across its back.

"And so you do have a body to show us," Ashton said, his eyes following the approach of the lifeless man. "How am I to know that he was killed by the same man who killed Rufus?"

Stanford shrugged as the man draped across the horse was brought to Ashton for closer inspection. "All I can tell you is that this man was my best sheepherder and someone broke his neck sometime during the night," he said, the lie on his lips coming as easily as breathing. "I've lost a valuable property

256

in this man—as well as several prime head of sheep!"

Ashton lowered his rifle and slipped it into his gunboot. He gazed at the dead man, then looked slowly back at Stanford, the evidence too strong not to believe him. They had both lost a sheepherder in the same ugly way—and both had lost several head of sheep.

"So it seems there's someone we both have to keep an eye out for," Ashton finally said. He glanced at Crispin and saw in his glare that Crispin was not buying Stanford's story as quickly as Ashton. He looked back at the dead man, then at Stanford. "Any ideas who it might be?"

Stanford took a half-smoked cigar and a match from his inside coat pocket. He placed the cigar between his lips and scraped a thumbnail against the head of the match, lighting it. "Do you remember the kangarooer Ajax?" he said, placing the flaming match to his cigar. He sucked on the cigar until it was lit, then shook the match out and tossed it aside.

"Who could forget that son of a bitch?" Ashton said, patting his horse's head when the horse whinnied and began pawing the ground with its hoof. He forked an eyebrow. "What about him?"

"He came by here the other day," Stanford said matter-of-factly, closely watching Ashton as he talked. "He laid a few threats on me. Did he do the same to you?"

Ashton raked his fingers through his hair as he tried to recall what Ajax had said exactly. "Somewhat," he said finally. "What of it?"

"I think he's the one you should be accusin' of

murder and thievery instead of me," Stanford said, chewing on the tip of his cigar.

"You think so, do you?" Ashton said, glancing down at the dead sheepherder again. He remembered now that Ajax had tossed around one threat after another. He could be responsible for Rufus's death—possibly even for Lightning's disappearance. He had showed no love at all for the pet dingo.

Crispin edged his horse closer to Ashton. "Don't listen to him," he urged Ashton. "You know he can't be trusted."

Stanford frowned at Crispin, thinking that perhaps the wrong man had been murdered during the storm. Crispin was an interfering bastard. Without him in the way, Stanford would have a much easier time succeeding in his plans to get at the chest filled with riches.

"Our men could join forces in searching for Ajax," Stanford quickly interjected, focusing his full attention on Ashton now. "We could string him up for what he's done to us."

Ashton leaned forward and looked Stanford square in the eyes. "It'll be a cold day in hell when I ride anywhere with you," he said, his teeth clenched. "As for who is guilty and who is not, I'll find out—and, if you've lied to me today, I'll be back to finish what I had originally planned for you."

Stanford's eyes narrowed. He took his cigar from his mouth and flipped it across his shoulder. "The next time you come on my land, you'd best bring more than your sidekick," he growled. "A pantywaist like him wouldn't do you no good against the kind of men under my employ." He wheeled his horse around and kicked the heels of his boots into the animal's flanks unmercifully, then rode away in a fury, his men following him.

Ashton and Crispin watched them for a moment. Crispin was the first to speak. "You don't truly believe that Ajax killed Rufus, do you?" he asked, thrusting his rifle into his gunboot.

"If I hadn't seen the body of a man killed the identical way that Rufus was, I'd have been less apt to listen to Stanford," Ashton said, turning his horse toward the river. "Because there was a body, and the man was under Stanford's employ, I have to give the bastard con artist the benefit of the doubt." He smiled sardonically over at Crispin. "At least he thinks so anyhow, doesn't he?"

"Then you don't believe him," Crispin said, spurring his horse to stay at a steady stride beside Ashton's steed.

"Not on your life," Ashton said. "But I aim to get proof. Ajax'll be glad to point an accusing finger at his old enemy. He'll even help place the noose around his neck."

"But there ain't no love lost between you and Ajax, either," Crispin said.

"True," Ashton said, nodding. "And he just might be the one who is guilty of this horrendous crime today. Perhaps he's even killed Lightning. I'm going to hunt him down and get answers out of him." He lowered his eyes. "But first we must give Rufus a proper burial."

"Let's bury him where the stars will shine upon his grave all night long," Crispin said, his voice emotion-filled. "And where he can hear the bleating of the sheep both night and day. Perhaps then he can rest in peace."

Ashton nodded. Tears shone at the corners of his eyes.

The sky had shed its clouds, and the sun overhead was so brilliant it made Sasha draw her eyes into a squint as Ashton finished reading words from a Bible over the fresh mound of earth dug on the top of the knoll that overlooked The Homestead and the vast spaces of the outback. Sheep grazed peacefully nearby and birds sang in the eucalyptus trees that swayed with the wind only a few yards away.

"And so, Rufus, my good friend, I shall say my final good-bye," Ashton said, closing the Bible. He clutched it with one hand and held it behind him. "Mate, we shall meet again—in that great beyond."

Sasha lowered her eyes and sniffled, then looked guiltily up at Ashton again, knowing that what she had planned would make him rant and rave at her again for her stubbornness.

But she would not allow him to order her to stay behind while he rode off with his men to search for Ajax. She felt that she had as much right to go on this manhunt as anyone else. She had respected and loved Rufus. She might even get a chance to finally find out what had happened to sweet Lightning!

And she did not want to stay behind at The Homestead, not knowing when she might see Ashton again. There was no doubt of the danger he would be in by searching for men like the kangarooers. Nor was there any doubt that she was putting herself in danger by wanting to be with Ashton should he have an encounter that might delay his ever coming home to her again!

Running her hand down the front of her skirt, she could feel the bulkiness of the breeches that she wore beneath it. For her plan to follow behind Ashton on horseback, she had decided it would be best to wear men's attire again. And as soon as Ashton rode away all she had to do was jerk off her skirt, slip into a loose shirt, and yank on her boots. She would follow behind him far enough so that he would not notice until they were deep into the outback that he could not chance sending her back alone. He would be forced to let her join the manhunt, whether he liked it or not!

Crispin cleared his voice noisily as he stepped closer to Rufus's grave. He clutched his hat, squeezing it hard between his long, narrow fingers. "My friend, what can I say?" he began, choking back a sob. "So much is missing in my life without you. You always made me laugh, even when I wanted to cuss. What can I say? Except good-bye and . . . and make 'em laugh wherever you are, do you hear?"

Ashton looked over his shoulder at his men waiting for him on their horses, their saddlebags filled with enough equipment and food to last for several days in the outback.

He then turned to Sasha and placed his fingers gently to her shoulders. "I've got to go," he murmured. "I'm glad you've not caused a fuss about wanting to go with me. It's not a place for a woman."

"I understand," Sasha said, blinking her eyes up at him. "Please be careful, Ashton. That bunch of kangarooers looked so dangerous."

"Don't worry about me," he said, drawing her into his embrace. He hugged her tightly. "But I'll be worrying about you. Don't take any risks. Stay close to home and keep a rifle loaded at all times."

"I shall," Sasha said, reveling in the feel of his arms around her. When he discovered that she had not stayed true to her words and had followed him, he might never hold her again!

"I must go," Ashton said, stepping away from her. He gave Crispin a nod, and Crispin brought his horse to him. "But first I'll see you safely back to the house."

"That's not necessary," Sasha said, smoothing her skirt down as the wind threatened to lift it and reveal the breeches beneath it. "It's not that far."

She glanced over at a thick stand of eucalyptus trees and got a glimpse of the horse that she had left hidden there, her boots, shirt and travel attire waiting for her in the saddlebag.

She then looked innocently up at Ashton and melted inside when his mouth lowered and met her lips in a sweet and lingering kiss.

Then he swung away from her and mounted his horse. She waved at him as he rode away, then smiling mischievously, ran toward her horse.

Chapter Twenty-One

After a full day in the saddle, her eyes never losing sight of Ashton as he and his men rode ahead of her, Sasha had felt a sense of dread as shadows began to lengthen when the sun dipped behind the mountains in the distance. Night had too quickly dropped a dark purple blanket over the world, but not before Sasha was able to see Ashton's campsite for the night. She had just as quickly chosen one for herself, yet she was alone—totally alone—in it.

Her horse grazing close by, her hat still firmly on her head to hide her hair coiled in tight braids, Sasha huddled beneath a blanket up against a gum tree, shivering. "I'm hungry," she whispered to herself, having gotten her travel gear together so quickly that she had forgotten to put food in her saddlebag. "I'm cold." Her gaze moved slowly around her. She swallowed hard. "And I'm frightened."

Her rifle was on her lap, and she slipped a hand around it for comfort. She peered into the distance where Ashton and his men had made camp. Strangely, she saw no signs of a campfire.

"Then what are they eating?" Sasha further worried aloud. She licked her lips and closed her eyes, leaning her head against the trunk of the tree. She could envision herself eating her homemade yeast cakes, fried chicken, and potatoes. The mere thought made her stomach growl unmercifully, filling the silent night air with the strangest of sounds.

Her eyes flew wildly open. "What am I doing to myself?" she uttered. "I can't allow myself to think of food. Not tonight, anyhow. Perhaps by daylight I can find something to eat."

She drew the blanket more snugly around her shoulders, watching Cloud munching on grass a few yards away from her. "Cloud, what will tomorrow bring?" she asked softly. "Will Ashton find the kangarooers, or will I be forced to ride endlessly onward in this empty land?"

She became lost in thought, remembering how the landscape she had traveled through too often faded to brindle, stunted gray stuff in yellow grass. The outback was dangerous—its emptiness, its lack of definition, the bizarre, even threatening, character of its flora and fauna.

Yet it could just as quickly become a place of awesome beauty—the red monoliths rising out of the flat land; the rare waterholes cold, clear and deep; and the primordial splendor of the vast, patterned landscapes laid out under a cerulean sky.

"And then there is now," Sasha fussed aloud, her stomach aching from emptiness. She looked skyward, glad to see the moon slipping out from behind the clouds, lighting the ground and trees around her.

She surveyed the land around her, then her eyes widened and her mouth watered. Not that far away, in a growth of tangles and silence, were what some Australians referred to as an exotic plague—vines of blackberries crowding out tree ferns.

Tossing her blanket aside, Sasha rushed to the vines and began plucking the round, thick, juicy morsels, eagerly plopping them into her mouth. They not only fed her hunger, but quenched her thirst!

Then she felt her heart drop to her feet when a hand clasped suddenly over her mouth, and another grabbed her around the waist. Her eyes were wild with fear. In her haste to get nourishment, she had left her rifle beside the tree!

She started to fight back but stood perfectly still when, all cold and menacing, the barrel of a revolver was thrust against her back.

"You've strayed a mite too far from the rest of the *kangarooers*, haven't you?" the man said in a low growl. "When I came to pluck some of these berries that I saw before making camp, I didn't plan to find something even more valuable. When I slip my fingers from your mouth easy-like, tell me where Ajax is making camp—or else when tomorrow comes you won't be in any shape to tell anyone anything."

Sasha's eyes widened above the heavy hand, recognizing the voice and relieved because of it. It was Ashton!

Yet, when he realized who he had just captured, she knew there would be hell to pay.

But wasn't it time to give up her charade, anyhow? They were far enough from home for Ashton not to send her back after scolding her!

As the hand slipped away from her mouth, Sasha smiled devilishly to herself. What if she played this game just a bit longer? It was apparent that the moonlight had not yet given away her true identity to Ashton. In her breeches, and with her hat covering her head and shadowing her face, she could go on teasing him indefinitely.

Except she did not dare take it too far. His finger could get itchy on the trigger of his revolver. . . .

Cloud whinnied suddenly, drawing Ashton's attention away from Sasha. Beneath the covering of the clouds earlier, he had not seen the reined horse. But now, the moonlight so bright and revealing, Cloud was plain to see and looked like a great white ghost against the backdrop of night.

"What?" Ashton exclaimed, lowering his revolver. "Cloud? Damn it, I'd know that horse anywhere!"

Knowing that her game was up, Sasha turned slowly around and faced Ashton. She slipped her hat off and looked up at him, her eyes dancing.

Ashton glared down at her, his gaze taking in her attire, and then the mischief in her eyes. "You never learn, do you?" he finally said, his own eyes stormy. "Here you are in men's clothing again, and this time you almost got your head blown off because of it."

He twirled his revolver into its holster and grabbed Sasha roughly by the shoulders. "What are you doing here?'' he demanded hotly. ''Or need I ask?''

''I wanted to come with you and you know it,'' she said stubbornly.

''But you said that you would stay home,'' he growled back.

''Sometimes it is necessary to go back on one's word,'' Sasha defended herself. ''I have as much right to search for Rufus's killer as you. Do you forget so easily that we are in partnership together?''

Ashton gave her a little shake. ''I intend to change the status of that partnership one day, he said. ''When you become my wife, I hope you will know your place—and it won't be to accompany me on manhunts!''

Sasha was torn with feelings—wondrous feelings to think that he cared enough to make her his legal wife, yet angry feelings to realize that he still set her apart from him in that she did not have the ability to participate in all sorts of exciting ventures.

Sasha shook herself free of his hands. ''One cannot be sure of anything except the present,'' she said, rubbing her shoulder where it still stung from his tight grip. ''And as for now, you can quit being so bullish. Yes, perhaps I did make a mistake riding off without telling you, but I am here and there is nothing you can do about it.''

Ashton sighed heavily and wove his fingers frustratingly through his hair. ''I suppose you are right.'' His eyes softened as he gazed down at her. ''Do you truly know the danger you put yourself in by traveling alone? My God, woman, were you intending to sleep here all alone? Anyone could've come up on you in the middle of the night and taken advantage of you. Men are always hungry for women in the outback."

"Don't forget that I am dressed like a man," Sasha reminded him, lifting her chin stubbornly. "*You* were fooled."

His lips tugged into a smile. "So, Spike, what am I to do with you? Leave you here to prove that you can defend yourself from all sorts of animals, two and four-legged, or do I take you to my camp and to bed with me?"

A hot flush rose up to Sasha's cheeks at the prospect of sharing any sort of bed with him again, be it beneath the roof of their cabin or beneath the stars. She smiled bashfully up at Ashton. "Do I have a choice?" she teased.

"Do you need one?" Ashton countered.

Sasha smiled up at him a moment longer, then flung herself into his arms. "Oh, Ashton, I am so glad that you aren't really all that angry with me," she said, sighing. "And, yes, I want to go back to your camp with you. It's—it's been horrid being alone. Just horrid!"

He placed his hands to her cheeks and lifted her face so that their eyes could meet. "I will bed you tonight, but tomorrow you must return home with one of our men as your escort," he said firmly. "It can't be any other way, Sasha. Do you hear?"

Her blood running hot with a sudden anger, Sasha jerked herself away from him. Grabbing up her blanket and rifle, she marched to her horse and, fitting a foot in a stirrup, swung herself up into the saddle. Taking the reins, she gave Ashton an angry stare as he hurried to her horse's side.

"On second thought, Ashton, I choose to sleep alone tonight after all," she said icily. "And as for tomorrow, no one is going to escort me anywhere. I shall be riding along with you and our men unless you want to shoot me to stop me."

She started to snap the reins but Ashton was too quick and grabbed them from her hands. "You drongo," he growled. "If you want to go with me tomorrow, then so be it. But when blood is shed, do not come to me with shocked, teary eyes. I will not comfort you. You will learn your lesson of violence without my shoulder to cry on. Do you understand?"

Eyes wide, Sasha swallowed hard. "Yes, I understand," she said faintly. She flinched when Ashton quickly mounted behind her, his one arm possessively around her waist. When he flicked the reins and clucked to Cloud, the horse obeyed.

They rode beneath the moonlight in silence, Sasha very aware of Ashton's firm body pressed against her. Without looking, she could easily define his narrow hips, his hard, flat stomach, and his long, firm legs.

In her mind's eye, she could even see his brooding expression, his brow knit in worried thought.

Surrounded by his hard, strong arm pressing her against him, she could not deny the fires that were being ignited inside her, her desire a sharp, hot pain deep within her soul.

When Ashton drew rein and dismounted, he led Cloud to graze among the other horses. As he took Sasha from the saddle, his hands hot through the thin fabric of her shirt, her breathing became harsh

269

and her heart was beating so profoundly, she felt as though it might consume her.

With no conscious thought for the other men lying around—some in small tents, others sleeping beneath the stars—Sasha melted into Ashton's embrace as he wrapped his arms around her, his mouth lowering to her lips. His tongue brushed her lips lightly, teasing her. His hands were slipping up her shirt.

Everything within Sasha turned to sweetness when Ashton's large, warm hands cupped her breasts. She twined her fingers through his hair and drew his lips more fully into hers, kissing him with a wild abandon.

With yearning, their bodies strained together. Sasha sighed when Ashton gyrated himself against her, and she felt his hard readiness pressing into her abdomen through their layers of clothing.

Someone snoring from close by brought Sasha to her senses. Dizzy with rapture but feeling that she should have more control, she eased away from Ashton. "We can't," she whispered, looking up into his burning eyes. She glanced around again at the sleeping men. "What if they should see . . .?"

Ashton's response was to sweep her up into his arms and carry her toward a small tent. When they reached it, he set her on her feet and motioned to the tent with a silent sweep of the hand.

Understanding his bidding, Sasha fell to her knees and crawled inside the small shelter of canvas, Ashton crawling behind her. When they were both inside, Sasha turned and faced Ashton, then drifted toward him, her heart pounding.

Again they kissed, tongues meeting and dancing. Ashton's eager hands fluttered among Sasha's clothes until she was undressed, his hands sliding along her silken flesh until he found the wet spot at the juncture of her thighs. As he kissed her deep and long, his fingers separated her dark bush of hair and began caressing her, drawing soft whimpering sounds from deep within her.

And then, when he felt her body tremble, too near to that point of no return, he drew away from her and knelt over her as he parted with his own clothes. Sasha ran her hands over his lean, bronzed, and handsome face, the sinews of his shoulders, his flat belly, and then to that place that nestled his velvet tautness.

Trembling, her fingers circled his shaft. Sucking in a wild breath of rapture as he slipped a finger inside her, she, in turn, began moving her hand over his hardness. Eyes closed, breathing harshly, she bit her lower lip to stifle a sigh of pleasure, then smiled and giggled when he was not that successful at keeping his own emotion so quietly intact. A husky groan from the depths of his throat made her aware that he could not stand much more of this sort of pampering.

"Darling, take me now," Sasha whispered, shimmering with ecstasy as his lips grazed against her pulsing love mound, then made a slow journey up her body, kissing her every sensitive part. When he gently sucked a nipple between his teeth, Sasha had to cover her mouth with a hand to keep from crying out from the wondrous splashes of desire enveloping her.

"Please," she whispered. "You are torturing me, darling. I am near to swooning clean away. Love me totally now, Ashton. Please?"

Too wrapped up in passion's reverie of need, Ashton could not voice anything aloud to Sasha at this moment. He just did her bidding. His hands cupped the rounded flesh of her bottom, moulding her to him as he drove into her swiftly and surely. Their bodies strained together hungrily as Ashton surged into her over and over again. He buried his face in her breasts, catching his breath, then not daring to breathe. Each thrust brought fresh desire, and he wanted to postpone that final moment when the ecstasy was too quickly gone. . . .

A splendid joy spreading through her, Sasha clung to Ashton as he continued to come to her, thrusting deeply. Her hips strained upward, arching to receive him, the blaze of urgency building within her. She trembled with ecstasy as once again he kissed her, his mouth forcing her lips apart. When he darted his tongue moistly into her mouth, she was overcome by an unbearable, sweet pain. Her breasts pulsing warmly beneath his fingers, she emitted a cry of blissful agony.

And then she felt a great shuddering in his loins, and a flood of rapture swept raggedly through her. She strained her hips up at him, crying out to him of her fulfillment as he surged wildly into her. Ashton groaned against her lips as he relinquished his soul to receive the ultimate of pleasure as it exploded through every cell in his body, cleansing him with light. . . .

Ashton's body then subsided, exhausted, into

Sasha's. They lay there for some time as she stroked his neck gently.

Then he spoke.

"Well, Spike, how about another round?" he said, chuckling low as she doubled a fist and teasingly hit him in the chest.

Chapter Twenty-Two

Leaving Ashton asleep in the tent, Sasha crept from its close confines and stood just outside, rebraiding her hair. The other men were just stirring. No one seemed to have noticed her yet, giving her time to enjoy the morning and revel in wondrous memories of the previous night. She never felt as loved, as desired, as now. And wasn't the morning just too wonderful? The air was so crisp and clear it made her want to kneel down and kiss the earth!

A sudden breath teased her ear, then lips brushed the nape of her neck. "Good morning, Spike," Ashton whispered, sending ripples of desire down her body.

Her hair now neatly braided and pinned to the top of her head, Sasha spun around and looked adoringly up into dark and knowing eyes. She draped her arms around Ashton's neck and pulled his head down so that their lips could meet.

"Good morning to you," she whispered.

She closed her eyes and shivered with ecstasy as his tongue brushed her lips lightly and his arms snaked around her and embraced her long and sweet. Their mouths met in a quivering kiss, but they were too soon torn apart by low chuckles behind them.

"I see Spike has rejoined us," Crispin said, stepping up beside them. His eyes were only for a moment alight with amusement, and then he frowned down at Sasha. "How did you get here? Why did you come? Ashton told you not to."

Sasha crept from Ashton's arms. She blushed when she discovered that not only were Crispin's eyes on her, but so were those of the rest of the men, who were now completely awake and dressed, their tents dismantled and their horses loaded with the bulky gear.

Then she centered her attention back on Crispin, ready to defend herself against any scolding he might decide to give her. "I came because I wanted to," she said. "And as for Ashton ordering me around, well I don't take to that too much, Crispin." She smiled slowly up at Ashton. "And he doesn't truly mind that I am here, do you, Ashton?"

Ashton's eyes wavered, getting her meaning. He had taken quick advantage of her presence, taking her to his bed as though he had been without a woman for a month of Sundays!

And, it was true, he had enjoyed her company.

But he did not want to announce it to the world

that she had been able to sway his opinions so easily!

He exhaled a frustrated breath, for the first time ever feeling awkward with Sasha's stubbornness. It was all right to display it when it was just between the two of them—but not when they had a damn audience!

"We've talked enough this morning," he fussed, turning away from Sasha and Crispin. He went into his tent and started throwing bedding gear from inside it. "Get the hell to work, Crispin. The kangarooers probably are up at the crack of dawn doing their dirty work, and here we are just standing around talking like we've no better thing to do!"

Sasha eyed the stakes that held up the tent. She giggled behind her hand, knowing of a sure-fire way to get Ashton's mood changed back to something more amiable. She smiled into Crispin's angry eyes, wanting to get him in on the mischief, also. It was bad enough to envision what might lie ahead of them, without everyone riding out to search for the kangarooers with long faces and set jaws. She wanted to lighten up everyone's mood—not only Ashton's.

"Help me, Crispin," she said, bending to a knee to yank on one of the stakes that supported the tent.

Crispin scratched his brow idly. "But Ashton ain't left the tent yet," he said, arching an eyebrow.

"I know," Sasha said, grunting as she yanked and pulled. She paused for a moment and smiled over her shoulder at Crispin. "That's the general idea, Crispin. Now are you going to help me or not?"

"But, why, ma'am?" Crispin said, fidgeting nervously with the handle of his holstered pistol.

Sasha sighed heavily. "Oh, Crispin, do I have to paint you a picture?" she said, yanking on the stake again. "Hurry up. Help me."

Ashton had heard everything. He smiled smugly, ready to crawl outside. But he was too late. A sudden splat of canvas falling on him spilled him awkwardly to the ground. His arms got tangled as he tried to fight the canvas off, and he cursed loudly enough so that everyone in the camp could hear.

"Oh, Ashton, I fear you have had a mishap," Sasha teased, Crispin laughing so hard beside her that tears were rushing from his eyes. She fell to her knees and began working with the tent, trying to free Ashton. But just as she yanked at it, he did the same, drawing the canvas taut between them.

"Just leave it alone!" Ashton shouted, finally seeing a light at one corner. "Haven't you done enough already?"

Sasha moved back to her feet. The sight of Ashton groping and fighting with the tent made her laugh so hard she had to grip Crispin's arm to keep herself from falling.

And then Ashton broke free. He cursed low beneath his breath again as he shoved the tent aside. He stood over Sasha, his long legs spread, his doubled fists on his hips. "So you want to play, do you?" he growled. "We'll see about that."

He picked her up and threw her across his shoulder as though she were no more than a sack of potatoes. He carried her toward an avenue of hardy gums that lined a creekbed. "I think you deserve a dunking this morning, sweet darlin'," he said, grinning from ear to ear. "The water is crisp and cold this early in the morning. It ought to rid you of

278

whatever mischief your mind might conjure up the rest of the day."

Sasha was kicking her legs and pummeling her fists against his back. "No, Ashton, I'll freeze to death," she pleaded. "Ashton, I did what I did just to make you laugh. What you plan to do to me will make me miserable!"

"It will, will it?" Ashton teased, boldly holding her up over the water that pooled shallowly around rocks. Fish darted around, silver against the morning light. Water spiders skipped across the surface, and a snake was curled up at the other bank, sunning itself. "I think I might be persuaded to change my mind."

"Anything," Sasha said, breathless as she watched the snake uncurl and slither away into high grass.

"Anything?" Ashton teased, lowering her to the ground so that she faced him. He framed her face with his hands, their eyes locked.

"Well, just about anything," Sasha murmured, not wanting to have to agree to return to The Homestead. "Like perhaps another one of those kisses I stole from you a moment ago?" Ashton said, drawing her lips to his mouth.

"Oh, Ashton," Sasha said, giggling. She locked her arms around his neck and kissed him passionately, straining her body into the curve of his, so loving him.

"All right, you two, let's cut that out," Crispin said, coming to bodily separate them. His eyes danced as he smiled from one to the other. "Let's leave the lovin' for tonight. I think we've got some quick breakfast to eat and some kangarooers to hunt down."

Ashton smiled warmly. "Well, Sasha, it looks as though Crispin has suddenly taken charge of this whole affair," he said, placing an arm around his friend's shoulder. "Do you know? I kind of like it."

"Me too," Sasha said, worming her way between the two men and placing an arm about each of them.

They joined the others. Again no fire was built, for they did not want to give the kangarooers a whiff of the smoke. Everyone had to postpone their morning cups of scalding hot coffee for a while longer. They sat around chatting and eating a breakfast of dried pumpkin, jerked beef, and fruit.

Then they all mounted their steeds and set out for another day of hunting. Sasha felt proud riding beside Ashton, glad that he had accepted her presence.

But she could not shake the dread of what lay ahead of them.

Perhaps even their deaths. . . .

Sasha rode straight-backed on Cloud, though everything in her rebelled at the thought of having to go another inch on the horse. It had been a long, uneventful day riding through the outback. She looked over at Ashton sullenly, wanting to ask him if he thought they would ever find the kangarooers, and how many days he was going to continue riding before he gave up. Though she had loved Rufus as though he were her brother and wanted to find his assailant as badly as Ashton did, she could not bear to think that the search would go endlessly onward. They needed to get on with the rest of their lives. Rufus would want that!

The tall yellow grasses swayed and whipped around in the wild winds. The mountains in the distance were washed in purplish hues as the sun glanced off their sides. Eagles soared overhead, screeching, their wide wings casting cooling shadows across the land.

Then the silence of the outback was broken by gunfire and the shouts of men just over a slight rise in the distance. Through the air also came the cries of animals in pain.

Sasha's heart skipped a beat and her throat went dry at the thought of having surely found the murdering, vile kangarooers. She looked over at Ashton, swallowing hard as she watched him grab his rifle from its leather sheath at the side of his horse. She reached for her own rifle, steadying herself in the saddle as she clasped harder to the horse's reins. For a moment Ashton's eyes silently met hers, then he reined in his horse closer to Cloud.

"Sasha, I'll ask you one last time to forget this foolishness of going any farther with me," he said. "You hear the gunfire. We've come upon a kangaroo slaughter. It won't be pretty."

Sasha paled. "But I can't stay behind by myself," she said, suddenly afraid, and for the first time wishing that she had not come.

"I can leave someone with you," Ashton said.

"From the sounds of things you are going to need all of the men and guns you have," Sasha said, tightening her grip on the rifle. "I cannot allow you to leave even one of your men behind to babysit me." She thrust her chin out boldly. "I have come this far, Ashton. I shall continue even now."

Ashton shook his head sorrowfully, then shrugged. "Have it your way," he grumbled. He gave her a stern look. "Don't ever say I didn't warn you."

Sasha nodded, trying not to show her true fear to Ashton. When he turned away from her and raised his rifle in the air as a warning to the men who awaited his command, she closed her eyes and sucked in a wild breath. Never had she been as afraid, or as unsure of herself, as now. How quickly things in life changed! She recalled how abruptly her parents had been taken from her. She remembered, too, how cruelly Woodrow Rutherford had abandoned her.

And now, when everything seemed to be falling into place for her, to have some meaning, would it all fall apart again?

Would she even live to know?

It was as though a dark cloud was hovering over her, at any moment ready to enclose her in its black depths and smother her.

"Let's go!" Ashton shouted, thrusting his heels into the flanks of his horse. He leaned low over his horse's flying mane, cursing himself over and over again that he had not tied Sasha to a tree to keep her from being involved in this fracas. He did not need her there to distract him! What had he been thinking when he had allowed it? Even now she was somewhere behind him on her horse. If he took the time to check on her, it was time taken away from keeping his wits about him for the battle ahead. He knew Ajax well enough to know that at this point in their relationship, there would be no talking—only shooting!

Sasha clutched her rifle as she led her horse into a

thunderous gallop close behind Ashton. The air was hot on her face—the sun scorching. Her breathing was quick, yet shallow. Her bottom ached as it bounced up and down in the hard saddle.

And then the rise in the land was met and quickly left behind, and down below her along the flat stretch of land was a sight that turned Sasha's stomach inside out. Everywhere she looked lay slaughtered kangaroos, blood curling from their bodies. The shooting had stopped, and the men were off their horses cutting into the slain animals, some for meat, others for their pelts. It was a gruesome sight, making a bitter bile rise into Sasha's throat.

She swallowed hard, but that did not seem to quell her need to retch. She pulled hard on her reins and drew her horse to a halt, then slipped from the saddle and hung her head. Her throat spasmed over and over again as she emptied her stomach onto the ground.

The kangarooers were taken offguard and rose quickly with their hands in the air as Ashton and his men made a wide, threatening circle around them on their horses, their rifles drawn. Trying to ignore the slaughter of the beautiful animals, Ashton began sorting through the faces of the kangarooers, trying to find Ajax among them.

His spine stiffened.

Ajax was not there.

But Ashton was sure that these were the men who rode with Ajax.

"Okay, where is he?" Ashton finally shouted, aiming his rifle into the throng of bloody, whiskered men. "Where's Ajax? He's the only one I'm interested in. Hand him over to me and you can get back to your butchering."

Sasha coughed, her throat stinging from the vomit. Glad that it was over, she wiped her mouth clean with the sleeve of her shirt. Slowly she raised her eyes and again she felt the icy claws of dread gripping her insides when she looked around at the massacred animals—too many to even count.

Sasha gazed sadly at one animal close by her, its short forelimbs looking almost like human arms, its long, thin powerful hind legs never again to be used for jumping. Its head was small, its ears large and rounded, with a small mouth and prominent lips. Its fur looked soft and wooly, and there were stripes on its head, back, and upper limbs.

Averting her gaze, Sasha choked back a sob when her attention was drawn to another kangaroo. A baby kangaroo was in its pouch, bleeding, its mouth still attached to one of its mother's four teats. But the baby was lifeless.

Hardly able to stand anymore of this, Sasha rushed away to lean against a lone eucalyptus tree. She looked at Ashton and the men, seeing that they had everything under control—except that something did seem suddenly awry. She could see it in Ashton's expression—the surprise that quickly changed to disappointment.

"You can't mean that Ajax is dead," Ashton said after one of the kangarooers explained that they were now riding without Ajax, that he was dead.

"He's been dead two nights now," the kangarooer further explained. "He was killed in his sleep by some stranger. Now why don't you ride on? These are our kangaroos. We killed 'em fair and square."

Ashton's gaze roamed over the bloody mass of kangaroos. "Fair and square, huh?" he grumbled. "That depends on whether or not you're the kangaroo, don't you think?"

Ashton swung around, and his men followed his lead. He rode to Sasha and swung himself out of the saddle to go to her. He held her face between his hands. "Are you all right?" he murmured.

"Yes, but I will be much better after we leave this place of death," she said, shuddering. She searched Ashton's eyes. "Where is Ajax?"

"He's dead," Ashton said, glancing at Crispin as he dismounted and stepped to his side. "Do you believe the kangarooer, Crispin? Do you truly think he's dead?"

"There ain't no reason for them to lie to us," Crispin said, shrugging. "They're too interested in killin' the kangaroos to worry about reasons for lyin' to you."

Ashton nodded his head. "Then Ajax couldn't have killed Rufus," he said solemnly. "The bastard kangarooer was already dead." He kneaded his chin contemplatively. "So who in the hell did it?"

"Need you think further on it?" Crispin said, his eyes flashing angrily. "It was the son of a bitch Stanford Sidwell. And damn it, Ashton, he sent us on a wild goose chase and he's probably back home laughin' at us because of it."

"Do you mean that he killed his own sheepherder, tore down his own fence, and scattered his own sheep, just to cover up what he did to Rufus?" Sasha gasped.

"Seems likely enough," Ashton grumbled. He gazed down at Sasha. "But there is no proof." He did not tell her that his main concern was her. He did not want her in the middle of a major confrontation between two retired bushrangers. Her life was already in enough danger because of him!

"But he'll slip up soon enough," Crispin said, slapping the handle of his holstered revolver, holding firmly onto his rifle with the other. "And then he'll have hell to pay."

"For now, let's go home," Ashton said, taking Sasha by the arm and leading her to her horse. "We've got to see if things are all right there. Who knows what Stanford Sidwell has been up to while we've been gone."

Sasha looked up at him and heaved a heavy sigh. "Yes, let's," she murmured. "I wish that I had never left."

Ashton lifted her up into her saddle, wanting so badly to say that he had told her so—but too happy that she had not been harmed by her decision to scold her.

Chapter Twenty-Three

Sasha was slouched over and weaving in the saddle. Her eyes jerked open as she caught herself falling asleep again. Forcing herself to straighten up in the saddle, she looked woefully at Ashton as he rode determinedly ahead of her. He had refused to stop for the night. Hate for Stanford Sidwell had kept him riding onward, and not trusting Stanford's intentions after he had sent them all on a wild goose chase, he dreaded what he might find back at The Homestead. Although several hands had stayed behind to guard the sheep station, it seemed nothing could stop Stanford in his search for vengeance against Ashton York.

The sun was at the midpoint in the sky, hot on Sasha's skin as its heat penetrated her clothes. She drew her hat farther down on her brow, glad to be able at least to protect her face from the dreaded rays that were never-ending during the day. It was hard to believe that she had witnessed a storm at all. As she gazed down at the ground over which her horse was now traveling, she could see wide cracks, and when the horse traveled beneath the widespread branches of gum trees, the fallen leaves beneath them crunched and sprayed dust in all directions.

Although it had only been a few days since the torrential rains, the parched earth showed signs of the beginning of a drought. She couldn't help but recall the time Ashton had told her about the Aborigines—that they set fires in order to frighten animals out of the forest and onto their spears for food. If the natives set a fire now, it would spread quickly, burning everything in its wake—perhaps even The Homestead!

She forced such terrifying thoughts from her mind, and her eyes lit up when, just ahead, she saw grazing sheep—hers and Ashton's! Home! She was almost home!

Then something gruesome and heart-stopping made Sasha grow pale. She was now close enough to the sheep to see that things were not right. Several were on the ground, blood covering their heads.

Even as she stared at the flock, she witnessed a sight that seemed too grotesque to be real. Several crows suddenly appeared from out of nowhere and landed on several of the surviving sheep's heads. Their talons sank into the sheep and held steadfast when the frightened animals began bleating and crying, running in crazed circles as they tried to shake the large black birds off.

Ashton reined in his horse as Sasha led Cloud quickly up beside him.

"Ashton, do you see—?" Sasha said, looking wildly over at him.

"My God!" he gasped, almost paralyzed by the sight as the crows began pecking at the eyes of the sheep. He drew his rifle and along with his men rode in a hard gallop away from Sasha toward the sheep. Gunshots filled the air, and the crows flopped every which way off the wounded sheep's bloody bodies.

Sasha turned her eyes away, tears streaming down her cheeks, but as she did, one of the blinded sheep came running madly toward her horse and ran into its legs, bleating noisily. The blood and the clumsiness of the sheep knocking against Cloud's legs caused the horse to rear up on its hind legs, its wide nostrils flaring and its eyes wild.

Sasha screamed. She tightened her knees against her horse's sides and clung desperately to the reins. "Cloud, please calm down!" she cried, looking down at the pitiful sheep that was not aware of the havoc it was causing.

Nothing Sasha could say or do eased the dilemma she had found herself in. She lost her grip on the reins and the saddle when Cloud reared again, his hooves landing on the blind sheep. Slipping backwards, she fell from the horse and landed painfully on her backside on the hard, cracked ground. She rolled quickly away from Cloud, who was now bucking his hindlegs up in the air, his teeth tearing at the sheep that was now trampled and lifeless.

Trying to get her breath, Sasha lay there for a moment on her back, her eyes closed. Then she rolled over to her side to push herself up. And when she did she found herself looking square into the face of another blinded sheep that had wandered aimlessly away from the others, a dreaded crow still perched on his head, pecking away at the hollow, bloody sockets.

Sasha heard a blast of gunfire, then saw the crow's head pop from its body. She became aware of hearing someone's terrifying screams, and suddenly realized they were her own.

When strong arms circled her waist and drew her up from the ground—when a voice so familiar and loving came to her through this fog that seemed to have so quickly enveloped her senses—she grabbed for Ashton and clung to him for dear life.

"It's so horrible," she sobbed, pressing her cheek against his chest, her eyes clenched closed. "The poor sheep."

"It's over," he said thickly, lovingly caressing her back. "The crows are all dead. Damn them. Damn them all to hell."

"I've heard about things like this before but—but I never thought it would happen to our sheep," Sasha cried, still clinging hard to Ashton.

Ashton sighed hard. "Sweet darlin', you are just beginning to see the hardships of living in the outback. Nothing comes easy here." He eased her away from him and looked down into her tear-filled eyes. "Are you sorry that you came with me to the outback? Would you rather be back in Melbourne?"

She swallowed hard and choked back a sob. She

wiped tears from her cheeks with the back of a hand. "No, never would I want to be back in Melbourne, not if you aren't there," she said softly. "And Ashton, I'm sorry I'm behaving like a child. I'm sorry. Truly I am."

Ashton smoothed more tears from her cheeks with a thumb. "Sasha, if you weren't behaving like this right now, after all you've seen, I'd begin to worry about you," he said, chuckling.

"You would . . . ?" Sasha asked, her voice faint. "Why would you, Ashton? I must seem so weak."

"Sweet darlin', you're not weak," he said tenderly. "You just have a heart that's in good working order."

Ashton drew away from her when he heard the thunder of approaching horses. He turned and shaded his eyes as he gazed intently at riders approaching on the horizon. He took steps toward them as the riders wheeled their horses to a halt a few yards away and dismounted.

Sasha recognized them as men from The Homestead. She grew cold inside as she surveyed their expressions. None was pleasant; most of their faces were knit with worry.

"It looks like I didn't come home any too soon," Ashton acknowledged as the men came to him, their heavy holstered pistols flapping at their hips. "How much of this has gone on while I've been gone?" he asked, gesturing with a hand toward the dead and bloody sheep that had been shot to put them out of their misery. "Just how many of these damn crow attacks were there besides the one I just witnessed?"

"Too many to keep track of," was the solemn

answer. "But that ain't all we've got to report, Ashton."

Ashton stiffened and inhaled a nervous, shaky breath. His thoughts went to Stanford Sidwell. Surely he had taken advantage of his absence. What the hell sort of havoc had he wrought on his property while he was gone? Ashton would have been surprised even to see his cabin still standing!

"Well? Don't take all day," he said, looking from one man to the other. "Give me the bad news. I'm getting used to it."

His lips parted and an icy coldness swept through him as he listened to tales of rats and black caterpillars eating their vegetables, and hordes of bright, screaming parrots eating the seeds that had been stored in the barn.

Ashton hung his head. Sasha felt helpless. It seemed that not only was Stanford Sidwell against them—but all of nature too!

Ashton looked at Crispin. "See to all of this for me," he said. "I—I just can't take any more today."

"It's as good as done," Crispin said, watching in disbelief as Ashton mounted his horse and rode away, his head still down. Never had Crispin seen Ashton so despondent and so willing to give up.

Then he watched Sasha quickly mount her horse and ride up next to Ashton, reaching over to touch his cheek while speaking soothing words to him. Crispin was touched to the soul by her show of love for Ashton, and he saw her as Ashton's only true salvation.

The sun was lowering in the sky, and the birds were scampering for shelter in the trees outside the cabin. In the distance a dingo barked in staccato fashion. In the pasture, the sheep that had lived through the ordeal of the crows were bleating peacefully.

Still in her riding gear, Sasha was sitting on a kangaroo pelt with Ashton in front of a roaring fire in the cabin. Quiet, scarcely breathing, she looked disbelievingly at Ashton as he poured himself another tin cup full of whiskey and drank it down in one swallow. Over and over again he did this, even though his eyes were already bloodshot and he was so drunk he could hardly hold his head up.

"I've let you down," Ashton said, his words slurring. He poured another drink and gulped it down. "My sweet little Sasha. I promised so much and am giving so little. I don't blame you if you hate me."

Sasha's heart was aching for Ashton. She eased the cup from his hand, the half-emptied bottle of whiskey from the other, and set them aside. Moving to her knees, she wrapped her arms around Ashton, cradling her face against his chest.

"Ashton," she murmured. "My darling Ashton. If you're drinking because you feel you are a failure, and you think that I hate you because of it, you are so wrong. Darling, I could never hate you. Don't you see? I love you with all of my heart."

She stroked his back lovingly. "As for our sheep station, you knew the risks," she continued softly. "You just didn't expect them to come piling on you all at one time. First Lightning disappears, then Rufus is killed, and now we've seen so much destruction by the birds and caterpillars."

She dared not to think of the large cracks that she had seen in the soil, expecting the ravages of a drought to be their next ordeal. Or perhaps a fire . . .

Ashton drew away from her and rose shakily to his feet. He started walking in a weaving fashion toward the door. "Come on, Sasha," he said. "I'm taking you back to Melbourne. I can't leave you out here. There are too many unknowns. I can't let anything happen to you."

Sasha scurried to her feet. She went to Ashton and grabbed him by the arm. "Ashton, you aren't going anywhere but to bed," she said, letting him lean into her.

"You've got to sleep this off," she said, leading him toward the bed. "Lord, Ashton, all the time that I worked with you at the pub I never saw you drunk. And now . . . Oh, Ashton, this is the worst time of all to get drunk!"

Ashton looked down at her, seeing her as only a blur through his drunken haze. "Where are you?" he stammered. "I can't see you."

She gave him a harried look. "I'm here," she reassured him. "After you get some sleep, you'll see and feel better."

She helped him onto the bed, and he fell immediately into a heavy sleep. Sighing, Sasha removed his boots and dropped them to the floor, then struggled with his shirt until she had it over his head.

Then she eyed his breeches, and his muscled legs. No. She would leave his breeches on. Asleep and drunk, his legs would be a dead weight.

Worn out, despondent, and missing Ashton so fiercely while he was in this drunken state, Sasha crumpled down before the fireplace again. She stared into the fire, then got a whiff of something unpleasant. She sniffed at her clothes and realized that she was smelling herself. The journey had been hot and tiring. A bath—Lord, how she needed a bath! Then she could crawl into bed with Ashton and get the sleep that she so badly needed. Who knew what horrors would be awaiting them tomorrow?

"What will go wrong next?" she whispered to herself, moving back to her feet. She went around the cabin gathering up a clean, fresh-smelling dress, a towel, a fragrant piece of soap, and soft slippers to take the place of the stiff boots that she had worn for what seemed weeks.

"The drought," she fussed. "We are surely in for a drought. Will it wipe out what is left? If so, what then shall we do?"

She took the time to unbraid her hair, then left the cabin and walked toward the river. She did not look over her shoulder at the activity at the sheep station. She did not want to know how many sheep had died, or how many vegetables had been destroyed in the garden. Something told her that Ashton had been right to find solace in the bottle of whiskey. Perhaps tomorrow she might join him if things did not improve!

Moving through thick, tangled brush, Sasha finally saw the shine of the river just ahead. And in the fast-falling dusk, she saw something else. Bianca. She was sitting beside the river seemingly lost in thought. Her back to Sasha, she did not hear her approach. And when Sasha came up behind her, Bianca bolted to her feet, paling with fright.

"It's only me, Bianca," Sasha said, dropping her clothes and bathing paraphernalia to go to her to take her hands. "I'm sorry I frightened you." She searched Bianca's face. The contusions had faded, yet they were still there all the same to remind Sasha of how concerned she had been for Bianca the last time she had seen her. Through all of the nightmare at The Homestead, she had forgotten about Bianca.

She felt a pang of regret deep within her soul because of it.

"I hoped you would come," Bianca said, her green eyes wide with a hidden fear. "I need to talk to you. Do you have time to listen?"

Sasha gazed up through the branches of the trees and saw that the sky was hazed over with purple and orange streaks as the sun dipped lower. Soon it would be dark. The constant threat of dingoes and all sorts of things that crawled around in the outback made her uneasy over the prospect of not getting back to the cabin before night fell in its total blackness.

She looked back at Bianca, seeing that she needed her. "Yes, I have time to talk," she murmured. "Before my bath. But only for a few moments, Bianca. We both should return home before it gets much darker."

Bianca squeezed Sasha's hands desperately. "What I have to say won't take long," she said in a rush.

"What is it, Bianca?" Sasha asked, sensing so much about this woman that made an overwhelming uneasiness creep through her. Surely it was Stanford Sidwell and the rest of the men. Her sheepherder husband was dead. They could all be taking turns at abusing this woman whose life up until now had been ruled by how many men she took to her bed each day and night, but who wanted to change her life because of a child.

"Tell me," Sasha encouraged her. "What's troubling you?"

"I am not a strong person," Bianca cried, tears streaming from her eyes. "I thought I was. But out here in this emptiness, I am discovering much about myself that is not good." She eased her hands from Sasha's and covered her abdomen with them. "I fear for my child. I could never be a fit mother. Sasha, will you take my child and raise it as your own? You are a woman with heart and Ashton is a man who cares for people. You could be wonderful parents to a child."

She suddenly grabbed Sasha by the shoulder, her eyes wild. "Please tell me that you will take my child and raise it as your own. Please, Sasha. Please promise me that!"

Sasha was taken aback by the request. "Bianca, you know that I will do anything to help you," Sasha said, taking Bianca's hands, holding them tightly. "Are you asking me to take your child because of who you were married to? Because you are treated so terribly? Is it that you truly fear for your child's safety, not that you will be an unfit mother? Let me send Ashton to Stanford's sheep station to teach whoever is responsible for frightening you a lesson. There is no reason on this earth to live in fright like you do. Better yet, come and stay with us, Bianca. We'll make do until we can get you back to Melbourne."

Bianca emitted a low sob. She jerked her hands

free and once again cupped them around her abdomen. "No," she said, her voice quavering, fearing Stanford too much to accept any assistance other than Sasha's word to take her child. "Bianca cannot do that. Oh, Sasha, don't you see? I was never married. I live with Stanford Sidwell. He brought me to the outback. I am his woman!"

"Bianca, I don't know what to say," Sasha said in a low gasp. "Oh, please let me and Ashton help you. You don't have to live with that horrid man!"

"It is my choice to," Bianca said, having to lie again to Sasha. "But my child deserves better." Tears rushed from her eyes again. "You promise? You will take my child? You will raise my child as your own?"

Sasha was compelled to embrace Bianca. She drew her into her arms and stroked her long hair. "Yes," she murmured. "If that is what you wish. Now please stop worrying."

"Thank you," Bianca sobbed. "Oh, thank you."

"Bianca, please let me send Ashton to make things right for you at Stanford's sheep station," Sasha said softly. "There is no need for you to live in fear from day to day. Let us take you away from there."

Bianca yanked away from her. Pale, her eyes wild, she shook her head frantically from side to side. "Do not come to Stanford's," she said, near to hysterics. "Leave me be!"

She turned to run away, then stopped and faced Sasha again. "It is only the child that should concern you," she said, then turned and ran up the river to the clay bank that reached across to the other side.

Sasha felt numb from the talk with Bianca. She was unnerved by everything that happened today. Her heart heavy, she undressed and dove into the river, letting the water be her solace, as whiskey had been Ashton's.

Chapter Twenty-Four

The aroma of coffee brewing over hot coals awakened Sasha. Leaning up on an elbow, she looked toward the fireplace, wiping sleep from her eyes. She was surprised to see Ashton up and around, just now slipping his fringed shirt over his head. She gazed out the window and saw that it was still dark outside, then back at Ashton who was now so determinedly yanking on a boot.

"Ashton?" Sasha questioned, tossing blankets aside and sitting up. "Why are you up so early?" She remembered all too well the night before, when Ashton had been so drunk that she could hardly get him to the bed. "Do you even feel like being up?"

Ashton gave Sasha a somber look as he yanked his other boot on. "I behaved like a drongo, last night," he said, determined. "I'm going to make up for that behavior today."

"What do you mean?" Sasha said, sweeping her legs from the bed. But her feet had scarcely touched the floor when Ashton came to her and lifted her legs back on the bed and had her comfortably covered.

"There isn't any need for you to get up this early, Sasha," Ashton scolded. "Get another wink of sleep, because you and I have quite a journey laid out before us tomorrow."

Sasha's mouth parted in an effort to question him further, but his lips were there, silencing her with a sweet brush of a kiss.

Ashton drew away from her and took his gunbelt from a peg on the wall. "I've decided to get what sheep are left standing sheared, and we'll take the wool to market tomorrow," he offered, fastening his gunbelt around his waist. "I'm tired of waiting to see what tragedy might befall us next. I'm going to beat the odds this time. I'm going to take the wool and get what we can while it's there for the taking."

Sasha stared at him, surprised, yet she knew that she shouldn't be. He was right to do this. Tragedies seemed to be following them around like the plague! She was beginning to wonder if anything they did would save their dream of being a success as owners of a sheep station. So far the odds had been against them.

She suddenly recalled Bianca pleading with her at the river—and why. Had Sasha actually agreed to take Bianca's child? What would Ashton think? Would he ever understand?

She wanted to tell him about it now, yet something deep inside her warned her against it. Now was not the time to stir up more problems. And he was too insistent about his other plan to even listen to something that had nothing at all to do with the success of their sheep station.

Ashton nodded toward the coffee brewing over the fire. "I made the coffee for you this morning, Sasha, in hopes that might make up to you for last night," he said. He smiled slowly at her. "I've got one hell of a headache—one I don't think I'll ever forget."

Sasha laughed softly and swung herself from the bed again. Barefoot, the hardwood floor cold against the soles of her feet, she went to Ashton and twined her arms about his neck. She looked adoringly up at him, then drew his mouth down close to her lips. "My darling, you don't want to go to work with a headache," she whispered. "Let me kiss it away."

She drew his mouth to her lips and kissed him long and sweet, arching her body into the curve of his. But too soon he placed his hands to her waist and set her away from him. "I don't think that's the way to help me with my misery," he chuckled. "It'll just start another one—one that'll keep me in this cabin all day long if you're not careful."

"Well we can't have that, now can we?" Sasha teased, trying to wriggle into his arms again, yet again being pushed gently away.

"We'll save this sort of pastime for when we're on the riverboat," Ashton said, walking toward the door. He grabbed his wide-brimmed hat from a peg on the wall.

Sasha scampered after him. She took his hand and stepped around to gaze up at him. "Riverboat?" she said. "What riverboat?"

"The one we'll be on tomorrow, traveling on the Murray River to Narrung to deliver the wool we shear from our sheep today," he said.

He lifted Sasha's chin with his free hand. "That is, if you'll let me get to work this morning," he said, his eyes dancing down into hers. "You know that you're threatening to spoil my whole day's plans, don't you? Even tomorrow's? Don't you think it'd be a lot more romantic to make love on the riverboat than now, in our cabin? Consider the possibilities, sweet darlin'. The moonlight, the gentle splash of the water against the sides of the boat, the birds singing in the trees overhead."

"Why, it sounds wonderful," Sasha marveled, sighing. "Too wonderful to be true."

"It won't be if I don't get out of here," Ashton said, swinging away from her. He opened the door and stepped out into the morning air. Dawn was just seeping along the horizon in streaks of purple.

Inhaling deeply, Ashton was suddenly invigorated and hopeful. He looked forward to shearing the sheep. It would give him a sense of belonging—of ownership—to pile the wool on the back of a packhorse to take to market.

"I'm going to help you today," Sasha said, jerking her nightgown off, grabbing up her breeches, and slipping into them.

Ashton turned and stared into the cabin at her. "Sasha, shearing is a man's job," he scolded. "Go on back to bed and get some more rest." His lips quivered into a smile. "Save your energy for our nights on the riverboat. I guarantee you're going to need it."

"I've always been able to manage whatever energy is needed to keep up with you," Sasha said, now fully clothed except for her boots. She sat down on the floor and began yanking one on, then stopped and smiled mischievously up at him. "In bed, or otherwise."

Ashton shook his head, then laughed as she came to him and locked an arm through his. "I didn't know what I was getting myself into when I brought you in from the streets and made you my partner, did I?"

"I think not," Sasha said, smiling sweetly up at him. "And you're not sorry, are you?"

He gazed down at her. "Sweet darlin', what do you think?" he said, his eyes filled with affection.

Sasha felt his love for her clean from her head to her toes.

The newborn lambs had been put with their mothers in a separate pen, making sure that the ewes mothered them. Several waterholes had been dug close to the tubbo shed, the place that had been erected specifically for shearing the sheep. Every shearer, shed-hand, and roustabout was busy today with the shearing.

Along with Crispin, Sasha helped hold a sheep in a waterhole while Ashton scrubbed it. The same process was going on all around them as many sheep bleated and cried.

Then Sasha stepped aside, her whole front drenched, as Crispin and Ashton wrestled the sheep into a dry pen, where the ground was thickly covered with the boughs of gum trees.

Ashton stepped to Sasha's side and smiled down at her, wiping a bead of perspiration from his brow.

"Ready to go back to woman chores?" he taunted, seeing exhaustion in her eyes. "The day has just begun here with the sheep, you know. Perhaps you need to go back to making bread. It doesn't take as much muscle."

Sasha placed her hands on her hips and gave Ashton a set stare. "I would like to challenge that statement," she declared. "Kneading dough takes a lot of muscle."

"I am sure that it does," Ashton said, reaching for her arm and feeling around for her muscle. "But sweet darlin', where is that muscle you are bragging about?"

She yanked her arm away, and her cheeks coloring with a blush. Ashton's eyes raked over her disheveled breeches and the wet shirt that clung to her breasts. "As I see it, today part of you could answer to the name Spike, the other to—"

Sasha did not give him the chance to continue his teasings. She spun around on a booted heel and stamped toward the tubbo shed, where the sheep were being taken for shearing.

Ashton chuckled beneath his breath, repositioned his hat on his head, and sauntered after her. Once inside the shearing shed, they stood aside and watched the shearing take place in the twenty-six stands, as the men worked quickly and skillfully at their craft.

"Sheepshearers are the most respected group of manual workers in Australia," Ashton explained to Sasha, admiring the shearers under their employ. "It is not simply a means of making money—it is a competition with each man bidding to be the champion, or ringer, as some call themselves."

"I see how earnestly they are working," Sasha said, her gaze settling on one man in particular. He was a strapping fellow with a dark beard, whose hands guided the shears over the sheep so quickly that they blurred before her eyes.

Ashton's gaze settled on the same man, and he rested his hands on his holstered revolvers. "See that man there?" he said, nodding toward him. "That's Adam Beaumont. That stripling from Sydney can outdo anyone with a pair of hand shears. It's rumored that he's going to try to beat the world shearing record."

"Do you mean shearers actually compete in such a way?" Sasha marveled, still watching Adam as he turned away the ragged locks of a sheep, leaving a track of snowy fleece from the brisket to the nose. It was lovely how he could peel off the fleece so smoothly.

"In 1802, a shearer created a world record at Alice Downs by shearing three hundred and twenty-one sheep in a day, using hand shears." Ashton said. "I don't doubt that this fellow will break that record."

The air filled with dust and lint, and Sasha sneezed as a bit of floating fleece tickled her nose. Her eyes watering, she started for the door. "I must get some fresh air," she said, sniffling and wiping at her eyes. "I can't seem to stop sneezing." She laughed softly as she looked through her blurred eyes at Ashton, as he followed her outside. "Here I am, an owner of sheep, and the fleece makes me sneeze."

Ashton swept an arm about her waist and swung her around to face him. "Thank God I don't make you sneeze," he teased. "Now how about you forgetting about the shearing and getting ready for our journey on the Murray? Once you're on that paddlewheeler, your mind should be clear of everything but me."

Sasha touched his face gently. "But can you think of only me?" she murmured. "We'll be gone from our sheep station for several days. Do you think you can trust Stanford Sidwell for that length of time? What if he hears that we're gone?"

"Sasha, I can't spend the rest of my life worrying about Stanford Sidwell's activities," Ashton said, frowning down at her. "And Crispin and the rest of our hands are going to stay behind to keep an eye on things. If Stanford tries anything, Crispin will be ready for him."

Sasha smiled weakly up at him, not as confident as he was. In her mind's eye she was seeing Bianca's bruised face. Any man capable of abusing a woman like that was capable of anything vile and criminal. Sasha so badly wanted to confide in Ashton about Bianca's plea for Sasha to take her baby to raise should anything happen to her.

But Sasha still could not find the words to tell him. It was evident that Bianca was afraid for her life, yet she had discouraged intervention of any sort. Sasha was torn between wanting to tell Ashton everything, and being afraid to.

Stanford rose from the bed and scooted his breeches up his legs quickly when he heard the approach of horses outside his cabin. He looked down at Bianca, his eyes roaming over her nudity. He was disgusted with her swollen stomach, having hoped that by now she would have miscarried. It seemed now that he was saddled not only with her, but also her bastard child.

Bianca gazed fearfully up at Stanford and drew a blanket up over her. Without his saying anything, it was obvious that he was disgusted with the sight of her. He wished that her child was dead!

Her thoughts went to Sasha and the kind offer she had made—to take her in if she left Stanford and let her live with Sasha and Ashton until they took another trip into Melbourne.

But Bianca was too afraid to involve anyone but herself in this ordeal that she was living through. If only she had found the strength to say no to Stanford back in Melbourne!

But even then, fearing him was the reason she had accompanied him to the outback.

"Get up and get dressed," Stanford said, slipping a shirt on. "Get to cleaning up this place. It's beginning to smell like you."

Stung by his cruel words, Bianca cowered as she crept from the bed, hurriedly slipping a loose-fitted kangaroo-hide dress over her head. She glanced his way as he went to the door and pulled it open, cursing beneath his breath as he stepped out onto the porch.

She went to the door and stood behind it, listening intently as the horsemen stopped just outside the cabin and began talking to Stanford.

"Ashton's up to something," one of the men said.

"Like what?" Stanford asked, squinting up at one of his loyal gunmen whom he had sent to spy on Ashton and Sasha.

"Like he's having all of the sheep sheared," the

man grumbled. "All 'cept the ewes, o' course."

"It ain't the time of year to do shearing," Stanford said, kneading his chin. "Heard anything that could give us a hint about why he's doin' this?"

"I heard one of his men sayin' somethin' about Ashton takin' a journey on a paddlewheeler up the Murray tomorrow," the man said.

"Up the Murray in a paddlewheeler?" Stanford said, forking an eyebrow. Then he smiled slowly. "Damn him. He's tryin' to con me. He's takin' the wool to market early to get a jump ahead of me." He straightened his shoulders. He chuckled. "The fool. Don't he know better than to try and con the best con artist in Australia?"

"What do you intend to do about it?" the man asked.

"Give me time to think about it," Stanford said, then swung around and went back inside the cabin. He caught Bianca before she had a chance to move away from the door. He grabbed her by a wrist and jerked her close to him so that he was glaring into her face. "You forget everything you just heard," he growled. "I don't need you meetin' up with Sasha to spill the beans."

Bianca nodded anxiously.

Chapter Twenty-Five

The Murray River meandered and twisted through tangles of exotic willows and a forest of stringybark trees with their rough, yellow-brown trunks, manna gums with leaves that glinted like ice when the sun was behind them, and lianas draping their dense veiling over the green wilderness.

Ashton and Sasha stood at the rail of the paddlewheeler, their bales of wool secured in the hold of the boat. "It's so beautiful, Ashton," Sasha said, not having realized before how desperately she needed to relax. She sighed deeply. "I'm not sure if you can ever get me off this boat. Our troubles seem so distant from this deck."

"Aye, it is easy to place our recent tragedies from our mind while watching the river rippling along so peacefully," Ashton said, watching the white foam of the Murray. Slipping an arm around Sasha's waist, he drew her next to him. He looked down at her, thinking that he had never seen her look so beautiful. He had almost gotten used to seeing her in a man's breeches and shirt. In the soft, flowing cotton dress with its gathering of lace at her lowswept bodice and at the cuffs of her sleeves, and with her hair drifting like warm, black satin down her slim back, she stirred him into needing her as never before.

Feeling his eyes on her, Sasha smiled up at him. "I hope you approve of what you are looking at so studiously, darling," she murmured. "It seems as though you are looking at me for the very first time." She lowered her eyes, blushing. "It unnerves me a little, Ashton."

"You look so lovely," he said, leaning his face low to kiss her cheek gently. He inhaled the sweet fragrance of her. "And you smell so good. How am I expected to wait until nightfall to take you to bed?"

Sasha laughed softly and looked up into his eyes. "It would look very improper, Ashton, if we slipped away into our cabin without enjoying the evening meal with the rest of the passengers," she said, yet thrilling inside at the thought of being with him alone in this romantic setting. "So let us just enjoy the view till then, shall we?"

"How am I expected to take my eyes off you?" Ashton said, brushing her lips with a light kiss.

Sasha blushed again and peered around her at the other passengers standing along the rail. Although no one was paying her and Ashton any mind, still it seemed a foolish thing to display such affection for one another so openly.

In an effort to draw Ashton's attention elsewhere, Sasha pointed toward the forest. "Ashton, look at the animals and birds that are roaming the banks so calmly you could almost reach out and touch them," she said, truly amazed at what she was seeing. "There are black swans, and pelicans—and look at that strange-looking wading bird."

Then her breath was taken clear away when suddenly a lyrebird dashed overhead, its head low and its long tail feathers trailing. "How exquisite!" Sasha exclaimed, placing her hands to her cheeks.

And then many budgerigars flew up from the boughs of trees in green clouds so dense they cast long, rippling shadows on the water.

"I'm glad you're enjoying yourself so much," Ashton said, again drawing her close to his side.

"Never in my wildest dreams had I expected to see so many beautiful creatures," Sasha murmured. "In England everything is so—so drab."

They cuddled close as the paddlewheeler plied its way through the water, a *whump-whump-whump* throbbing through the boat as the helmsman eased her over a sandbar.

Koalas clambered about in the gum trees overhead, looking more cuddlesome than they were, while grey 'roos hopped about. White clusters of Christmas bush filled the air with spicy sweetness. . . .

The clanging of a bell was the warning that the dinner hour was near. The sun now dipped low and turned crimson behind the gum trees, turning everything on shore into lengthening shadows.

Ashton escorted Sasha to a dining room, where

candles flickered low on the tables. Helping her to her chair, he then sat down opposite her and took her hands across the table.

"I'm not hungry for food," he whispered huskily, his violet eyes gleaming into hers. "But since we are forced to be proper about this, taking time to eat with the others, I have a surprise for you, sweet darlin'."

"A surprise?" Sasha said, her eyes widening. She gasped low and her face lit up when a cabin boy brought a bottle of champagne to the table, and two long-stemmed glasses. "Why, Ashton, champagne again? Can we truly afford it?"

"We will soon be selling our wool for a substantial price," Ashton reassured her. "And after all you've been through, partner, I think you deserve a special reward tonight."

"And also you, Ashton," Sasha said, squeezing his hands before releasing them so that he could pour the champagne.

Her gaze went over him, admiring his finely chiseled face that was now sun-bronzed from his outdoor activities. This evening he looked so handsome in his fringed kangaroo-hide shirt that clung to the expanse of his sleekly muscled chest and wide shoulders beneath, and with his golden-red hair combed to just above his collar. When he returned her loving gaze, it felt as though he was scorching her skin with his intense gaze, a look of possession in his eyes.

Ashton poured two glasses of champagne and slid one over to Sasha. He lifted his glass as she circled her fingers around the long stem, also lifting it and holding it before her.

"Here's to tonight," Ashton whispered, clinking his glass against hers. He took a long swallow while Sasha only sipped at hers, looking at him with passion-heavy lashes, her eyes darkening with emotions forced to remain hidden for now.

Two cabin boys came to their table and each placed a plate of food before them. "You have your choice of fruit," one of the cabin boys said, gesturing with a hand toward a mahogany sideboard that was piled high with mounds of peaches, pears, grapes, figs, bananas, plums, and great dripping pink wedges of watermelon.

Sasha and Ashton nodded without looking. Ashton filled their glasses with champagne again and they resumed sipping and gazing with wonder over the tips of the glasses.

Then Sasha giggled as the aroma of the food wafted upward, tantalizingly enticing. "If I don't eat now, I'm afraid I may embarrass you," she murmured, setting her glass down.

"Oh? And how could you ever embarrass me?" Ashton said. His lips tugged into an amused smile. "Unless you're thinking about turning yourself into that character named Spike while on this elegant paddlewheeler. I'd hate to explain why I'm sharing champagne and holding hands with someone named Spike."

Sasha giggled. She placed her hands on her stomach, already feeling the rumbling beginning. "No, you drongo," she teased. She glanced around her as her stomach erupted into a low, drawn-out growl. "Now do you see? My stomach, Ashton. I must eat before it growls again."

Ashton laughed, eyeing the platter of hare smothered with cherries. He reached for her fork and stabbed a cherry and lifted it to her mouth. "Open wide, sweet darlin'," he said, his eyes twinkling. "We must get you fed, mustn't we?"

Sasha blushed and took the fork from him. "Ashton, please stop this foolishness," she scolded softly. "You are embarrassing me."

Realizing how hungry he was himself, Ashton began eating along with Sasha, yet never taking his eyes off her. This was a moment in time that he wanted to cherish. Once they left the paddlewheeler, who could say what might await them? There was much talk of a drought. Along with droughts came fires. The thought of what a fire would mean to him and Sasha made his gut ache.

And suddenly there was entertainment. Their plates emptied, they sipped on champagne again as moonlight flooded through the small windows along the top of the dining room wall, and Sasha and Ashton enjoyed the music of a tall, thin Aborigine dressed in only a brief loincloth. Using a long gum leaf which gave a resonant music when held taut at his lips, the dark-skinned native worked his way around the room, serenading everyone so simply, yet so beautifully.

The candle's glow, the moonlight, the music, the champagne—and Sasha's innocent loveliness— was more than Ashton could bear. He set his glass aside and took Sasha's from her, then took her hands and urged her up from the chair. Taking a wide turn around the end of the table, Ashton went to Sasha and swept an arm around her waist.

He leaned down close to her ear as he walked her from the room. "We've waited long enough," he whispered. "It's time I show my lady just how much I love her."

Sasha trembled with the promise of what was to come. She walked with Ashton beneath the moonlight until they reached the small confines of their cabin, in which was only a bunk attached to the wall, a basin of water on a stand secured to the floor, and a porcelain chamber pot. Though quaint and hardly roomy enough to undress in, Sasha and Ashton managed quite well to shed their clothes in record time.

The cabin was lit only by a soft ray of moonlight filtering through the small, round porthole at the top of the outside wall, when Ashton gazed at Sasha for a moment, feasting his eyes on her exquisite creamy skin, the soft pink crests of her breasts, and her passion-moist lips. He surrounded her with his hard, strong arms and pressed her against him, her mouth responding hot and sweet as he kissed her.

Sasha felt Ashton's hunger in the hard, seeking pressure of his lips, matching her own. She clung to his sinewed shoulders as he lifted her up into his arms and placed her on the bunk, then came to her, anchoring her fiercely to him as he entered her. She clung and rocked with him, her whole body quivering as the slow thrusting of his body promised more, assuring fulfillment.

And then he leaned away from her, only to allow himself room to worship her with his lips and hands. Her ragged breathing slowed as he made his way down her body. His lips moved over the glossy texture of her breasts, lapping at the taut nipples, and down over her ribs until he was sending ripples of pleasure through her as his tongue made a wet descent across the soft flesh of her belly, stopping then where he had parted the soft down of hair between her thighs. When his tongue touched her there, her body jolted with alarm, then pleasure spread and spread as he began the slow caress, making everything seem to go dim, except where her feelings were now centered.

Tossing her head from side to side, making whimpering sounds that she did not recognize as her own, Sasha gave herself over to the wild ecstasy and sensual abandonment that Ashton was creating by this different sort of lovemaking.

But before she went over the edge to enter that place inhabited only by lovers, he moved over her and entered her again and began making wild thrusts within her, his lips drugging her as he kissed her hard and long. As her passion rose, her whole body seemed fluid with fire. She clung to Ashton, arching to meet him, their bodies fusing as though one soul, one heartbeat, one moonbeam of sensuous pleasure.

Ashton moved his lips from her mouth and slithered them down her neck, groaning as he felt passion engulfing him in wild, fiery splashes. It was agony and bliss, these moments of mindlessness with Sasha!

His hands could not stay still. He smoothed them over the slimness of her body below her breasts, the supple broadening into the hips with their central muff of dark hair, her long, satiny thighs.

His lips then moved upward, brushing the smooth skin of her breast, moving over her nipple. He kissed the nipple, sucking it. Sasha drew in her breath sharply and gave a little cry.

Their bodies suddenly jolted and quivered. Ashton pressed endlessly deeper, over and over again, then sighed heavily and lay limply on her, both having reached the ultimate joy almost simultaneously.

Sasha stroked Ashton's back, then moved her hands down to the tightness of his buttocks. "My darling," she whispered. "How I do love you."

Ashton rolled away from her and lay at her side, gazing at her with wonder. "You make me feel like a man is supposed to feel," he said, smiling over at her. He smoothed a fallen lock of hair back from her eyes. "Never have I felt more like a man than tonight."

Sasha giggled. She leaned over and kissed his brow gently. "You always think that each time is better than the last," she teased. "What if I disappoint you one of these times, Ashton?" He cuddled her close. She could feel his manhood growing against her abdomen again, causing her heart to flutter with eagerness.

"Never will you disappoint me," Ashton whispered, entering her again. He could feel her gasp with pleasure as he began his gentle strokes within her again. He cupped a breast and squeezed it. "Sweet darlin', I vow never to disappoint you."

Sasha became flushed with desire. She placed her lips close to his and whispered against them. "You could never disappoint me," she said. "My Lord, Ashton, how you do delight me in so many ways!"

Ashton twined his fingers through her hair and drew her lips hard into his. He kissed her, and their bodies strained hungrily together, all velvet and fire. . . .

Deep in the shadows where the moonlight could not touch him, Stanford Sidwell rode through the forest with his men, never far enough from the paddlewheeler to lose sight of it through the thick brush and twisting willows. Wheeling his horse to a halt, he turned and faced his men as they edged up around him in a circle.

"You know what we must do now," he said, his voice soft, yet threatening. "You've been instructed, so get on with you. We've got to make sure Ashton York will have the surprise of his life at the break of dawn. We want to catch everyone on that paddlewheeler offguard. But don't kill Ashton. Just make sure we get all of his bales of wool from the hold of the ship. We've got to make Ashton see the senselessness of going on with his life as a grazier. I want to see him leave it all behind like a dog leaving a fight with its tail tucked between its legs."

He cleared his throat. "Now it's understood that Ashton shouldn't see me," he said, searching the faces of his men for this understanding. "I'll be close by enjoyin' his humiliation." He doubled a fist at his side. "But still, remember, it's of the utmost importance that no matter what happens, Ashton York must come out of this fracas alive!"

He waved his fist in the air. "Now get goin'!" he commanded. "Get way ahead of that paddlewheeler then get to work cuttin' them damn trees!"

The men rode away, Stanford behind them. He laughed throatily. The men still did not understand his motivation. But because they were getting wages they were happy with, they had no reason to question anything.

"With luck, my need of them will soon run out," he whispered to himself. "Surely Ashton will break soon and lead me to that damn chest!"

As he rode beneath the shadowy trees, his thoughts went to Bianca. She had become a sudden threat to his plans. But for now he was safe. He had left her well-guarded at his sheep station. Until he was running his fingers through the coins and jewels in the chest, he must keep his eye on Bianca. Then he would kill her. She would be of no use to him anymore.

"Nor anyone," Stanford said to himself, laughing throatily.

Chapter Twenty-Six

Restless, Ashton stirred from the bunk, careful not to awaken Sasha. No amount of star gazing or drinking champagne could erase the doubts that were consuming him about being a grazier. Every way he turned it seemed that he was running into obstacles. If things had been right, he would not have chosen to go to market now with his wool. He would have waited until the fleece was thicker and longer on his sheep, guaranteeing a heftier price.

As it was, he would have to pretend that the price paid him was enough while Sasha stood at his side, trusting that he was not going to let any more of their world fall apart around them.

The cabin was dusky with the morning light seeping through the small porthole above the bunk as Ashton slipped into his breeches. He gazed down at Sasha, curled up on her side, her dark lashes pressed against her pink cheeks in her sleep. With her cotton nightgown lying loosely around her, she looked no less than adorable.

Bending over her, Ashton brushed her lips with a kiss, tingling all over from the pleasure of even this little contact with her.

But not wanting to awaken her, he stepped back away from the bunk and finished dressing. He eyed his gunbelt and shrugged as he slipped it around his waist. He had gotten so used to wearing his revolvers that he felt naked without them. He had learned long ago not to trust anything that crawled, walked, or talked in Australia.

There were only three exceptions—Sasha, Crispin, and Rufus.

He choked back a lump that formed in his throat every time he thought of Rufus. It still did not seem real that he was dead.

Shaking off memories that filled him with an aching despair, Ashton went to the door and slowly opened it. He took one last look at Sasha, smiled, then stepped out onto the deck and closed the door quietly behind him.

The air was cool and fragrant as he walked past the other closed doors of the cabins along the top deck, then went to the rail and clasped his hands around it, leaning his full weight against it. Yellow sprays of mimosa flashed in the morning sun, and in the tall and stately trees that lined the river, several kinds of parrots thronged the bush—galahs, bold-eyed corellas, and pink leadbetter cockatoos. The yellow-and-black cockatoos cried *brrrarrrk*, alert as sentinels. A kookaburra jeered from somewhere in the distance.

There was a sudden *whumping* sound and then the paddles of the boat suddenly ground to a halt. Ashton jumped with alarm. He leaned out over the rail and peered ahead, then grew cold inside when he saw the reason the boat had stopped. He automatically reached for one of his revolvers and slung it out of its holster, warily eyeing the pile of lumber that was blocking the progress of the paddle-wheeler.

"What's going on?" a man spoke from behind him, followed by other curious men who had felt the delay of the boat and had emerged from their cabins.

Ashton turned to them and was glad to see that they had all very intelligently slipped their gunbelts on, because he knew that at any moment they would probably have to use them. The boat was targeted for an attack!

Charles Kelton, the captain of the ship, rushed to the rail armed with a hefty shotgun, the helmsman and other crew members following his lead with long-barreled pistols and rifles.

"I think we'd best scatter along the rail on both sides of the boat and prepare ourselves for an attack," Ashton shouted, scrutinizing the heavy vegetation along the banks that was capable of hiding many horsemen. "And quick!"

The men scattered and none too soon, for out of the thicket on the right side of the boat came a thundering of horsemen shooting their firearms at the paddlewheeler. The men who had gone to the opposite rail came scurrying back, and in a moment there was a barrage of gunfire, discouraging the riders from moving any closer.

Sasha was awakened abruptly by the gunfire. With her eyes wide and frightened, she searched the cabin for Ashton. "No," she cried to herself. "Oh, Ashton, what now?"

She rose from the bunk and hurried into her clothes. Combing her fingers through her hair, she ran from the cabin. Her heart pounding, she looked for Ashton among the men at the rail, and when she found him she scurried to his side and without even asking him yanked his other revolver from its holster. Aiming into the horsemen, she fired, then was shaken to the core when Ashton discovered her there and jerked the gun from her hand.

"Sasha, get back to the cabin!" he shouted. "Lord, woman, can't you see danger when it's staring you square in the eye?"

Sasha stood her ground, flinching when a bullet whizzed by her head, making a strange sort of zinging sound. Although her knees were shaking and her heart was pounding, she grabbed the revolver back from Ashton.

"Ashton, you choose the craziest times to fuss at me," she scolded. "While you are doing so we could both be shot. Now leave me be. I can shoot a gun. Let me!"

The pinging of bullets scraping against the deck and rail close beside them caused Ashton to wheel back around and begin shooting at the horsemen again. Sasha steadied her aim, closed her eyes, and fired again; this time the jolt of the firing threw her off balance. Awkwardly she fell backwards, her backside making painful contact with the wooden deck.

But not to be dissuaded, knowing that every gun

was needed to protect the people on the ship, she pushed herself back up beside Ashton and started to fire. Then she stopped and gasped when, at the outer edge of the attackers, was a man she instantly recognized.

"Stanford Sidwell!" she whispered, paling. "So he is the cause—"

Her lips parted, and another gasp escaped them when Stanford's body lurched with the impact of a bullet and he grabbed at his left arm as blood began rolling from a wound, down across the sleeve of his elegant suit jacket.

"I got the son of a bitch," Ashton grumbled, laughing throatily.

"You saw him also?" Sasha asked, edging closer to Ashton, glad that the gunfire had stopped and that they were quickly retreating. "You saw Stanford Sidwell?"

Ashton aimed his revolver and fired into the retreating men, then slung his smoking firearm into its holster. "Aye, I saw him, and I'm sure it was not his intention to be seen—most definitely not to be shot," he said, easing his revolver from Sasha's hand and twirling it back into its holster also. "The bastard. He's not going to stop until I reveal—"

Sasha peered up at him as he suddenly broke his words off, looking down at her with a strange light in his eyes. "Until you reveal what?" she asked. "What were you about to say?"

Ashton gazed down at her a moment longer, then looked away from her into the brush where the horsemen had disappeared. "It was nothing," he said, kneading his brow. "Nothing at all."

Frustrated, knowing that Ashton was lying to her,

Sasha stepped around in front of him, forcing him to look at her again. "Ashton, don't you think it's time to let me in on what this thing is between you and Stanford?" she asked, placing her hands on her hips. "It is not entirely because there is hate between you. There is something else. Don't you think I deserve to know since I am constantly the target of that man's vengeance as well as you? Ashton, it is only fair."

Captain Kelton stepped up to Ashton just then with his hand extended. "Son, I want to thank you for taking charge this morning," he said, shaking Ashton's hand vigorously. "It is not every day that my paddlewheeler is attacked by gunmen. Though well equipped with firearms, it is not in my line to command those who are firing them." A large man in a dark blue suit with gold buttons gracing the front and a thick, dark mustache that bounced as he talked, he continued shaking Ashton's hand. "You saved the day, lad. You saved the day."

Ashton's lips lifted slowly into a smile, the flattery making his face take on a crimson color beneath his bronze tan. "I was glad to oblige, sir," he said, in truth feeling guilty that he was the cause of the attack. "Glad to oblige."

"When we reach Narrung, I want to set you and your lady up in one of the finest hotels and make sure you get the finest of champagne and food for your entire stay there," Captain Kelton said, finally dropping his hand from Ashton's.

He smiled down at Sasha, his dark eyes showing their appreciation of her delicate loveliness. "How does that sound to you, ma'am?" he said. "You and your husband can have a holiday before headin' back to hard work at your sheep station."

Sasha's face colored at the mention of her "husband." She lowered her eyes, then when Ashton took her hand, looked back up at the captain. "Why, it would be a pleasure, sir, and Ashton and I appreciate your thoughtfulness," she murmured, a wave of ecstasy flooding her insides as Ashton snaked an arm possessively around her waist.

The events of the previous night were still fresh in her mind. Oh, how he had loved her—how she had loved him back!

Enough to be married?

Yes, that was what she wanted. She had begun to be able to place Woodrow Rutherford and the way he had abandoned her from her mind. She could not envision Ashton ever turning his back on her.

Yes, she wanted to be Ashton's wife! How wonderful it was to have finally made up her mind to trust and totally love him!

She looked adoringly up at him and blushed anew when he gazed down at her, surely seeing something wonderfully different in her eyes.

"Then let us rid the river of the debris, and after the boat is on its way again, I would like to have the honor of having you two at my table for breakfast," Captain Kelton said, smiling from Ashton to Sasha.

"That sounds delightful," Sasha said, exchanging glances with Ashton again.

Then she cast a worried look toward the riverbank, wondering if Stanford and his men had truly fled. Was it safe for Ashton to leave the ship to help move the stacked limbs? What if Stanford and his men returned?

Again she looked up at Ashton, wondering what

he was avoiding telling her about his past relationship with Stanford Sidwell. Surely it was something quite intense for Stanford to take such elaborate steps to get back at Ashton.

Captain Kelton walked away from them and began shouting orders to his men.

Ashton turned to Sasha and held her gently by the shoulders. "You return to the cabin until the boat is moving in the water again," he ordered flatly.

"But, Ashton, what if Stanford should return?" she argued. "I proved that I could help defend the boat the same as the men. I want to stay at the rail and keep watch and be prepared should they return."

Ashton sighed heavily. "Sasha, for once do as I say?" he said, his dark eyes boring down into hers. "There are enough men to see to things." He looked over his shoulder. "Anyhow, there isn't any sign of the scalawags anywhere. Once Stanford was wounded, he surely gave the command to return to his sheep station." His jaw tightened. "But if he knows what's good for him, he'll hightail it out of this part of the country while the gettin' is good. I won't stand by any longer and let him destroy our lives."

Sasha flung herself into Ashton's arms and hugged him. "Please be careful," she murmured. "Ashton York, I love you with all of my heart. I can't bear the thought of losing you."

"Sasha," Ashton said, weaving his fingers through her long and lustrous hair. "My sweet Sasha. Do you think I would let anything happen to me now that I've found someone like you to spend the rest of my life with?"

He held her away from him and smiled down at her, his eyes gleaming. "Darling, while in Narrung, let's make the celebration complete," he said softly. "Let's look us up a preacher and let him speak words over us that will make us man and wife. That's the sort of partnership I have always wanted with you—a total commitment of the heart."

Tears flooded Sasha's eyes. Again she flung herself into his arms. "Yes, darling, that is also what I want," she whispered, pressing her cheek against his chest. "It just took a while for me to trust such feelings. Because of Woodrow—"

Ashton eased her away from him and gently placed a hand over her lips. "Shh," he whispered. "Let's not speak of that man again. From now on it is just the two of us—and perhaps one day a daughter in your image, darling."

Radiant, Sasha felt tears running down her cheeks. She drew Ashton's mouth to her lips and kissed him with a sweet ardor.

His wounded arm limp, his shirt sleeve stained with dried blood, Stanford stumbled into his cabin and collapsed on the bed. Bianca stood back away from him, her hands at her throat, then jumped with alarm as he turned and faced her with utter contempt in his eyes.

"Whore, don't just stand there," he said, his voice too weak to shout at her. "See to my wound." He winced as pain stabbed away at his flesh. "Get the bullet out of my arm and be easy while doin' it. I don't like the idea of being scarred anymore than I have to be."

Bianca inched toward him, her heart racing. If

ever there was an opportunity to rid herself of this evil man, now was the time. But, as though he had read her mind, Stanford yanked a pistol from his holster and aimed it at her.

"Don't get any ideas, whore," he hissed. "This gun will be on you the whole time you're cuttin' on me. If you make any suspicious slips I'll shoot you faster than you can bat an eye."

"Why didn't you have one of your men do it?" Bianca complained. She bent over him and tore his shirt sleeve away from the wound. "You've lost a lot of blood by waiting for me to do it."

"Any one of them would've liked stickin' a knife in me, but not to help me," Stanford growled. "I gave all of them their walkin' papers as soon as we got free and clear of the guns on the paddlewheeler."

Bianca's mind was spinning. "You no longer have need of men to help you?" she gasped. "And what is this about a paddlewheeler? Is that where you were wounded? How could a gun battle erupt on a paddlewheeler?"

She paled and straightened her back to stare down at Stanford. "Unless it was you who instigated such gunplay. . . ." she said, her words trailing off to nothing.

"Stanford, what did you do?" she then continued. "Did it have anything to do with Ashton and Sasha? Oh, Lord, did you hurt either one of them?"

"Quit talkin' and askin' so many questions, whore," Stanford warned, sweat dampening his brow as the pain worsened in his arm. He yanked his knife from its sheath and handed it to Bianca.

"Use this. Scald it good over the fire and then get this damn bullet out of my arm."

Bianca took the knife, her pulse racing at the thought of plunging it into Stanford's dark heart. But it was just a thought, a deep desire that was to be denied, for he still held her at bay with the loaded pistol.

"Just tell me one thing," she dared to ask. "Are Sasha and Ashton harmed?"

"Damn it, no, they're not harmed," Stanford said, licking his parched lips. "Now get busy. We've got to get out of here. I don't want to be here when Ashton comes lookin' for me."

"Please leave me behind," Bianca begged. "I'll just get in your way if you take me with you."

She flinched and her throat went dry when Stanford placed his finger on the trigger of his pistol. "You're goin' wherever I go," he snarled. "I need you to take care of my wound." He laughed, and his eyes took on a evil glint. "Then I'll let you go. I'll leave you in the outback with the others of your own kind. But I doubt if the Aborigines will want you either. You're worthless to anyone. Worthless, do you hear?"

Hate spiraled through Bianca. Her grip grew tighter on the handle of the knife. She would not be able to kill Stanford now—but one day soon she would find the opportunity. She would wait until the time was exactly right. She wanted to watch him squirm, even beg for mercy!

Stanford kept a close eye on Bianca as she held the blade of the knife over the flames of the fire. He smiled smugly. He was rid of the men who had become too much extra baggage for him. He did not need them around to interfere in his plans for Ashton any longer. They had proved worthless today. Always before he had worked alone. He had only needed the hired hands to make him look legitimate.

"But only to a point," he thought to himself.

His original plan had failed, but he thought mother nature would take up the attack where he had left off. He had seen the cracks in the ground and the dried vegetation. He knew the danger of fires under these conditions. One careless Aborigine setting fire to the brush with a firestick and the devastation would be vast.

He smiled at the thought.

Chapter Twenty-Seven

NARRUNG, AUSTRALIA

"I now pronounce you man and wife," the minister said, slowly closing his Bible.

Beneath a bonnet of white satin enveloped in the folds of a most exquisite rich white veil, and dressed in a pale pink satin dress with a gorgeous barege shawl draped loosely over her shoulders, Sasha looked through teary eyes up at Ashton.

He gazed down at her, as if she were a vision of awe-inspiring beauty. With trembling fingers, he lifted the veil and bent over her, pressing his lips softly against hers.

"My wife," he whispered. "My adorable wife."

Feeling as if she were floating, Sasha hugged his words to her. And when he stepped to her side, sweeping his arm around her waist, her gaze raked over him. Wearing a suit with an ascot at his throat, his hair neatly trimmed to lie just above his shirt collar, his face dark and finely chiseled, he was the handsomest of men.

And he was hers!

Oh, how blessed she was!

"Congratulations," the preacher said, stepping aside as Captain Kelton stepped forward, a diamond stickpin glistening in the folds of his ascot.

"Yes, congratulations are in order," Captain Kelton said. "And may your future be blessed with much happiness."

"Thank you," Sasha said, smiling up at him as he took her hand and kissed it gallantly. She had been amazed to discover that this riverboat captain was a wealthy man, having acquired his riches from a vast fleet of ships he had owned. After retiring from the sea, he had fulfilled his fantasies by purchasing a paddlewheeler to live a simple and carefree life along Australia's Murray River.

She gazed around her at the sumptuousness of this hotel that Captain Kelton also owned. The lobby in which she had just been married was a spacious, airy room. It was filled with many eye-catching things—a stunning mural of an Australian bush fire, mirrored walls, chandeliers, exuberant bouquets of flowers, and inviting sofas.

The linen-covered chairs were perfect for sipping champagne. Tea and biscuits were being served among the guests who were sitting on plush sofas before a roaring fire in a marble fireplace.

"Sasha? Sweet darlin'?" Ashton said, breaking her trance. "Are you ready to go to our suite?"

Sasha blinked her eyes and dropped her hand, damp with Captain Kelton's kiss, to her side. She laughed softly as she looked blushingly up at

Ashton. "I'm sorry, darling," she murmured. "What did you say? For a moment I was caught up in admiring Captain Kelton's hotel."

"The captain has said that our suite is ready," Ashton said, leaning down so close to her his breath teased her ear. "Shall we depart, my love, and enjoy a full evening and night of privacy?"

Again Sasha blushed, a warmth blossoming within her. "Yes, darling, let's," she whispered back. "But a suite? Did you say that we are to have a suite?"

"The captain says that he wouldn't have it any other way than for us to have the fanciest room in his hotel," Ashton said, smiling over his shoulder at Captain Kelton who was now puffing on a thin cheroot, seeming to enjoy making two lovebirds the happiest people in Narrung.

"How kind," Sasha said, then tingled all over when Ashton placed an arm around her waist and drew her close to his side, walking her toward a magnificent spiral staircase at the far end of the room.

"Thank you, Captain," he said, looking over his shoulder at the captain. He mocked a half salute toward him, then suddenly swept Sasha up into his arms and began carrying her up the staircase.

"My word, Ashton," Sasha said, giggling as she held onto her hat. She gazed behind her at the people gaping at them from the lobby. "Please put me down. We are making a spectacle of ourselves."

"We are expected to," Ashton chuckled. "We are newlyweds."

"Perhaps," Sasha said, resignedly removing her hat so that it would not tumble from her head and down the stairs. "But it is not something that I am used to." She glanced down at her dress. "Nor am I used to such beautiful clothes." She gave him a worried stare. "Ashton, we shouldn't have spent so much money. Not for my dress and hat, nor for your suit. Those coins could have paid for supplies for The Homestead."

"They could have," Ashton said, reaching the first floor landing. He began carrying Sasha down a narrow corridor dimly lit by candles in wall sconces. "But, Sasha, this is our wedding day and I wanted it to be a day that you remember with pride and gladness in your heart."

He stopped at a closed door and turned the knob. When the door opened, he carried Sasha over the threshold. "Anyhow, we were paid well for our wool," he tried to reassure her. "And that is only the beginning. When we come to market again, our supply of wool will be twice what it was today." He smiled down at her. "So then shall the price."

Sasha didn't have the heart to argue with him, even as she doubted that their future could be as bright as the picture he was painting for her today. She was so filled with concern over their sheep station's even surviving that it made a bitter taste in her mouth just to think of it.

But not wanting to ruin this very special day that a woman had only once in a lifetime, Sasha cast all worries and doubts aside, to cling to the present—to now when, if she let herself, she could imagine that everything in the world was brilliantly wonderful and carefree as her heart ached for it to be.

She gazed around the room, its magnificence momentarily stealing her breath away. It was easy to forget that down below on the streets of Narrung could be found jinkers, bullock carts, hay wagons, sleepy hacks hung up to hitching posts, and tired Aborigines leaning against verandah posts. She had even seen a few brooding Chinese prospectors smoking thin, yellow cigarettes, and a row of mongrel dogs asleep along the earthen pavement. All had seemed to be stilled into a strange sort of inertia in the summer heat.

Like the lobby, this room was large, airy and opulent. Everything was white and lacy, from the satin draperies at the one window to the satin bedspread and bedskirt, white lace adorning its edges to match the pillows that were trimmed with thickly gathered lace.

Freshly cut flowers were in abundance throughout the room, filling the air with the fragrance of an English garden. Two overstuffed chairs flanked a wide, white velveteen-covered sofa in front of a fireplace. The carpet was white at Ashton's feet as he carried her to the bed and gently laid her upon it. She scarcely noticed a bottle of champagne and two tall-stemmed glasses on a nightstand beside the bed, for Ashton's fingers were already eagerly undressing her.

"My wife," Ashton said, his violet eyes darkening with passion. "Is it true, Sasha? Did you speak words of forever with me only moments ago? Did you truly become my wife?"

"My husband," Sasha said, trembling as Ashton smoothed her dress down from her shoulders, and then her underthings, freeing her breasts. "Are you truly my husband? I thought such a man as you only existed in a woman's fantasies. How can you be real? You are so handsome, so gentle, so wonderful."

She sucked in a wild breath and closed her eyes in ecstasy when his way of answering her was to brush her throat with his lips, then close over the nipple of her breast with his mouth.

Shaken with desire, Sasha wriggled herself free of the rest of her clothes. Gently he enveloped her with his powerful arms and touched her lips wonderingly with his mouth. His tongue brushed her lips lightly, then he kissed her with a lazy warmth that left her weak.

A tremor went through her body when his hand found her warm and secret place. Parting her thighs, she let him caress the damp valley. Her throat arched backward and he buried his lips along its delicate column.

When he rose from the bed, her eyes followed him and her pulse raced as he shed his clothing a piece at a time, slowly revealing his magnificently muscled body to her feasting eyes.

After the last garment and his boots were discarded, Ashton joined Sasha on the bed. Moving over her, fitting himself into the curve of her softly pliant limbs, he plunged deeply within her. Sasha clung and rocked with him, her hips responding in a rhythmic movement to meet the slow thrusting of his pelvis. His lean, sinewy buttocks moving, he plunged more deeply within her. Her breasts pulsed warmly beneath his fingers; her lips were on fire as he nibbled on them.

"Sweet darlin', how I love you," Ashton whispered, now stroking the satiny line of her inner thighs.

She traced the line of his jaw with her finger. "I have loved you for so long," she whispered. "For so very, very long."

"If I had only known," Ashton said, stilling his thrusts to momentarily just look at her flawless features, so vibrant and glowing in her love.

"Oh, Ashton, you had to know," Sasha said, smoothing her hand over his cheek, reveling in the mere touch of his flesh against hers. "It was in my eyes. It was in my every breath spoken to you."

"Aay, I saw and I heard, yet I could not be sure," he said softly. "There were so many things crowding your heart at that time."

"But never again," Sasha whispered, draping her arms around his neck, bringing him down to her so that she could hug him tightly. "Never again." She kissed his cheek. "Make love to me, Ashton. All night long, make love to me."

"How easy it is to obey my woman's wishes," he said, chuckling. He resumed his rhythmic strokes within her, the pleasure building within him, as though he were being swept along by the touch of the wild winds of Australia.

Their bodies tangled. Their passions crested. Their bodies exploded in spasms of desire, the silent explosion of their needs accompanied by their sighs and groans.

Then a great calm filled them both.

Her abdomen now uncomfortably large, and feeling clumsy, Bianca trailed along behind Stanford as he rode on a horse, his shoulders stooped, his wounded arm hanging heavy at his side. She had not been offered a horse, and she would not have mounted one if she had been. She feared too much for her unborn child. She was too near to the birthing date. Since accompanying Stanford to the outback, she had experienced enough hardships to last a lifetime—and so many that had threatened her and her child.

If only she could last just a little while longer. . . .

Finding it hard to place one foot after another for even one more step along the dry, parched ground, Bianca faltered in her steps, then stopped. "Stanford," she cried, the sun beating down on her as if her head were in an oven. "Please go no farther. I . . . don't . . . know if I can. . . ."

Stanford wiped beads of perspiration from his brow. He cast Bianca a glaring look over his shoulder. "We've not traveled even a mile and you are complaining?" he growled. His eyes narrowed as he looked down at her stomach and the way she was holding onto it. "If not for that load you are carrying in front of you, you'd have no cause to complain." He shook his head with disgust. "All those years of bedding up with men and you let yourself get pregnant?"

"Bianca is glad that you are not the father," she blurted out, tears streaming down her face as she met his steady stare with her own. "I did not even know you when I became with child. I am blessed, at least, because of that. I do not have to have nightmares of my child turning out to be like you."

Stanford glared down at her a moment longer, then looked away from her and flicked his horse's reins. "Come along, whore," he grumbled. "We've only a little way to go."

Bianca looked to her left, realizing that she and

Stanford were still traveling along grazing land that belonged to Ashton and Sasha. Along the horizon, beneath the glare of the sun, she could see several sheep grazing, and farther still, a sheepherder tending the flock, with a dog yapping and circling the sheep as they momentarily scattered.

Then she looked up at Stanford and trudged onward behind him.

Finally he wheeled his horse to a stop and dismounted, anchoring his wounded arm with his hand.

"This'll do," he growled, looking at the thick cover of eucalyptus that blocked the entrance of a cave that led underground. "No one should find us here. I only happened along and found this cave the other day. Its entrance was hidden behind brush that I cleared away."

Bianca placed her hands at the small of her back and groaned, then straightened her shoulders and walked past Stanford, eyeing the cave entrance warily. "Do you intend for us to —to live in there?" she asked, her voice weak. She turned to Stanford, her shoulders slouching again. "Why, Stanford? Why couldn't we have just stayed at the cabin?" She shuddered. "There could be any amount of wild things running around in that—that hole in the ground."

"Quit complainin'," Stanford said, securing his horse's reins on a tree limb. "Always complainin'. You're worthless, whore. Worthless."

"Then why couldn't you have left me at the cabin?" Bianca whined. "Or better yet, why did you bring me to the outback at all? I've only been in the way."

Stanford shrugged. "For the most part, yes," he said, kicking tangled weeds away from the cave entrance with the toe of his boot. "But I can recall some moments when you came in right handy." He smiled wickedly over at her. "If you know what I mean." He grabbed her by the wrist. "And I'm only havin' you taggin' along now because I don't trust that mouth of yours. I can't have you runnin' to Sasha about me and my plans."

"What plans?" Bianca asked shallowly, yet knowing that he wouldn't disclose any of them to her.

Stanford ignored her. He released his grip on her wrist and gazed into the distance, his eyes narrowing. "I hope we'll not be stayin' here long," he grumbled. "That bastard Ashton York'll surely decide to go for that chest soon. How could he not? There are riches in it just for the taking!"

Bianca paled. She started to question him about what he had just said about a chest—and riches. She did not want to remind him that he had spoken out of turn and had perhaps revealed too much to her. Although she was intrigued to the core with what he had said, she now had a vague suspicion of what had been behind everything that Stanford Sidwell had done these past months. He hoped to become wealthy by means other than being a con artist. This time he was going to take what he wanted by force—the taking most surely endangering not only Ashton, but Sasha!

Bianca eyed Stanford's holstered pistols, then smiled to herself. He had been getting careless. He was too trusting of her. Rarely did he hold her at bay anymore with his pistols. And he had somehow forgotten that she still had possession of the knife that had been used to remove the bullet from his flesh. In due time, when he least expected it, she would plunge the knife into the evil man and end his life. She would protect Sasha at all costs, for whether Bianca lived or died, she had already decided that Sasha would raise her child. Her child deserved a better life than she had been given. Her child would be raised in a home filled with love. Her child would be respected!

"Help me get the gear inside the cave," Stanford ordered.

Bianca went to the horse and removed the saddle-bag. Somehow, she felt suddenly filled with hope. If Sasha and Ashton were to one day be the recipient of a chest filled with treasure, wouldn't her child also share in this wealth?

She turned and frowned at Stanford. Yes, he had to die, but it must be at a time that would hurt him the most.

Perhaps just when he thought he was going to get his hands on the chest . . . ?

She smiled and carried the saddlebag toward the dark hole in the ground, not even caring when she saw a rodent scampering from inside it.

Chapter Twenty-Eight

THE OUTBACK
THE HOMESTEAD

*The carefree days and nights away from The Home-*stead were now like a dream to Sasha. As soon as she and Ashton arrived home it seemed that they stepped right back into a nightmare —one that seemed endless. Stirred by the spiraling updrafts of wind known as *willy willies*, a haze of red dust hung over their sheep station; their pastureland was scorched by the sun stretching into a dusty horizon.

Blowing a stray strand of sweat-dampened hair back from her eyes, Sasha stood at the kitchen table filled with a hopeless disgust. "Oh, Ashton, nothing will keep even overnight anymore," she groaned, staring down at the meat laid out before her eyes on the table. She turned her head away, shuddering. "This meat that we butchered last night? It's—it's crawling with maggots."

Ashton grabbed the piece of meat and slung it out the door, where it would bake on the ground as though it were cooking in an oven. "Damn it all to hell," he growled. He leaned against the frame of the door and crossed his arms angrily, staring out at the sheep that stood like painted beasts on the parched earth. In this dry spell, the sheep had been forced to resort to digging the bare earth with their hooves for roots.

"I knew the danger of drought in the outback, but never had I thought it could be this devastating," Ashton solemnly added. "Our land can't tolerate much more blowing away in the wind. The pulverized soil is disappearing into thin air."

Sasha went to Ashton and stood beside him. She followed his gaze and felt sick inside when she looked at the sheep. Fretting in the sun, some were shoving their heads under one another's bellies for a spot of shade, while others were staring into infinity with their hungry, vacant eyes, their flanks sunken in. The young and weak were gone, burned and buried in mass graves.

She looked skyward. As the sun slid upward, the heat rose with it, and the swirling dust glowed golden in the back light. "Will it ever end?" she asked.

"You might ask *how* will it end?" Ashton said, slowly shaking his head back and forth. "The outback is baked tawny by the summer heat. Its ground is mantled in a crackling skin of dry gum leaves, grasses, and fallen strips of eucalyptus bark. One spark of fire and—"

Sasha grabbed his arm, her eyes wide with fear. "Don't even think it," she said, swallowing hard.

"Ashton, we must pray for rain. Surely it will rain soon. It's been so long."

Ashton frowned as he looked up at the sky. "Aye, I think that we should get a storm soon," he said, yet doubting it.

Sasha swung away from him. She took a wet cloth from a basin of water and began washing the stain of the meat and maggots from the tabletop. "I don't want to hear any more talk of fires or drought," she said, her voice weak. "I want to work this day away just like yesterday, and tomorrow I shall do the same until one day I will work myself right into seeing myself dancing outside in the rain."

Ashton chuckled. He took the damp cloth from Sasha and dropped it on the table, then drew her into his arms.

"I smell so sweaty," Sasha complained, yet did not pull away from him. He was her solace. He and his arms, and his wonderful kisses.

"No sweatier than me," Ashton said, brushing a light kiss across her lips. He smoothed her damp hair back from her brow. "Darling, I must go and check on things in the pasture. Will you promise that you won't work so hard today? It's too hot. It will drain your energy too quickly." Again he brushed a kiss across her lips. "I can't let anything happen to my bride, now can I?"

"Ashton, how can you think of me when it is you who will be out in that baking sun," Sasha worried, touching his cheek gently with her hand. "Look at your flesh. It's baked almost as tight as shoe leather. Even your hat isn't helping keep the sun away from you."

"That's just a part of being in this tough, dry, and

uncompromising land," Ashton grumbled. "It takes a strong man to wrest a living from it." He framed her face between his hands and smiled down at her. "Also a strong woman. And I think I've got the strongest of them all."

Sasha laughed lightly. "I'm not sure how to take that," she said. "Yes, I'm glad that you think of me as strong and capable enough to be with you in the outback, but I hope you still see me as—as feminine, Ashton." Never had she felt as feminine as now. She wanted to touch her abdomen to feel that part of her that soon would be growing with a child. Only in these past few days had she realized that she must be pregnant. She had not shared the news with Ashton yet—not until she was sure.

And now she was sure!

"Sweet darlin', the only time I have ever questioned your femininity was when you chose to disguise yourself as Spike," he said, chuckling.

"Will you ever forget that I went by that terrible name?" Sasha said, her lower lip curving into a pout.

"Only when I am given cause to," Ashton said, his eyes twinkling.

"Oh?" Sasha said, tracing his lips with her forefinger. "And just what must I do? Perhaps tell you that I am with child? Would that be proof enough of my femininity? I don't think anyone named Spike has ever had a child, do you?"

Ashton paled and his lips parted in a surprised gasp. "What are you saying?" he said, taking a step back from her. "Are you—"

"Pregnant?" Sasha said, smiling devilishly up at him. "Well, yes, I do believe so."

Ashton let out a loud shout. He grabbed Sasha around the waist and lifted her up in the air, then placed her gingerly back to the floor and enveloped her within his arms. His mouth moved over her lips. He kissed her reverently, then held her at arm's length, beaming with pride as he raked his eyes over her, stopping at her stomach.

Sasha placed her hands on her abdomen. "Our child is growing within me, Ashton," she murmured, tears of joy rolling down her cheeks. "Never have I been as happy as now."

Ashton's hands trembled as he placed them atop Sasha's. "Our child," he said thickly, then he once again wrapped his arms around Sasha and drew her into his embrace. "Damn this drought. It can't be good for either you or the child. What are we going to do to protect you from it?" He held her away from him again. "Perhaps I should take you to Melbourne, where you can be more comfortable in your pregnancy."

Sasha was taken aback by such a suggestion. "Never," she said, squaring her shoulders stubbornly. "I shall stay with you. I belong here. I shall not deprive you of one moment of this pregnancy. I could not bear not to be with you at such a precious time as this."

"But the heat—" Ashton worried, swinging away from her to go to the open door to stare out at the dry and open spaces again. "Damn this heat."

"It will pass, Ashton," Sasha murmured, going to his side. She looked adoringly up at him. "Until it does, I promise not to overtire myself." She took his hand and led him out the door, onto the porch. "Now you go on and see about our sheep. Those pitiful creatures need more attention than I do.''

Sasha leaned back inside the house and grabbed Ashton's hat from a peg on the wall. On tiptoe, she plopped it on his head, then gave him a playful smack on his rear. "There," she said, clasping her hands together behind her. "Go and tell Crispin I said hello and to stop in tonight for a cup of tea. It would be a good time to tell him our good news."

"He'll be happy to hear it," Ashton said, rushing on down the steps. "He'll be like a second daddy to our child."

"He can be our child's godfather, if you like," Sasha said, waving at Crispin in the distance as he rode up to the barn on his horse.

Ashton turned and gave Sasha an endearing look, then went to saddle his horse. Sasha watched him until he was riding away into the sunburnt country that was as dry as a sunstruck bone. She was afraid of what he might find while traveling across their pastureland. In this intense heat, most of the lambs born between dawn and late afternoon would not survive their first day. Too many had died this past week even to count.

Squinting into the sun dazzle and peering through the haze of dust, Sasha became aware of someone approaching in a covered wagon. Wanting to remain in the shade of the porch, she waited for the wagon to come to her. When it came to a shuddering halt, its two heat-exhausted horses clammy with sweat, their heads bowed, Sasha still remained on the porch. The driver gave her a sense of foreboding in his pitch-black suit and wiry gray hair tangled and twisted around his gaunt, narrow face. His gray eyes seemed pitiless as he looked up at her; his teeth were yellow as he gave her a slow smile.

"Good-day to you ma'am," the man said, making an effort to bow from where he sat on the seat. He dropped the reins from his long fingers, stepped down from the wagon, and came to stand at the foot of the steps to peer intensely up at Sasha.

"Might I interest you in my wares today, ma'am?" he asked, gesturing toward his wagon. "I've many sizes and shapes of slabs for you to choose from."

Sasha forked an eyebrow questionably. "Slabs?" she said, looking in wonder at the canvas that covered the wagon. "What sort of slabs?"

"Why, tombstones, ma'am," the vendor said, as though offended by her ignorance. "I've come prepared to engrave on the spot any that you might choose."

The vendor smiled slowly up at her again, his gray eyes squinting. "One never knows when the good Lord is going to call one home," he said, hunching over somewhat as he began to rub his hands together. "One must be prepared to meet one's maker with the right words of everlasting peace on one's gravestone."

Sasha paled and swallowed hard, feeling that this itinerant vendor's appearance with such morbid wares could be a bad omen. She started to tell him to leave, but he had already hurried to his wagon and had slung open the canvas at one side, revealing all sizes and shapes of stones, as though his wagon was a portable cemetery!

"Sir, please go elsewhere with—with your wares," Sasha said, turning her eyes away. "I . . . am not interested."

The vendor was not to be dissuaded. He rambled on. "I can fix up one real nice for you, lady," he said, lifting one of the stones and carrying it with him back to the porch. "I know verses that are right pretty." He paused, then continued, his eyes never leaving Sasha. "You look like an educated lady. Perhaps you even write poetry? I could engrave your own poem on the stone, miss, if you like."

Anger welling up in her, Sasha turned her eyes back to the man and glared down at him. "Sir, if you don't leave my premises now, I shall be forced to show you how educated I am with a firearm," she threatened. She placed her hands on her hips. "Now take your stones with you and sell them to someone else. I've other things in mind today besides—besides death."

"Ma'am, during these times of drought and desolation, death never leaves one's mind for long," the vendor said solemnly. "And with death comes the proper way to identify one's burial spot. That is with a stone, ma'am. And I sell the best stones in Australia."

Ashton came riding in a hard gallop toward the cabin. Sasha sighed with relief when he wheeled his horse to a stop next to the vendor. She rushed down the steps and stood beside Ashton as he quickly dismounted.

"Tell this man to leave, Ashton," she said, her voice trembling. "He does not seem to understand that I do not want to—to be bothered by him any longer."

Ashton's hands resting on his holstered revolvers was all the message that the vendor needed. He swallowed hard and marched back to his wagon to put the stone back inside it. He was soon driving away, the creaking wheels stirring up more rust-colored dust in their wake.

"Lord, I am so glad that you saw him here pestering me," Sasha said, raking her fingers through her heat-dampened hair. "I'm afraid I would have been forced to make him leave by gunpoint."

"I didn't return home because of the vendor," Ashton said, looking toward the river. "I came to tell you what one of our men discovered yesterday while snooping around close to Stanford Sidwell's sheep station."

"Discovered?" Sasha said, a strange sort of sudden fear gripping her. Bianca. She had not had a chance to go and see Bianca since she and Ashton had returned from Narrung. "What, Ashton? Tell me."

"Stanford has abandoned his sheep station and all of his cattle and sheep," Ashton said in a low rumble. "The cattle and sheep that weren't already dead were wasted away to nothing and had to be shot. As for Stanford and his men, no one knows where they are."

Fear for Bianca gripped Sasha's insides. "Ashton," she said, grabbing his arm. "What of Bianca? Did—did Stanford abandon her also?"

"Seems not," Ashton said, inhaling a shaky breath. "At least he didn't abandon her there. There's no sign of her."

Sasha screwed her face up into a frown. "Poor Bianca," she murmured. "And what of her child once it is born? It doesn't have a chance, Ashton. Not a chance in the world of living a normal life."

"Child?" Ashton said, idly scratching his brow. "She's pregnant?"

"Yes," Sasha said, sighing. "She is with child." She gave Ashton a pensive stare, recalling Bianca begging her to take her child to raise as her own. That would now be an impossibility—and Sasha doubted if Bianca or the child would survive. Being at the mercy of Stanford Sidwell was surely a death sentence in itself.

Sitting just inside the cave where the sun couldn't reach with its pounding heat, Bianca dropped wild onions into a pot of stew slowly cooking over a fire. Stanford was keeping them well supplied with meat, since every hour it seemed that another hare would drop in its tracks because of the intense heat. Except for the smoke that filled the small spaces of the cave that snaked underground, Bianca felt blessed that she was being spared the ravages of the drought. The nights and days were pleasantly cool and Stanford had quit touching her since her stomach had grown so large and distasteful to his eyes. She was finding it not all that hard to wait out the weather and Stanford's decision on when he was going to move on.

Stanford came into the cave, sweat rolling down his face. He ran his hand over his brow and flicked the perspiration from his fingers. "It can't be much longer now," he said, settling down beside the fire opposite where Bianca was preparing their evening meal. He reached inside his shirt pocket and removed a half-smoked cheroot. "And I'd say it's about time. I'm almost out of cigars."

Bianca gazed at his arm and how easily he was

able to maneuver it. It had healed well enough. She had hoped that gangrene would set in so that she would have to amputate it. Being so vain, he would not have been able to live with such an imperfection!

"Are you saying that we may leave this place soon?" Bianca dared to ask. "That we will be traveling back to Melbourne?"

"I never promised that I'd take you back to Melbourne," Stanford grumbled, leaning his cigar into the flames of the fire and puffing on it until it was well lighted. "But I think I can safely say that we will be leavin' this place soon enough," he volunteered. "The mitchell grass that Ashton's sheep survive on has long since been nibbled away and no new growth has come in to replace what has been grazed to the nubbin. Grass needs water to sprout." He chuckled. "Why, even the acacia thickets are providing only a fourth of the shade they usually do. Their leaves have all shriveled and fallen."

"But the clouds that roll by overhead are empty," Bianca said. "They are waterless clouds."

"And so I hope it continues for just a while longer," Stanford said smugly. "What's left of Ashton's stock won't survive much longer in this drought. He'll lose everything." He flicked ashes into the fire. "He'll have to resort to lookin' elsewhere for the means of survival. He'll soon be goin' to that fancy chest to get the coins so that he can guarantee that pretty lady won't leave him. Mark my word, he'll be leadin' me to that chest soon."

Bianca placed her hand to her abdomen. The mention of Sasha reminded her of what she must do with her child after it was born. Sasha must become the child's mother in every sense of the word!

Eyeing Stanford warily, then the pistols holstered at his hips, Bianca knew that one day soon she would have to be brave enough to go up against the man and his weapons with her only weapon—a knife. But she had one thing in her favor that even Stanford didn't know about her. At one time in her life she had lived with a circus performer—a knife thrower. He had taught her many ways to throw a knife. Even today she could flip a knife through the air so quickly it seemed to be only a smear in the sky. And never had she missed her target!

Smiling to herself, Bianca moved to her feet and walked heavily to the entrance of the cave. Not that far from where she stood, a dingo was running down a grey kangaroo, closing in for the kill. The dingo was killing for its survival, just as she would kill for her child's survival.

She looked into the distance. The hot, wild wind was raising dust into a vivid sunset.

Chapter Twenty-Nine

DEEP IN THE OUTBACK

*Lifting their firesticks high over their heads, the Aborig-*ines rushed over the strand, waving the flaming brands from bush to bush, tree to tree. With rapid steps they ran until the whole forest began to blaze to the sky, driving the terrified marsupials out onto waiting spears.

Out of control, the red torrent rushed over the plain.

The night had been miserable. Sasha had tossed and turned in her sleep, her cotton nightgown soaked clear through with sweat. At dusk, the winds had died down and not even a trace of a breeze blew through the opened windows and door the whole night through.

The morning sunshine, already scorching hot, was now spilling through the windows onto the bed, awakening Sasha. She rolled away from the splash of heat and, reaching around her, she awakened with a start when she discovered that Ashton wasn't there.

"I couldn't sleep," he said, moving to the bed to lean over her to kiss her brow. "I've been watching you. Seems you were struggling with sleep, also."

Sasha twined her arms around his neck and returned his kiss, then eased away from him to climb from the bed. "I've never been so miserable," she said, eager to get her perspiration-dampened nightgown off. She slipped it over her head and draped it over the back of a chair to dry, then hurried into her underthings and cotton dress.

Once dressed she strolled listlessly to the door and looked heavenward. There still were no clouds; the sky was azure from horizon to horizon.

"No, no rain today," Ashton said, pouring coffee grounds into the coffee pot. "Perhaps in the distant mountains, but not here."

"We came to the outback for pure, fresh air and what do we get from dusk to dawn but the harsh smell of parched earth and dust," Sasha said, watching some of the men riding toward the pasture, their horses' hooves stirring up clouds of dust. As far as she could see, there was nothing but flat, brown land, with a horizon of sunburned grass.

Then she sniffed the air more closely. There was something peculiarly different about the air today—something carried in by the wind from far out in the outback?

"Ashton, come here," she said, waving him to her side with a hand. "Take a whiff. What is that I am smelling?"

Ashton stepped past her onto the porch. He wrapped his fingers around the porch railing and leaned his full weight against it, his nose twitching as it also picked up something besides the harsh smell of the parched earth and dust.

"What is it, Ashton?" Sasha asked, stepping gingerly beside him. She sniffed again, then she grew pale when in the distance she saw something blackish gray covering the azure sky.

"Damn it," Ashton suddenly exclaimed. "Smoke. What we're smelling is smoke! Look yonder! It's a bush fire! And, by God, it's headed our way!"

Sasha felt faint at the thought of what a fire could do in this withered country, where the wild winds moved incessantly through the trees from morning until night. A bush fire would be fueled by the dead vegetation. Nothing would survive in its path!

"Sasha, grab some blankets and hurry to the river! Wet the blankets and wrap them around you!" Ashton ordered. "There's no use trying to save anything but our lives. There won't be enough time!"

"But what about our sheep? Our horses? Our cattle?" Sasha cried, panic grabbing her insides. "What about all of our hired help?"

"We can't worry about our stock. The human life is all that is important here. I'm going to ride out and warn the men and try my damndest to get everyone back to the protection of the river," Ashton said, hurrying from the porch. "Hurry, Sasha! Don't waste time trying to save anything but yourself! Get to the river! Now!"

"What about Cloud?" Sasha cried after Ashton,

gripping the porch rail so hard her knuckles were white.

Ashton turned and glared at her. "Save yourself, Sasha," he said flatly. "Save our child!"

Sasha nodded. She hurried back inside the house and grabbed blankets from their storage places. She took one last look at her belongings inside the cabin, then fled and began running toward the shine of the river in the distance.

Her breath was stolen away when something else grabbed her quick attention. She was no longer just smelling smoke—she was seeing fire!

The sight stunned her for a moment, so much that she felt frozen to the ground. Her lips parted in a quiet gasp as she stared with horror at the approaching fire. The wind had picked up again, and the fire moved through the dry summer forest at an appalling rate—a cliff of flames moving forward speedily, igniting treetop after treetop.

"Ashton!" she cried, turning to yell at him to come with her now, for she feared that if he didn't, he would not have the chance later. Her heart sank, for he had already ridden away to the pasture to warn the others.

"Oh, Ashton, please hurry," Sasha sobbed, then with tears blinding her she broke into a run again. She could hear the crackling and popping of the fire in the trees as it made its quick approach. The smoke was thickening, moving like drum rolls of black toward her. As quickly as the red torrent was rushing over the plain and through the forest, she very well understood that no human power could ever restrain it. It was going to burn everything in its wake—leaving nothing of Sasha and Ashton's dream untouched.

"It will all be gone," Sasha sobbed, stumbling as she moved into the thicker, tangled vegetation. "Everything! Perhaps even we won't survive! Can the river truly be protection enough with the size of this raging fire? Won't I ever get the chance to hold my child in my arms? Oh, what in life is fair? Everything is taken from me! Always!"

Finally at the river, Sasha waded in until she was waist deep. Her fingers trembling, she doused the armful of blankets in the water. She wrapped one around herself and then held on to the others to share with Ashton and Crispin.

While she breathlessly awaited their arrival, she looked cautiously at the trees that were bent over the river like lovers. When they caught fire they would snap in two and fall into the water! When that happened, she and everyone else would have to be in the middle of the river away from them. She feared growing tired while treading water. How long would she last?

"I must keep my wits about me," she whispered, willing herself to calm down. "It isn't good for the baby. I must, first and foremost, think of my baby. My—and Ashton's—baby!"

Overhead, she could no longer see the azure blue of the sky. Smoke was everywhere—black, swirling smoke! That meant that the fire was dangerously close!

"Ashton!" Sasha cried, panic once again seizing her. He must get there soon or else . . .

The sound of horses approaching, like thunder

against the parched ground, made Sasha soar with a relieved joy. When she caught sight of Ashton as he swung himself out of his saddle, Crispin following his lead beside him, she began crying and silently thanking the Lord for looking out for the man she loved.

The rest of the men soon appeared. Everything became frantic as the horses were slapped and shoved into the river, the men following. Some ran into the water, others dove in headfirst, until they were all standing in a tight circle, breathlessly awaiting their fate.

Sasha gave the soaked blankets to Crispin and Ashton and as many other men as she could, then moved into Ashton's arms. She scarcely breathed as she watched the trees overhead catch fire. Then she could not help herself. She screamed and clung more tightly to Ashton when the gale-force winds driving the fire caused a vacuum into which fireballs were sucked, then bounced from tree to tree until not a tree was spared from the red torrent rushing through them.

"It's time to swim to the center of the river!" Ashton shouted. He held onto Sasha and swam with her alongside him until they were out of the reach of the falling, flaming limbs.

Still clinging to Ashton, treading water alongside him, Sasha gaped openly at the spectacle. The water at the riverbank seemed to be on fire as the burning limbs piled up one on top of the other. The gushing sound of the racing fire and winds made a sound like that of a speeding train.

"Oh, Ashton," Sasha cried, turning her eyes away from the horrors of the fire. "What are we to do?"

Ashton was cold inside as he watched his world going up in flames around him. Every last coin that he and Sasha had saved and spent on the sheep station was going up in smoke. His and Sasha's livelihood and future was turning to smoke! What were they to do? He did not like to think of having to return to Melbourne a loser. He did not want to put Sasha through the grind of eking out a living again as pub owners!

That was a laugh! Even that would not be available to him. He did not have the funds to buy back York's Pub. He was broke. He and his wife had nothing to fall back on.

Except . . .

Ashton's eyes lit up with a thought—a ray of hope that he had placed at the far recesses of his mind for the past several years. Perhaps this was the time to take advantage of the chest that he had vowed never to touch! The circumstances warranted that he forget his damn vows and stubborn pride and take what he had fought so hard to get from the damnable Superintendent Silas Howland.

Sasha peered up at Ashton, seeing a spark of life in his eyes which only a moment ago were dull and filled with the torment that only failure could cause. "Ashton, what is it?" she asked, touching his cheek gently. "What are you thinking about? You look as though you are no longer filled with despair. Why is that, Ashton? We have lost everything!"

Ashton drew her closer and hugged her. "Not everything," he said. "We have each other. And also . . ."

"Also what?" Sasha asked, her eyes wide.

"I'll explain later," Ashton said, his gaze moving

along the land that had been left smoldering from the raging fire, which had now moved onward. "We'll wait a while longer, then I think it'll be safe enough to go back to shore." He looked down at Sasha. "It won't be pretty, Sasha."

"And poor Cloud," Sasha said, burying her face against Ashton's powerful chest. "Poor, beautiful Cloud."

"Cloud?" Ashton said, placing a finger beneath Sasha's chin, urging her eyes to meet his. "Didn't you see? I had time to save your horse. He's in the river with the rest."

Sasha stared disbelievingly up at Ashton, then flung her arms around his neck and hugged him. "Oh, thank you," she cried. "Thank you so very, very much!"

"I think we can leave the river now," he said, releasing his hold on Sasha. "Are you up to swimming by yourself, Sasha?"

"Yes, I think so," she murmured, the strength having returned to her knees since her initial fear of the fire was past.

"Stay close beside me and watch for any falling limbs from the scorched trees," Ashton said, taking long strokes in and out of the water. "And don't despair, darling. I have a plan that could solve all of our problems."

Bianca stifled another scream behind her hand as flames shot into the cave entrance, then whipped out again.

Stanford held a dampened blanket up to the entrance. "Come on and help hold this in place!" he shouted. "We can't allow the smoke to get in here.

366

That is our true danger. We're safe from the fire. It's the smoke that can kill us!"

Sobbing, Bianca grabbed the end of the blanket and held it tightly between herself and Stanford. "I'm frightened," she cried. "Everything outside the cave is burning! Everything!"

Stanford's eyes gleamed as he looked at Bianca. "Everything," he boasted. "Ashton's sheep station and everything he owns will be destroyed by the bush fire. That will finally break his will. He'll be forced to go to the chest."

He chuckled low. "But I won't be far behind him. As soon as he gets the chest out in the open for me to see, I'm going to place a bullet square between his shoulder blades. It's been a long time comin'. Finally I'll be rid of that bastard and have the riches all to myself."

Bianca listened intently, shivering at the thought of Stanford sneaking up on Ashton to murder him. Would Sasha be with Ashton?

"Tell me about the chest," Bianca dared to say. "Please tell me. Before long I will see it anyway."

Stanford laughed throatily. "You?" he said in a mocking tone. "Whore, if you think I plan to share those riches with the likes of you, you've got another think coming."

Bianca paled. "What are your plans for me?" she asked shallowly. "Or need I ask? You're going to murder me also, aren't you?"

"Good guess," Stanford said, his eyes narrowing with hate. "As I see it, you're no longer of any use to me. I'd have killed you and left you behind at the sheep station except that Ashton would've found you. Now, here in this cave, I doubt anything but rats will ever come across your body. As soon as this damnable fire burns itself out, you may as well begin saying your prayers."

Shaken to the core by his heinous confession, Bianca dropped the blanket and started taking short steps backward. "I should've known," she sobbed. "I shouldn't ever have trusted you!"

"Come back here and hold on to the other end of the blanket!" Stanford shouted, choking as smoke began rolling into the cave.

Bianca tensed, then grabbed at her stomach when a sharp pain tore suddenly through it, followed by another one which took her breath away. "My baby!" she gasped. She sank to the floor of the cave, grabbing at her abdomen again. Sweat pearled from her brow as she pleaded up at Stanford with her eyes. "Help me. I am in labor. My child. Nothing can happen to my child!"

Stanford stood over her, his eyes gleaming. "Do you think I care about your stupid baby?" he said, laughing. "Don't you see, Bianca? Everything is working out perfectly for me. I wanted to be rid of you and the baby, and you're doing me the honors. Left unattended, both you and your heathen child will die."

He shrugged. "I couldn't have planned it better myself," he said, chuckling.

Turning, he stared outside. The flames were gone, leaving behind only the strong stench of scorched ash. "As it is, it's simply done," he bragged. "The fire has burned itself out just in time. I'm getting out of here."

"You can't just leave me—" Bianca said, gritting

her teeth as another pain tightened her abdomen. "How can you—be so cruel?"

"How?" Stanford gloated. "Just watch me." He took a cautious step outside, feeling the heat of the ash penetrating through the soles of his shoes. Shielding his eyes with his hands, he looked into the distance. He must make his move now and prepare to watch for Ashton. If he was wrong—if Ashton never intended to go for the chest at all—then everything that Stanford had gone through would be for naught.

But if Ashton did leave his sheep station and did head in the direction away from Melbourne, then Stanford had been the wisest of them both.

Kicking the hot ash aside, Stanford began moving beneath scorched trees and through smoke rising up from the burned debris that covered the ground. He would position himself close enough to Ashton's sheep station so that he could see all the comings and goings.

With sheer will and hate guiding her, Bianca rose up on an elbow and peered at the cave entrance. Pushing herself up from the ground, she stumbled out of the cave and moved lethargically over the ash-strewn ground, her gaze never leaving Stanford as he walked ahead of her, unaware that he was being followed. Somehow she would manage to get close enough to kill him. She must! He . . . must . . . be killed!

Her hand trembled as she lifted her skirt. Fighting off nausea as fresh pain gripped her, she removed the knife from where she had tied it at her right thigh.

Another pain drew her suddenly to her knees. She bit her lower lip to keep herself from crying out, then rose to her feet again and became gripped with panic when she did not see Stanford. But she knew that he couldn't be all that far ahead of her. She would find him. She would find him. . . .

Chapter Thirty

Sasha and Ashton stood with their arms linked, staring around them. Everything was gone—The house, the animals, the garden. Looking at the devastation was surely the same as looking at the pits of hell. The black remains were still smouldering. Across the pastureland were charred carcasses of sheep and cattle; the crows that had survived the fire swooped down over them, surveying what was left for them to consume.

"It's even worse than I imagined," Sasha said, shuddering. "Ashton, seeing this gives me such a—such an empty feeling. We worked so hard and now have nothing left to show for it."

Ashton turned to her. He placed his hands at her cheeks and gazed sternly down at her. "Didn't I tell you that I have a plan that will give this all back to us?" he said. "We shall rebuild our house. We shall purchase more sheep. We can't give up our dream, ever, Sasha.''

"Oh, Ashton, you are making me feel hopeful when I see no reason to," Sasha said, sighing. "What sort of a plan? There is nothing left to work with to begin anew. All of our money was invested in what is now only ashes.''

"Sasha, it's time I tell you more about my past," Ashton said, gripping her shoulders gently. "And this time, I vow to you, I will tell you everything.''

Sasha winced at the way he was talking about his past. It was as though he expected her to reject him because of what he was. Did he not know that nothing he revealed to her now would surprise her? And didn't he know that nothing he told her would ever make her love him less?

But what was there about his past that had anything to do with this tragedy today? It seemed to be linked with the plan he had mentioned—a plan that would return their dreams to them twofold!

"What is it, Ashton?" Sasha asked, looking devotedly up at him. "I want to hear it all. Please feel free to tell me. I love you. With all of my heart, I love you. Nothing you say will change that.''

Ashton chuckled, his eyes dancing. "Sweet darlin', what I am going to reveal to you will not give you cause to hate me," he said. "What I did in my past was only for the good of the honest, hard-working people of Australia. I took it upon myself a few years back to find evidence of the corrupt ways of Melbourne's head of police at the time, but I became the hunted before I had the chance to show the proof of Superintendent Silas Howland's dirty deeds.''

"You were caught and placed in prison," she said. "You said that was where you became acquainted with Stanford Sidwell."

"And so I did," Ashton said, dropping his hands to his sides. He took Sasha by the elbow and began walking her around the smouldering ruins of their cabin. "It's like this, Sasha. I discovered a chest of coins and jewels stashed away in Superintendent Howland's house. It had been stolen from the government and the people of Australia. I took the chest and fled, wounding Howland in the process."

"And then what happened?" Sasha asked, attentive to his intriguing tale, discovering that he was even more wonderful than she had until now thought him to be.

"I did not achieve my goals that day," Ashton went on. "The superintendent's men were loyal to him, not to the government. But luck was partially with me. I had time to hide the loot before being captured."

A saddlebag slung across his arm, a shovel in his right hand, Crispin stepped up to Ashton and Sasha. He rested his free hand on a holstered pistol as he walked with them around the property while Ashton explained about that day when he had tried to become Melbourne's hero, only to be scorned and sent to prison for his deed.

"And Ashton, who was then known as Lawrence Proffitt to all who knew him, spent time in prison while I looked for a way to win his release," Crispin added. "But all of my efforts were futile. It seems that I was as scorned by everyone as Ashton, except that I did not have to spend time in prison. The day Ashton was arrested, he was working alone."

"And I sure as hell did not reveal the names of my two partners," Ashton said. "Crispin and Rufus. The best two friends a man could ever have." He gave Crispin an appreciative look.

Crispin went to Ashton and held the saddlebag out before him. "Fill it to the brim, Ashton," he said, his voice breaking. "It's time you got paid for your wrongful time in prison. Pay yourself well."

Sasha's lips parted in surprise. "What are you talking about?" she then asked, her eyes wide. She turned to Ashton. "What does he mean, Ashton?"

Ashton slung the saddlebag across his shoulder, took the shovel from Crispin, and slipped an arm around Sasha's waist. He winked at Crispin, then began walking Sasha across the ash-strewn ground. "It's time I went and dug up that chest I was telling you about," he said, smiling down at Sasha. "For now I plan to take some of its contents for our own personal use. Then, after we get back to Melbourne, I will tell the authorities where the chest is. Now that Superintendent Howland is no longer in charge in Melbourne, the authorities will be delighted to get their hands on this chest. It will also prove, once and for all, the superintendent's guilt."

Ashton frowned down at Sasha. "But first and foremost, I plan to take my fair share of the loot for what I have had to endure," he said. "The coins I plan to take as payment for my service to the country will give us another start, Sasha. I would say we are deserving of reward."

"Ashton, it's wonderful that you feel you have found a way to ensure our dream again," Sasha murmured. "And I want it as badly as you. But why did you wait until now? If you knew the coins were there all along, why didn't you take them earlier? Wouldn't things have been easier for you?"

She did not want to seem selfish by saying that having the coins would have made things easier for her as well! It had been gratifying to know that she had worked for what she had gotten. Things were appreciated more if earned, not taken!

"To be truthful, Sasha," Ashton told her, kicking up ash as he trudged onward. "I never wanted to see those coins again. I had never planned to. They had caused enough grief and trouble. As I saw it, they were best forgotten by everyone. They were accumulated by greedy people. But now that I have decided to dig up the damnable chest, I may as well get full worth out of it. I shall clear my name once and for all—and we shall take what we need to get a fresh start in life."

Sasha looked over her shoulder at Crispin, and then around her at the men who were busy going through the ruins to rescue anything they could that had not been completely incinerated by the fire.

Then she looked into the distance, all hazy with smoke. "But, Ashton, if you are going to dig up that chest, don't you think you should go by horseback?" she questioned softly. "And are you actually letting me accompany you without my having to ask? I usually have to almost get on my hands and knees and beg to be a part of each of your new adventures."

Ashton's eyes glistened, so beautifully violet through the ash smudges on his face. "Darling, no horses are needed," he said, smiling down at her. "We don't have that far to go to get to the digging spot. I purposely chose the land on which we established our sheep station for more reason than because it was available and prime land for raising sheep. Not far from it is the hiding place of the chest. Although I had not ever wanted to see it again, for some strange reason I felt as though I should at least be near it."

Sasha laughed softly. "Ashton, you are a scheming man," she said, locking her arm through his as they walked farther and farther from their sheep station. She cast him a mischievous look. "Or should I call you Lawrence Proffitt?"

"Should I call you Spike?" Ashton teased.

Again Sasha laughed. "Touché," she murmured.

They walked on, leaving the burned fence that had once bordered their sheep station behind them, on past skeletal remains of trees, to a sandy terrain that was even now being whipped by the wind.

Ashton's footsteps faltered as he gazed with a furrowed brow around him. "Damn it," he grumbled, stopping to take in the terrain more closely with his eyes. Everywhere he looked, things seemed unfamiliar to him. All identifying points that he had chosen for the chest's burial spot had been changed. What the fire hadn't ravaged, the wild winds had.

"What is it?" Sasha asked as Ashton stepped away from her, poking his shovel here and there in the hills of sand and ash.

"Never in a hundred years can I find the burial spot now," Ashton said, his voice strained. "Nothing is as I remembered it. It's changed even since the time I came to check on the land for squatting." He threw the shovel down and yanked the saddlebag from his shoulder, tossing it angrily to the ground.

"Do you mean that you truly don't know where the chest is now?" Sasha asked, paling. For a while, she had allowed herself a faint ray of hope for their future.

But now?

Just like everything else, from the moment they had reached the outback, even this was not meant to be!

Ashton slung a wild hand in the air, gesturing toward the fallen trees, the windblown sand, the burned debris all around them. "It's impossible," he said. "The fire and the winds have changed the terrain." He raked his hands frustratingly through his hair. "It's gone forever, Sasha! Forever!"

Feeling desperation seize her, Sasha grabbed the shovel and began fitfully digging. "It can't be," she cried. "It can't be! Ashton, we must find it!"

Stunned at Sasha's reaction to having lost a chance at their dream again, Ashton watched her for a moment; then, because of the dangers to their unborn child, he became alarmed. He went to her and grabbed the shovel from her.

"Stop it, Sasha," he said brusquely. "Just because we can't find that damnable chest, it is not the end of the world. We'll find another way to make things right for us. By God, we'll return to Melbourne and borrow money if we have to and open another pub. That wasn't all that horrible, you know."

Tears streamed from Sasha's eyes as she looked up at Ashton. "It all seems so hopeless, Ashton," she sobbed.

"Nothing is ever hopeless," Ashton said, giving Sasha a gentle shake. "And it's not like you to give up so easily. Darling, we have each other. We soon will have a child. Can't you see how blessed we are?"

Sighing deeply, Sasha wiped the torrent of tears from her eyes with the back of a hand. "I am suddenly so tired," she whispered. "So very, very tired."

Ashton drew her into his embrace and held her close. "Sasha, I'm sorry that I have not been able to make things work out for you," he said hoarsely. "Can you forgive me?"

Sasha sniffled back another urge to cry, now feeling guilty for letting Ashton down by her selfish behavior. She eased from his arms and looked up at him. "Ashton, I'm—"

Her words—her apologies—were cut short by a sudden burst of gunfire from somewhere close by. They turned with a start and peered through the haze of blowing smoke and sand and made out a movement just ahead. Ashton quickly drew one of his revolvers.

"Who can that be?" Sasha asked, grabbing for Ashton's arm. She squinted her eyes, then gasped when the smoke and sand momentarily thinned and she could see two bodies lying on the ground, several feet apart. She felt faint when she recognized them both. "Lord, no," she cried, breaking into a run, ignoring Ashton's warning not to.

"I must go to her!" Sasha cried, lifting the skirt of her dress as it threatened to tangle around her legs. "Bianca! Bianca!"

Sasha fell to her knees beside Bianca. Ashton twirled his revolver back into its holster and supported himself on a knee as he knelt over Stanford Sidwell. Stanford was sprawled out on his stomach, a knife lodged squarely in his back. His head lay sidewise, his eyes locked in a death trance.

Sasha smoothed Bianca's heavy hair back from her face, relieved to discover her breathing and looking up at her. "Thank God, you're alive," she said, cradling Bianca's head on her lap. Her gaze swept over her, seeing only a small spattering of blood on the sleeve of Bianca's upper right arm.

"I'm not hurt badly," Bianca reassured her in a faint whisper. "His bullet only grazed my flesh."

"How did this happen?" Sasha asked. "Why were you here? Oh, Lord, Bianca, I have been so worried about you. Where did Stanford take you after he abandoned his sheep station? Where have you been?"

"He took me to . . . to a cave close to your sheep station," Bianca said, her voice drawn with pain. "He watched and waited for Ashton to go to . . . to the chest. After the fire, he left me in the cave to have my baby alone, surely to die. I . . . I began following him. I followed him here. When I got the chance, I sneaked up on him and threw the knife into his back. Before he died, he managed to shoot me."

She closed her eyes and groaned, her hands clutching at her abdomen. Then she opened her eyes and looked wildly at Sasha. "The child," she cried. "It is coming! I feel it! I cannot help but bear down!"

Sasha's pulse raced. She looked frantically over at Ashton. "Ashton!" she cried. "Come quickly! Come and help me. Bianca is having the baby!"

"God," Ashton said, hurrying to kneel down at Bianca's feet. He spread her legs apart, lifted her skirt, and slipped her bloomers down her legs and threw them aside. He felt a strange sort of dizziness assail him when he saw that the child's head was already visible.

He gave Sasha a grimacing look, then had no recourse but to place his hands gently on either side of the child's head and wait for Bianca to do the rest.

"It hurts so!" Bianca cried, her face twisted with pain. She grunted and groaned, then gave a great push.

Sasha felt faint when she saw the child slide from Bianca's body into Ashton's waiting arms. She placed her hands to her throat and felt tears welling up in her eyes when she saw that the child was a boy—a healthy, pinkish-colored boy with ten fingers and toes, and the most perfectly shaped head sporting a full cropping of black hair. Streaked with blood, the umbilical cord still attaching him to his mother, the baby began crying and kicking his legs.

"He's so beautiful!" Sasha said, ripping some material from the skirt of her dress to clean the baby with, while Ashton took a knife from his pocket and detached mother from son.

Bianca breathed hard, her eyes closed. "I do not want to see him," she said, sobbing. "He is yours, Sasha! He is yours!"

"Bianca, surely you don't mean that," she murmured. "Look at him. He's perfect in every way. He's your child. You have to want him!"

"I want my child to have a good life," Bianca said, still refusing to look at her son. "He—he could never have a good life with me." She opened her eyes and grabbed wildly for Sasha's hands. She held onto them desperately. "Please take him. You are so good. You would be a good mother!"

Sasha gave Ashton a frustrated look, seeing the compassion in his eyes as he held the child in his arms. Then she gazed down at Bianca again. "For now, please take your child and hold him," she urged. "He should be fed soon. Bianca, only you are capable of feeding him."

Bianca choked back a sob. She gazed a moment up into Sasha's eyes, then looked slowly toward Ashton. Tears rolled down her cheeks as she held her arms out to Ashton. "I will feed my son," she said. "Give him to me."

Ashton took the child to Bianca and gently placed him in her arms.

"His skin is white," Bianca murmured. "That is good. That will make it easier for you to raise him as your son than if he were dark-skinned like my people."

A knot formed in Sasha's throat when Bianca unbuttoned her dress and eased her son's lips to her breast.

"We must get her to Melbourne where she and the child can be looked after properly," Ashton said. "You stay with her, Sasha. I will search until I find enough wood to make a travois. Surely I can find enough limbs that didn't burn completely. That will be a hell of a way to travel to Melbourne, but since all of our wagons burned in the fire I see no other way to transport her there."

Sasha nodded. She sat down beside Bianca, feeling as though God had found a way to perform a miracle today to take away the dread and horror from everything else that they had lost. A child had been born, and perhaps hope too, which had seemed so elusive, of late, would renew itself.

"He will be yours," Bianca said, reaching for Sasha's hand. She held it tightly. "I will make it so, Sasha. I . . . will make it so. . . ."

Chapter Thirty-One

MELBOURNE

The aroma was the same. The sounds were the same. If Sasha closed her eyes, she could see herself downstairs in the pub, barefoot and serving drinks to the rowdy men whose hands more often than not tried to roam beneath the skirt of her dress.

"Sweet darlin', are you awake?"

Ashton's voice beside her in the bed made tears come to Sasha's eyes. She knew the humiliation that he must be feeling. He had struggled and fought to make their dreams become a reality and no matter how valiantly he had fought the battle, he had lost. They had lost. They were back to their beginnings—in Melbourne, upstairs over York's Pub.

"I just awakened," Sasha murmured, rolling over to face Ashton. In truth she had not slept a wink since they had arrived from the outback late the previous evening. Even though they had been given a room and a comfortable bed until they made plans again for their future, it did not ease her mind into sleep. Her mind had been filled with tumultuous thoughts, trying to come up with a way to make Ashton feel less at fault for what had happened.

But she knew that no matter what she said or did, he would blame himself forever for their losses.

"Good, that means you slept," Ashton said, gently smoothing fallen locks of hair back from Sasha's eyes. He drew her next to him and cuddled her close. "I've got to think of a way to repay Sam for his generosity in letting us stay over his pub. We'd best check on Bianca and the baby soon. Though they are in the room next to us, I feel uneasy about leaving them alone. Bianca was behaving quite strangely last night, don't you think?"

"Yes, quite," Sasha whispered, straining her ear for any sounds coming from the next room. She hadn't wanted to leave Bianca and the baby alone, yet when Sam had been generous enough to lend them two of his vacant rooms instead of one, it had been Bianca who had insisted that they sleep in separate rooms. Her excuse had been the baby— that he might cry through the night and disturb Ashton's and Sasha's sleep.

And because Sasha had known how tired Ashton was, she had not had the heart to say no.

"I'm going to try to get a loan today, Sasha," Ashton said, changing the subject. He eased her from his arms and rose from the bed, slipping into his breeches. "We can either put money down on another pub, or we can take one more stab at making a go of it in the outback."

He leaned down close to Sasha, supporting himself on either side of her with the palms of his hands. "What do you want to do, Sasha?" he asked softly. "It's entirely up to you."

Sasha exhaled a nervous breath as she gazed up into his troubled violet eyes. She knew the chances of his getting a loan were slim. If he was refused, what then of his self-respect? Could she even bear the thought of how such a rejection would make him feel? Her heart would be bleeding for him, for there would be nothing she could do, ever.

"Must I be forced to make such a decision alone?" she asked, pleading up at him with her eyes. "Ashton, that isn't fair. And can't we wait a few days before we do anything at all? We've been through so much."

"Sam's generosity can go just so far, Sasha," Ashton said sternly. He swung up away from her and drew on his fringed shirt. "And my pride can take just so much. The decision must be made now." He turned and gazed down at her, his jaw tight. "We have no other choice, Sasha. I hardly have enough coins in my pocket to feed us this one day, let alone tomorrow and all the tomorrows after that."

Swallowing hard, Sasha rose from the bed and began dressing, the stench of perspiration strong on her body and clothes. All of her clothes but what she wore had been burned in the fire; she did not even own a bar of soap with which to bathe herself! Things could not be much worse!

Fully clothed, her fingers untangling several witch's knots from her raven-black hair, Sasha turned to Ashton. "Do what you must, Ashton," she murmured. "I understand."

He gripped her shoulders gently with his fingers. "You haven't said which you would prefer," he reminded her. "A pub or the outback."

She winced at the thought of either. The aroma of the pub wafting through the floorboards of this room was enough reminder of how unpleasant it was to be around groping, drunken men from morning to night.

Yet the memory of all that she had been through in the outback sent a shiver of fear up and down her spine.

But could all of those tragedies happen again? Surely fate would not have it so!

"The outback," she said, without much further thought. She squared her shoulders and looked proudly up at Ashton. "If at all possible, we must return to the outback. We can't be beaten all that easily, Ashton."

But still, she was afraid that they had already been beaten. Getting a loan would be the deciding factor in whether or not they had a decent future together. She placed a hand to her abdomen, fearing for her unborn child.

"Then the outback it will be," Ashton said, fastening his gunbelt around his waist. He placed his arms around her and drew her into his strong embrace and kissed her before making a quick exit.

Sasha went to the window and, drawing back the sheer curtain, watched Ashton cross the street, his stride filled with confidence and pride.

Choking back a sob, she turned away from the window and hung her head. When Ashton returned, would his gait be so confident?

386

Or would it be slow and heavy, his eyes vacant of hope?

"I must busy myself," Sasha whispered to herself. She went to the bed and fluffed up the pillows; their cases were torn and ugly. She smoothed down the mattress, which had no sheet on it and pulled the heavy blanket up over it.

She placed her hands to her cheeks and looked around the dismal room. There was a knock on it. Smiling, expecting to find Bianca and the baby there, Sasha rushed to the door and jerked it open.

She was taken aback when she found a very well-dressed man standing in the corridor, a valise tucked beneath his left arm.

"Sasha?" the man said, his voice distinguished. "Sasha Seymour?"

Sasha gazed into the man's dark eyes, her own filled with wonder. "Yes, I am Sasha," she murmured. "Why do you ask?"

"Ma'am, I have been trying to locate you for at least a month," the man said, clearing his throat irritably. "Word was sent to my hotel this morning that you had taken a room in this—in this—ahem, place." He looked past her, over her shoulder, then back down at her. "May I?"

Sasha stepped aside. "Oh, yes, please do come in," she said, watching his stiff stride as he stepped past her into the drab room.

"Reginald VanCleave at your service, ma'am," the man said, reaching out a white-gloved hand to Sasha. "It is my sincere pleasure to make your acquaintance."

Sasha noticed that his nose was twitching and she

was embarrassed to think that her dire need of a bath was the reason.

She took his hand and shook it, then when he took it away to grip the valise, she took a step away from him to give him more breathing space.

"Ma'am, I have ventured from England in search of you," Reginald said, unsnapping his valise.

Sasha's eyes were wide as she watched the man reach inside the valise and bring out several legal-appearing documents. "What is your reason for wanting to find me?" she asked guardedly.

Reginald lay his valise aside and spread the legal documents atop the nightstand beside the bed. "These are for your perusal," he said, motioning toward them. "Please read them slowly so that you will understand them."

He reached into his inside vest pocket and withdrew a leather drawstring bag. "And then I have something else for you," he said, opening the bag which displayed a vast number of coins and banknotes.

Having never before seen such a massive amount of money, Sasha's heart skipped a beat. She looked slowly up at the dignified man, then back at the money, then at the documents.

Trembling, filled with so many questions that she was afraid to ask, Sasha went and picked up the documents. Breathlessly, she began to read. Her face became flushed with excitement and her knees became weaker the more she read.

When she had scanned quickly over them all, she clutched them to her and turned to Reginald with tear-filled eyes.

"He didn't abandon me after all?" she murmured, holding the proof in her hands that Woodrow Rutherford had loved her to his last dying breath. "Woodrow . . . Woodrow willed his riches to me? Oh, can it be true? My dear Woodrow loved me so much? And he . . . he is dead?"

"Woodrow Rutherford contracted an illness aboard ship on his voyage from Australia to England," Reginald said, his eyes sad. "On his death bed, after receiving his title of Baronet and an immeasurable inheritance, he summoned me, his attorney and a man he could trust, to his bedside. There he dictated his will to me. He left everything but his lands and title to you."

He cleared his throat nervously as he raked his eyes over Sasha. "I promised the baronet that I would deliver the news to you personally," he continued. "I apologize for the length of time that it took me to find you."

Sasha was speechless. She was so grateful to know that Woodrow had never truly abandoned her. He had loved her all along! He had been true to his promise to her!

A keen sense of loneliness swept over her at the thought that Woodrow was dead and she had not been there to comfort him in his sickness. And while he was dying, she had been cursing him! If only she had known!

Then another thought seized her. She was rich! Her eyes widened as she looked at the large bag of money, then up at the attorney. She could hardly believe it when he took her hand and placed the heavy bag in it.

"The rest of the money is in safekeeping in a bank in London," Reginald quickly reassured her. "I brought you enough to tide you over until you were free to travel to London to claim your inheritance."

He clasped his hands tightly behind him and looked thoughtfully at Sasha. "I presume that is enough to last until you reach London?" he said, again his eyes raking over her disapprovingly. "Perhaps, ma'am, you can purchase a new wardrobe? Perhaps you can meet with a—a hairdresser?"

"Oh, yes, I shall do all of those things," she cried, clutching the bag close to her chest.

Her thoughts went to Ashton and what she could do for him. At last she had a way to repay him for all his kindnesses to her!

Oh, but wouldn't he be surprised?

"Then I shall be on my way," Reginald said, snatching up his valise. "I shall arrange for your passage on the next ship to London."

Sasha followed him to the door. "Sir, I do not wish to go to London now—or ever," she murmured. She held her chin up proudly. "There is too much to be done here in Australia. I trust that you will see that my money is transferred from London to Melbourne? You shall be paid well for your trouble."

Reginald paled. "But, ma'am, so many opportunities await you in London," he protested. "You are now a wealthy woman."

"Sir, there are also many opportunities here in Australia," she said softly. "This is where I want my dreams to come true. Not London."

Reginald shrugged. "Whatever you say," he said,

nodding at her. "I shall arrange for your monies to be transferred." He smiled down at her. "Good day, ma'am."

"Good day," Sasha said, returning his smile. "And thank you so much for keeping your word to Woodrow."

When he had walked away down the stairs, Sasha was still in a state of shock. She stared down at the bag of money, then gasped with joy when Ashton suddenly appeared on the stairs, taking them two at a time as he came to where she waited, on the landing.

"We did it!" he said, placing his hands on her waist. He picked her up and swung her around, laughing. "I had no trouble getting the loan. I earned the reputation of being reliable when I was a pubkeep. I was told that I could borrow any amount of money that I wanted to get our sheep station established again."

Becoming dizzy not only from the spinning around, but from everything wonderful that was suddenly happening to her and Ashton, Sasha began giggling drunkenly. "Let me down, Ashton," she said, holding onto the bag of money with all her might. "Lord, Ashton, if you don't, I am going to spill this money all over the floor."

Ashton stopped suddenly and set her to the floor. He looked down at the bulging bag, then up at Sasha. "Money?" he said, rubbing his brow. "What are you talking about? Where did you get it?"

Sasha began laughing softly, then forced the bag into Ashton's hands. "I haven't counted it yet, but I believe enough is there to purchase plenty of sheep and supplies for our station." She giggled again when she saw Ashton's total shock as he opened the bag and peered inside. "And there is more where that came from, Ashton. Lots, lots more!"

Ashton measured the wealth with his eyes as he shook some of the coins into the palm of his hands. "I don't understand," he said, his voice breaking. Afraid that someone might see or hear them, Sasha grabbed Ashton's arm and half dragged him into their room and closed the door behind them.

She went to the table and picked up the legal documents and waved them before Ashton's wide eyes. "Just wait until you hear," she said, torn between being so happy she could shout and being saddened over knowing that Woodrow, wonderful Woodrow, was dead.

"Hear what?" Ashton said, plunking the bag onto the bed. He took the documents and began reading them. The further he read, the faster his eyes scanned the pages.

Then he looked up at Sasha, wordless.

"It's true, Ashton," Sasha said, her eyes dancing. "We are rich beyond belief."

Ashton was not certain how to feel. A part of him was glad that Woodrow hadn't actually abandoned Sasha as she had suspected, and a part of him was sad that he alone could not have given her the world.

Yet it was enough, it seemed, to see her so happy over her sudden wealth. And he had not come up empty-handed himself. He had gained a foothold on his self-esteem by knowing that he was able to get a loan just by asking.

"Ashton, say something," Sasha said, her eyes

wavering. "Aren't you happy about our sudden wealth? We can buy anything we want, Ashton. We can have our dream!"

Ashton tossed the legal documents aside and drew Sasha into his arms. "Sweet darlin', we would have even without the money you've inherited," he said softly.

"But, don't you see, Ashton?" Sasha said, pleading up at him with her eyes. "What I have received today, on top of the loan that you've been promised, is like icing on a cake! We are blessed twofold."

"Aye, we are," Ashton said, cradling her close. "And we shall have us the best sheep station in Australia for our children to be raised on."

"Children," Sasha whispered, a tremor of happiness surging through her. "How wonderful that sounds."

The sound of a baby crying drew them instantly apart. They looked toward the door, then questioned each other with their eyes.

"Bianca's baby," Sasha said, rushing to the door. "I wonder if he's all right."

"All babies cry sometimes," Ashton said, following after her.

They went to Bianca's room and knocked on the door. When there was no response, Ashton gingerly opened it. Sasha felt a pang of fear when she stepped into the room and found that Bianca wasn't there— only the baby wrapped snugly in his blanket on the bed, crying.

"Where is Bianca?" Ashton wondered, approaching the bed.

Sasha's fingers trembled as she picked up a note

that lay beside the baby. Although Bianca had never had any formal schooling, she had learned a few scribblings from some of the men she had bedded.

"What does it say?" Ashton asked, frowning down at Sasha.

Sasha glanced at the note, reading it to herself first. Then she read it slowly aloud to Ashton. "It says, 'Sasha, Bianca go. Take baby. Love him. He is yours. Thank you.'" Sasha, choked on a sob. She read further. "'Bianca named son Tobias.'"

"Damn her," Ashton grumbled, doubling a fist at his side.

Sasha paled as she looked up at Ashton. "You are angry because you do not want the child?" she asked, her voice breaking. "I doubt if you would ever be able to find Bianca should you even try. She was determined that we raise her son. She—she did not think of herself as a fit mother."

Ashton bent over the bed and scooped the baby up into his arms. His eyes softened as he looked down at the tiny pink facial features. "I'm not upset because I don't want to raise the child," he explained. "I'm upset because of the reason Bianca felt she must do this. There is so much injustice in the world. Bianca is one of the best examples of it."

"Yes, she is," Sasha said, tears wetting the corners of her eyes. "I hope that she can eventually find at least a small measure of happiness wherever she has decided to go."

"I'll try and find Bianca to reassure her about the child and that we will give him a good home," he said, gently touching the baby's cheek.

"Well, Tobias, it looks as though you've found

yourself a mama and daddy," he said, laughing softly as Tobias's tiny soft lips quivered into a smile.

Sasha placed an arm around Ashton's waist and smiled adoringly up at him.

Chapter Thirty-Two

ONE YEAR LATER
THE OUTBACK
THE HOMESTEAD—REBUILT

"Let him go, Ashton," Sasha said, *holding her arms* out for Tobias as he clung to Ashton, his chunky legs wobbly. She smiled at Tobias and beckoned to him with her hands. "Come on, darling. You're a year old today. Let's see you take your first step."

"Come on, son, you can do it," Ashton said, releasing his grip on Tobias's arms. Pride swelled through him when Tobias stood his ground instead of falling to his hands and knees as he had done every other time they had tried to encourage him to walk. Ashton held his breath when Tobias shakily placed one foot ahead of the other, then balanced himself to hold his arms out to the child.

Ashton inched around Tobias and went to stand beside Sasha. "That-away, son," he encouraged him softly. "You've taken one step. Let me see you take another."

Tears came to Sasha's eyes as she watched Tobias gingerly take another step as he grinned from ear to ear.

"Da-da?" Tobias uttered, taking several more steps in a rush as he hurried and fell into Ashton's waiting arms.

Laughing, Ashton grabbed Tobias up and swung him around. "You did it!" he shouted. "By God, you did it! Now that you can walk, you can conquer the world."

The cooing of a baby close by drew Sasha around. Wiping tears of joy from her eyes, she went to the crib on the far side of the wall where it was guarded from the vicious rays of the morning sun.

"Paulette, did you see your brother?" Sasha murmured, lifting her five-month-old daughter from the crib, the baby's soft cotton gown trimmed with tiny ruffles of eyelet lace. She held her baby close to her bosom. "You're next, Paulette. In a few months you'll be taking your first steps too."

"Our son needs no more coaxing," Ashton said, carrying Tobias to Sasha's side. "Isn't he quite advanced for his age, Sasha? Did you see how he walked? Did you hear him say Da-da? Soon he'll be reading books!"

"Yes, I'm sure he will if you have anything to say about it," Sasha said, smiling down at Tobias. He was so healthy and content!

A pang of sadness gripped her when she allowed herself to think of Bianca. The search for her had only recently been called off. There had not been a trace of her anywhere since the day she left Tobias behind to become someone else's child.

"And when do we leave for Melbourne to sign the papers that will make Tobias legally ours?" Ashton said, as though he had read Sasha's troubled thoughts about Bianca. "When he calls me Da-da, I would feel much better if I knew that it was official."

"You sent Crispin ahead to meet with the attorney for us," Sasha said, placing Paulette back in her crib. "When he returns and tells us that it has all been arranged, then I think that we should go immediately to Melbourne and finalize the procedure. We've done everything within our power to find Bianca, to give her one last chance to claim her son. I think we've earned the right to claim him as ours now. Morally, and otherwise."

Ashton set Tobias down and laughed throatily when the tot went immediately for the floor on his hands and knees and began crawling away toward a large pile of birthday toys. "Well, so much for walking today," he said, shrugging.

He placed an arm around Sasha's waist and walked her to a window where together they looked out at their thriving empire. "Just look at it," he said proudly, gesturing with his free hand toward the sheep grazing in the distance, along the horizon splashed with the golden rays of the sun. "A year ago, who would have thought that any of this would have been possible?"

"It's not only the money that bought this all for us," Sasha said, sidling closer to Ashton and hugging him to her side. "Mother Nature has finally cooperated. We've had a good year, without the scab, Aborigines setting uncontrollable fires, or throngs of crows diving down on our sheep to peck out their eyes."

She looked to the heavens that were dotted with fluffy, white clouds. "And we've had a good measure of rain to help us with our garden," she said.

She sighed and leaned her head against Ashton. "Everything is so wonderful," she murmured. "It frightens me, Ashton. Everything seems just too perfect."

"Sometimes I look back over my shoulder, wondering what is going to be there to interrupt our contented life," Ashton agreed. He hugged her more closely to him. "But so far, all I have found is happiness."

He turned Sasha around so that they could gaze around them. "A year ago, when our cabin burned on this spot, did you ever imagine rebuilding something as grand as this?" he said, pride thick in his words.

He was glad that he did not have Woodrow Rutherford to thank for all of their blessings. To keep his self-esteem, he had accepted the loan and had used it solely to purchase their sheep and rebuild their house. It had been the sale of the wool from those sheep that had netted them a profit that was spent to pay back the loan and to purchase all of the fancy fineries in the house that he felt Sasha deserved.

She had left a good portion of her inheritance in the bank, using only what she wanted to purchase things for the children, who delighted her so that she could not resist treats for them.

The rest was in trust for the children's education. Bianca had depended on Sasha and Ashton to give her son a home filled with love, and an education.

And so it was coming to pass—all of it.

"It is so very lovely, Ashton," Sasha murmured. "So often I think I am imagining it all and that I will suddenly find myself barefoot and hungry again."

"Never," Ashton growled.

Sasha gazed at the parlor with its gold wainscoting, damask curtains, and a serpentine-front Hepplewhite sofa. Chairs with slender, crane-necked elbows on their arms, and outlined with carved reeding, sat on each side of the fireplace. In her mind's eye she pictured the other rooms—a fireplace was in every room, with fine paneling and molding. In the bedroom there was a four-poster bed with its rolling pin headboard, dressed in crewel-work linen, handwoven and embroidered in India.

In the family room, a settle was pulled up to the cooking fireplace, a tin kitchen partly obscuring the opening for the lower oven, and a collection of rat-tail cooking utensils hanging above it. Just over the fireplace was a swing-out drying rack. A pair of cupboards with butterfly shelves was built symmetrically on either side of the fireplace, within them a pair of Minton ironstone-covered serving dishes flanking an inlaid mahogany knife box. Above it hung a gilt wood mantel mirror, a massive chandelier reflected in it.

Everything seemed perfect. Paulette was sweet and precious and healthy. Tobias was their son in every sense of the word, except . . .

"I hope Crispin doesn't run into any problems with the adoption procedures," Sasha said, looking up at Ashton with wide and troubled eyes.

MELBOURNE

Crispin sat at the bar at York's Pub, a drunken smile smeared across his face. He swallowed another drink of ale, then reached inside his pocket and withdrew a piece of folded paper. Unfolding it, he held it out before his eyes and read it, then thrust it back inside his pocket again.

Carrying a mug of ale, a tall and muscled man with a guarded expression on his long, narrow face sat down on a stool beside Crispin. "Mate, what's your reason for smilin' so broad and drinkin' yourself blind?" he asked, motioning with a gesture of his hand and nod of his head to the pubkeep for a refill for Crispin. "If you don't mind, I'd like to join you."

Crispin watched the ale being poured into his mug at the expense of the man at his side, and turned a grateful smile to him. "Glad to have you," he said, lifting his mug and tapping the stranger's with it. "Here's to you."

The man smiled darkly and took a quick swallow of ale, then set his mug down and began turning it slowly around in the spilled alcohol on the countertop. "You new in these parts?" he asked, challenging Crispin with a set stare.

"Naw," Crispin said, hiccoughing. He chuckled as he gazed over at the stranger. "You? I don't remember seein' you around Melbourne." He patted the man on the back good-naturedly. "But in my condition, I'm not sure who I would and wouldn't remember."

"You didn't say what you're celebratin'," the stranger said, eyeing the folded piece of paper that was partially hanging from Crispin's shirt pocket. "Care to share some good news with me?"

Crispin shrugged. "Guess so," he said. He laughed into his ale as he took another deep swallow, then once again grabbed the paper from his pocket. He began waving it in the air for all to see. "In fact I'm goin' to share the news with everyone and then buy a round of drinks."

"Sounds good to me," the stranger said, casting a look over his shoulder at a man slouched over in a wheelchair in a shadowed corner of the pub. "I'm sure there's more than one person who's interested in what you have to say."

"I know two people in particular who're waitin' to hear the good news," Crispin said, thrusting the paper back inside his pocket. "They're goin' to become parents legally to a damn fine boy. And I'm goin' to be the proudest godfather ever there was in Australia."

"Oh?" the stranger prodded. "And who are these parents?"

"Ashton and Sasha York," Crispin announced loudly. He stood up and looked around the room. For an instant his gaze stopped at the man in the wheelchair, seeing something about him that was familiar, yet through his drunken haze unable to make out what.

He shrugged and continued looking around the room. "I'm sure you all know Ashton," he boasted.

"He's served many an ale in this establishment. This pub was named after him!"

"And the baby you are talkin' about," the stranger said, leaning his face closer to Crispin's, to draw his undivided attention. "You say they're adoptin' the baby?"

"That's right," Crispin said, setting his mug down on the counter for a refill. "And it's been a long enough wait for them. A whole damn year. They waited a whole damn year."

"And why is that?" the stranger asked, casting the man in the wheelchair another quick glance.

"Because they wanted to be fair about it," Crispin said, slapping a coin on the counter for the ale, then smiling a thank-you to the stranger as he slipped his coin out ahead of Crispin's to pay for the drink.

"Fair?" the stranger asked, placing the mug of ale in Crispin's hand for him. "What was there to play fair about?"

Crispin gulped down another swallow of ale. He set the mug down and wiped his mouth clean with the back of a hand. "It was because of Bianca Whitelaw," he explained. "It's her child. They tried to find her to be sure she didn't want it. They looked but they couldn't find her."

Feeling good and carefree, Crispin lifted his mug again and waved it in the air, slopping ale over its sides. "If there is a father for Bianca's child, step forward or forever hold your peace!" he shouted drunkenly, laughing as he again took another quick drink.

When he had somewhat regained his composure, he looked for the stranger but was stupified to find that he had suddenly disappeared.

"Oh well," he whispered to himself. "Anyhow, the drongo didn't even tell me his name."

The stranger wheeled the man in the wheelchair out of the pub, took him to a horse and buggy, and lifted the wheelchair into it, placing it where normally there would be a seat for the driver. Locking the wheelchair in place and handing the reins to the crippled man, the stranger stepped back from the buggy, resting his hands on his holstered revolvers.

"Now I have absolute proof that Bianca bore a child," the crippled man said, in his sunken eyes a strange sort of light. "That's all I need to know to make my next move."

"Are you sure you want to follow Crispin to Ashton York's sheep station alone?" the stranger asked, concern showing in his eyes. "What if he doesn't leave tonight? He's so drunk he may not even be able to get into the saddle."

"He'll go tonight," the crippled man growled. "He checked out of the hotel this afternoon."

"I want to at least follow close behind you in case you need me," the stranger said. "You've never traveled that far alone since your accident."

"It's about time then, don't you think?" the crippled man snarled. "Now that I know that I've got a grandson I sure as hell don't plan to spend the rest of my life in bed thinkin' about the days when I wasn't a cripple."

"You ought to kill the son of a bitch that's responsible for your condition," the stranger said, his eyes narrowing.

"I'm not out for vengeance," the crippled man said. "I'm just looking for something to put meaning back in my life." He brushed his feeble hand across his bald head. "My grandson will do that for me."

"You're sure he's your grandson?" the stranger questioned. "How do you know that his grandmother didn't shack up with everything on two legs, like his mother?"

"I knew her well," the crippled man said. "And I know that she only had eyes for me." He looked down at his lifeless legs, then sidewise at his twisted back. "At one time in my life, I could've had any woman I wanted. My choice was a woman with dark skin."

He lifted the reins and gave the stranger a determined look. "I'll be waiting in the shadows over there for Crispin to leave the pub," he said. "And if it will make you feel better, you have my permission to follow once we head for the outback. I'm not daft. I know the dangers of traveling alone in my condition."

The crippled man frowned at the stranger. "In fact, I'm glad you're taggin' along in case I need you," he said. "If the child isn't handed over to me—by damn, I'll send you in to take it."

The stranger gave the crippled man a smile and a nod, then swung himself up into his saddle and rode away. He positioned himself between two buildings and watched for Crispin to leave York's Pub.

Chapter Thirty-Three

THE HOMESTEAD

Carrying Tobias on her hip, Sasha went to the door and found Crispin there wearing a broad smile and a thin layer of dust on his face from his long journey from Melbourne.

"Everything is set," Crispin said, yanking the crumpled sheet of paper from his shirt pocket. "Read this. It's a note from your attorney explaining a surprising development in the adoption procedures. Everything is set for the adoption. All you and Ashton need to do now is go to Melbourne and meet with the attorney and sign the papers."

Sasha eyed the paper anxiously as Crispin handed it to her. She smiled a thank-you up at him as he grabbed Tobias into his arms, playfully lifting him up in the air while talking to him.

"Soon you'll be my godson," Crispin said, laughing up at Tobias as he giggled from the bouncing around. "And aren't you a cute one?" He gathered him in his arms and cuddled him close. "Did you have a happy birthday, Tobias, while I was in Melbourne?"

"Quite," Sasha said, unfolding the paper. "Ashton and I did, also. We proudly watched our son take his first step."

"He did, did he?" Crispin said, his eyes twinkling. "I've got something for Tobias for his birthday. Can I take him out with me to the horse? I left the stuffed animal in my saddlebag."

"Stuffed animal?" Sasha said, half hearing what Crispin was saying, for she was too busy scanning the page and getting a rapid pulsebeat from what she was reading. Bianca had somehow received word that she and Ashton wanted to legally adopt Tobias! She had come out of hiding long enough to go to the attorney to sign the documents which gave up all her rights to the child, giving them to Ashton and Sasha! Her doing this erased all their fears that the document might not be truly binding. Once she and Ashton signed the papers, Tobias would be theirs, forever and ever!

"Yeah, I didn't think he was too old just yet for something to cuddle up with at night when the candles are blown out," Crispin said, frowning at Sasha when he saw a sparkling of tears in her eyes. He knew why. He had already celebrated the good news.

Sasha refolded the paper and placed it inside the pocket of her dress. She wiped tears from her eyes. "Bianca still wants us to raise Tobias as our own," she said softly. "Although I have felt sad over Bianca having given her child up, I have so feared that in time she would change her mind." She sighed heavily. "I am so glad that she hasn't."

"If it's all right, I'm going to take Tobias out with me to get his present," Crispin said, holding Tobias gently within his arms.

"What present is that?" Ashton said as he walked into the house.

Crispin smiled broadly at Ashton. "Sasha will tell you all about it," he said, then carried Tobias from the house.

Sasha looked up at Ashton, tears again burning at the corners of her eyes. She flung herself into his arms, radiantly happy. "We need no longer fear any sort of problem with the adoption," she said. "Bianca has signed documents which relinquish her claim to Tobias forever."

Stunned by the news, Ashton held Sasha out away from himself and gazed intently down at her. "How can that be?" he gasped. "Bianca has as good as disappeared from the face of the earth. You know how damn hard I've tried to find her. And you say she has been in Melbourne? She met with our attorney?"

"Yes," Sasha said, wiping tears from her cheeks. "And all we have to do now is go into Melbourne and sign the papers. Tobias will be ours, Ashton. Our very own son."

Crispin came back into the house with Tobias, who was hugging a stuffed toy in the shape of a koala, his eyes proud.

"He likes it," Crispin said as he handed Tobias over to Ashton. "It's something to always remember his godfather by."

"That was very thoughtful of you, Crispin," Sasha

said, giving him a big hug. "Thank you."

Crispin hugged her back, then eased her away from him. "I don't think you want to stay close enough to me to get a whiff of me or my clothes," he said, chuckling. "I'm in dire need of a bath." He swung around and walked toward the door. "I'll talk to you more about my experiences in Melbourne after I get to smellin' better."

"Come for supper?" Sasha asked, walking him to the door. "We've missed you, you know."

"I'll be there with bells on," Crispin said over his shoulder, giving Sasha a sly wink.

She closed the door after him, then turned to Ashton. It looked so natural for him to be holding Tobias in his arms and talking to him the way a father does to a son. Always before she had doubted that this could be an everlasting relationship. If anything could go wrong, she had expected it would for them.

But now, thanks to Bianca's generous heart, there would never be any doubts again. Soon Tobias would be hers and Ashton's, and nobody could lay claim to him.

Nobody!

The sound of an approaching buggy drew Sasha's attention. She opened the door and gazed into the distance, squinting her eyes against the brilliance of the sun. As the horse and buggy moved closer, she tried to make out who the driver was, then was taken aback when she realized that it wasn't just any driver. It was a man in a wheelchair in charge of the two spirited black mares.

"Who is it?" Ashton asked, coming to Sasha's side, Tobias now on the floor behind them playing with his stuffed toy. The buggy was now close enough for him to make out the facial features of the man driving it. He stiffened and looked from the man's thin, pale face to his crippled and twisted body, then to the wheelchair in which he sat where usually there was a buggy seat.

"I have no idea who that is," Sasha said, looking guardedly up at Ashton, realizing that his breathing was now coming in short intervals. She turned cold inside when she discovered his jaw tight and alarm and hate in his violet eyes.

And he had grown quite pale.

"Ashton, you look as though you've seen a ghost," Sasha said, inhaling a quivering breath when Ashton looked icily down at her, then slowly back at the approaching horse and buggy.

"I think I have," Ashton finally said, resting a hand on one of his holstered revolvers. "Damn it, how did he find out where I live? Why has he come? And why alone?"

"Who?" Sasha said, raking her fingers frustratedly through her hair. "Who is that, Ashton? Tell me. How do you know him?"

Ashton glared at the man as he wheeled his horse and buggy to a halt at the foot of the steps to the porch. "Sweet darlin', that crippled and twisted man is none other than Superintendent Silas Howland," he said, his voice drawn. "I had hoped that he had forgotten about me. Seems he never will."

"Superintendent Howland?" Sasha gasped, placing a hand to her throat. "Oh Lord, Ashton, has he come to arrest you?"

"He no longer has the power to arrest me or anyone," Ashton assured her. "There's only one reason he'd bother to come to the outback to look for me—to ruin our lives."

Sasha grabbed Ashton's arm and held tightly to it. "Ashton, is he crippled and twisted like that because—because of you?" she asked, shuddering at the sight of the man.

"You might say that," Ashton said, his eyes narrowing as Superintendent Howland gazed intently toward the door, surely having caught sight of Ashton and Sasha standing there in the shadows. "One of my bullets went clean through him and lodged in his spine. As fate would have it, he came through it alive. I had meant for him to be dead."

"Lawrence Proffitt!" Superintendent Howland shouted. "I've come to have a talk with you." He cleared his throat nervously. "Or should I be asking for Ashton York? Did you think that changing your name would keep me from finding you once I set my mind to doing it?"

Ashton turned to Sasha. "You stay here," he said sternly. "I'll take care of this."

Sasha's lips parted to argue with him, but he was too quick. In two wide steps he was already outside on the porch. She was momentarily distracted when Tobias came to her and began yanking on her dress. She turned to him and lifted him into her arms, now knowing that Ashton had been right to ask her to stay inside. She had to protect their children from all harm—especially from evil men like Superintendent Silas Howland!

But she could not help stepping closer to the opened door, leaning an ear closer. What if Ashton was in danger?

Yet how much harm could the crippled old man

cause? He did not look even capable of pulling the trigger of a gun.

"Why have you come?" Ashton asked, his hands resting on his holstered revolvers. "How did you find out where I lived and the name I now go by?"

"Did you think that you could keep your identity from me?" Silas Howland said, his voice thin and dry. "It took me a while, but I finally found out where you and your wife established a sheep station."

He frowned up at Ashton. "I also know that you are raising my grandson," he said, gazing past Ashton to Sasha and Tobias standing in the shadow of the opened door. "I've come to lay claim to him."

"You've what?" Ashton exclaimed, paling. "What is this about a grandson?"

Silas smiled crookedly. "You chose to call him Tobias?" he said. "I think that name will suit him just fine once I give him my last name."

Ashton was stunned speechless by what Silas's continued ramblings were disclosing. He looked quickly back at Sasha and realized that she had also heard, for never had he seen her so pale and stunned.

His gaze moved to Tobias and something tugged at his heart. Then he turned back to Silas. "You don't know what you're saying," he said, his voice drawn. "Now get that damn buggy turned around and get the hell off my property. I think the lead of my bullet did more than cripple you. It turned you into a mindless fool."

"No matter what you think of me, Lawrence, I have come for my grandson," Silas hissed. "He belongs to me. And you owe me, Lawrence. Your bullet robbed me of my youthful body and I have been forced to live the life of a twisted old man ever since. I can never father another child. I want an heir. Tobias is my heir! I demand that you give him to me!"

Sasha could not bear to stand by any longer and only listen. Clutching Tobias, she stepped out on the porch beside Ashton. Dry-mouthed, she glowered down at the twisted old man, feeling no pity for him since she knew exactly why Ashton had been forced to shoot him those years ago. This man had lived off the poor. He was rich because he took from the poor!

And now he wanted to take her son away?

She turned her eyes slowly to Ashton's revolvers. If not for Tobias in her arms, she would have been tempted to finish what Ashton had failed to do.

"How could you on God's earth lay claim to this boy?" Ashton asked, taking a step closer to Silas, his hands clasping more tightly to the handles of his revolvers. "Is this how you chose to make me pay for crippling you? For having taken the chest of riches from your house? By making up a crazed story of being this child's grandfather? I would have expected you to come and demand to be told where I hid the chest—not to take away what is so precious to my heart."

"I care not for the chest," Silas grumbled. "I lost interest in it the day I realized that I would not have the opportunity to freely spend what was inside it. I had planned to sail the seas with beautiful women at my side. Now I rarely venture further than from my bed to my parlor. Coming to the outback to get my grandson is very daring for me, to say the least. And, by God, I will not depart from your sheep station without him."

Trembling, Sasha inched up beside Ashton. "You say that Tobias is your grandson," she said, her voice breaking. "Though we will not let you take him with you, before you go I would like to know exactly how you came up with this plan to get our son from us. You had to know that it would not work—that we would never hand Tobias over to you, or anyone."

"By birthright he is not your son," Silas stated flatly. "He is Bianca Whitelaw's son."

"Yes, we know that," Sasha said, growing agitated. She held Tobias more snugly in her arms, aware that Superintendent Howland's beady eyes were on him, watching him, studying him. "What does that have to do with you?"

Ashton gave Sasha a quick glance, then glared down at Silas. "Enough of this," he said, yanking a revolver from his holster. "I see no need to go any further with this conversation. I told you before— turn that buggy around and get the hell off my property."

Silas was not dissuaded by the threat of the revolver. He gave Ashton an icy stare, then smiled slowly as he looked back at the child. "What does Bianca being Tobias's true mother have to do with me?" he drawled. "Bianca is my daughter."

The confession came to Sasha as though someone had slapped her. She teetered for a moment, then felt Ashton's strong arm around her waist, steadying her.

Ashton was taken aback, again rendered speechless by what Silas had revealed. He leveled his aim at the man's chest. "I don't want to hear any more of this contrived nonsense," he said from between clenched teeth. "I'll give you two minutes to get that damn buggy turned around and then two more to get off my property, or by God, the next bullet I put into your body won't just cripple you. I plan for this one to go straight into that black heart of yours."

"I've not told too many people what I'm about to tell you," Silas said, his eyes wavering as once again he gazed at Tobias. "Long ago I was involved in a forbidden love. I fell in love with Bianca's mother. She was a full-blooded Aborigine, but more beautiful than any other woman I'd ever seen. But I was a magistrate, looked up to as a pillar of the community. I was forced to relinquish the woman I loved because of that and cast her aside, even when she told me that she was pregnant with my child. My position in the community was more important to me than the woman I loved, or her child, Bianca. I stayed my distance. I never laid claim to my daughter. I made sure never to go near her mother because I knew that she would kill me for how Bianca turned out. A whore. A cheap whore."

Sasha's mind was spinning with the tale and its implications. He did sound so sincere! He could be Tobias's grandfather!

Oh, how she wanted to run away with Tobias and hide! She could not let this evil, twisted man stand in the way of adopting Tobias. He was already too much a part of her, as though she had carried him within her womb and borne the pain of his birth!

Surely the pain of that birthing could be no less than the pain that she was feeling now!

"And you expect us to believe that?" Ashton said, yet fearing that what he heard was the absolute truth. Looking into this crippled man's eyes was almost the same as looking into Bianca's! The few times he had seen her face to face, he had been intrigued by her green eyes, since most Aborigines' eyes were dark.

"I turned my back on my daughter," Silas said, his voice weakening. "I won't on my grandson." He lifted his arms toward the child. "Give him to me. Since his mother, my daughter, has abandoned him, he is now rightfully mine."

"If you think I would ever consider handing over my son to the likes of you, grandfather or not, you are even more daft than I thought," Ashton growled.

He took a step closer to the edge of the porch, flipping his other revolver from its holster. He cocked both guns, steading his aim on Silas. "I won't bother to count this time," he warned. "I aim to just shoot. If you want to live to see another day, then I'd suggest you not try any more talk on us and get the hell out of here."

He inched his way off the porch, taking the steps slowly and calculatingly. "Don't ever come out here again with your threats," he warned. "You won't be allowed to get near my wife and children again."

"You owe me," Silas said, his eyes wet with tears.

"You son of a bitch, I owe you nothing," Ashton said. "Now get!"

Silas emitted a low throaty sob, almost choking on it as he gazed with a deep longing at Tobias, then slapped the horse's rump with the reins, made a wide circle in the drive, and rode off.

His heart pounding, Ashton watched until Silas was only a dot on the horizon.

Then he spun his revolvers back into their holsters and turned to look at Sasha. His gut twisted when he saw the tears streaming down her face, wetting Tobias's face where he had fallen asleep against her bosom.

"What are we to do?" Sasha sobbed. "What if he comes back?"

"If he does, we'll be ready," Ashton said, moving up the steps, wrapping his arms around both Tobias and Sasha. "But, darling, I now see the need to get that adoption legalized quickly. We'll leave for Melbourne tomorrow."

"What if he tries to stop it?" Sasha asked, pleading up at Ashton through her tear-filled eyes.

"He won't, for the same reason he didn't before. He is not about to make an announcement for all to hear that he fathered a daughter by an Aborigine woman," Ashton said. "His pride won't allow it."

"Lord, I hope you're right," Sasha said, blinking tears from her thick lashes. "Ashton, I can't imagine life without Tobias. He is my heart—my very soul!"

"And mine also," Ashton whispered, gently kissing Sasha's brow.

"We can't let anything happen to our family," Sasha whispered, looking down at Tobias as he slept so peacefully, so trustingly in her arms.

Ashton nodded, yet he feared the journey to Melbourne. Even though there was no one with Silas as he had come on their property, that did not mean he did not have many armed friends hidden in the outback just waiting for instructions from him —enough to fight off Ashton's men before he took Tobias by force.

He tried to reassure Sasha. "Things will be all

right," he said, caressing her back. "You'll see. Things'll be just fine."

A sudden cold fear gripping her, Sasha looked up at Ashton. She knew him too well not to recognize the worry in his voice. Nor could he hide the strange sort of light that always entered his violet eyes when he was wary about something.

Oh, Lord, why had she ever thought that keeping Tobias as their own would be all that simple?

Chapter Thirty-Four

Sasha awakened from a troubled sleep, sweat pearling her brow. She turned to Ashton in the bed, sighing with relief when she found him still there. In her dream, she had been stranded in the middle of the outback, alone. She had searched frantically for Ashton and her children, but never found them. Just before she awakened, she had fainted beneath the pounding rays of the sun. . . .

A knock on the door startled her from the bed. As Ashton leaned up on an elbow, wiping sleep from his eyes, she slipped on a robe and rushed to the door. Her knees grew weak when she opened it to Crispin and saw dried blood on his forehead where a purplish knot loomed from his scalp.

"My Lord, what happened?" Sasha gasped, grabbing the door to steady herself against it. Then she paled as she gazed down the corridor toward

Tobias's bedroom. The door was ajar. She could see inside to his crib. It was empty!

"No!" she screamed, brushing past Crispin. "He can't be gone! Crispin, you were supposed to be on guard outside his door! Tell me he's all right. Oh, Crispin, tell me Tobias is all right."

Ashton jumped from the bed and jerked on his breeches. He ran from the room and caught up with Sasha as she entered Tobias's bedroom. They clutched feverishly at one another when it became evident that the child was gone.

"I'm sorry," Crispin said, holding his pounding head as he came teetering into the room. "I didn't even hear anyone approach. I was hit from behind. I imagine I fared better than the others who were on guard outside—they were knifed."

Ashton gazed blankly down into the empty crib, then drew Sasha into his arms and comforted her as she cried.

"I don't even know how long I was unconscious," Crispin said dejectedly. "Ashton? Sasha? What can I say but that I'm sorry?"

Ashton looked over Sasha's shoulder at Crispin. "How are you?" he asked, his voice breaking. "Are you going to be all right? It looks like you've got a nasty head wound."

"Pounding like hell, but I'll survive," Crispin grumbled. "I'm sure as hell well enough to ride with you to go after Tobias."

Sasha jerked away from Ashton. "I'm going with you," she cried. She straightened her shoulders and wiped the tears from her eyes. "And don't try to stop me, Ashton. Nothing would keep me from going after my son."

"But what about Paulette?" Ashton worried.

"She'll be safe here," Sasha said, walking determinedly toward the door. "No one is interested in stealing Paulette away. Tobias is the only one that was ever in danger."

Crispin and Ashton followed Sasha from the room. "I'll see how things are outside," Crispin said, rushing down the stairs. "I'll also get the men together!"

Ashton grabbed Sasha's wrist, stopping her. "It's best you don't go with us, Sasha," he said. "Whoever abducted Tobias has probably had a full night's jump on us. Before we can catch up with them, I'm sure they'll make it into Melbourne. It could be a long search, Sasha."

"I've got to go," Sasha said, fighting back her tears of frustration. "When Tobias is found I must be there to comfort him. I'm his mother. He'll need me."

"Of course, you're right," Ashton said, his eyes wavering. "Tobias is probably frightened to death. If you are there when we find him, it could help dispel his fears. Yes, it is best for Tobias that you be with us when we find him."

"Who could have done this?" Sasha sobbed.

"Do you really have to ask?" Ashton said sarcastically. "Silas Howland, that's who."

"But he is a helpless cripple," Sasha said, wiping her cheeks with the back of her hand.

"Sweet darlin', that helpless cripple has money enough to pay an army if he wanted to," Ashton grumbled. "I should have known that he hadn't come here alone. When he left, I should've known that he was giving up way too easy. His hired hand was waiting on his instructions even then. No matter how many guards I would have placed around our house, it wouldn't have been enough."

"If Silas Howland is responsible for Tobias's disappearance, then surely we don't have to worry about our son's safety," Sasha said softly. "The old man wouldn't harm his own grandson."

"That old man is capable of anything at any time," Ashton said, then regretted having said it when he saw fresh tears trickling from Sasha's eyes.

The sun was barely creeping up along the horizon. Straight-backed on Cloud, Sasha rode beside Ashton. Her hair was flying in the wind and her riding skirt was hiked up above her knees.

She glanced over her shoulder at the men following them. His head bandaged, Crispin was in the lead.

Again she looked straight ahead, her heart aching every time she allowed herself even the briefest thought of her beloved Tobias in the arms of that wretched, crippled man. Her lower lip trembled and she fought against crying again. She did not want to upset Ashton any more than he already was. He was grieving as much as she, for he loved his son with the passion that all fathers gave their sons—no matter whether they were of the same blood or not.

Ashton suddenly thrust a hand in the air, gesturing for everyone to stop. He leaned over his saddlehorn, peering intently ahead.

"What is it, Ashton?" Sasha asked, shielding her eyes from the glare of the morning sun with one hand. "Why did you stop? Do you see something?"

Something grabbed at her insides when her gaze

settled on something at the edge of the road just ahead. It was an overturned buggy. "Oh, no," she moaned, recognizing the buggy. "Please, God—no!"

Ashton cast her a worried glance. He edged his horse closer to hers and grabbed her by the hand. "Sasha, I'm going ahead and check things out," he said, unable to keep the fear out of his voice. He too had realized whose buggy it was. Silas Howland's.

"Oh, Ashton, I don't think I could go an inch closer if I tried," Sasha cried, looking wildly at him. "I can't bear to see if . . . if Tobias . . ."

Ashton reached a hand to her lips and silenced her words. "I'll be back as quickly as I can," he reassured her, then rode on ahead, dizzy with a building fear.

Crispin rode up next to him. "It's him, isn't it?" he shouted. "It's Silas Howland. He's had an accident."

"It seems that way," Ashton shouted back. He tried to steady his heartbeat as he grew closer to the buggy, but when he saw the broken wheelchair at the side of the road, he knew for sure that what he had feared was fact. He wheeled his horse to a stop when he discovered Silas Howland's body not far from the wheelchair, a bullet wound in his chest.

Feeling as though every inch of him had been rendered numb, Ashton then discovered the body of another man not far from the overturned buggy, the cause of his death also a bullet wound.

"Damn," Crispin gasped, quickly dismounting to check Silas for a heartbeat. When he found none, he gave Ashton a slow nod.

Ashton dismounted, and in a crazed fashion began searching through the brush for any signs of

Tobias. When he found his blanket, he knew for certain that he had been taken in the raid and could now be far into the outback, possibly never to be seen again.

Ashton buried his face in his hands, a sob tearing through his body. "Christ," he moaned. "Oh, Christ, what am I going to tell Sasha? Our son. Our sweet son!"

Sasha rode up to the scene of the crime and in a state of shock dismounted and went to Ashton. "You don't need to tell me," she murmured, dazed. "I already know. Tobias is gone. But why, Ashton?"

Ashton raised his head from his hands and looked at Sasha. "Bushrangers," he said hoarsely. "They can get top dollar for a healthy child like Tobias. There are many in Australia who are childless. Tobias will be sold to the highest bidder." He gestured toward the buggy. "They also took the horses."

Sasha stared blankly up at Ashton for a moment, then ran to the edge of the road and hung her head. Her throat spasmed over and over again until there was nothing else to spill from her stomach.

Ashton came to her and turned her to face him, wiping her mouth clean with his handkerchief.

"I'm going to be all right," Sasha reassured, blinking back tears. "I must. We have to find Tobias. We can't let anyone sell him as though—as though he were a sheep or a bale of wool."

"There will be a search party formed, Sasha, but not before I take you home," Ashton said, his voice firm. "We have another child. She needs you, too, Sasha. Paulette needs you."

As though in a trance, Sasha nodded. "Yes,

Paulette needs me," she said thinly. "I must hurry home to her. I can't let anything happen to her."

"That's my girl," Ashton said, drawing her into his embrace. He cradled her close, burying his face in the perfumed depths of her hair. "Let's go home. I'll get you settled in and then I'll go and find our son if I have to search to the ends of the earth for him."

"Thank you, Ashton," Sasha whispered, clinging to him for dear life. "Oh, darling, thank you."

Arm in arm, they went to Sasha's horse. Ashton helped her into the saddle, then mounted himself and rode protectively beside Sasha until they were home again. Seeing how drawn she was, Ashton went to her and lifted her from her horse. As they walked toward the porch, something on the ground in the shadows of the steps grabbed their attention.

"My Lord, that dingo is having pups at our doorstep!" Sasha said in a rush of words.

Then her eyes widened and she inhaled a quivering breath of air when she recognized the dingo. There never could be another dingo with that identical marking on its head. There never could be another dingo that would come in out of the wilds of the outback to have her pups so close to humans, normally the enemy.

"Lightning?" Ashton said, kneeling down beside the dingo and the three pups that had already been born, just in time to see a fourth slip from inside the mother.

"Oh, it is Lightning," Sasha sighed, so badly wanting to scoop the dingo up into her arms to give her a welcome hug. "You've come home. And you've brought us some special gifts! You wanted to share your pups with us."

A fifth pup was born, and then a sixth, the last of the litter. Ashton and Sasha busied themselves carrying the pups into the house, and then Lightning. Sasha fixed a bed for Lightning in one of her wicker laundry baskets, then smiled down at the dingo as the pups were placed with her. One by one the pups began to snuggle up to their mother to nurse. Tears of joy at having Lightning home again flowed freely from Sasha's eyes, but too soon she was again swept up into remorse for having lost Tobias.

"I'm going to go up with you to see to Paulette, and then I must leave to go and search for Tobias," Ashton said, giving Lightning a last pat before rising.

Sasha smoothed a hand over one of the pups and over Lightning's smooth fur, then walked slowly with Ashton up the stairs. When they made a turn to go to Paulette's room, a noise from Tobias's room drew them quickly to a halt.

"That sounds like the rocking chair squeaking," Sasha whispered, peering intently at the closed door that led into Tobias's room. "Someone is in there rocking."

"It's probably the maid rocking Paulette," Ashton said, shrugging. "Let's go and see."

Walking lightly to the door, Sasha stood aside as Ashton turned the knob. When the door opened and Sasha could see who was sitting in the rocker in the faint light of a candle, she felt a dizziness claim her. Ashton gasped and grabbed for Sasha, steadying her.

"Bianca?" Sasha said, tears pooling in her eyes when she looked down and saw Tobias asleep in Bianca's arms. "Tobias?"

Ashton led Sasha on into the room. They stood

over Bianca, staring disbelievingly down at her and Tobias.

Continuing to rock, Bianca smiled up at them. "Bianca stopped Silas Howland," she said softly. "Bianca returns your son to you." She rose from the rocker and eased Tobias into Sasha's arms. "See how he sleeps? He was not harmed. He is back home where he belongs."

Sasha looked through her tears at Tobias. He was sleeping so soundly, so trustingly, as though nothing had happened to disturb his contented life. She then looked at Bianca. "How did you know about Silas?" she whispered.

"I have friends in Melbourne who hear everything good and evil," Bianca whispered back. "That is how I knew that Silas came to get Tobias. I also knew why he was doing this. He had to be stopped. I stopped him. I killed the man with him and then returned the horses that were with them to the wild."

"Then you must know what Silas was to you and Tobias?" Ashton said, placing a gentle hand on Bianca's shoulder.

"He was my father," Bianca said matter-of-factly. "He was Tobias's grandfather."

"This you also found out from your spies in Melbourne?" Sasha asked, rocking Tobias back and forth in her arms.

"No," Bianca murmured. "My mother told me."

"Ever since you left us you have been with your mother?" Ashton asked, seeing how Bianca looked so adoringly at her son.

"I have been with my people, where I always belonged. Always, I felt drawn to the white man's world because a part of me was white," Bianca said, reaching to touch Tobias gently on the cheek. "I am now at peace with myself and who I am. I will now return to my true people. Their future is my future. I will no longer do what disgraces them."

"But, Tobias . . . ?" Sasha dared to say.

"Your future is Tobias's future," Bianca said, smiling softly at Sasha. "That is only the way it should be for my son who is now yours."

Bianca turned to walk toward the door. "I must return to my people," she said over her shoulder. "We must move deep into the outback so that the authorities can never find me and enslave me for having killed two white men. They would never understand why it had to be done."

She turned and gazed in longing at Ashton, then at Sasha. "And do not fear that you will be accused for the crime," she said. "I have sent a written confession to the authorities, stating my part in it. I did this to protect you. You can live in peace now with your children. Perhaps sometime in the future our paths will cross again. Until then, be happy."

Ashton and Sasha were wordless as Bianca left the room. They stared down at Tobias, then gazed in wonder at one another.

"Nothing good is ever gained easily, it seems," Ashton said, gently touching Sasha's cheek.

"Oh, Ashton, dear Ashton, that does seem so," Sasha said, choking back a sob. "But we do have our son back—and this time forever."

They went to the window together, and Ashton drew back the sheer curtain. They leaned closer when they saw an elderly Aborigine woman with gray hair step from the shadows to walk beside

Bianca. Hand in hand, they walked toward the outback.

"Her mother!" Sasha whispered. "That must be Bianca's mother!"

"Though hard-won, I think that Bianca has finally found contentment in her life," Ashton said gravely. "It was there all along with her mother and her people."

Sasha looked up at Ashton, her heart filled with love and adoration for him, realizing that she had been one of the lucky ones. She had known the moment she gave her heart to Ashton York where her contentment lay—and that his contentment would be hers.

She had been blessed—oh, so blessed!

Night Wind's Woman
By Shirl Henke

OUR STORY SO FAR . . .

Proud and untameable as a lioness, Orlena had fled the court of Spain and a forced marriage to an aging lecher. But in the savage provinces of New Spain, the golden-haired beauty was destined to clash with another man—one whom her aristocratic blood dictated that she loathe, one whom her woman's heart demanded that she love . . .

Half white, half Apache, he was a renegade who attacked when least expected, then disappeared like the wind in the night. He would take his revenge against the hated Spaniards by holding hostage the beautiful Orlena.

We pick up the story, on the trail, as Night Wind takes Orlena back to the Apache camp . . . .

Orlena cursed the plodding, foul-tempered little beast that smelled even worse than she did. After three days without a bath, she was filthy. The hot, parching days in the sun had wind-blistered her delicate golden skin until it peeled painfully; the cold night air drove her to seek the most unwelcome body heat of her captor.

As if conjured up, Night Wind reined in his big piebald stallion alongside her. He inspected her bedraggled condition, finding her distressingly desirable in spite of burned skin, tangled hair and torn boy's clothing. In fact, the shirt and pants outlined her flawlessly feminine curves all too well now that she had discarded the binding about her breasts.

Orlena watched his cool green eyes examine her and felt an irrational urge to comb her fingers through her hair in a vain attempt to straighten it. Instead she said waspishly, "Why do you stare at me? To take pleasure in my misery?"

He chuckled, a surprisingly rich sound, vaguely familiar. Indeed the eyes, too, seemed familiar, but that was only because in his swarthy face such an obviously white feature stood out.

"Look you ahead. Relief for your misery is at hand, Doña. Your bath awaits." He gestured to a dense cluster of scrub pine and some rustling alders. They ringed a small lake of crystal-clear water fed from some underground spring.

Orlena's first impulse was to leap into its cool, inviting depths, but her reason quickly asserted itself. She fixed him with a frosty glare and replied, "A lady requires privacy for her ablutions. Also some clean clothes to wear afterward."

"Unfortunately for you, my men and I travel light. We have no silk dresses in our saddlebags."

"Then you should not have abducted me," she snapped as her burro skittered, smelling the water.

"You should not have worn your brother's clothes

and my men would not have taken you by mistake," he replied evenly as he dismounted by the water's edge.

Her eyes narrowed. They were back at the original impasse. "Why did you want Santiago?"

His face became shuttered once more as he considered his plan gone awry. "I did not plan to kill him," was all he would say.

Or ransom him either. Orlena was certain of that much. His motives regarding both of them centered on Conal in some way. Before she could argue further he strode over to the burro and swept her from it, tossing her into the deep clear water. At first she shrieked in shock as her blistered, sweaty body met the icy cold water. But when she began to swim, the cold became refreshing. However, her clothes and boots were a decided impediment. With a couple of quick yanks she freed the boots and tossed them onto the bank.

Night Wind watched her glide through the water like a sleek little otter. He was surprised that she could swim. He had expected her to flounder and cry out to be rescued from drowning. Smiling grimly to himself, he shed his moccasins and breechclout and dove in after her.

"Ladies do not know how to swim, Lioness," he said as he caught up with her in several swift strokes.

She gasped in surprise, then recovered. "Conal taught Santiago and me when we were children."

His face darkened ominously. "He has taught you much—too much for a Spanish female of the noble class."

"Some Spaniard has taught you also—too much for an Apache male of the renegade class," she replied in a haughty tone as cold as his expression.

He reached out and one wet hand clamped on her arm, pulling her to him. "Come here. Take off your clothes," he whispered.

Her eyes scanned the banks. As if by prearrangement, the Lipan and Pascal had vanished downstream. She could dimly hear them unpacking the animals and making camp, but a thick stand of juniper bushes and alder trees provided complete privacy. She jerked free and kicked away from him, but he was a stronger swimmer. In a few strokes he caught up to her, this time grabbing her around her waist.

"You will drown us both if you are not sensible," he said as he struggled with the shirt plastered to her body.

"I told you the last time you asked me to disrobe that I would never do it for you," she gasped, flailing at him. Blessed Virgin, she could see through the water! He was completely naked! "No!" The cry was torn from her as he finally succeeded in freeing her from the shredded remnants of her shirt.

"You are burned and filthy. If you do not cleanse your skin properly you will become ill," he gritted out as he began to unfasten the buttons on her trousers. She continued struggling. "I am not going to rape you, little Lioness," he whispered roughly.

"I do not believe you," she panted. "You only waited, tricked me—"

He silenced her with a kiss. It was most difficult to remain coldly rigid with her lips closed when she was gasping for breath and flailing in the water. The hot interior of his mouth was electrifying as he opened it over hers. His tongue plunged in to twine with hers in a silent duel. Orlena pushed at his chest ineffectually as he propelled them effortlessly toward the bank where shade from an overhanging alder beckoned.

The sandy soil was gritty and full of rocks away from the water's edge, but an uneven carpet of tall grass grew out of the water and up the gently sloping bank. He carried her dripping from the water and tossed her on it. Before she could regain her breath or roll up, he seized her sagging, loose pant legs and yanked, straightening her legs and raising her buttocks off the ground. Unbuttoned at the top, the trousers slid off with a whoosh, taking with them the ragged remains of her undergarments.

He looked down at her naked flesh, sun and wind burned, covered with scratches and bruises. Orlena shivered as the dry air quickly evaporated the cold water from her skin. She tried ineffectually to cover herself with her hands as she rolled to one side, unable to meet his piercing gaze. He reached down and scooped her into his arms again.

"Now, I am going to let you swim for a few moments while I get some medicine from my saddle-bags. I do not think it wise to try to escape with no clothing. You are already burned enough!" With that he tossed her back into the icy embrace of the water and strolled off, heedless of his own nakedness.

Orlena fumed as she treaded water, watching him carry off the last remnants of her clothes. He was right. Where could she go in the mountain wilderness, naked and afoot? In only a moment he returned, leading the big black-and-white stallion. He took something from the buckskin pouch on what passed on an Apache mount for a saddle and waded back into the shallows. "Spanish ladies seem to set great store by this," he said mockingly, holding up a piece of what looked to be soap—real soap! "It is not the jasmine scent you favor, but it is all I could find for our unplanned bathing." He held out the soap for her inspection. The unspoken command was in his eyes as he waited, waist-deep in the water, for her to come to him.

Orlena warred within herself. She could not outrun him and had nowhere to go, yet she hated to let him humble her by begging for the soap—not to mention having to expose her nakedness once again to his lascivious green eyes in order to reach the bribe. She treaded water, careful not to let her breasts bob above the surface.

"Toss it to me. I can catch quite well."

He smiled blackly. "Allow me to guess. Conal taught you. No, Doña Orlena, you must come to me—or stay in the lake until that lovely little body turns blue and freezes at nightfall." With that he sauntered toward the shallows, tossing the soap casually from hand to hand.

"Wait!" Orlena was growing cold already and the sun was beginning to arc toward its final descent beyond the mountain peaks to the west.

He turned with one arched black eyebrow raised and said, "I will meet you half way, but you must do as I command. I have already given my word not to take you against your will. Unlike your Spanish soldiers, the word of a Lipan is never broken."

That a savage could talk to her thus made bile rise in her throat, but she was trapped in the freezing water, hungry, naked, completely at his mercy. "I suppose I must trust your Apache honor," she replied through chattering teeth. Was it only the cold that made her shiver?

Very slowly she swam toward him. Very slowly he walked across the smooth lake bottom toward her. Orlena watched the sunlight filtering through the trees trace a shifting design on his bronzed skin. His arm and chest muscles rippled with every step he took. He had taken off the leather headband along with his other apparel and his wet black hair hung free, almost touching his shoulders. Without the band, he seemed less Apache, more white, but not less dangerous.

"Come," he whispered, watching her, knowing what this was costing her Spanish pride. Waiting for her, touching her without taking her, was exacting a price from him as well. He observed the swell of her breasts swaying as she moved through the clear water. Darkened almost bronze by soaking, her hair floated like a mantle, covering her as she touched bottom and rose from the water.

He reached out and drew her to him, unresisting at first, until he pushed back the wet heavy hair from one pale shoulder. "No," she gasped, but it was too late. He had one slim wrist imprisoned. Slowly he worked a rich, sensuous lather against her collarbone, moving lower, toward her breast. When his soap-slicked fingers made contact, she forgot to breathe. The tip of her breast puckered to a hard rosy point and the tingling that began there quickly spread downward. When he released her wrist, Orlena did not notice. His free hand lifted the wet hair from her shoulder and he spread the lather across to capture her other breast, gently massaging both of them in rhythm. She swayed unsteadily in the water. Although it was still cold, Orlena Valdiz had become hot. Night Wind cupped her shoulders and then worked the sensuous, slick suds down her arms.

She stood glassy-eyed and trembling in the waist-deep water, studying the rippling muscles beneath the light dusting of black hair on his chest. It narrowed in a pattern that vanished beneath the water. Just as her eyes began to trespass to that forbidden place, she felt a jolt as he reached that selfsame location on her! Quickly and delicately, he skirted the soft mound of curls and lathered over her hips, then around, cupping her buttocks.

"Raise your hair and turn," he commanded hoarsely, maneuvering her like a porcelain doll into shallow water. He could feel the quivering thrill that raced through her as he performed the intimate toilette. His own body responded, hard and aching, but he ignored his need and massaged the delicate vertebrae of her back, down past her tiny waist to the flair of hips and rounding of buttocks. "Now, kneel so I can wash your hair."

Like a sleepwalker she responded to his slight pressure on her shoulders and knelt with her back to him. He lathered the masses of hair, massaging her scalp with incredibly gentle fingers. Orlena imagined her maid back in Spain performing this familiar ritual, but this was not Maria and she was far from Madrid, alone in a foreign land, the prisoner of a savage!

His voice, low and warm, with its disquietingly educated accent, cut into her chaotic thoughts. "Lower your head and rinse away the soap."

Orlena did so, working all traces of the lather from her hair. Then she rose from the water, eyes tightly closed against the sting of the soap, and began to squeeze the excess water from her hair. Night Wind watched the way her breasts curved as she raised her arms above her head. Her waist was slim, her skin pale; she was so fragile and lovely that it made his heart stop.

He had used many white women over the years, but none had any more claim on him than to assuage his lust, more often to please his masculine pride. A despised Apache could seduce a fine white lady, have her begging him to make love to her. Make love! Those other times had been more acts of war than love to Night Wind. Never had he played a waiting game, balancing gentleness with iron authority. Never before had he taken a white woman's virginity. And it was still far too soon, he knew, for that to occur unless he forced her. The feelings she evoked were dangerous and he did not like them. The anger betrayed itself in his voice.

"Now, I have bathed you. You will bathe me."

Orlena's eyes flew open and she blinked in amazement. "Surely you jest, but it does not amuse me!"

"So, I can play lady's maid to you," he said in a quiet deadly voice, "but you will not be body servant to a dirty savage."

She reddened guiltily, recalling her thoughts of Maria a moment earlier. He held out the soap in one open palm, waiting once more.

"No! I will not—I *cannot*." She hated the way her voice cracked.

"Yes, you will and you can—else the young deer Broken Leg is now roasting will not fill that lovely little belly tonight."

Ever since her first temper tantrum with the bowl of beans and the water gourd, she had learned the power of hunger and thirst over human pride. She had not been fed all the following day, only given water, until they camped last night. By then the mush of bean paste had actually been palatable. Now the fragrance of roasting meat wafted on the evening breeze. She salivated and her stomach rumbled. They had broken their morning fast at dawn with cold corn cakes and water, but she had eaten nothing since.

"I have clothes for you, in Warpaint's saddlebag," he motioned to the horse grazing untethered nearby. "Or, you can stay here all night, freezing and starving."

With a remarkable oath she had overhead a Spanish sailor use, Orlena stalked over to him and grabbed the soap.

Forcing her hands to remain steady was nearly impossible as she flattened her lathered palms against his sleek dark skin and began to rub in small circles across his chest, then down the hard biceps on his arms. His chest was lightly furred with curly black hair. Trusting the steadiness of her voice only slightly more than that of her hands, she said curiously, "All the other men are smooth-skinned. Why do you—."

"You may think me a savage, but I am half white," was the stormy reply. Then he added in a lighter tone, "You have never seen any man's bared chest before, have you, Lioness?"

She stiffened at the intimacy of his voice, hating herself for her stupid words. "Of course not!"

"Then how did Conal teach you to swim—fully clothed?"

A small smile warmed her face as she recalled being a little girl with a toddler brother, cavorting in the pond at the villa in Aranjuez. "In fact, we all wore light undergarments. I was a child and never thought on it. But I do not remember him furred as are you."

He frowned. "Conal's hair is red. It would not show as easily as dark hair. Body hair is considered ugly among my people."

She looked up suddenly. "Then the Apache must think you uncomely indeed," she said with asperity.

"No. The Lipan accept me as one of their own," he replied with an arrogant grin, adding, "Woman, red or white, have never found me unattractive."

"Well now you have met the first one who does," she hissed.

"Liar," he whispered softly, watching as she lowered her eyes and busily applied herself to the disconcerting task he had set her.

Orlena felt the steady thud of his heart, angry at its evenness when her own pulse was racing.

Night Wind was having a far more difficult time looking calm than the furious, golden-haired woman before him could imagine. Lord, her small rounded breasts arched up enticingly as she raised her arms to lather him. Intent on winning this contest of wills with her, he clenched his fists beneath the water to keep from caressing the impudently pointed nipples. Smiling, he watched how she bit her lip in concentration as she was forced to touch his body. She kept her eyes fastened on her busy hands, not looking up into his face.

Orlena could feel him shrug and flex his muscles as he turned, allowing her such casual access to his body. She thought she knew it well from lying wrapped in his arms the past nights. She was wrong —how much different this was, with both of them naked, slicked by the cool water and warm sun.

"Turn so I may wash your back." She tried to emulate his command and was rewarded with a rich, low chuckle. When he did not move at once, she added, "You do not, for a surety, fear to turn your back on a mere female?"

"Not as long as my knife and any other weapons lay well beyond your reach," he replied with arched eyebrows. Then kneeling in front of her he added, "It will be far easier for you to wash my hair than me yours."

His thick, night-black hair was coarse and straight, shiny black as a raven's wing. She worked a rich lather into it, finding the massaging motion of her fingertips on his scalp soothing. Angry with herself, she shoved his head under the water abruptly, saying, "Rinse clean."

He came up coughing and splattering her with droplets. "You try a man's patience overmuch, Lioness." Then a slow smile transformed his face as he said with arrogant assurance, "Wash below the water, also, as I did to you."

She dropped the soap with a splash, but he quickly recovered it in the clear water. When he handed it to her silently, she moved around him and began with his back. Touching his tight, lean buttock made her quiver with a strange seeping warmth in spite of the cold water. She finished quickly, forgetting to breathe as he turned around to face her again.

His eyes burned into her as he took her wrist and began to work her small, soapy palm in circles around his navel, then lower, beneath the water. When she touched that mysterious, frighteningly male part of him, she could feel its heat and hardness.

In spite of his best resolution, Night Wind let out a sharp gasp and his hips jerked reflexively when he closed her soap-filled little hand around his phallus. Orlena jumped back, jerking her hand free. At first she was uncertain what had happened, but then she realized what it was, and a small smirk curved her lips.

So, he is not as indifferent to me as he would pretend. On a few occasions when she escaped her *dueña*, she had seen animals mate in their stables. Always the male's staff had seemed an ugly, threatening thing to her. But those were merely horses and dogs. This was different . . . frightening, yes, but not ugly. . . .

She dragged her thoughts from their horrifying direction. Blessed Virgin, what was happening to her? She surely had not found the naked body of a man pleasing! And a savage at that! Like mares and bitches, women had to subject themselves to male lust in the marriage bed. But she knew well from her own mother's plight what the consequences were—a swollen belly and an agonizing childbirth. She backed away from him, clenching the soap unconsciously in her hands.

Night Wind struggled with his desire for her, but at last let her go, deciding the game had been played out long enough for now. Then he realized that she continued slowly backing away from him, all the spitting fury and innocent sexual awakening of moments ago evaporated. Her face was chalky, and she wrapped her arms protectively about her body as if warding off a blow.

"I did not intend to frighten you, Lioness," he said softly. "I gave my word not to force you, and I will keep it."

"I see evidence to the contrary," she spat, but refused to look at his lower body, clearly outlined beneath the water.

One long arm shot out and grabbed her wrist, prying the soap from her fingers. "We are both clean enough," he said gruffly, pulling the shivering woman behind him as he splashed to the bank.

Feeling her resistance, he released her in the shallows and said, "I have cloth to dry you and an ointment for your burns."

"And what of the small matter of clothing? You have destroyed the pitiful remnants of Santiago's shirt and trousers."

"I have more suitable garments—women's clothing with which to replace them," he replied reasonably, ignoring her as he pulled a long cloth from the piebald's saddlebag and tossed it at her.

Orlena dried herself carefully with the rough cotton towel, wincing at its abrasion on her tender skin. In a moment he returned from another foray into his pack with a small tin. "Pascal says this is a miracle cure for sun and wind burn. It will serve until the women of my band can tend you."

She eyed him suspiciously. His hair and chest were still wet but he had slipped on a pair of sleek buckskin pants and his moccasins. He held out the ointment like a peace offering. "Come here." A smile played about his lips. "After all, I need not repeat the rest of the sentence. You are already rid of your clothes."

"You promised me women's clothing," she replied with rising anger, but still she clutched the towel protectively in front of herself.

He waited until she approached, warily, then commanded, "Raise your hair first so I may treat your shoulders.

Still holding the towel draped around herself with one hand, she lifted her hair up with the other. Santiago's thin shirt had been ripped on the brushy shrubs and trees as they rode and her skin was both scratched and sunburned. His fingers were calloused, yet warm and soothing as he spread the salve on her skin with surprising gentleness. The sting evaporated magically, but she did not voice her appreciation, only turned to let him minister to her throat and arms, then her hands.

When he tipped up her chin to touch her wind-burned cheeks and nose, she was forced to meet his eyes. Again a sense of recognition niggled, then vanished as she observed his reaction to her.

"Ah, Lioness, you are too delicate for New Mexico. You should have stayed in Spain," he said with what almost sounded like regret in his voice.

She looked at him oddly, puzzled and afraid. Of him . . . or of herself? She honestly did not know.

Don't miss
NIGHT WIND'S WOMAN
by Shirl Henke

**On Sale in April
At Booksellers Everywhere**

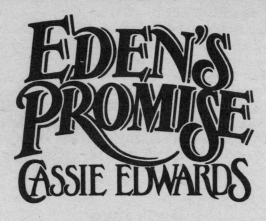